The Inspector Rebus Novels

'Rankin ranks alongside P D James and Michael Dibdin as Britain's finest detective novelist' *Scotland on Sunday*

'Rankin captures, like no one else, that strangeness that is Scotland at the end of the twentieth century. He has always written superb crime fiction ... but what he's also pinning down is instant history' *Literary Review*

'Rankin writes laconic, sophisticated, well-paced thrillers' *The Scotsman*

'One of the fastest-rising contemporary British sleuths is Ian Rankin's Inspector John Rebus, a character who's just begging for the right television treatment. Powerful characterisation and a strong sense of place dominate the Rebus novels ... A talent not to be ignored' *Time Out*

'Rankin strips Edinburgh's polite facade to its gritty skeleton' *The Times*

'The internal police politics and corruption in high places are both portrayed with bone-freezing accuracy. This novel should come with a wind-chill factor warning' *Daily Telegraph*

'A brutal but beautifully written series ... Rankin pushes the procedural form well past conventional genre limits' *New York Times*

Born in the Kingdom of Fife in 1960, Ian Rankin graduated from the University of Edinburgh and has since been employed as grape-picker, swineherd, taxman, alcohol researcher, hi-fi journalist and punk musician. His first Rebus novel, *Knots & Crosses*, was published in 1987 and the Rebus books are now translated into several languages as well as being increasingly popular in the USA. Ian Rankin has been elected a Hawthornden Fellow, and is also a past winner of the prestigious Chandler-Fulbright Award, as well as two CWA short story 'Daggers' and the 1997 Macallan Gold Dagger for Fiction for *Black & Blue*, which was also shortlisted for the Mystery Writers of America 'Edgar' award for best novel. He lives in Edinburgh and is married with two sons.

Ian Rankin

Mortal Causes

An Inspector Rebus Novel

ORION

An Orion paperback
First published in Great Britain by Orion in 1994
This paperback edition published in 1995 by Orion Books Ltd,
Orion House, 5 Upper St Martin's Lane, London WC2H 9EA

Sixth impression 1998

A CIP catalogue record for this book is available
from the British Library

ISBN: 1 85797 863 3

Typeset by Selwood Systems, Midsomer Norton
Printed and bound in Great Britain by
Clays Ltd, St Ives plc

Acknowledgements

A lot of people helped me with this book. I'd like to thank the people of Northern Ireland for their generosity and their 'crack'. Particular thanks need to go to a few people who can't be named or wouldn't thank me for naming them. You know who you are.

Thanks also to: Colin and Liz Stevenson, for trying; Gerald Hammond, for his gun expertise; the officers of the City of Edinburgh Police and Lothian and Borders Police, who never seem to mind me telling stories about them; David and Pauline, for help at the Festival.

The best book on the subject of Protestant paramilitaries is Professor Steve Bruce's *The Red Hand* (OUP, 1992). One quote from the book: 'There is no "Northern Ireland problem" for which there is a solution. There is only a conflict in which there must be winners and losers.'

The action of *Mortal Causes* takes place in a fictionalised summer, 1993, before the Shankill Road bombing and its bloody aftermath.

Perhaps Edinburgh's terrible inability to speak out,
Edinburgh's silence with regard to all it should be saying,
Is but the hush that precedes the thunder,
The liberating detonation so oppressively imminent now?

Hugh MacDiarmid

We're all gonna be just dirt in the ground.

Tom Waits

He could scream all he liked.

They were underground, a place he didn't know, a cool ancient place but lit by electricity. And he was being punished. The blood dripped off him onto the earth floor. He could hear sounds like distant voices, something beyond the breathing of the men who stood around him. Ghosts, he thought. Shrieks and laughter, the sounds of a good night out. He must be mistaken: he was having a very bad night in.

His bare toes just touched the ground. His shoes had come off as they'd scraped him down the flights of steps. His socks had followed sometime after. He was in agony, but agony could be cured. Agony wasn't eternal. He wondered if he would walk again. He remembered the barrel of the gun touching the back of his knee, sending waves of energy up and down his leg.

His eyes were closed. If he opened them he knew he would see flecks of his own blood against the whitewashed wall, the wall which seemed to arch towards him. His toes were still moving against the ground, dabbling in warm blood. Whenever he tried to speak, he could feel his face cracking: dried salt tears and sweat.

It was strange, the shape your life could take. You might be loved as a child but still go bad. You might have monsters for parents but grow up pure. His life had been neither one nor the other. Or rather, it had been both, for he'd been cherished and abandoned in equal measure. He was six,

1

and shaking hands with a large man. There should have been more affection between them, but somehow there wasn't. He was ten, and his mother was looking tired, bowed down, as she leaned over the sink washing dishes. Not knowing he was in the doorway, she paused to rest her hands on the rim of the sink. He was thirteen, and being initiated into his first gang. They took a pack of cards and skinned his knuckles with the edge of the pack. They took it in turns, all eleven of them. It hurt until he belonged.

Now there was a shuffling sound. And the gun barrel was touching the back of his neck, sending out more waves. How could something be so cold? He took a deep breath, feeling the effort in his shoulder-blades. There couldn't be more pain than he already felt. Heavy breathing close to his ear, and then the words again.

'*Nemo me impune lacessit.*'

He opened his eyes to the ghosts. They were in a smoke-filled tavern, seated around a long rectangular table, their goblets of wine and ale held high. A young woman was slouching from the lap of a one-legged man. The goblets had stems but no bases: you couldn't put them back on the table until they'd been emptied. A toast was being raised. Those in fine dress rubbed shoulders with beggars. There were no divisions, not in the tavern's gloom. Then they looked towards him, and he tried to smile.

He felt but did not hear the final explosion.

1

Probably the worst Saturday night of the year, which was why Inspector John Rebus had landed the shift. God was in his heaven, just making sure. There had been a derby match in the afternoon, Hibs versus Hearts at Easter Road. Fans making their way back to the west end and beyond had stopped in the city centre to drink to excess and take in some of the sights and sounds of the Festival.

The Edinburgh Festival was the bane of Rebus's life. He'd spent years confronting it, trying to avoid it, cursing it, being caught up in it. There were those who said that it was somehow atypical of Edinburgh, a city which for most of the year seemed sleepy, moderate, bridled. But that was nonsense; Edinburgh's history was full of licence and riotous behaviour. But the Festival, especially the Festival Fringe, was different. Tourism was its lifeblood, and where there were tourists there was trouble. Pickpockets and house-breakers came to town as to a convention, while those football supporters who normally steered clear of the city centre suddenly became its passionate defenders, challenging the foreign invaders who could be found at tables outside short-lease cafes up and down the High Street.

Tonight the two might clash in a big way.

'It's hell out there,' one constable had already commented as he paused for rest in the canteen. Rebus believed him all too readily. The cells were filling nicely along with the CID in-trays. A woman had pushed her drunken husband's fingers into the kitchen mincer. Someone was applying superglue to cashpoint machines then chiselling the flap open later to get at the money. Several bags had been snatched around Princes Street. And the Can Gang were on the go again.

The Can Gang had a simple recipe. They stood at bus stops and offered a drink from their can. They were imposing figures, and the victim would take the proffered drink, not knowing that the beer or cola contained crushed up Mogadon tablets, or similar fast-acting tranquillisers. When the victim passed out, the gang would strip them of cash and valuables. You woke up with a gummy head, or in one severe case with your stomach pumped dry. And you woke up poor.

Meantime, there had been another bomb threat, this time phoned to the newspaper rather than Lowland Radio. Rebus had gone to the newspaper offices to take a statement from the journalist who'd taken the call. The place was a madhouse of Festival and Fringe critics filing their reviews. The journalist read from his notes.

'He just said, if we didn't shut the Festival down, we'd be sorry.'

'Did he sound serious?'

'Oh, yes, definitely.'

'And he had an Irish accent?'

'Sounded like it.'

'Not just a fake?'

The reporter shrugged. He was keen to file his story, so Rebus let him go. That made three calls in the past week, each one threatening to bomb or otherwise disrupt the Festival. The police were taking the threat seriously. How could they afford not to? So far, the tourists hadn't been scared off, but venues were being urged to make security checks before and after each performance.

Back at St Leonard's, Rebus reported to his Chief Superintendent, then tried to finish another piece of paperwork. Masochist that he was, he quite liked the Saturday back-shift. You saw the city in its many guises. It allowed a salutory peek into Edinburgh's grey soul. Sin and evil weren't black – he'd argued the point with a priest – but were greyly anonymous. You saw them all night long, the grey peering faces of the wrongdoers and malcontents, the wife beaters and the knife boys. Unfocused eyes, drained of all concern save for themselves. And you prayed, if you were John Rebus, prayed that as few people as possible ever had to get as close as this to the massive grey nonentity.

Then you went to the canteen and had a joke with the lads, fixing a smile to your face whether you were listening or not.

'Here, Inspector, have you heard the one about the squid with the moustache? He goes into a restaurant and –'

Rebus turned away from the DC's story towards his ringing phone.

'DI Rebus.'

He listened for a moment, the smile melting from his face. Then he put down the receiver and lifted his jacket from the back of his chair.

'Bad news?' asked the DC.

'You're not joking, son.'

The High Street was packed with people, most of them just browsing. Young people bobbed up and down trying to instil enthusiasm in the Fringe productions they were supporting. Supporting them? They were probably the *leads* in them. They busily thrust flyers into hands already full of similar sheets.

'Only two quid, best value on the Fringe!'

'You won't see another show like it!'

There were jugglers and people with painted faces, and a cacophony of musical disharmonies. Where else in the world would bagpipes, banjos and kazoos meet to join in a busking battle from hell?

Locals said this Festival was quieter than the last. They'd

been saying it for years. Rebus wondered if the thing had ever had a heyday. It was plenty busy enough for him.

Though it was a warm night, he kept his car windows shut. Even so, as he crawled along the setts flyers would be pushed beneath his windscreen wipers, all but blocking his vision. His scowl met impregnable drama student smiles. It was ten o'clock, not long dark; that was the beauty of a Scottish summer. He tried to imagine himself on a deserted beach, or crouched atop a mountain, alone with his thoughts. Who was he trying to kid? John Rebus was *always* alone with his thoughts. And just now he was thinking of drink. Another hour or two and the bars would sluice themselves out, unless they'd applied for (and been granted) the very late licences available at Festival time.

He was heading for the City Chambers, across the street from St Giles' Cathedral. You turned off the High Street and through one of two stone arches into a small parking area in front of the Chambers themselves. A uniformed constable was standing guard beneath one of the arches. He recognised Rebus and nodded, stepping out of the way. Rebus parked his own car beside a marked patrol car, stopped the engine and got out.

'Evening, sir.'

'Where is it?'

The constable nodded towards a door near one of the arches, attached to the side wall of the Chambers. They walked towards it. A young woman was standing next to the door.

'Inspector,' she said.

'Hello, Mairie.'

'I've told her to move on, sir,' the constable apologised.

Mairie Henderson ignored him. Her eyes were on Rebus's. 'What's going on?'

Rebus winked at her. 'The Lodge, Mairie. We always meet in secret, like.' She scowled. 'Well then, give me a chance. Off to a show, are you?'

6

'I was till I saw the commotion.'

'Saturday's your day off, isn't it?'

'Journalists don't get days off, Inspector. What's behind the door?'

'It's got glass panels, Mairie. Take a keek for yourself.'

But all you could see through the panels was a narrow landing with doors off. One door was open, allowing a glimpse of stairs leading down. Rebus turned to the constable.

'Let's get a proper cordon set up, son. Something across the arches to fend off the tourists before the show starts. Radio in for assistance if you need it. Excuse me, Mairie.'

'Then there *is* going to be a show?'

Rebus stepped past her and opened the door, closing it again behind him. He made for the stairs down, which were lit by a naked lightbulb. Ahead of him he could hear voices. At the bottom of this first flight he turned a corner and came upon the group. There were two teenage girls and a boy, all of them seated or crouching, the girls shaking and crying. Over them stood a uniformed constable and a man Rebus recognised as a local doctor. They all looked up at his approach.

'This is the Inspector,' the constable told the teenagers. 'Right, we're going back down there. You three stay here.'

Rebus, squeezing past the teenagers, saw the doctor give them a worried glance. He gave the doctor a wink, telling him they'd get over it. The doctor didn't seem so sure.

Together the three men set off down the next flight of stairs. The constable was carrying a torch.

'There's electricity,' he said. 'But a couple of the bulbs have gone.' They walked along a narrow passage, its low ceiling further reduced by air- and heating-ducts and other pipes. Tubes of scaffolding lay on the floor ready for assembly. There were more steps down.

'You know where we are?' the constable asked.

'Mary King's Close,' said Rebus.

7

Not that he'd ever been down here, not exactly. But he'd been in similar old buried streets beneath the High Street. He knew of Mary King's Close.

'Story goes,' said the constable, 'there was a plague in the 1600s, people died or moved out, never really moved back. Then there was a fire. They blocked off the ends of the street. When they rebuilt, they built over the top of the close.' He shone his torch towards the ceiling, which was now three or four storeys above them. 'See that marble slab? That's the floor of the City Chambers.' He smiled. 'I came on the tour last year.'

'Incredible,' the doctor said. Then to Rebus: 'I'm Dr Galloway.'

'Inspector Rebus. Thanks for getting here so quickly.'

The doctor ignored this. 'You're a friend of Dr Aitken's, aren't you?'

Ah, Patience Aitken. She'd be at home just now, feet tucked under her, a cat and an improving book on her lap, boring classical music in the background. Rebus nodded.

'I used to share a surgery with her,' Dr Galloway explained.

They were in the close proper now, a narrow and fairly steep roadway between stone buildings. A rough drainage channel ran down one side of the road. Passages led off to dark alcoves, one of which, according to the constable, housed a bakery, its ovens intact. The constable was beginning to get on Rebus's nerves.

There were more ducts and pipes, runs of electric cable. The far end of the close had been blocked off by an elevator shaft. Signs of renovation were all around: bags of cement, scaffolding, pails and shovels. Rebus pointed to an arc lamp.

'Can we plug that in?'

The constable thought they could. Rebus looked around. The place wasn't damp or chilled or cobwebbed. The air seemed fresh. Yet they were three or four storeys beneath road level. Rebus took the torch and shone it through a doorway. At the end of the hallway he could see a wooden toilet, its seat raised. The next door along led into a long vaulted room, its walls whitewashed, the floor earthen.

'That's the wine shop,' the constable said. 'The butcher's is next door.'

So it was. It too consisted of a vaulted room, again whitewashed and with a floor of packed earth. But in its ceiling were a great many iron hooks, short and blackened but obviously used at one time for hanging up meat.

Meat still hung from one of them.

It was the lifeless body of a young man. His hair was dark and slick, stuck to his forehead and neck. His hands had been tied and the rope slipped over a hook, so that he hung stretched with his knuckles near the ceiling and his toes barely touching the ground. His ankles had been tied together too. There was blood everywhere, a fact made all too plain as the arc lamp suddenly came on, sweeping light and shadows across the walls and roof. There was the faint smell of decay, but no flies, thank God. Dr Galloway swallowed hard, his Adam's apple seeming to duck for cover, then retreated into the close to be sick. Rebus tried to steady his own heart. He walked around the carcass, keeping his distance initially.

'Tell me,' he said.

'Well, sir,' the constable began, 'the three young people upstairs, they decided to come down here. The place had been closed to tours while the building work goes on, but they wanted to come down at night. There are a lot of ghost stories told about this place, headless dogs and –'

'How did they get a key?'

'The boy's great-uncle, he's one of the tour guides, a retired planner or something.'

'So they came looking for ghosts and they found this.'

'That's right, sir. They ran back up to the High Street and bumped into PC Andrews and me. We thought they were having us on at first, like.'

9

But Rebus was no longer listening, and when he spoke it wasn't to the constable.

'You poor little bastard, look what they did to you.'

Though it was against regulations, he leaned forward and touched the young man's hair. It was still slightly damp. He'd probably died on Friday night, and was meant to hang here over the weekend, enough time for any trail, any clues, to grow as cold as his bones.

'What do you reckon, sir?'

'Gunshots.' Rebus looked to where blood had sprayed the wall. 'Something high-velocity. Head, elbows, knees, and ankles.' He sucked in breath. 'He's been six-packed.'

There were shuffling noises in the close, and the wavering beam of another torch. Two figures stood in the doorway, their bodies silhouetted by the arc lamp.

'Cheer up, Dr Galloway,' a male voice boomed to the hapless figure still crouched in the close. Recognising the voice, Rebus smiled.

'Ready when you are, Dr Curt,' he said.

The pathologist stepped into the chamber and shook Rebus's hand. 'The hidden city, quite a revelation.' His companion, a woman, stepped forward to join them. 'Have the two of you met?' Dr Curt sounded like the host at a luncheon party. 'Inspector Rebus, this is Ms Rattray from the Procurator Fiscal's office.'

'Caroline Rattray.' She shook Rebus's hand. She was tall, as tall as either man, with long dark hair tied at the back.

'Caroline and I,' Curt was saying, 'were enjoying supper after the ballet when the call came. So I thought I'd drag her along, kill two birds with one stone ... so to speak.'

Curt exhaled fumes of good food and good wine. Both he and the lawyer were dressed for an evening out, and already some white plaster-dust had smudged Caroline Rattray's black jacket. As Rebus moved to brush off the dust, she caught her first sight of the body, and looked away quickly. Rebus didn't blame her, but Curt was advancing on the

10

figure as though towards another guest at the party. He paused to put on polythene overshoes.

'I always carry some in my car,' he explained. 'You never know when they'll be needed.'

He got close to the body and examined the head first, before looking back towards Rebus.

'Dr Galloway had a look, has he?'

Rebus shook his head slowly. He knew what was coming. He'd seen Curt examine headless bodies and mangled bodies and bodies that were little more than torsos or melted to the consistency of lard, and the pathologist always said the same thing.

'Poor chap's dead.'

'Thank you.'

'I take it the crew are on their way?'

Rebus nodded. The crew were on their way. A van to start with, loaded with everything they'd need for the initial scene of crime investigation. SOC officers, lights and cameras, strips of tape, evidence bags, and of course a bodybag. Sometimes a forensic team came too, if cause of death looked particularly murky or the scene was a mess.

'I think,' said Curt, 'the Procurator Fiscal's office will agree that foul play is suspected?'

Rattray nodded, still not looking.

'Well, it wasn't suicide,' commented Rebus. Caroline Rattray turned towards the wall, only to find herself facing the sprays of blood. She turned instead to the doorway, where Dr Galloway was dabbing his mouth with a handkerchief.

'We'd better get someone to fetch me my tools.' Curt was studying the ceiling. 'Any idea what this place was?'

'A butcher's shop, sir,' said the constable, only too happy to help. 'There's a wine shop too, and some houses. You can still go into them.' He turned to Rebus. 'Sir, what's a six-pack?'

'A six-pack?' echoed Curt.

11

Rebus stared at the hanging body. 'It's a punishment,' he said quietly. 'Only you're not supposed to die. What's that on the floor?' He was pointing to the dead man's feet, to the spot where they grazed the dark-stained ground.

'Looks like rats have been nibbling his toes,' said Curt.

'No, not that.' There were shallow grooves in the earth, so wide they must have been made with a big toe. Four crude capital letters were discernible.

'Is that Neno or Nemo?'

'Could even be Memo,' offered Dr Curt.

'Captain Nemo,' said the constable. 'He's the guy in *2,000 Leagues Beneath the Sea*.'

'Jules Verne,' said Curt, nodding.

The constable shook his head. 'No, sir, Walt Disney,' he said.

2

On Sunday morning Rebus and Dr Patience Aitken decided to get away from it all by staying in bed. He nipped out early for croissants and papers from the local corner shop, and they ate breakfast from a tray on top of the bedcovers, sharing sections of the newspapers, discarding more than they read.

There was no mention of the previous night's grisly find in Mary King's Close. The news had seeped out too late for publication. But Rebus knew there would be something about it on the local radio news, so he was quite content for once when Patience tuned the bedside radio to a classical station.

He should have come off his shift at midnight, but murder tended to disrupt the system of shifts. On a murder inquiry, you stopped working when you reasonably could. Rebus had hung around till two in the morning, consulting with the night shift about the corpse in Mary King's Close. He'd contacted his Chief Inspector and Chief Super, and kept in touch with Fettes HQ, where the forensic stuff had gone. DI Flower kept telling him to go home. Finally he'd taken the advice.

The real problem with back shifts was that Rebus couldn't sleep well after them anyway. He'd managed four hours since arriving home, and four hours would suffice. But there was a warm pleasure in slipping into bed as dawn neared, curling against the body already asleep there. And even more pleasure in pushing the cat off the bed as you did so.

Before retiring, he'd swallowed four measures of whisky. He told himself it was purely medicinal, but rinsed the glass and put it away, hoping Patience wouldn't notice. She complained often of his drinking, among other things.

'We're eating out,' she said now.

'When?'

'Lunch today.'

'Where?'

'That place out at Carlops.'

Rebus nodded. 'Witch's Leap,' he said.

'What?'

'That's what Carlops means. There's a big rock there. They used to throw suspected witches from it. If you didn't fly, you were innocent.'

'But also dead?'

'Their judicial system wasn't perfect, witness the ducking-stool. Same principle.'

'How do you know all this?'

'It's amazing what these young constables know now-adays.' He paused. 'About lunch ... I should go into work.'

'Oh no, you don't.'

'Patience, there's been a –'

'John, there'll be a murder *here* if we don't start spending some time together. Phone in sick.'

'I can't do that.'

'Then *I'll* do it. I'm a doctor, they'll believe me.'

They believed her.

They walked off lunch by taking a look at Carlops Rock, and then braving a climb onto the Pentlands, despite the fierce horizontal winds. Back in Oxford Terrace, Patience eventually said she had some 'office things' to do, which meant filing or tax or flicking through the latest medical journals. So Rebus drove out along Queensferry Road and parked outside the Church of Our Lady of Perpetual Hell,

14

noting with guilty pleasure that no one had yet corrected the mischievous graffiti on the noticeboard which turned 'Help' into 'Hell'.

Inside, the church was empty, cool and quiet and flooded with coloured light from the stained glass. Hoping his timing was good, he slipped into the confessional. There was someone on the other side of the grille.

'Forgive me, father,' said Rebus, 'I'm not even a Catholic.'

'Ah good, it's you, you heathen. I was hoping you'd come. I want your help.'

'Shouldn't that be my line?'

'Don't be bloody cheeky. Come on, let's have a drink.'

Father Conor Leary was between fifty-five and seventy and had told Rebus that he couldn't remember which he was nearer. He was a bulky barrelling figure with thick silver hair which sprouted not only from his head but also from ears, nose and the back of his neck. In civvies, Rebus guessed he would pass for a retired dockworker or skilled labourer of some kind who had also been handy as a boxer, and Father Leary had photos and trophies to prove that this last was incontrovertible truth. He often jabbed the air to make a point, finishing with an upper-cut to show that there could be no comeback. In conversation between the two men, Rebus had often wished for a referee.

But today Father Leary sat comfortably and sedately enough in the deckchair in his garden. It was a beautiful early evening, warm and clear with the trace of a cool sea-borne breeze.

'A great day to go hot-air ballooning,' said Father Leary, taking a swig from his glass of Guinness. 'Or bungee jumping. I believe they've set up something of the sort on The Meadows, just for the duration of the Festival. Man, I'd like to try that.'

Rebus blinked but said nothing. His Guinness was cold

enough to double as dental anaesthetic. He shifted in his own deckchair, which was by far the older of the two. Before sitting, he'd noticed how threadbare the canvas was, how it had been rubbed away where it met the horizontal wooden spars. He hoped it would hold.

'Do you like my garden?'

Rebus looked at the bright blooms, the trim grass. 'I don't know much about gardens,' he admitted.

'Me neither. It's not a sin. But there's an old chap I know who does know about them, and he looks after this one for a few bob.' He raised his glass towards his lips. 'So how are you keeping?'

'I'm fine.'

'And Dr Aitken?'

'She's fine.'

'And the two of you are still . . . ?'

'Just about.'

Father Leary nodded. Rebus's tone was warning him off. 'Another bomb threat, eh? I heard on the radio.'

'It could be a crank.'

'But you're not sure?'

'The IRA usually use codewords, just so we know they're serious.'

Father Leary nodded to himself. 'And a murder too?'

Rebus gulped his drink. 'I was there.'

'They don't even stop for the Festival, do they? Whatever must the tourists think?' Father Leary's eyes were sparkling.

'It's about time the tourists learned the truth,' Rebus said, a bit too quickly. He sighed. 'It was pretty gruesome.'

'I'm sorry to hear that. I shouldn't have been so flippant.'

'That's all right. It's a defence.'

'You're right, it is.'

Rebus knew this. It was the reason behind his many little jokes with Dr Curt. It was their way of avoiding the obvious, the undeniable. Even so, since last night Rebus had held in his mind the picture of that sad strung-up

16

figure, a young man they hadn't even identified yet. The picture would stay there forever. Everybody had a photographic memory for horror. He'd climbed back out of Mary King's Close to find the High Street aglow with a firework display, the streets thronged with people staring up openmouthed at the blues and greens in the night sky. The fireworks were coming from the Castle; the night's Tattoo display was ending. He hadn't felt much like talking to Mairie Henderson. In fact, he had snubbed her.

'This isn't very nice,' she'd said, standing her ground.

'This is very nice,' Father Leary said now, relaxing back further into his seat.

The whisky Rebus had drunk hadn't rubbed out the picture. If anything, it had smeared the corners and edges, which only served to highlight the central fact. More whisky would have made this image sharper still.

'We're not here for very long, are we?' he said now.

Father Leary frowned. 'You mean here on earth?'

'That's what I mean. We're not around long enough to make any difference.'

'Tell that to the man with a bomb in his pocket. Every one of us makes a difference just by being here.'

'I'm not talking about the man with the bomb, I'm talking about stopping him.'

'You're talking about being a policeman.'

'Ach, maybe I'm not talking about anything.'

Father Leary allowed a short-lived smile, his eyes never leaving Rebus's. 'A bit morbid for a Sunday, John?'

'Isn't that what Sundays are for?'

'Maybe for you sons of Calvin. You tell yourselves you're doomed, then spend all week trying to make a joke of it. Others of us give thanks for *this* day and its meaning.'

Rebus shifted in his chair. Lately, he didn't enjoy Father Leary's conversations so much. There was something proselytising about them. 'So when do we get down to business?' he said.

17

Father Leary smiled. 'The Protestant work ethic.'

'You haven't brought me here to convert me.'

'We wouldn't want a dour bugger like you. Besides, I'd more easily convert a fifty-yard penalty in a Murrayfield cross-wind.' He took a swipe at the air. 'Ach, it's not really your problem. Maybe it isn't a problem at all.' He ran a finger down the crease in his trouser-leg.

'You can still tell me about it.'

'A reversal of roles, eh? Well, I suppose that's what I had in mind all along.' He sat further forward in the deckchair, the material stretching and sounding a sharp note of complaint. 'Here it is then. You know Pilmuir?'

'Don't be daft.'

'Yes, stupid question. And Pilmuir's Garibaldi Estate?'

'The Gar-B, it's the roughest scheme in the city, maybe in the country.'

'There are good people there, but you're right. That's why the Church sent an outreach worker.'

'And now he's in trouble?'

'Maybe.' Father Leary finished his drink. 'It was my idea. There's a community hall on the estate, only it had been locked up for months. I thought we could reopen it as a youth club.'

'For Catholics?'

'For both faiths.' He sat back in his chair. 'Even for the faithless. The Garibaldi is predominantly Protestant, but there are Catholics there too. We got agreement, and set up some funds. I knew we needed someone special, someone really dynamic in charge.' He punched the air. 'Someone who might just draw the two sides together.'

Mission impossible, thought Rebus. This scheme will self-destruct in ten seconds.

Not least of the Gar-B's problems was the sectarian divide, or the lack of one, depending on how you looked at it. Protestants and Catholics lived in the same streets, the same tower blocks. Mostly, they lived in relative harmony

18

and shared poverty. But, there being little to do on the estate, the youth of the place tended to organise into opposing gangs and wage warfare. Every year there was at least one pitched battle for police to contend with, usually in July, usually around the Protestant holy day of the 12th.

'So you brought in the SAS?' Rebus suggested. Father Leary was slow to get the joke.

'Not at all,' he said, 'just a young man, a very ordinary young man but with inner strength.' His fist cut the air. 'Spiritual strength. And for a while it looked like a disaster. Nobody came to the club, the windows were smashed as soon as we'd replaced them, the graffiti got worse and more personal. But then he started to break through. *That* seemed the miracle. Attendance at the club increased, and both sides were joining.'

'So what's gone wrong?'

Father Leary loosened his shoulders. 'It just wasn't quite right. I thought there'd be sports, maybe a football team or something. We bought the strips and applied to join a local league. But the lads weren't interested. All they wanted to do was hang around the hall itself. And the balance isn't there either, the Catholics have stopped joining. Most of them have even stopped attending.' He looked at Rebus. 'That's not just sour grapes, you understand.'

Rebus nodded. 'The Prod gangs have annnexed it?'

'I'm not saying that exactly.'

'Sounds like it to me. And your . . . outreach worker?'

'His name's Peter Cave. Oh, he's still there. Too often for my liking.'

'I still don't see the problem.' Actually he could, but he wanted it spelling out.

'John, I've talked to people on the estate, and all over Pilmuir. The gangs are as bad as ever, only now they seem to be working together, divvying the place up between them. All that's happened is that they've become more organised. They have meetings in the club and carve up the surrounding territory.'

'It keeps them off the street.' Father Leary didn't smile. 'So close the youth club.'

'That's not so easy. It would look bad for a start. And would it solve anything?'

'Have you talked with Mr Cave?'

'He doesn't listen. He's changed. That's what troubles me most of all.'

'You could kick him out.'

Father Leary shook his head. 'He's lay, John. I can't *order* him to do anything. We've cut the club's funding, but the money to keep it going comes from somewhere nevertheless.'

'Where from?'

'I don't know.'

'How much?'

'It doesn't take much.'

'So what do you want me to do?' The question Rebus had been trying not to ask.

Father Leary gave his weary smile again. 'To be honest, I don't know. Perhaps I just needed to tell someone.'

'Don't give me that. You want me to go out there.'

'Not if you don't want to.'

It was Rebus's turn to smile. 'I've been in safer places.'

'And a few worse ones, too.'

'I haven't told you about half of them, Father.' Rebus finished his drink.

'Another?'

He shook his head. 'It's nice and quiet here, isn't it?'

Father Leary nodded. 'That's the beauty of Edinburgh, you're never far from a peaceful spot.'

'And never far from a hellish one either. Thanks for the drink, Father.' Rebus got up.

'I see your team won yesterday.'

'What makes you think I support Hearts?'

20

'They're Prods, aren't they? And you're a Protestant yourself.'

'Away to hell, Father,' said John Rebus, laughing.

Father Leary pulled himself to his feet. He straightened his back with a grimace. He was acting purposely aged. Just an old man. 'About the Gar-B, John,' he said, opening his arms wide, 'I'm in your hands.'

Like nails, thought Rebus, like carpentry nails.

3

Monday morning saw Rebus back at work and in the Chief Super's office. 'Farmer' Watson was pouring coffee for himself and Chief Inspector Frank Lauderdale, Rebus having refused. He was strictly decaf these days, and the Farmer didn't know the meaning of the word.

'A busy Saturday night,' said the Farmer, handing Lauderdale a grubby mug. As inconspicuously as he could, Lauderdale started rubbing marks off the rim with the ball of his thumb. 'Feeling better, by the way, John?'

'Scads better, sir, thank you,' said Rebus, not even close to blushing.

'A grim business under the City Chambers.'

'Yes, sir.'

'So what do we have?'

It was Lauderdale's turn to speak. 'Victim was shot seven times with what looks like a nine-millimetre revolver. Ballistics will have a full report for us by day's end. Dr Curt tells us that the head wound actually killed the victim, and it was the last bullet delivered. They wanted him to suffer.'

Lauderdale sipped from the cleaned rim of his mug. A Murder Room had been set up along the hall, and he was in charge. Consequently, he was wearing his best suit. There would be press briefings, maybe a TV appearance or two. Lauderdale looked ready. Rebus would gladly have tipped the mug of coffee down the mauve shirt and paisley-pattern tie.

'Your thoughts, John,' said Farmer Watson. 'Someone mentioned the words "six-pack".'

'Yes, sir. It's a punishment routine in Northern Ireland, usually carried out by the IRA.'

'I've heard of kneecappings.'

Rebus nodded. 'For minor offences, there's a bullet in each elbow or ankle. For more serious crimes, there's a kneecapping on top. And finally there's the six-pack: both elbows, both knees, both ankles.'

'You know a lot about it.'

'I was in the army, sir. I still take an interest.'

'You were in Ulster?'

Rebus nodded slowly. 'In the early days.'

Chief Inspector Lauderdale placed his mug carefully on the desktop. 'But they normally wouldn't then kill the person?'

'Not normally.'

The three men sat in silence for a moment. The Farmer broke the spell. 'An IRA punishment gang? *Here?*'

Rebus shrugged. 'A copycat maybe. Gangs aping what they've seen in the papers or on TV.'

'But using serious guns.'

'Very serious,' said Lauderdale. 'Could be a tie-in with these bomb threats.'

The Farmer nodded. 'That's the line the media are taking. Maybe our would-be bomber had gone rogue, and they caught up with him.'

'There's something else, sir,' said Rebus. He'd phoned Dr Curt first thing, just to check. 'They did the knees from behind. Maximum damage. You sever the arteries before smashing kneecaps.'

'What's your point?'

'Two points, sir. One, they knew exactly what they were doing. Two, why bother when you're going to kill him anyway? Maybe whoever did it changed his mind at the last minute. Maybe the victim was meant to live. The probable handgun was a revolver. Six shots. Whoever did it must have stopped to reload before putting that final bullet in the head.'

Eyes were avoided as the three men considered this, putting themselves in the victim's place. You've been six-packed. You think it's over. Then you hear the gun being reloaded...

'Sweet Jesus,' said the Farmer.

'There are too many guns around,' Lauderdale said matter-of-factly. It was true: over the past few years there had been a steady increase in the number of firearms on the street.

'Why Mary King's Close?' asked the Farmer.

'You're not likely to be disturbed there,' Rebus guessed. 'Plus it's virtually soundproof.'

'You could say the same about a lot of places, most of them a long way from the High Street in the middle of the Festival. They were taking a big risk. Why bother?'

Rebus had wondered the same thing. He had no answer to offer.

'And Nemo or Memo?'

It was Lauderdale's turn, another respite from the coffee. 'I've got men on it, sir, checking libraries and phone directories, digging up meanings.'

'You've talked to the teenagers?'

'Yes, sir. They seem genuine enough.'

'And the person who gave them the key?'

'He didn't give it to them, sir, they took it without his knowledge. He's in his seventies and straighter than a plumb-line.'

'Some builders I know,' said the Farmer, 'could bend even a plumb-line.'

Rebus smiled. He knew those builders too.

'We're talking to everyone,' Lauderdale went on, 'who's been working in Mary King's Close.' It seemed he hadn't got the Farmer's joke.

'All right, John,' said the Farmer. 'You were in the army, what about the tattoo?'

Yes, the tattoo. Rebus had known the conclusion everyone would jump to. From the case notes, they'd spent most of Sunday jumping to it. The Farmer was examining a photograph. It had been taken during Sunday's post-mortem examination. The SOCOs on Saturday night had taken photos too, but those hadn't come out nearly as clearly.

The photo showed a tattoo on the victim's right forearm. It was a rough, self-inflicted affair, the kind you sometimes saw on teenagers, usually on the backs of hands. A needle and some blue ink, that's all you needed; that and a measure of luck that the thing wouldn't become infected. Those were all the victim had needed to prick the letters SaS into his skin.

'It's not the Special Air Service,' said Rebus.

'No?'

Rebus shook his head. 'For all sorts of reasons. You'd use a capital A for a start. More likely, if you wanted an SAS tattoo you'd go for the crest, the knife and wings and "Who dares wins", something like that.'

'Unless you didn't know anything about the regiment,' offered Lauderdale.

'Then why sport a tattoo?'

'Do we have any ideas?' asked the Farmer.

'We're checking,' said Lauderdale.

'And we still don't know who he is?'

'No, sir, we still don't know who he is.'

Farmer Watson sighed. 'Then that'll have to do for now. I know we're stretched just at the minute, with the Festival threat and everything else, but it goes without saying this takes priority. Use all the men you have to. We need to clean this up quickly. Special Branch and the Crime Squad are already taking an interest.'

Ah, thought Rebus, so that was why the Farmer was

25

being a bit more thorough than usual. Normally, he'd just let Lauderdale get on with it. Lauderdale was good at running an office. You just didn't want him out there on the street with you. Watson was shuffling the papers on his desk.

'I see the Can Gang have been at it again.'

It was time to move on.

Rebus had had dealings in Pilmuir before. He'd seen a good policeman go wrong there. He'd tasted darkness there. The sour feeling returned as he drove past stunted grass verges and broken saplings. Though no tourists ever came here, there was a welcome sign. It comprised somebody's gable-end, with white painted letters four feet high: ENJOY YOUR VISIT TO THE GAR-B.

Gar-B was what the kids (for want of a better term) called the Garibaldi estate. It was a mish-mash of early-'60s terraced housing and late-'60s tower blocks, everything faced with grey harling, with boring swathes of grass separating the estate from the main road. There were a lot of orange plastic traffic cones lying around. They would make goalposts for a quick game of football, or chicanes for the bikers. Last year, some enterprising souls had put them to better use, using them to divert traffic off the main road and into the Gar-B, where youths lined the slip-road and pelted the cars with rocks and bottles. If the drivers ran from their vehicles, they were allowed to go, while the cars were stripped of anything of value, right down to tyres, seat-covers and engine parts.

Later in the year, when the road needed digging up, a lot of drivers ignored the genuine traffic cones and as a result drove into newly dug ditches. By next morning, their abandoned vehicles had been stripped to the bone. The Gar-B would have stripped the paint if they could.

You had to admire their ingenuity. Give these kids money and opportunity and they'd be the saviours of the capitalist state. Instead, the state gave them dole and daytime TV. Rebus was watched by a gang of pre-teens as he parked. One of them called out.

'Where's yir swanky car?'

'It's no' him,' said another, kicking the first lazily in the ankle. The two of them were on bicycles and looked like the leaders, being a good year or two older than their cohorts. Rebus waved them over.

'What is it?' But they came anyway.

'Keep an eye on my car,' he told them. 'Anyone touches it, you touch them, okay? There's a couple of quid for you when I get back.'

'Half now,' the first said quickly. The second nodded. Rebus handed over half the money, which they pocketed.

'Naebody'd touch *that* car anyway, mister,' said the second, producing a chorus of laughter from behind him.

Rebus shook his head slowly: the patter here was probably sharper than most of the stand-ups on the Fringe. The two boys could have been brothers. More than that, they could have been brothers in the 1930s. They were dressed in cheap modern style, but had shorn heads and wide ears and sallow faces with dark-ringed eyes. You saw them staring out from old photographs wearing boots too big for them and scowls too old. They didn't just seem older than the other kids; they seemed older than Rebus himself.

When he turned his back, he imagined them in sepia.

He wandered towards the community centre. He'd to pass some lock-up garages and one of the three twelve-storey blocks of flats. The community centre itself was no more than a hall, small and tired looking with boarded windows and the usual indecipherable graffiti. Surrounded by concrete, it had a low flat roof, asphalt black, on which lay four teenagers smoking cigarettes. Their chests were naked, their t-shirts tied around their waists. There was so much broken glass up there, they could have doubled as fakirs in a magic show. One of them had a pile of sheets of paper, and was folding them into paper planes which he released from the roof. Judging by the number of planes littering the grass, it had been a busy morning at the control tower.

Paint had peeled in long strips from the centre's doors, and one layer of the plywood beneath had been punctured by a foot or a fist. But the doors were locked fast by means of not one but two padlocks. Two more youths sat on the ground, backs against the doors, legs stretched in front of them and crossed at the ankles, for all the world like security guards on a break. Their trainers were in bad repair, their denims patched and torn and patched again. Maybe it was just the fashion. One wore a black t-shirt, the other an unbuttoned denim jacket with no shirt beneath.

'It's shut,' the denim jacket said.

'When does it open?'

'The night. No polis allowed though.'

Rebus smiled. 'I don't think I know you. What's your name?'

The smile back at him was a parody. Black t-shirt grunted an undeveloped laugh. Rebus noticed flecks of white scale in the youth's hair. Neither youth was about to say anything. The teenagers on the roof were standing now, ready to leap in should anything develop.

'Hard men,' said Rebus. He turned and started to walk away. Denim jacket got to his feet and came after him.

'What's up, Mr Polisman?'

Rebus didn't bother looking at the youth, but he stopped walking. 'Why should anything be up?' One of the paper planes, aimed or not, hit him on the leg. He picked it up. On the roof, they were laughing quietly. 'Why should anything be up?' he repeated.

'Behave. You're not our usual plod.'

'A change is as good as a rest.'

'Arrest? What for?'

Rebus smiled again. He turned to the youth. The face

28

was just leaving acne behind it, and would be good looking for a few more years before it started to decline. Poor diet and alcohol would be its undoing if drugs or fights weren't. The hair was fair and curly, like a child's hair, but not thick. There was a quick intelligence to the eyes, but the eyes themselves were narrow. The intelligence would be narrow too, focusing only on the main chance, the next deal. There was quick anger in those eyes too, and something further back that Rebus didn't like to think about.

'With an act like yours,' he said, 'you should be on the Fringe.'

'I fuckn *hate* the Festival.'

'Join the club. What's your name, son?'

'You like names, don't you?'

'I can find out.'

The youth slipped his hands into his tight jeans pockets. 'You don't want to.'

'No?'

A slow shake of the head. 'Believe me, you really don't want to.' The youth turned, heading back to his friends. 'Or next time,' he said, 'your car might not be there at all.'

Sure enough, as Rebus approached he saw that his car was sinking into the ground. It looked like maybe it was taking cover. But it was only the tyres. They'd been generous; they'd only slashed two of them. He looked around him. There was no sign of the pre-teen gang, though they might be watching from the safe distance of a tower-block window.

He leaned against the car and unfolded the paper plane. It was the flyer for a Fringe show, and a blurb on the back explained that the theatre group in question were uprooting from the city centre in order to play the Garibaldi Community Centre for one night.

'You know not what you do,' Rebus said to himself.

Some young mothers were crossing the football pitch. A crying baby was being shaken on its buggy springs. A toddler was being dragged screaming by the arm, his legs frozen in protest so that they scraped the ground. Both baby and toddler were being brought back into the Gar-B. But not without a fight.

Rebus didn't blame them for resisting.

4

Detective Sergeant Brian Holmes was in the Murder Room, handing a polystyrene cup of tea to Detective Constable Siobhan Clarke, and laughing about something.

'What's the joke?' asked Rebus.

'The one about the hard-up squid,' Holmes answered.

'The one with the moustache?'

Holmes nodded, wiping an imaginary tear from his eye. 'And Gervase the waiter. Brilliant, eh, sir?'

'Brilliant.' Rebus looked around. The Murder Room was all purposeful activity. Photos of the victim and the locus had been pinned up on one wall, a staff rota not far from it. The staff rota was on a plastic wipe-board, and a WPC was checking names from a list against a series of duties and putting them on the board in thick blue marker-pen. Rebus went over to her. 'Keep DI Flower and me away from one another, eh? Even if it means a slip of the pen.'

'I could get into trouble for that, Inspector.' She was smiling, so Rebus winked at her. Everyone knew that having Rebus and Flower in close proximity, two detectives who hated one another, would be counter productive. But of course Lauderdale was in charge. It was Lauderdale's list, and Lauderdale liked to see sparks fly, so much so that he might have been happier in a foundry.

Holmes and Clarke knew what Rebus had been talking about with the WPC, but said nothing.

'I'm going back down Mary King's Close,' Rebus said quietly. 'Anyone want to tag along?'

He had two takers.

Rebus was keeping an eye on Brian Holmes. Holmes hadn't tendered his resignation yet, but you never knew when it might come. When you joined the police, of course, you signed on for the long haul, but Holmes's significant other was pulling on the other end of the rope, and it was hard to tell who'd win the tug o' war.

On the other hand, Rebus had stopped keeping an eye on Siobhan Clarke. She was past her probation, and was going to be a good detective. She was quick, clever and keen. Police officers were seldom all three. Rebus himself might pitch for thirty per cent on a good day.

The day was overcast and sticky, with lots of bugs in the air and no sign of a dispersing breeze.

'What are they, greenfly?'

'Maybe midges.'

'I'll tell you what they are, they're disgusting.'

The windscreen was smeared by the time they reached the City Chambers, and there being no fluid in the wiper bottle, the windscreen stayed that way. It struck Rebus that the Festival really was a High Street thing. Most of the city centre streets were as quiet or as busy as usual. The High Street was the hub. The Chambers' small car park being full, he parked on the High Street. When he got out, he brought a sheet of kitchen-towel with him, spat on it, and cleaned the windscreen.

'What we need is some rain.'

'Don't say that.'

A transit van and a flat-back trailer were parked outside the entrance to Mary King's Close, evidence that the builders were back at work. The butcher's shop would still be taped off, but that didn't stop the renovations.

'Inspector Rebus?'

An old man had been waiting for them. He was tall and fit looking and wore an open cream-coloured raincoat despite the day's heat. His hair had turned not grey or

32

silver but a kind of custard yellow, and he wore half-moon glasses most of the way down his nose, as though he needed them only to check the cracks in the pavement.

'Mr Blair-Fish?' Rebus shook the brittle hand.

'I'd like to apologise again. My great-nephew can be such a –'

'No need to apologise, sir. Your great-nephew did us a favour. If he hadn't gone down there with those two lassies, we wouldn't have found the body so fast as we did. The quicker the better in a murder investigation.'

Blair-Fish inspected his oft-repaired shoes, then accepted this with a slow nod. 'Still, it's an embarrassment.'

'Not to us, sir.'

'No, I suppose not.'

'Now, if you'll lead the way . . . ?'

Mr Blair-Fish led the way.

He took them in through the door and down the flights of stairs, out of daylight and into a world of low-wattage bulbs beyond which lay the halogen glare of the builders. It was like looking at a stage-set. The workers moved with the studied precision of actors. You could charge a couple of quid a time and get an audience, if not a Fringe First Award. The gaffer knew police when he saw them, and nodded a greeting. Otherwise, nobody paid much attention, except for the occasional sideways and appraising glance towards Siobhan Clarke. Builders were builders, below ground as above.

Blair-Fish was providing a running commentary. Rebus reckoned he'd been the guide when the constable had come on the tour. Rebus heard about how the close had been a thriving thoroughfare prior to the plague, only one of many such plagues to hit Edinburgh. When the denizens moved back, they swore the close was haunted by the spirits of those who had perished there. They all moved out again and the street fell into disuse. Then came a fire, leaving only the first few storeys untouched. (Edinburgh tenements back then could rise to a precarious twelve storeys or more.) After which, the city merely laid slabs across what remained and built again, burying Mary King's Close.

'The old town was a narrow place, you must remember, built along a ridge or, if you enjoy legend, on the back of a buried serpent. Long and narrow. Everyone was squeezed together, rich and poor living cheek by jowl. In a tenement like this you'd have your paupers at the top, your gentry in the middle floors, and your artisans and commercial people at street level.'

'So what happened?' asked Holmes, genuinely interested.

'The gentry got fed up,' said Blair-Fish. 'When the New Town was built on the other side of Nor' Loch, they were quick to move. With the gentry gone, the old town became dilapidated, and stayed that way for a long time.' He pointed down some steps into an alcove. 'That was the baker's. See those flat stones? That's where the oven was. If you touch them, they're still warmer than the stones around them.'

Siobhan Clarke had to test this. She came back shrugging. Rebus was glad he'd brought Holmes and Clarke with him. They kept Blair-Fish busy while he could keep a surreptitious eye on the builders. This had been his plan all along: to appear to be inspecting Mary King's Close, while really inspecting the builders. They didn't look nervous; well, no more nervous than you would expect. They kept their eyes away from the butcher's shop, and whistled quietly as they worked. They did not seem inclined to discuss the murder. Someone was up a ladder dismantling a run of pipes. Someone else was mending brickwork at the top of a scaffold.

Further into the tour, away from the builders, Blair-Fish took Siobhan Clarke aside to show her where a child had been bricked up in a chimney, a common complaint among eighteenth-century chimney sweeps.

'The Farmer asked a good question,' Rebus confided to Holmes. 'He said, why would you bring anyone down here?

Think about it. It shows you must be local. Only locals know about Mary King's Close, and even then only a select few.' It was true, the public tour of the close was not common knowledge, and tours themselves were by no means frequent. 'They'd have to have been down here themselves, or know someone who had. If not, they'd more likely get lost than find the butcher's.'

Holmes nodded. 'A shame there's no record of the tour parties.' This had been checked, the tours were informal, parties of a dozen or more at a time. There was no written record. 'Could be they knew about the building work and reckoned the body would be down here for weeks.'

'Or maybe,' said Rebus, 'the building work is the reason they were down here in the first place. Someone might have tipped them off. We're checking everyone.'

'Is that why we're here just now? Giving the crew a once-over?' Rebus nodded, and Holmes nodded back. Then he had an idea. 'Maybe it was a way of sending a message.'

'That's what I've been wondering. But what kind of message, and who to?'

'You don't go for the IRA idea?'

'It's plausible and implausible at the same time,' Rebus said. 'We've got nothing here to interest the paramilitaries.'

'We've got Edinburgh Castle, Holyrood Palace, the Festival . . .'

'He has a point.'

They turned towards the voice. Two men were standing in torchlight. Rebus recognised neither of them. As the men came forwards, Rebus studied both. The man who had spoken, the slightly younger of the two, had an English accent and the look of a London copper. It was the hands in the trouser pockets that did it. That and the air of easy superiority that went with the gesture. Plus of course he was wearing old denims and a black leather bomber-jacket. He had close cropped brown hair spiked with gel, and a heavy pockmarked face. He was probably in his late-thirties but looked like a fortysomething with coronary problems. His eyes were a piercing blue. It was difficult to meet them. He didn't blink often, like he didn't want to miss any of the show.

The other man was well-built and fit, in his late-forties, with ruddy cheeks and a good head of black hair just turning silver at the edges. He looked as if he needed to shave two or even three times a day. His suit was dark blue and looked straight off the tailor's dummy. He was smiling.

'Inspector Rebus?'

'The same.'

'I'm DCI Kilpatrick.'

Rebus knew the name of course. It was interesting at last to have a face to put to it. If he remembered right, Kilpatrick was still in the SCS, the Scottish Crime Squad.

'I thought you worked out of Stuart Street, sir,' Rebus said, shaking hands.

'I moved back from Glasgow a few months ago. I don't suppose it made the front page of the *Scotsman*, but I'm heading the squad here now.'

Rebus nodded. The SCS took on serious crimes, where cross-force investigations were necessary. Drugs were their main concern, or had been. Rebus knew men who'd been seconded to the SCS. You stayed three or four years and came out two things: unwillingly, and tough as second-day bacon. Kilpatrick was introducing his companion.

'This is DI Abernethy from Special Branch. He's come all the way from London to see us.'

'That takes the biscuit,' said Rebus.

'My grandad was a Jock,' Abernethy answered, gripping Rebus's hand and not getting the joke. Rebus introduced Holmes and, when she returned, Siobhan Clarke. From the colouring in Clarke's cheeks, Rebus reckoned someone along the way had made a pass at her. He decided to rule out Mr Blair-Fish, which still left plenty of suspects.

'So,' said Abernethy at last, rubbing his hands, 'where's this slaughterhouse?'

'A butcher's actually,' Mr Blair-Fish explained.

'I know what I mean,' said Abernethy.

Mr Blair-Fish led the way. But Kilpatrick held Rebus back.

'Look,' he whispered, 'I don't like this bastard being here any more than you do, but if we're tolerant we'll get rid of him all the quicker, agreed?'

'Yes, sir.' Kilpatrick's was a Glaswegian accent, managing to be deeply nasal even when reduced to a whisper, and managing, too, to be full of irony and a belief that Glasgow was the centre of the universe. Usually, Glaswegians somehow added to all this a ubiquitous chip on their shoulder, but Kilpatrick didn't seem the type.

'So no more bloody cracks about biscuits.'

'Understood, sir.'

Kilpatrick waited a moment. 'It was you who noticed the paramilitary element, wasn't it?' Rebus nodded. 'Good work.'

'Thank you, sir.' Yes, and Glaswegians could be patronising bastards, too.

When they rejoined the group, Holmes gave Rebus a questioning look, to which Rebus replied with a shrug. At least the shrug was honest.

'So they strung him up here,' Abernethy was saying. He looked around at the setting. 'Bit melodramatic, eh? Not the IRA's style at all. Give them a lock-up or a warehouse, something like that. But someone who likes a bit of drama set this up.'

Rebus was impressed. It was another possible reason for the choice of venue.

'Bang-bang,' Abernethy continued, 'then back upstairs to melt into the crowd, maybe take in a late-night revue before toddling home.'

Clarke interrupted. 'You think there's some connection with the Festival?'

Abernethy studied her openly, causing Brian Holmes to straighten up. Not for the first time, Rebus wondered about Clarke and Holmes.

'Why not?' Abernethy said. 'It's every bit as feasible as anything else I've heard.'

'But it was a six-pack.' Rebus felt obliged to defend his corner.

'No,' Abernethy corrected, 'a *seven*-pack. And that's not paramilitary style at all. A waste of bullets for a start.' He looked to Kilpatrick. 'Could be a drug thing. Gangs like a bit of melodrama, it makes them look like they're in a film. Plus they do like to send messages to each other. Loud messages.'

Kilpatrick nodded. 'We're considering it.'

'My money'd still be on terrorists,' Rebus added. 'A gun like that –'

'Dealers use guns, too, Inspector. They *like* guns. Big ones to make a big loud noise. I'll tell you something, I'd hate to have been down here. The report from a nine-millimetre in an enclosed space like this. It could blow out your eardrums.'

'A silencer,' Siobhan Clarke offered. It wasn't her day. Abernethy just gave her a look, so Rebus provided the explanation.

'Revolvers don't take silencers.'

Abernethy pointed to Rebus, but his eyes were on Clarke's. 'Listen to your Inspector, darling, you might learn something.'

Rebus looked around the room. There were six people there, four of whom would gladly punch another's lights out.

He didn't think Mr Blair-Fish would enter the fray.

Abernethy meantime had sunk to his knees, rubbing his fingers over the floor, over ancient dirt and husks.

'The SOCOs took off the top inch of earth,' Rebus said, but Abernethy wasn't listening. Bags and bags of the stuff had been taken to the sixth floor of Fettes HQ to be sieved and analysed and God knew what else by the forensics lab.

It occurred to Rebus that all the group could now see of Abernethy was a fat arse and brilliant white Reeboks. Abernethy turned his face towards them and smiled. Then he got up, brushing his palms together.

'Was the deceased a drug user?'

'No signs.'

'Only I was thinking, SaS, could be Smack and Speed.'

Again, Rebus was impressed, thoroughly despite himself. Dust had settled in the gel of Abernethy's hair, small enough motes of comfort.

'Could be Scott and Sheena,' offered Rebus. In other words: could be anything. Abernethy just shrugged. He'd been giving them a display, and now the show was over.

'I think I've seen enough,' he said. Kilpatrick nodded with relief. It must be hard, Rebus reflected, being a top cop in your field, a man with a rep, sent to act as tour guide for a junior officer . . . and a Sassenach at that.

Galling, that was the word.

Abernethy was speaking again. 'Might as well drop in on the Murder Room while I'm here.'

'Why not?' said Rebus coldly.

'No reason I can think of,' replied Abernethy, all sweetness and bite.

5

St Leonard's police station, headquarters of the city's B
Division, boasted a semi-permanent Murder Room. The
present inquiry looked like it had been going on forever.
Abernethy seemed to favour the scene. He browsed among
the computer screens, telephones, wall charts and photographs. Kilpatrick touched Rebus's arm.

'Keep an eye on him, will you? I'll just go say hello to
your Chief Super while I'm here.'

'Right, sir.'

Chief Inspector Lauderdale watched him leave. 'So that's
Kilpatrick of the Crime Squad, eh? Funny, he looks almost
mortal.'

It was true that Kilpatrick's reputation – a hard one to
live up to – preceded him. He'd had spectacular successes
in Glasgow, and some decidedly public failures too. Huge
quantities of drugs had been seized, but a few terrorist
suspects had managed to slip away.

'At least he looks human,' Lauderdale went on, 'which
is more than can be said for our cockney friend.'

Abernethy couldn't have heard this – he was out of
earshot – but he looked up suddenly towards them and
grinned. Lauderdale went to take a phone call, and the
Special Branch man sauntered back towards Rebus, hands
stuffed into his jacket pockets.

'It's a good operation this, but there's not much to go
on, is there?'

'Not much.'

'And what you've got doesn't make much sense.'

'Not yet.'

'You worked with Scotland Yard on a case, didn't you?'

'That's right.'

'With George Flight?'

'Right again.'

'He's gone for retraining, you know. I mean, at *his* age. Got interested in computers, I don't know, maybe he's got a point. They're the future of crime, aren't they? Day's coming, the big villains won't have to move from their living rooms.'

'The big villains never have.'

This earned a smile from Abernethy, or at least a lopsided sneer. 'Has my minder gone for a jimmy?'

'He's gone to say hello to someone.'

'Well tell him ta-ta from me.' Abernethy looked around, then lowered his voice. 'I don't think DCI Kilpatrick will be sorry to see the back of me.'

'What makes you say that?'

Abernethy chuckled. 'Listen to you. If your voice was any colder you could store cadavers in it. Still think you've got terrorists in Edinburgh?' Rebus said nothing. 'Well, it's *your* problem. I'm well shot of it. Tell Kilpatrick I'll talk to him before I head south.'

'You're supposed to stay here.'

'Just tell him I'll be in touch.'

There was no painless way of stopping Abernethy from leaving, so Rebus didn't even try. But he didn't think Kilpatrick would be happy. He picked up one of the phones. What did Abernethy mean about it being Rebus's problem? If there *was* a terrorist connection, it'd be out of CID's hands. It would become Special Branch's domain, M15's domain. So what did he mean?

He gave Kilpatrick the message, but Kilpatrick didn't seem bothered after all. There was relaxation in his voice, the sort that came with a large whisky. The Farmer had

41

stopped drinking for a while, but was back off the wagon again. Rebus wouldn't mind a drop himself...

Lauderdale, who had also just put down a telephone, was staring at a pad on which he'd been writing as he took the call.

'Something?' Rebus asked.

'We may have a positive ID on the victim. Do you want to check it out?' Lauderdale tore the sheet from the pad.

'Do Hibs fans weep?' Rebus answered, accepting it.

Actually, not all Hibs fans were prone to tears. Siobhan Clarke supported Hibernian, which put her in a minority at St Leonard's. Being English-educated (another minority, much smaller) she didn't understand the finer points of Scottish bigotry, though one or two of her fellow officers had attempted to educate her. She wasn't Catholic, they explained patiently, so she should support Heart of Midlothian. Hibernian were the Catholic team. Look at their name, look at their green strip. They were Edinburgh's version of Glasgow Celtic, just as Hearts were like Glasgow Rangers.

'It's the same in England,' they'd tell her. 'Wherever you've got Catholics and Protestants in the same place.' Manchester had United (Catholic) and City (Protestant), Liverpool had Liverpool (Catholic) and Everton (Protestant). It only got complicated in London. London even had Jewish teams.

Siobhan Clarke just smiled, shaking her head. It was no use arguing, which didn't stop her trying. They just kept joking with her, teasing her, trying to convert her. It was light-hearted, but she couldn't always tell how light-hearted. The Scots tended to crack jokes with a straight face and be deadly serious when they smiled. When some officers at St Leonard's found out her birthday was coming, she found herself unwrapping half a dozen Hearts scarves. They all went to a charity shop.

She'd seen the darker side of football loyalty, too. The

collection tins at certain games. Depending on where you were standing, you'd be asked to donate to either one cause or the other. Usually it was for 'families' or 'victims' or 'prisoners' aid', but everyone who gave knew they might be perpetuating the violence in Northern Ireland. Fearfully, most gave. One pound sterling towards the price of a gun.

She'd come across the same thing on Saturday when, with a couple of friends, she'd found herself standing at the Hearts end of the ground. The tin had come round, and she'd ignored it. Her friends were quiet after that.

'We should be doing something about it,' she complained to Rebus in his car.

'Such as?'

'Get an undercover team in there, arrest whoever's behind it.'

'Behave.'

'Well why not?'

'Because it wouldn't solve anything and there'd be no charge we could make stick other than something paltry like not having a licence. Besides, if you ask me most of that cash goes straight into the collector's pocket. It never reaches Northern Ireland.'

'But it's the *principle* of the thing.'

'Christ, listen to you.' Principles: they were slow to go, and some coppers never lost them entirely. 'Here we are.'

He reversed into a space in front of a tenement block on Mayfield Gardens. The address was a top floor flat.

'Why is it always the top floor?' Siobhan complained.

'Because that's where the poor people live.'

There were two doors on the top landing. The name on one doorbell read MURDOCK. There was a brown bristle welcome-mat just outside the door. The message on it was GET LOST!

'Charming.' Rebus pressed the bell. The door was opened by a bearded man wearing thick wire-framed glasses. The beard didn't help, but Rebus would guess the man's age at

43

mid-twenties. He had thick shoulder-length black hair, through which he ran a hand.

'I'm Detective Inspector Rebus. This is –'

'Come in, come in. Mind out for the motorbike.'

'Yours, Mr Murdock?'

'No, it's Billy's. It hasn't worked since he moved in.'

The bike's frame was intact, but the engine lay disassembled along the hall carpet, lying on old newspapers turned black from oil. Smaller pieces were in polythene bags, each bag tied at the neck and marked with an identifying number.

'That's clever,' said Rebus.

'Oh aye,' said Murdock, 'he's organised is Billy. In here.' He led them into a cluttered living area. 'This is Millie, she lives here.'

'Hiya.'

Millie was sitting on the sofa swathed in a sleeping bag, despite the heat outside. She was watching the television and smoking a cigarette.

'You phoned us, Mr Murdock.'

'Aye, well, it's about Billy.' Murdock began to pad around the room. 'See, the description in the paper and on the telly, well ... I didn't think about it at the time, but as Millie says, it's not like Billy to stay away so long. Like I say, he's organised. Usually he'd phone or something, just to let us know.'

'When did you last see him?'

Murdock looked to Millie. 'When was it, Thursday night?'

'I saw him Friday morning.'

'So you did.'

Rebus turned to Millie. She had short fair hair, dark at the roots, and dark eyebrows. Her face was long and plain, her chin highlighted by a protruding mole. Rebus reckoned she was a few years older than Murdock. 'Did he say where he was going?'

'He didn't say anything. There's not a lot of conversation in this flat at that hour.'

'What hour?'

She flicked ash into the ashtray which was balanced on her sleeping bag. It was a nervous habit, the cigarette being tapped even when there was no ash for it to surrender. 'Seven thirty, quarter to eight,' she said.

'Where does he work?'

'He doesn't,' said Murdock, resting his hand on the mantelpiece. 'He used to work in the Post Office, but they laid him off a few months back. He's on the dole now, along with half of Scotland.'

'And what do you do, Mr Murdock?'

'I'm a computer consultant.'

Sure enough, some of the living room's clutter was made up of keyboards and disk drives, some of them dismantled, piled on top of each other. There were piles of fat magazines too, and books, hefty operating manuals.

'Did either of you know Billy before he moved in?'

'I did,' said Millie. 'A friend of a friend, casual acquaintance sort of thing. I knew he was looking for a room, and there was a room going spare here, so I suggested him to Murdock.' She changed channels on the TV. She was watching with the sound turned off, watching through a squint of cigarette smoke.

'Can we see Billy's room?'

'Why not?' said Murdock. He'd been glancing nervously towards Millie all the time she'd been talking. He seemed relieved to be in movement. He took them back into where the narrow entrance hall became a wider rectangle, off which were three doors. One was a cupboard, one the kitchen. Back along the narrow hall they'd passed the bathroom on one side and Murdock's bedroom on the other. Which left just this last door.

It led them into a very small, very tidy bedroom. The room itself would be no more than ten feet by eight, yet it managed to contain single bed, wardrobe, a chest of drawers and a writing desk and chair. A hi-fi unit, including speakers, sat atop the chest of drawers. The bed had been made, and there was nothing left lying around.

'You haven't tidied up, have you?'

Murdock shook his head. 'Billy was always tidying. You should see the kitchen.'

'Do you have a photograph of Billy?' Rebus asked.

'I might have some from one of our parties. You want to look at them?'

'Just the best one will do.'

'I'll fetch it then.'

'Thank you.' When Murdock had gone, Siobhan squeezed into the room beside Rebus. Until then, she'd been forced to stay just outside the door.

'Initial thoughts?' Rebus asked.

'Neurotically tidy,' she said, the comment of one whose own flat looked like a cross between a pizza franchise and a bottle bank.

But Rebus was studying the walls. There was a Hearts pennant above the bed, and a Union Jack flag on which the Red Hand of Ulster was centrally prominent, with above it the words 'No Surrender' and below it the letters FTP. Even Siobhan Clarke knew what those stood for.

'Fuck the Pope,' she murmured.

Murdock was back. He didn't attempt to squeeze into the narrow aisle between bed and wardrobe, but stood in the doorway and handed the photo to Siobhan Clarke, who handed it to Rebus. It showed a young man smiling manically for the camera. Behind him you could see a can of beer held high, as though someone were about to pour it over his head.

'It's as good a photo as we've got,' Murdock said by way of apology.

'Thank you, Mr Murdock.' Rebus was almost sure. Almost. 'Billy had a tattoo?'

'On his arm, aye. It looked like one of those things you do yourself when you're a daft laddie.'

Rebus nodded. They'd released details of the tattoo, looking for a quick result.

'I never really looked at it close up,' Murdock went on, 'and Billy never talked about it.'

Millie had joined him in the doorway. She had discarded the sleeping bag and was wearing a modestly long t-shirt over bare legs. She put an arm around Murdock's waist. 'I remember it,' she said. 'SaS. Big S, small a.'

'Did he ever tell you what it stood for?'

She shook her head. Tears were welling in her eyes. 'It's him, isn't it? He's the one you found dead?'

Rebus tried to be non-committal, but his face gave him away. Millie started to bawl, and Murdock hugged her to him. Siobhan Clarke had lifted some cassette tapes from the chest of drawers and was studying them. She handed them silently to Rebus. They were collections of Orange songs, songs about the struggle in Ulster. Their titles said it all: *The Sash and other Glories*, *King Billy's Marching Tunes*, *No Surrender*. He stuck one of the tapes in his pocket.

They did some more searching of Billy Cunningham's room, but came up with little excepting a recent letter from his mother. There was no address on the letter, but it bore a Glasgow postmark, and Millie recalled Billy saying something about coming from Hillhead. Well, they'd let Glasgow deal with it. Let Glasgow break the news to some unsuspecting family.

In one of the drawers, Siobhan Clarke came up with a Fringe programme. It contained the usual meltdown of *Abigail's Party*s and *Krapp's Last Tape*s, revues called things like *Teenage Alsatian Orgy*, and comic turns on the run from London fatigue.

'He's ringed a show,' said Clarke.

So he had, a country and western act at the Crazy Hose

Saloon. The act had appeared for three nights back at the start of the Festival.

'There's no country music in his collection,' Clarke commented.

'At least he showed taste,' said Rebus.

On the way back to the station, he pushed the Orange tape into his car's antiquated machine.

The tape played slow, which added to the grimness. Rebus had heard stuff like it before, but not for a wee while. Songs about King Billy and the Apprentice Boys, the Battle of the Boyne and the glory of 1690, songs about routing the Catholics and why the men of Ulster would struggle to the end. The singer had a pub vibrato and little else, and was backed by accordion, snare and the occasional flute. Only an Orange marching band could make the flute sound martial to the ears. Well, an Orange marching band or Iain Anderson from Jethro Tull. Rebus was reminded that he hadn't listened to Tull in an age. Anything would be better than these songs of ... the word 'hate' sprang to mind, but he dismissed it. There was no vitriol in the lyrics, just a stern refusal to compromise in any way, to give ground, to accept that things could change now that the 1690s had become the 1990s. It was all blinkered and backward-looking. How narrow a view could you get?

'The sod is,' said Siobhan Clarke, 'you find yourself humming the tunes after.'

'Aye,' said Rebus, 'bigotry's catchy enough all right.'

And he whistled Jethro Tull all the way back to St Leonard's.

Lauderdale had arranged a press conference and wanted to know what Rebus knew.

'I'm not positive,' was the answer. 'Not a hundred per cent.'

'How close?'

'Ninety, ninety-five.'

Lauderdale considered this. 'So should I say anything?'

'That's up to you, sir. A fingerprint team's on its way to the flat. We'll know soon enough one way or the other.'

One of the problems with the victim was that the last killing shot had blown away half his face, the bullet entering through the back of the neck and tearing up through the jaw. As Dr Curt had explained, they could do an ID covering up the bottom half of the face, allowing a friend or relative to see just the top half. But would that be enough? Before today's potential break, they'd been forced to consider dental work. The victim's teeth were the usual result of a Scottish childhood, eroded by sweets and shored up by dentistry. But as the forensic pathologist had said, the mouth was badly damaged, and what dental work remained was fairly routine. There was nothing unusual there for any dentist to spot definitively as his or her work.

Rebus arranged for the party photograph to be reprinted and sent to Glasgow with the relevant details. Then he went to Lauderdale's press conference.

Chief Inspector Lauderdale loved his duels with the media. But today he was more nervous than usual. Perhaps it was that he had a larger audience than he was used to, Chief Superintendent Watson and DCI Kilpatrick having emerged from somewhere to listen. Both sported faces too ruddy to be natural, whisky certainly the cause. While the journalists sat towards the front of the room, the police officers stood to the back. Kilpatrick saw Rebus and sidled over to him.

'You may have a positive ID?' he whispered.

'Maybe.'

'So is it drugs or the IRA?' There was a wry smile on his face. He didn't really expect an answer, it was the whisky asking, that was all. But Rebus had an answer for him anyway.

'If it's anybody,' he said, 'it's not the IRA but the other lot.' There were so many names for them he didn't even begin to list them: UDA, UVF, UFF, UR ... The U stood for Ulster in each case. They were proscribed organisations, and they were all Protestant. Kilpatrick rocked back a little on his heels. His face was full of questions, fighting their way to the surface past the burst blood vessels which cherried nose and cheeks. A drinker's face. Rebus had seen too many of them, including his own some nights in the bathroom mirror.

But Kilpatrick wasn't so far gone. He knew he was in no condition to ask questions, so he made his way back to the Farmer instead, where he spoke a few words. Farmer Watson glanced across to Rebus, then nodded to Kilpatrick. Then they turned their attention back to the press briefing.

Rebus knew the reporters. They were old hands mostly, and knew what to expect from Chief Inspector Lauderdale. You might walk into a Lauderdale session sniffing and baying like a bloodhound, but you shuffled out like a sleepy-faced pup. So they stayed quiet mostly, and let him have his insubstantial say.

Except for Mairie Henderson. She was down at the front, asking questions the others weren't bothering to ask; weren't bothering for the simple reason that they knew the answer the Chief Inspector would give.

'No comment,' he told Mairie for about the twentieth time. She gave up and slumped in her chair. Someone else asked a question, so she looked around, surveying the room. Rebus jerked his chin in greeting. Mairie glared and stuck her tongue out at him. A few of the other journalists looked around in his direction. Rebus smiled out their inquisitive stares.

The briefing over, Mairie caught up with him in the corridor. She was carrying a legal notepad, her usual blue fineliner pen, and a recording walkman.

'Thanks for your help the other night,' she said.

'No comment.'

She knew it was a waste of time getting angry at John

Rebus, so exhaled noisily instead. 'I was first on the scene, I could have had a scoop.'

'Come to the pub with me and you can have as many scoops as you like.'

'That one's so weak it's got holes in its knees.' She turned and walked off, Rebus watching her. He never liked to pass up the opportunity of looking at her legs.

6

Edinburgh City Mortuary was sited on the Cowgate, at the bottom of High School Wynd and facing St Ann's Community Centre and Blackfriars Street. The building was low-built red brick and pebbledash, purposely anonymous and tucked in an out of the way place. Steep sloping roads led up towards the High Street. For a long time now, the Cowgate had been a thoroughfare for traffic, not pedestrians. It was narrow and deep like a canyon, its pavements offering scant shelter from the taxis and cars rumbling past. The place was not for the faint-hearted. Society's underclass could be found there, when it wasn't yet time to shuffle back to the hostel.

But the street was undergoing redevelopment, including a court annexe. First they'd cleaned up the Grassmarket, and now the city fathers had the Cowgate in their sights.

Rebus waited outside the mortuary for a couple of minutes, until a woman poked her head out of the door.

'Inspector Rebus?'

'That's right.'

'He told me to tell you he's already gone to Bannerman's.'

'Thanks.' Rebus headed off towards the pub.

Bannerman's had been just cellarage at one time, and hadn't been altered much since. Its vaulted rooms were unnervingly like those of the shops in Mary King's Close. Cellars like these formed connecting burrows beneath the Old Town, worming from the Lawnmarket down to the Canongate and beyond. The bar wasn't busy yet, and Dr

Curt was sitting by the window, his beer glass resting on a barrel which served as table. Somehow, he'd found one of the few comfortable chairs in the place. It looked like a minor nobleman's perch, with armrests and high back. Rebus bought a double whisky for himself, dragged over a stool, and sat down.

'Your health, John.'

'And yours.'

'So what can I do for you?'

Even in a pub, Rebus would swear he could smell soap and surgical alcohol wafting up from Curt's hands. He took a swallow of whisky. Curt frowned.

'Looks like I might be examining your liver sooner than I'd hoped.'

Rebus nodded towards the pack of cigarettes on the table. They were Curt's and they were untipped. 'Not if you keep smoking those.'

Dr Curt smiled. He hadn't long taken up smoking, having decided to see just how indestructible he was. He wouldn't call it a death wish exactly; it was merely an exercise in mortality.

'How long have you and Ms Rattray been an item then?'

Curt laughed. 'Dear God, is that why I'm here? You want to ask me about Caroline?'

'Just making conversation. She's not bad though.'

'Oh, she's quite something.' Curt lit a cigarette and inhaled, nodding to himself. 'Quite something,' he repeated through a cloud of smoke.

'We may have a name for the victim in Mary King's Close. It's up to fingerprints now.'

'Is that why you wanted to see me? Not just to discuss Caro?'

'I want to talk about guns.'

'I'm no expert on guns.'

'Good. I'm not after an expert, I'm after someone I can talk to. Have you seen the ballistics report?' Curt shook his head. 'We're looking at something like a Smith and Wesson model 547, going by the rifling marks – five grooves, right-hand twist. It's a revolver, takes six rounds of nine millimetre parabellum.'

'You've lost me already.'

'Probably the version with the three-inch rather than four-inch barrel, which means a weight of thirty-two ounces.' Rebus sipped his drink. There were whisky fumes in his nostrils now, blocking any other smells. 'Revolvers don't accept silencers.'

'Ah.' Curt nodded. 'I begin to see some light.'

'A confined space like that, shaped the way it was ...' Rebus nodded past the bar to the room beyond. 'Much the same size and shape as this.'

'It would have been loud.'

'Bloody loud. Deafening, you might say.'

'Meaning what exactly?'

Rebus shrugged. 'I'm just wondering how professional all of this really was. I mean, on the surface, if you look at the *style* of execution, then yes, it was a pro job, no question. But then things start to niggle.'

Curt considered. 'So what now? Do we scour the city for recent purchasers of hearing-aids?'

Rebus smiled. 'It's a thought.'

'All I can tell you, John, is that those bullets did damage. Whether meant to or not, they were messy. Now, we've both come up against messy killers before. Usually the facts of the mess make it easier to find them. But this time there doesn't seem to be much evidence left lying around, apart from the bullets.'

'I know.'

Curt slapped his hand on the barrel. 'Tell you what, I've got a suggestion.'

'What is it?'

He leaned forward, as if to impart a secret. 'Let me give you Caroline Rattray's phone number.'

'Bugger off,' said Rebus.

That evening, a marked patrol car picked him up from Patience's Oxford Terrace flat. The driver was a Detective Constable called Robert Burns, and Burns was doing Rebus a favour.

'I appreciate it,' said Rebus.

Though Burns was attached to C Division in the west end, he'd been born and raised in Pilmuir, and still had friends and enemies there. He was a known quantity in the Gar-B, which was what mattered to Rebus.

'I was born in one of the pre-fabs,' Burns explained. 'Before they levelled them to make way for the high-rises. The high-rises were supposed to more "civilised", if you can believe that. Bloody architects and town planners. You never find one admitting he made a mistake, do you?' He smiled. 'They're a bit like us that way.'

'By "us" do you mean the police or the Wee Frees?' Burns was more than just a member of the Free Church of Scotland. On Sunday afternoons he took his religion to the foot of The Mound, where he spouted hellfire and brimstone to anyone who'd listen. Rebus had listened a few times. But Burns took a break during the Festival. As he'd pointed out, even his voice would be fighting a losing battle against steel bands and untuned guitars.

They were turning into the Gar-B, passing the gable end again with its sinister greeting.

'Drop me as close as you can, eh?'

'Sure,' said Burns. And when they came to the dead end near the garages, he slowed only fractionally as he bumped the car up first onto the pavement and then onto the grass. 'It's not my car,' he explained.

They drove beside the path past the garages and a high-rise, until there was nowhere else to go. When Burns stopped, the car was resting about twelve feet from the community centre.

'I can walk from here,' said Rebus.

Kids who'd been lying on the centre's roof were standing now, watching them, cigarettes hanging from open mouths. People watched from the path and from open windows, too. Burns turned to Rebus.

'Don't tell me you wanted to sneak up on them?'

'This is just fine.' He opened his door. 'Stay with the car. I don't want us losing any tyres.'

Rebus walked towards the community centre's wide open doors. The teenagers on the roof watched him with practised hostility. There were paper planes lying all around, some of them made airborne again temporarily by a gust of wind. As Rebus walked into the building, he heard grunting noises above him. His rooftop audience were pretending to be pigs.

There was no preliminary chamber, just the hall itself. At one end stood a high basketball hoop. Some teenagers were in a ruck around the grounded ball, feet scraping at ankles, hands pulling at arms and hair. So much for non-contact sports. On a makeshift stage sat a ghetto blaster, blaring out the fashion in heavy metal. Rebus didn't reckon he'd score many points by announcing that he'd been in at the birth. Most of these kids had been born after *Anarchy in the UK*, never mind *Communication Breakdown*.

There was a mix of ages, and it was impossible to pick out Peter Cave. He could be nodding his head to the distorted electric guitar. He could be smoking by the wall. Or in with the basketball brigade. But no, he was coming towards Rebus from the other direction, from a tight group which included black t-shirt from Rebus's first visit.

'Can I help?'

Father Leary had said he was in his mid-twenties, but he could pass for late-teens. The clothes helped, and he wore them well. Rebus had seen church people before when they wore denim. They usually looked as if they'd be more comfortable in something less comfortable. But Cave, in faded denim jeans and denim shirt, with half a dozen thin leather and metal bracelets around his wrists, he looked all right.

'Not many girls,' Rebus stated, playing for a little more time.

Peter Cave looked around. 'Not just now. Usually there are more than this, but on a nice night...'

It was a nice night. He'd left Patience drinking cold rose wine in the garden. He had left her reluctantly. He got no initial bad feelings from Cave. The young man was fresh-faced and clear-eyed and looked level headed too. His hair was long but by no means untidy, and his face was square and honest with a deep cleft in the chin.

'I'm sorry,' Cave said, 'I'm Peter Cave. I run the youth club.' His hand shot out, bracelets sliding down his wrist. Rebus took the hand and smiled. Cave wanted to know who he was, a not unreasonable request.

'Detective Inspector Rebus.'

Cave nodded. 'Davey said a policeman had been round earlier. I thought probably he meant uniformed. What's the trouble, Inspector?'

'No trouble, Mr Cave.'

A circle of frowning onlookers had formed itself around the two of them. Rebus wasn't worried, not yet.

'Call me Peter.'

'Mr Cave,' Rebus licked his lips, 'how are things going here?'

'What do you mean?'

'A simple question, sir. Only, crime in Pilmuir hasn't exactly dropped since you started this place up.'

Cave bristled at that. 'There haven't been any gang fights.'

Rebus accepted this. 'But housebreaking, assaults ... there are still syringes in the playpark and aerosols lying –'

'Aerosols to you too.'

Rebus turned to see who had entered. It was the boy with the naked chest and denim jacket.

'Hello, Davey,' said Rebus. The ring had broken long enough to let denim jacket through.

The youth pointed a finger. 'I thought I said you didn't want to know my name?'

'I can't help it if people tell me things, Davey.'

'Davey Soutar,' Burns added. He was standing in the doorway, arms folded, looking like he was enjoying himself. He wasn't of course, it was just a necessary pose.

'Davey Soutar,' Rebus echoed.

Soutar had clenched his fists. Peter Cave attempted to intercede. 'Now, please. Is there a problem here, Inspector?'

'You tell me, Mr Cave.' He looked around him. 'Frankly, we're a little bit concerned about this gang hut.'

Colour flooded Cave's cheeks. 'It's a youth centre.'

Rebus was now studying the ceiling. Nobody was playing basketball any more. The music had been turned right down. 'If you say so, sir.'

'Look, you come barging in here –'

'I don't recall barging, Mr Cave. More of a saunter. I didn't ask for trouble. If Davey here can be persuaded to unclench his fists, maybe you and me can have a quiet chat outside.' He looked at the circle around them. 'I'm not one for playing to the cheap seats.'

Cave stared at Rebus, then at Soutar. He nodded slowly, his face drained of anger, and eventually Soutar let his hands relax. You could tell it was an effort. Burns hadn't put in an appearance for nothing.

'There now,' said Rebus. 'Come on, Mr Cave, let's you and me go for a walk.'

They walked across the playing fields. Burns had returned to the patrol car and moved it to a spot where he could watch them. Some teenagers watched from the back of the community centre and from its roof, but they didn't venture any closer than that.

'I really don't see, Inspector –'

'You think you're doing a good job here, sir?'

Cave thought about it before answering. 'Yes, I do.'

'You think the experiment is a success?'

'A limited success so far, but yes, once again.' He had his hands behind his back, head bowed a little. He looked like he didn't have a care in the world.

'No regrets?'

'None.'

'Funny then . . .'

'What?'

'Your church doesn't seem so sure.'

Cave stopped in his tracks. 'Is that what this is about? You're in Conor's congregation, is that it? He's sent you here to . . . what's the phrase? Come down heavy on me?'

'Nothing like that.'

'He's paranoid. *He* was the one who wanted me here. Now suddenly he's decided I should leave, *ipso facto* I *must* leave. He's used to getting his way after all. Well, I don't choose to leave. I like it fine here. Is that what he's afraid of? Well there's not much he can do about it, is there? And as far as I can see, Inspector, there's nothing you can do about it either, unless someone from the club is found breaking the law.' Cave's face had reddened, his hands coming from behind his back so he could gesture with them.

'That lot break the law every day.'

'Now just a –'

'No, listen for a minute. Okay, you got the Jaffas and the Tims together, but ask yourself why they were amenable. If they're not divided, they're united, and they're united for a *reason*. They're the same as before, only stronger. You must see that.'

'I see nothing of the sort. People can change, Inspector.'

Rebus had been hearing the line all his professional life. He sighed and toed the ground.

'You don't believe that?'

'Frankly, sir, not in this particular case, and the crime stats back me up. What you've got just now is a truce of sorts, and it suits them because while there's a truce they can get busy carving up territory between them. Anyone threatens them, they can retaliate in spades ... or even *with* spades. But it won't last, and when they split back into their separate gangs, there's going to be blood spilled, no way round it. Because now there'll be more at stake. Tell me, in your club tonight, how many Catholics were there?'

Cave didn't answer, he was too busy shaking his head. 'I feel sorry for you, really I do. I can smell cynicism off you like sulphur. I don't happen to believe anything you've just said.'

'Then you're every bit as naive as I am cynical, and that means they're just using you. Which is good, because the only way of looking at this is that you've been sucked into it and you accept it, knowing the truth.'

Cave's cheeks were red again. 'How dare you say that!' And he punched Rebus in the stomach, hard. Rebus had been punched by professionals, but he was unprepared and felt himself double over for a moment, getting his wind back. There was a burning feeling in his gut, and it wasn't whisky. He could hear cheering in the distance. Tiny figures were dancing up and down on the community centre roof. Rebus hoped they'd fall through it. He straightened up again.

'Is that what you call setting a good example, Mr Cave?'

Then he punched Cave solidly on the jaw. The young man stumbled backwards and almost fell.

He heard a double roar from the community centre. The youth of the Gar-B were clambering down from the roof, starting to run in his direction. Burns had started the car and was bumping it across the football pitch towards him. The car was outpacing the crowd, but only just. An empty can bounced off its rear windscreen. Burns barely braked as he caught up with Rebus. Rebus yanked the door open and got in, grazing a knee and an elbow. Then they were off again, making for the roadway.

'Well,' Burns commented, checking the rearview, 'that seemed to go off okay.' Rebus was catching his breath and examining his elbow.

'How did you know Davey Soutar's name?'

'He's a maniac,' Burns said simply. 'I try to keep abreast of these things.'

Rebus exhaled loudly, rolling his sleeve back down. 'Never do a favour for a priest,' he said to himself.

'I'll bear that in mind, sir,' said Burns.

7

Rebus walked into the Murder Room next morning with a cup of delicatessen decaf and a tuna sandwich on whole-meal. He sat at his desk and peeled off the top from the styrofoam cup. From the corner of his eye he could see the fresh mound of paperwork which had appeared on his desk since yesterday. But he could ignore it for another five minutes.

The victim's fingerprints had been matched with those taken from items in Billy Cunningham's room. So now they had a name for the body, but precious little else. Murdock and Millie had been interviewed, and the Post Office were looking up their personnel files. Today, Billy's room would be searched again. They still didn't know who he was really. They still didn't know anything about where he came from or who his parents were. There was so much they didn't know.

In a murder investigation, Rebus had found, you didn't always need to know everything.

Chief Inspector Lauderdale was standing behind him. Rebus knew this because Lauderdale brought a smell with him. Not everyone could distinguish it, but Rebus could. It was as if talcum powder had been used in a bathroom to cover some less acceptable aroma. Then there was a click and the buzz of Lauderdale's battery-shaver. Rebus straight-ened at the sound.

'Chief wants to see you,' Lauderdale said. 'Breakfast can wait.'

Rebus stared at his sandwich.

'I said it can wait.'

Rebus nodded. 'I'll bring you back a mug of coffee, shall I, sir?'

He took his own coffee with him, sipping it as he listened for a moment at Farmer Watson's door. There were voices inside, one of them more nasal than the other. Rebus knocked and entered. DCI Kilpatrick was sitting across the desk from the Farmer.

'Morning, John,' said the Chief Super. 'Coffee?'

Rebus raised his cup. 'Got some, sir.'

'Well, sit down.'

He sat next to Kilpatrick. 'Morning, sir.'

'Good morning, John.' Kilpatrick was nursing a mug, but he wasn't drinking. The Farmer meantime was pouring himself a refill from his personal machine.

'Right, John,' he said at last, sitting down. 'Bottom line, you're being seconded to DCI Kilpatrick's section.' Watson took a gulp of coffee, swilling it around his mouth. Rebus looked to Kilpatrick, who obliged with a confirmation.

'You'll be based with us at Fettes, but you're going to be our eyes and ears on this murder inquiry, liaison if you like, so you'll still spend most of your time here at St Leonard's.'

'But why?'

'Well, Inspector, this case might concern the Crime Squad.'

'Yes, sir, but why me in particular?'

'You've been in the Army. I notice you served in Ulster in the late '60s.'

'That was quarter of a century ago,' Rebus protested. An age spent forgetting all about it.

'Nevertheless, you'll agree there seem to be paramilitary aspects to this case. As you commented, the gun is not your everyday hold-up weapon. It's a type of revolver used by terrorists. A lot of guns have been coming into the UK recently. Maybe this murder will connect us to them.'

'Wait a second, you're saying you're not interested in the shooting, you're interested in the *gun*?'

'I think it will become clearer when I show you our operation at Fettes. I'll be through here in –' he looked at his watch '– say twenty minutes. That should give you time to say goodbye to your loved ones.' He smiled.

Rebus nodded. He hadn't touched his coffee. A cooling scum had formed on its surface. 'All right, sir,' he said, getting to his feet.

He was still a little dazed when he got back to the Murder Room. Two detectives were being told a joke by a third. The joke was about a squid with no money, a restaurant bill, and the guy from the kitchen who washed up. The guy from the kitchen was called Hans.

Rebus was joining the SCS, the Bastard Brigade as some called it. He sat at his desk. It took him a minute to work out that something was missing.

'Which bollocks of you's eaten my sandwich?'

As he looked around the room, he saw that the joke had come to an untimely end. But no one was paying attention to him. A message was being passed through the place, changing the mood. Lauderdale came over to Rebus's desk. He was holding a sheet of fax paper.

'What is it?' Rebus asked.

'Glasgow have tracked down Billy Cunningham's mother.'

'Good. Is she coming here?'

Lauderdale nodded distractedly. 'She'll be here for the formal ID.'

'No father?'

'The father and mother split up a long time ago. Billy was still an infant. She told us his name though.' He handed over the fax sheet. 'It's Morris Cafferty.'

'What?' Rebus's hunger left him.

'Morris Gerald Cafferty.'

Rebus read the fax sheet. 'Say it ain't so. It's just Glasgow having a joke.' But Lauderdale was shaking his head.

'No joke,' he said.

Big Ger Cafferty was in prison, had been for several months, would be for many years to come. He was a dangerous man, runner of protection rackets, extortioner, murderer. They'd pinned only two counts of murder on him, but there had been others, Rebus knew there had been others.

'You think someone was sending him a message?' he asked.

Lauderdale shrugged. 'This changes the case slightly, certainly. According to Mrs Cunningham, Cafferty kept tabs on Billy all the time he was growing up, made sure he didn't want for anything. She still gets money from time to time.'

'But did Billy know who his father was?'

'Not according to Mrs Cunningham.'

'Then would anyone else have known?'

Lauderdale shrugged again. 'I wonder who'll tell Cafferty.'

'They better do it by phone. I wouldn't want to be in the same room with him.'

'Lucky my good suit's in my locker,' said Lauderdale. 'There'll have to be another press conference.'

'Best tell the Chief Super first though, eh?'

Lauderdale's eyes cleared. 'Of course.' He lifted Rebus's receiver to make the call. 'What did he want with you, by the way?'

'Nothing much,' said Rebus. He meant it too, now.

'But maybe this changes things,' he persisted to Kilpatrick in the car. They were seated in the back, a driver taking them the slow route to Fettes. He was sticking to the main roads, instead of the alleys and shortcuts and fast stretches unpoliced by traffic lights that Rebus would have used.

'Maybe,' said Kilpatrick. 'We'll see.'

Rebus had been telling Kilpatrick all about Big Ger Cafferty. 'I mean,' he went on, 'if it's a gang thing, then it's nothing to do with paramilitaries, is it? So I can't help you.'

Kilpatrick smiled at him. 'What is it, John? Most coppers I know would give their drinking arm for an assignment with SCS.'

'Yes, sir.'

'But you're not one of them?'

'I'm quite attached to my drinking arm. It comes in handy for other things.' Rebus looked out of the window. 'The thing is, I've been on secondment before, and I didn't like it much.'

'You mean London? The Chief Superintendent told me all about it.'

'I doubt that, sir,' Rebus said quietly. They turned off Queensferry Road, not a minute's walk from Patience's flat.

'Humour me,' said Kilpatrick stiffly. 'After all, it sounds like you're an expert on this man Cafferty too. I'd be daft not to use a man like you.'

'Yes, sir.'

And they left it at that, saying nothing as they turned into Fettes, Edinburgh's police HQ. At the end of the long road you got a good view of the Gothic spires of Fettes School, one of the city's most exclusive. Rebus didn't know which was uglier, the ornate school or the low anonymous building which housed police HQ. It could have been a comprehensive school, not so much a piece of design as a lack of it. It was one of the most unimaginative buildings Rebus had ever come across. Maybe it was making a statement about its purpose.

The Scottish Crime Squad's Edinburgh operation was run from a cramped office on the fifth floor, a floor shared with the city's Scene of Crime unit. One floor above worked the forensic scientists and the police photographers. There was a lot of interaction between the two floors.

The Crime Squad's real HQ was Stuart Street in Glasgow, with other branches in Stonehaven and Dunfermline, the latter being a technical support unit. Eighty-two officers in total, plus a dozen or so civilian staff.

'We've got our own surveillance and drugs teams,' Kilpatrick added. 'We recruit from all eight Scottish forces.' He kept his spiel going as he led Rebus through the SCS office. A few people looked up from their work, but by no means all of them. Two who did were a bald man and his freckle-faced neighbour. Their look wasn't welcoming, just interested.

Rebus and Kilpatrick were approaching a very large man who was standing in front of a wall-map. The map showed the British Isles and the north European mainland, stretching east as far as Russia. Some sea routes had been marked with long narrow strips of red material, like something you'd use in dressmaking. Only the big man didn't look the type for crimping-shears and tissue-paper cut-outs. On the map, the ports had been circled in black pen. One of the routes ended on the Scottish east coast. The man hadn't turned round at their approach.

'Inspector John Rebus,' said Kilpatrick, 'this is Inspector Ken Smylie. He never smiles, so don't bother joking with him about his name. He doesn't say much, but he's always thinking. And he's from Fife, so watch out. You know what they say about Fifers.'

'I'm from Fife myself,' said Rebus. Smylie had turned round to grip Rebus's hand. He was probably six feet three or four, and had the bulk to make the height work. The bulk was a mixture of muscle and fat, but mostly muscle. Rebus would bet the guy worked out every day. He was a few years younger than Rebus, with short thick fair hair and a small dark moustache. You'd take him for a farm labourer, maybe even a farmer. In the Borders, he'd definitely have played rugby.

'Ken,' Kilpatrick said to Smylie, 'I'd like you to show

John around. He's going to be joining us temporarily. He's ex-Army, served in Ulster.' Kilpatrick winked. 'A good man.' Ken Smylie looked appraisingly at Rebus, who tried to stand up straight, inflating his chest. He didn't know why he wanted to impress Smylie, except that he didn't want him as an enemy. Smylie nodded slowly, sharing a look with Kilpatrick, a look Rebus didn't understand.

Kilpatrick touched Smylie's arm. 'I'll leave you to it.' He turned and called to another officer. 'Jim, any calls?' Then he walked away from them.

Rebus turned to the map. 'Ferry crossings?'

'There isn't a ferry sails from the east coast.'

'They go to Scandinavia.'

'This one doesn't.' He had a point. Rebus decided to try again.

'Boats then?'

'Boats, yes. We think boats.' Rebus had expected the voice to be *basso profondo*, but it was curiously high, as though it hadn't broken properly in Smylie's teens. Maybe it was the reason he didn't say much.

'You're interested in boats then?'

'Only if they're bringing in contraband.'

Rebus nodded. 'Guns.'

'Maybe guns.' He pointed to some of the east European ports. 'See, these days things being what they are, there are a lot of weapons in and around Russia. If you cut back your military, you get excess. And the economic situation there being what it is, you get people who need money.'

'So they steal guns and sell them?'

'If they need to steal them. A lot of the soldiers kept their guns. Plus they picked up souvenirs along the way, stuff from Afghanistan and wherever. Here, sit down.'

They sat at Smylie's desk, Smylie himself spilling from a moulded plastic chair. He brought some photographs out of a drawer. They showed machine guns, rocket launchers, grenades and missiles, armour-piercing shells, a whole dusty armoury.

'This is just some of the stuff that's been tracked down. Most of it in mainland Europe: Holland, Germany, France. But some of it in Northern Ireland of course, and some in England and Scotland.' He tapped a photo of an assault rifle. 'This AK 47 was used in a bank hold-up in Hillhead. You know Professor Kalashnikov is a travelling salesman these days? Times are hard, so he goes to arms fairs around the world flogging his creations. Like this.' Smylie picked out another photograph. 'Later model, the AK 74. The magazine's made of plastic. This is actually the 74S, still quite rare on the market. A lot of the stuff travels across Europe courtesy of motorcycle gangs.'

'Hell's Angels?'

Smylie nodded. 'Some of them are in this up to their tattooed necks, and making a fortune. But there are other problems. A lot of stuff comes into the UK direct. The armed forces, they bring back souvenirs too, from the Falklands or Kuwait. Kalashnikovs, you name it. Not everyone gets searched, a lot of stuff gets in. Later, it's either sold or stolen, and the owners aren't about to report the theft, are they?'

Smylie paused and swallowed, maybe realising how much he'd been talking.

'I thought you were the strong silent type,' Rebus said.

'I get carried away sometimes.'

Rebus wouldn't fancy being on stretcher detail. Smylie began to tidy up the photographs.

'That's basically it,' he said. 'The material that's already here we can't do much about, but with the help of Interpol we're trying to stop the trafficking.'

'You're not saying Scotland is a target for this stuff?'

'A conduit, that's all. It comes through here on its way to Northern Ireland.'

'The IRA?'

'To whoever has the money to pay for it. Right now, we think it's more a Protestant thing. We just don't know why.'

'How much evidence do you have?'

'Not enough.'

Rebus was thinking. Kilpatrick had kept very quiet, but all along he'd thought there was a paramilitary angle to the murder, because it tied in with all of this.

'You're the one who spotted the six-pack?' Smylie asked. Rebus nodded. 'You might well be right about it. If so, the victim must've been involved.'

'Or just someone who got caught up in it.'

'That tends not to happen.'

'But there's another thing. The victim's father is a local gangster, Big Ger Cafferty.'

'You put him away a while back.'

'You're well informed.'

'Well,' said Smylie, 'Cafferty adds a certain symmetry, doesn't he?' He rose briskly from his chair. 'Come on, I'll give you the rest of the tour.'

Not that there was much to see. But Rebus was introduced to his colleagues. They didn't look like supermen, but you wouldn't want to fight them on their terms. They all looked like they'd gone the distance and beyond.

One man, a DS Claverhouse, was the exception. He was lanky and slow-moving and had dark cusps beneath his eyes.

'Don't let him fool you,' Smylie said. 'We don't call him Bloody Claverhouse for nothing.'

Claverhouse's smile took time forming. It wasn't that he was slow so much as that he had to calculate things before he carried them out. He was seated at his desk, Rebus and Smylie standing in front of him. He was tapping his fingers on a red cardboard file. The file was closed, but on its cover was printed the single word SHIELD. Rebus had just seen the word on another file lying on Smylie's desk.

'Shield?' he asked.

'The Shield,' Claverhouse corrected. 'It's something we keep hearing about. Maybe a gang, maybe with Irish connections.'

'But just now,' interrupted Smylie, 'all it is is a name.'

Shield, the word meant something to Rebus. Or rather, he knew it should mean something to him. As he turned from Claverhouse's desk, he caught something Claverhouse was saying to Smylie, saying in an undertone.

'We don't need him.'

Rebus didn't let on he'd heard. He knew nobody liked it when an outsider was brought in. Nor did he feel any happier when introduced to the bald man, a DS Blackwood, and the freckled one, DC Ormiston. They were as enthusiastic about him as dogs welcoming a new flea to the area. Rebus didn't linger; there was a small empty desk waiting from him in another part of the room, and a chair which had been found in some cupboard. The chair didn't quite have three legs, but Rebus got the idea: they hadn't exactly stretched themselves to provide him with a wholesome working environment. He took one look at desk and chair, made his excuses and left. He took a few deep breaths in the corridor, then descended a few floors. He had one friend at Fettes, and saw no reason why he shouldn't visit her.

But there was someone else in DI Gill Templer's office. The nameplate on the door told him so. Her name was DI Murchie and she too was a Liaison Officer. Rebus knocked on the door.

'Enter!'

It was like entering a headmistress's office. DI Murchie was young; at least, her face was. But she had made determined efforts to negate this fact.

'Yes?' she said.

'I was looking for DI Templer.'

Murchie put down her pen and slipped off her half-moon glasses. They hung by a string around her neck. 'She's moved on,' she said. 'Dunfermline, I think.'

71

'Dunfermline? What's she doing there?'

'Dealing with rapes and sexual assaults, so far as I know. Do you have some business with Inspector Templer?'

'No, I just ... I was passing and ... Never mind.' He backed out of the room.

DI Murchie twitched her mouth and put her glasses back on. Rebus went back upstairs feeling worse than ever.

He spent the rest of the morning waiting for something to happen. Nothing did. Everyone kept their distance, even Smylie. And then the phone rang on Smylie's desk, and it was a call for him.

'Chief Inspector Lauderdale,' Smylie said, handing over the receiver.

'Hello?'

'I hear you've been poached from us.'

'Sort of, sir.'

'Well, tell them I want to poach you back.'

I'm not a fucking salmon, thought Rebus. 'I'm still on the investigation, sir,' he said.

'Yes, I know that. The Chief Super told me all about it.' He paused. 'We want you to talk to Cafferty.'

'He won't talk to me.'

'We think he might.'

'Does he know about Billy?'

'Yes, he knows.'

'And now he wants someone he can use as a punch-bag?' Lauderdale didn't say anything to this. 'What good will it do talking to him?'

'I'm not sure.'

'Then why bother?'

'Because he's insisting. He wants to talk to CID, and not just any officer will do. He's asked to speak to *you*.' There was silence between them. 'John? Anything to say?'

'Yes, sir. This has been a very strange day.' He checked his watch. 'And it's not even one o'clock yet.'

8

Big Ger Cafferty was looking good.

He was fit and lean and had purpose to his gait. A white t-shirt was tight across his chest, flat over the stomach, and he wore faded work denims and new-looking tennis shoes. He walked into the Visiting Room like he was the visitor, Rebus the inmate. The warder beside him was no more than a hired flunkey, to be dismissed at any moment. Cafferty gripped Rebus's hand just a bit too hard, but he wasn't going to try tearing it off, not yet.

'Strawman.'

'Hello, Cafferty.' They sat down at opposite sides of the plastic table, the legs of which had been bolted to the floor. Otherwise, there was little to show that they were in Barlinnie Jail, a prison with a tough reputation from way back, but one which had striven to remake itself. The Visiting Room was clean and white, a few public safety posters decorating its walls. There was a flimsy aluminium ashtray, but also a No Smoking sign. The tabletop bore a few burn marks around its rim from cigarettes resting there too long.

'They made you come then, Strawman?' Cafferty seemed amused by Rebus's appearance. He knew, too, that as long as he kept using his nickname for Rebus, Rebus would be needled.

'I'm sorry about your son.'

Cafferty was no longer amused. 'Is it true they tortured him?'

'Sort of.'

'Sort of?' Cafferty's voice rose. 'There's no halfway house with torture!'

'You'd know all about that.'

Cafferty's eyes blazed. His breathing was shallow and noisy. He got to his feet.

'I can't complain about this place. You get a lot of freedom these days. I've found you can *buy* freedom, same as you can buy anything else.' He stopped beside the warder. 'Isn't that right, Mr Petrie?'

Wisely, Petrie said nothing.

'Wait for me outside,' Cafferty ordered. Rebus watched Petrie leave. Cafferty looked at him and grinned a humourless grin.

'Cosy,' he said, 'just the two of us.' He started to rub his stomach.

'What do you want, Cafferty?'

'Stomach's started giving me gyp. What's my point, Strawman? My point's this.' He was standing over Rebus, and now leant down, his hands pressing Rebus's shoulders. 'I want the bastard found.' Rebus found himself staring at Cafferty's bared teeth. 'See, I can't have people fucking with my family, it's bad for *my* reputation. Nobody gets away with something like that ... it'd be bad for business.'

'Nice to see the paternal instinct's so strong.'

Cafferty ignored this. 'My men are out there hunting, understood? And they'll be keeping an eye on *you*. I want a result, Strawman.'

Rebus shrugged off Cafferty's pressure and got to his feet. 'You think we're going to sit on our hands because the victim was your son?'

'You better not ... *that's* what I'm saying. Revenge, Strawman, I'll have it one way or the other. I'll have it on *some*body.'

'Not on me,' Rebus said quietly. He held Cafferty's stare, till Cafferty opened his arms wide and shrugged, then went to his chair and sat down. Rebus stayed standing.

'I need to ask you a few questions,' he said.

'Fire away.'

'Did you keep in touch with your son?'

Cafferty shook his head. 'I kept in touch with his mum. She's a good woman, too good for me, always was. I send her money for Billy, at least I did while he was growing up. I still send something from time to time.'

'By what means?'

'Someone I can trust.'

'Did Billy know who his father was?'

'Absolutely not. His mum wasn't exactly proud of me.' He started rubbing his stomach again.

'You should take something for that,' Rebus said. 'So, could anyone have got to him as a way of getting at you?'

Cafferty nodded. 'I've thought about it, Strawman. I've thought a lot about it.' Now he shook his head. 'I can't see it. I mean, it was my first thought, but nobody knew, nobody except his mum and me.'

'And the intermediary.'

'He didn't have anything to do with it. I've had people ask him.'

The way Cafferty said this sent a shiver through Rebus.

'Two more things,' he said. 'The word Nemo, mean anything?'

Cafferty shook his head. But Rebus knew that by tonight villains across the east of Scotland would be on the watch for the name. Maybe Cafferty's men *would* get to the killer first. Rebus had seen the body. He didn't much care who got the killer, so long as someone did. He guessed this was Cafferty's thinking too.

'Second thing,' he said, 'the letters SaS on a tattoo.'

Cafferty shook his head again, but more slowly this time. There was something there, some recognition.

'What is it, Cafferty?'

But Cafferty wasn't saying.

'What about gangs, was he in any gangs?'

'He wasn't the type.'

'He had the Red Hand of Ulster on his bedroom wall.'

'I've got a Pirelli calendar on mine, doesn't mean I use their tyres.'

Rebus walked towards the door. 'Not much fun being a victim, is it?'

Cafferty jumped to his feet. 'Remember,' he said, 'I'll be watching.'

'Cafferty, if one of your goons so much as asks me the time of day, I'll throw him in a cell.'

'You threw me in a cell, Strawman. Where did it get you?'

Unable to bear Cafferty's smile, the smile of a man who had drowned people in pigshit and shot them in cold blood, a cold devious manipulator, a man without morals or remorse, unable finally to bear any of this, Rebus left the room.

The prison officer, Petrie, was standing outside, shuffling his feet. His eyes couldn't meet Rebus's.

'You're an absolute disgrace,' Rebus told him, walking away.

While he was in Glasgow, Rebus could have talked to the boy's mother, only the boy's mother was in Edinburgh giving an official ID to the top half of her dead son's face. Dr Curt would be sure she never saw the bottom half. As he'd said to Rebus, if Billy had been a ventriloquist's dummy, he'd never have worked again.

'You're a sick man, doctor,' John Rebus had said.

He drove back to Edinburgh weary and trembling. Cafferty had that effect on him. He'd never thought he'd have to see the man again, at least not until both of them were of pensionable age. Cafferty had sent him a postcard the day he'd arrived in Barlinnie. But Siobhan Clarke had intercepted it and asked if he wanted to see it.

'Tear it up,' Rebus had told her. He still didn't know what the message had been.

Siobhan Clarke was still in the Murder Room when he got back.

'You're working hard,' he told her.

'It's a wonderful thing, overtime. Besides, we're a bit short of hands.'

'You've heard then?'

'Yes, congratulations.'

'What?'

'SCS, it's like a lateral promotion, isn't it?'

'It's only temporary, like a run of good games to Hibs. Where's Brian?'

'Out at Cunningham's digs, talking to Murdock and Millie again.'

'Was Mrs Cunningham up to questioning?'

'Just barely.'

'Who talked to her?'

'I did, the Chief Inspector's idea.'

'Then for once Lauderdale's had a good idea. Did you ask her about religion?'

'You mean all that Orange stuff in Billy's room? Yes, I asked. She just shrugged like it was nothing special.'

'It *is* nothing special. There are hundreds of people with the same flag, the same music-tapes. Christ, I've seen them.'

And this was the truth. He'd seen them at close quarters, not just as a kid, hearing the Sash sung by drunks on their way home, but more recently. He'd been visiting his brother in Fife, just over a month ago, the weekend before July 12th. There'd been an Orange march in Cowdenbeath. The pub they were in seemed to be hosting a crowd of the marchers in the dance hall upstairs. Sounds of drums, especially the huge drum they called the *lambeg*, and flutes and penny whistles, bad choruses repeated time and again. They'd gone upstairs to investigate, just as the thing was

77

winding down. *God Save the Queen* was being destroyed on a dozen cheap flutes.

And some of the kids singing along, sweaty brows and shirts open, some of them had their arms raised, hands straight out in front of them. A Nazi-style salute.

'Nothing else?' he asked. Clarke shook her head. 'She didn't know about the tattoo?'

'She thinks he must have done it in the last year or so.'

'Well, that's interesting in itself. It means we're not dealing with some ancient gang or old flame. SaS was something recent in his life. What about Nemo?'

'It didn't mean anything to her.'

'I've just been talking to Cafferty, SaS meant something to him. Let's pull his records, see if they tell us anything.'

'*Now?*'

'We can make a start. By the way, remember that card he sent me?' Clarke nodded. 'What was on it?'

'It was a picture of a pig in its sty.'

'And the message?'

'There wasn't any message,' she said.

On the way back to Patience's he dropped into the video store and rented a couple of movies. It was the only video store nearby that he hadn't turned over at one time or another with vice or Trading Standards, looking for porn and splatter and various bootleg tapes. The owner was a middle-aged fatherly type, happy to tell you that some comedy was particularly good or some adventure film might prove a bit strong for 'the ladies'. He hadn't commented on Rebus's selections: *Terminator 2* and *All About Eve*. But Patience had a comment.

'Great,' she said, meaning the opposite.

'What's wrong?'

'You hate old movies and I hate violence.'

Rebus looked at the Schwarzenegger. 'It's not even an 18. And who says I don't like old films?'

'What's your favourite black and white movie?'

'There are hundreds of them.'

'Name me five. No, three, and don't say I'm not fair.'

He stared at her. They were standing a few feet apart in the living room, Rebus with the videos still in his hands, Patience with her arms folded, her back erect. He knew she could probably smell the whisky on his breath, even keeping his mouth shut and breathing through his nose. It was so quiet, he could hear the cat washing itself somewhere behind the sofa.

'What are we fighting about?' he asked.

She was ready for this. 'We're fighting about consideration, as usual. To wit, your lack of any.'

'*Ben Hur.*'

'Colour.'

'Well, that courtroom one then, with James Stewart.' She nodded. 'And that other one, with Orson Welles and the mandolin.'

'It was a zither.'

'Shite,' said John Rebus, throwing down the videos and making for the front door.

Millie Docherty waited until Murdock had been asleep for a good hour. She spent the hour thinking about the questions the police had asked both of them, and thinking further back to good days and bad days in her life. She spoke Murdock's name. His breathing remained regular. Only then did she slip out of bed and walk barefoot to Billy's bedroom door, touching the door with her fingertips. Christ, to think he wasn't there, would never be there again. She tried to control her breathing, fast in, slow out. Otherwise she might hyperventilate. Panic attacks, they called them. For years she'd suffered them not knowing she was not alone. There were lots of people out there like her. Billy had been one of them.

She turned the doorknob and slipped into his room. His

mother had been round earlier on, hardly in a state to cope with any of it. There had been a policewoman with her, the same one who'd come to the flat that first time. Billy's mum had looked at his room, but then shook her head.

'I can't do this. Another time.'

'If you like,' Millie had offered, 'I can bag everything up for you. All you'd have to do is have his things collected.' The policewoman had nodded her gratitude at that. Well, it was the least ... She felt the tears coming and sat down on his narrow bed. Funny how a bed so narrow could be made wide enough for two, if the two were close. She did the breathing exercises again. Fast in, slow out, but those words, her instructions to herself, reminded her of other things, other times. Fast in, slow out.

'I've got this self-help book,' Billy had said. 'It's in my room.' He'd gone to find it for her, and she'd followed him into his room. Such a tidy room. 'Here it is,' he'd said, turning towards her quickly, not realising how close behind him she was.

'What's all this Red Hand stuff?' she'd asked, looking past him at his walls. He'd waited till her eyes returned to his, then he'd kissed her, tongue rubbing at her teeth till she opened her mouth to him.

'Billy,' she said now, her hands filling themselves with his bedcover. She stayed that way for a few minutes, part of her mind staying alert, listening for sounds from the room she shared with Murdock. Then she moved across the bed to where the Hearts pennant was pinned to the wall. She pushed it aside with a finger.

Underneath, taped flat against the wall, was a computer disk. She'd left it here, half hoping the police would find it when they searched the room. But they'd been hopeless. And watching them search, she'd become suddenly afraid for herself, and had started to hope they wouldn't find it. Now, she got her fingernails under it and unpeeled it, looking at the disk. Well, it was hers now, wasn't it? They might kill her for it, but she could never let it go. It was part of her memory of him. She rubbed her thumb across the label. The streetlight coming through the unwashed window wasn't quite enough for her to read by, but she knew what the label said anyway.

It was just those three letters, SaS.

Dark, dark, dark.

Rebus recalled that line at least. If Patience had asked him to quote from a poem instead of giving her movie titles, he'd have been all right. He was standing at a window of St Leonard's, taking a break from his deskful of work, all the paperwork on Morris Gerald Cafferty.

Dark, dark, dark.

She was trying to civilise him. Not that she'd admit it. What she said instead was that it would be nice if they liked the same things. It would give them things to talk about. So she gave him books of poetry, and played classical music at him, bought them tickets for ballet and modern dance. Rebus had been there before, other times, other women. Asking for something more, for commitment beyond the commitment.

He didn't like it. He enjoyed the basic, the feral. Cafferty had once accused him of liking cruelty, of being attracted to it; his natural right as a Celt. And hadn't Rebus accused Peter Cave of the same thing? It was coming back to him, pain on pain, crawling back along his tubes from some place deep within him.

His time in Northern Ireland.

He'd been there early in the history of 'the Troubles', 1969, just as it was all boiling over; so early that he hadn't really known what was going on, what the score was; none of them had, not on any side. The people were pleased to see them at first, Catholic and Protestant, offering food and drink and a genuine welcome. Then later the drinks were laced with weedkiller, and the welcome might be leading you into a 'honey trap'. The crunching in the sponge cake might only be hard seeds from the raspberry jam. Then again, it might be powdered glass.

Bottles flying through the dark, lit by an arc of flame. Petrol spinning and dripping from the rag wick. And when it fell on a littered road, it spread in an instant pool of hate. Nothing personal about it, it was just for a cause, a troubled cause, that was all.

And later still it was to defend the rackets which had grown up around that aged cause. The protection schemes, black taxis, gun-running, all the businesses which had spread so very far away from the ideal, creating their own pool.

He'd seen bullet wounds and shrapnel blasts and gashes left by hurled bricks, he'd tasted mortality and the flaws in both his character and his body. When not on duty, they used to hang around the barracks, knocking back whisky and playing cards. Maybe that was why whisky reminded him he was still alive, where other drinks couldn't.

There was shame too: a retaliatory strike against a drinking club which had gotten out of hand. He'd done nothing to stop it. He'd swung his baton and even his SLR with the rest of them. Yet in the middle of the commotion, the sound of a rifle being cocked was enough to bring silence and stillness . . .

He still kept an interest in events across the water. Part of his life had been left behind there. Something about his tour of duty there had made him apply to join the Special Air Service. He went back to his desk and lifted the glass of whisky.

Dark, dark, dark. The sky quiet save for the occasional drunken yell.

No one would ever know who called the police.

No one except the man himself and the police themselves.

He'd given his name and address, and had made his complaint about the noise.

'And do you want us to come and see you afterwards, sir, after we've investigated?'

'That won't be necessary.' The phone went dead on the desk officer, who smiled. It was very seldom necessary. A visit from the police meant you were involved. He wrote on a pad then passed the note along to the Communications Room. The call went out at ten to one.

When the Rover patrol car got to the community centre, it was clear that things were winding down. The officers debated heading off again, but since they were here ... Certainly there had been a party, a function of some kind. But as the two uniformed officers walked in through the open doors, only a dozen or so stragglers were left. The floor was a mess of bottles and cigarette butts, probably a few roaches in there too if they cared to look.

'Who's in charge?'

'Nobody,' came the sharp response.

There were flushing sounds from the toilets. Evidence being destroyed, perhaps.

'We've received complaints about the noise.'

'No noise here.'

The patrolman nodded. On a makeshift stage a ghetto-blaster had been hooked up to a guitar amplifier, a large Marshall job with separate amp and speaker-bin. Probably a hundred watts, none of it built for subtlety. The amplifier was still on, emitting an audible buzz. 'This thing belongs out at the Exhibition Centre.'

'Simple Minds let us borrow it.'

'Whose is it really though?'

'Where's your search warrant?'

The officer smiled again. He could see that his partner was itching for trouble, but though neither of them had a welter of experience, they weren't stupid either. They knew where they were, they knew the odds. So he stood there

83

smiling, legs apart, arms by his side, not looking for aggro.

He seemed to be having a dialogue with one of the group, a guy with a denim jacket and no shirt underneath. He was wearing black square-toed biker boots with straps and a round silver buckle. The officer had always liked that style, had even considered buying himself a pair, just for the weekends.

Then maybe he'd start saving for the bike to go with them.

'Do we need a search warrant?' he said. 'We're called to a disturbance, doors wide open, no one barring our entry. Besides, this is a community centre. There are rules and regulations. Licences need to be applied for and granted. Do you have a licence for this ... soirée?'

'Swaah-ray?' the youth said to his pals. 'Fuckin' listen to that! Swaaah-rrray!' And he came sashaying over towards the two uniforms, like he was doing some old-fashioned dance step. He turned behind and between them. 'Is that a dirty word? Something I'm not supposed to understand? This isn't your territory, you know. This is the Gar-B, and we're having our own wee festival, since nobody bothered inviting us to the other one. You're not in the real world now. You better be careful.'

The first officer could smell alcohol, like something from a chemistry lab or a surgery: gin, vodka, white rum.

'Look,' he said, 'there has to be someone running the show, and it isn't you.'

'Why not?'

'Because you're a short-arsed wee prick.'

There was stillness in the hall. The other officer had spoken, and now his partner swallowed, trying not to look at him, keeping all his concentration on the denim jacket. Denim jacket was considering, a finger to his lips, tapping them.

'Mmm,' he said at last, nodding. 'Interesting.' He started moving back towards the group. He seemed to be wiggling his bum as he moved. Then he stooped forward, pretending to tie a shoe-lace, and let rip with a loud fart. He straightened up as his gang enjoyed the joke, their laughter subsiding only when denim jacket spoke again.

'Well, sirs,' he said, 'we're just packing everything away.' He faked a yawn. 'It's well past our bedtimes and we'd like to go home. If you don't mind.' He opened his arms wide to them, even bowed a little.

'I'd like to –'

'That'll be fine.' The first officer touched his partner's arm and turned away towards the doors. They were going to get out. And when they got out, he was going to have words with his partner, no doubt about that.

'Right then, lads,' said denim jacket, 'let's get this place tidy. We'll need to put this somewhere for a start.'

The constables were near the door when, without warning, the ghetto-blaster caught both of them a glancing blow to the back of their skulls.

9

Rebus heard about it on the morning news. The radio came on at six twenty-five and there it was. It brought him out of bed and into his clothes. Patience was still trying to rouse herself as he placed a mug of tea on the bedside table and a kiss on her hot cheek.

'*Ace in the Hole* and *Casablanca*,' he said. Then he was out of the door and into his car.

At Drylaw police station, the day shift hadn't come on yet, which meant that he heard it from the horses' mouths, so to speak. Not a big station, Drylaw had requested reinforcements from all around, as what had started as an assault on two officers had turned into a miniature riot. Cars had been attacked, house windows smashed. One local shop had been ram-raided, with consequent looting (if the owner was to be believed). Five officers were injured, including the two men who had been coshed with a hi-fi machine. Those two constables had escaped the Gar-B by the skin of their arses.

'It was like Northern bloody Ireland,' one veteran said. Or Brixton, thought Rebus, or Newcastle, or Toxteth...

The TV news had it on now, and police heavy-handedness was being discussed. Peter Cave was being interviewed outside the youth club, saying that his had been the party's organising hand.

'But I had to leave early. I thought I had flu coming on or something.' To prove it, he blew his nose.

'At breakfast-time, too,' complained someone beside Rebus.

'I know,' Cave went on, 'that I bear a certain amount of responsibility for what happened.'

'That's big of him.'

Rebus smiled, thinking: we police invented irony, we live by its rules.

'But,' said Cave, 'there are still questions which need answering. The police seem to think they can rule by threat rather than law. I've talked to a dozen people who were in the club last night, and they've told me the same thing.'

'Surprise, surprise.'

'Namely, that the two police officers involved made threats and menacing actions.'

The interviewer waited for Cave to finish. Then: 'And what do you say, Mr Cave, to local people who claim the youth club is merely a sort of hang-out, a gang headquarters for juveniles on the estate?'

Juveniles: Rebus liked that.

Cave was shaking his head. They'd brought the camera in on him for the shot. 'I say rubbish.' And he blew his nose again. Wisely, the producer switched back to the studio.

Eventually, the police had managed to make five arrests. The youths had been brought to Drylaw. Less than an hour later, a mob from the Gar-B had gathered outside, demanding their release. More thrown bricks, more broken glass, until a massed charge by the police ranks dispersed the crowd. Cars and foot patrols had cruised Drylaw and the Gar-B for the rest of the night. There were still bricks and strewn glass on the road outside. Inside, a few of the officers involved looked shaken.

Rebus looked in on the five youths. They sported bruised faces, bandaged hands. The blood had dried to a crust on them, and they'd left it there, like war paint, like medals.

'Look,' one of them said to the others, 'it's the bastard who took a poke at Pete.'

'Keep talking,' retorted Rebus, 'and you'll be next.'

'I'm quaking.'

The police had stuck a video camera onto the rioters outside the station. The picture quality was poor, but after a few viewings Rebus made out that one of the stone throwers, face hidden by a football scarf, was wearing an open denim jacket and no shirt.

He stuck around the station a bit longer, then got back in his car and headed for the Gar-B. It didn't look so different. There was glass in the road, sounds of brittle crunching under his tyres. But the local shops were like fortresses: wire mesh, metal screens, padlocks, alarms. The would-be looters had run up and down the main road for a while in a hot-wired Ford Cortina, then had launched it at the least protected shop, a place specialising in shoe repairs and key-cutting. Inside, the owner's own brand of security, a sleepy-eyed Alsatian, had thrown itself into the fray before being beaten off and chased away. As far as anyone knew, it was still roaming the wide green spaces.

A few of the ground floor flats were having boards hammered into place across their broken windows. Maybe one of them had made the initial call. Rebus didn't blame the caller; he blamed the two officers. No, that wasn't fair. What would he have done if he'd been there? Yes, exactly. And there'd have been more trouble than this if he had...

He didn't bother stopping the car. He'd only be in the way of the other sight-seers and the media. With not much happening on the IRA story, reporters were here in numbers. Plus he knew he wasn't the Gar-B's most popular tourist. Though the constables couldn't swear who'd thrown the ghetto-blaster, they knew the most likely suspect. Rebus had seen the description back at Drylaw. It was Davey Soutar of course, the boy who couldn't afford a

88

shirt. One of the CID men had asked Rebus what his interest was.

'Personal,' he'd said. A few years back, a riot like this would have prompted the permanent closure of the community hall. But these days it was more likely the Council would bung some more cash at the estate, guilt money. Shutting the hall down wouldn't do much good anyway. There were plenty of empty flats on the estate – flats termed 'unlettable'. They were kept boarded up and padlocked, but could soon be opened. Squatters and junkies used them; gangs could use them too. A couple of miles away in different directions, middle class Barnton and Inverleith were getting ready for work. A world away. They only ever took notice of Pilmuir when it exploded.

It wasn't much of a drive to Fettes either, even with the morning bottlenecks starting their day's business. He wondered if he'd be first in the office; that might show *too* willing. Well, he could check, then nip out to the canteen until everyone started arriving. But when he pushed open the office door, he saw that there was someone in before him. It was Smylie.

'Morning,' Rebus said. Smylie nodded back. He looked tired to Rebus, which was saying something, the amount of sleep Rebus himself had had. He rested against one of the desks and folded his arms. 'Do you know an Inspector called Abernethy?'

'Special Branch,' said Smylie.

'That's him. Is he still around?'

Smylie looked up. 'He went back yesterday, caught an evening plane. Did you want to see him?'

'Not really.'

'There was nothing here for him.'

'No?'

Smylie shook his head. 'We'd know about it if there was. We're the best, we'd've spotted it before him. QED.'

'*Quod erat demonstrandum.*'

Smylie looked at him. 'You're thinking of Nemo, aren't you? Latin for nobody.'

'I suppose I am.' Rebus shrugged. 'Nobody seems to think Billy Cunningham knew any Latin.' Smylie didn't say anything. 'I'm not wanted here, am I?'

'How do you mean?'

'I mean, you don't need me. So why did Kilpatrick bring me in? He must've known it'd cause nothing but aggro.'

'Best ask him yourself.'

'Maybe I will. Meantime, I'll be at St Leonard's.'

'We'll be pining away in your absence.'

'I don't doubt it, Smylie.'

'What does the woman do?'

'Her name's Millie Docherty,' said Siobhan Clarke. 'She works in a computer retailer's.'

'And her boyfriend's a computer consultant. And they shared their flat with an unemployed postie. An odd mix?'

'Not really, sir.'

'No? Well, maybe not.' They were in the canteen, facing one another across the small table. Rebus took occasional bites from a damp piece of toast. Siobhan had finished hers.

'What's it like over at Fettes?' she asked.

'Oh, you know: glamour, danger, intrigue.'

'Much the same as here then?'

'Much the same. I read some of Cafferty's notes last night. I've marked the place, so you can take over.'

'Three's more fun,' said Brian Holmes, dragging over a chair. He'd placed his tray on the table, taking up all the available room. Rebus gave Holmes's fry-up a longing look, knowing it wouldn't square with his diet. All the same ... Sausage, bacon, eggs, tomato and fried bread.

'Ought to carry a government health warning,' said the vegetarian Clarke.

'Hear about the riot?' Holmes asked.

'I went out there this morning,' Rebus admitted. 'The place looked much the same.'

'I heard they threw an amplifier at a couple of our lads.'

The process of exaggeration had begun.

'So, about Billy Cunningham,' Rebus nudged, none too subtly.

Holmes forked up some tomato. 'What about him?'

'What have you found out?'

'Not a lot,' Holmes conceded. 'Unemployed deliverer of the royal mail, the only regular job he's ever had. Mum was overfond of him and kept gifting him money to get by on. Bit of a loyalist extremist, but no record of him belonging to the Orange Lodge. Son of a notorious gangster, but didn't know it.' Holmes thought for a second, decided this was all he had to say, and cut into his sliced sausage.

'Plus,' said Clarke, 'the anarchist stuff we found.'

'Ach, that's nothing,' Holmes said dismissively.

'What anarchist stuff?' asked Rebus.

'There were some magazines in his wardrobe,' Clarke explained. 'Soft porn, football programmes, a couple of those survivalist mags teenagers like to read to go with their diet of *Terminator* films.' Rebus almost said something, but stopped himself. 'And a flimsy little pamphlet called ...' She sought the title. '*The Floating Anarchy Factfile*.'

'It was years old, sir,' said Holmes. 'Not relevant.'

'Do we have it here?'

'Yes, sir,' said Siobhan Clarke.

'It's from the Orkneys,' said Holmes. 'I think it's priced in old money. It belongs in a museum, not a police station.'

'Brian,' said Rebus, 'all that fat you're eating is going to your head. Since when do we dismiss *anything* in a murder inquiry?' He picked a thin rasher of streaky from the plate and dropped it into his mouth. It tasted wonderful.

The Floating Anarchy Factfile consisted of six sheets of A4 paper, folded over with a single staple through the middle to keep it from falling apart. It was typed on an old and irregular typewriter, with hand printed titles to its meagre articles and no photographs or drawings. It was priced not in old money but in new pence: five new pence to be exact, from which Rebus guessed it to be fifteen to twenty years old. There was no date, but it proclaimed itself 'issue number three'. To a large extent Brian Holmes was right: it belonged in a museum. The pieces were written in a style that could be termed 'Celtic hippy', and this style was so uniform (as were the spelling mistakes) that the whole thing looked to be the work of a single individual with access to a copying machine, something like an old Roneo.

As for the content, there were cries of nationalism and individualism in one paragraph, philosophical and moral lethargy the next. Anarcho-syndicalism was mentioned, but so were Bakunin, Rimbaud and Tolstoy. It wasn't, to Rebus's eye, the sort of stuff to boost advertising revenue. For example:

'What Dalriada needs is a new commitment, a new set of mores which look to the existent and emerging youth culture. What we need is action by the individual without recourse or prior thought to the rusted machinery of law, church, state.

'We need to be free to make our own decisions about our nation and then act self-consciously to make those decisions a reality. The sons and daughters of Alba are the future, but we are living in the mistakes of the past and must change those mistakes in the present. If you do not act then remember: Now is the first day of the rest of your strife. And remember too: inertia corrodes.'

Except that 'mores' was spelt 'moeres' and 'existent' as 'existant'. Rebus put the pamphlet down.

'A psychiatrist could have a field day,' he muttered. Holmes and Clarke were seated on the other side of his desk. He noticed that while he'd been at Fettes, people had been using his desktop as a dumping ground for sandwich wrappers and polystyrene cups. He ignored these and turned the pamphlet over. There was an address at the bottom of the back page: Zabriskie House, Brinyan, Rousay, Orkney Isles.

'Now that's what I call dropping out,' said Rebus. 'And look, the house is named after *Zabriskie Point*.'

'Is that in the Orkneys too?' asked Holmes.

'It's a film,' said Rebus. He'd gone to see it a long long time ago, just for the '60s soundtrack. He couldn't remember much about it, except for an explosion near the end. He tapped his finger against the pamphlet. 'I want to know more about this.'

'You're kidding, sir,' said Holmes.

'That's me,' said Rebus sourly, 'always a smile and a joke.'

Clarke turned to Holmes. 'I think that means he's serious.'

'In the land of the blind,' said Rebus, 'the one-eyed man is king. And even *I* can see there's more to this than meets your eyes, Brian.'

Holmes frowned. 'Such as, sir?'

'Such as its provenance, its advanced years. What would you say, 1973? '74? Billy Cunningham wasn't even born in 1974. So what's this doing in his wardrobe beside up-to-date scud mags and football programmes?' He waited. 'Answer came there none.'

Holmes looked sullen; an annoying trait whenever Rebus showed him up. But Clarke was ready. 'We'll get Orkney police to check, sir, always supposing the Orkneys possess any police.'

'Do that,' said Rebus.

10

Like a rubber ball, he thought as he drove, I'll come bouncing back to you. He'd been summoned back to Fettes by DCI Kilpatrick. In his pocket there was a message from Caroline Rattray, asking him to meet her in Parliament House. He was curious about the message, which had been taken over the phone by a Detective Constable in the Murder Room. He saw Caroline Rattray as she'd been that night, all dressed up and then dragged down into Mary King's Close by Dr Curt. He saw her strong masculine face with its slanting nose and high prominent cheekbones. He wondered if Curt had said anything to her about him ... He would definitely make time to see her.

Kilpatrick had an office of his own in a corner of the otherwise open-plan room used by the SCS. Just outside it sat the secretary and the clerical assistant, though Rebus couldn't work out which was which. Both were civilians, and both operated computer consoles. They made a kind of shield between Kilpatrick and everyone else, a barrier you passed as you moved from your world into his. As Rebus passed them, they were discussing the problems facing South Africa.

'It'll be like on Uist,' one of them said, causing Rebus to pause and listen. 'North Uist is Protestant and South Uist is Catholic, and they can't abide one another.'

Kilpatrick's office itself was flimsy enough, just plastic partitions, see-through above waist height. The whole thing could be dismantled in minutes, or wrecked by a few judicious kicks and shoulder-charges. But it was definably an office. It had a door which Kilpatrick told Rebus to close. There was a certain amount of sound insulation. There were two filing-cabinets, maps and print-outs stuck to the walls with Blu-Tak, a couple of calendars still showing July. And on the desk a framed photograph of three grinning gap-toothed children.

'Yours, sir?'

'My brother's. I'm not married.' Kilpatrick turned the photo around, the better to study it. 'I try to be a good uncle.'

'Yes, sir.' Rebus sat down. Beside him sat Ken Smylie, hands crossed in his lap. The skin on his wrists had wrinkled up like a bloodhound's face.

'I'll get straight to the point, John,' said Kilpatrick. 'We've got a man undercover. He's posing as a long-distance lorry driver. We're trying to pick up information on arms shipments: who's selling, who's buying.'

'Something to do with The Shield, sir?'

Kilpatrick nodded. 'He's the one who's heard the name mentioned.'

'So who is he?'

'My brother,' Smylie said. 'His name's Calumn.'

Rebus took this in. 'Does he look like you, Ken?'

'A bit.'

'Then I dare say he'd pass as a lorry driver.'

There was almost a smile at one corner of Smylie's mouth.

'Sir,' Rebus said to Kilpatrick, 'does this mean you think the Mary King's Close killing had something to do with the paramilitaries?'

Kilpatrick smiled. 'Why do you think you're here, John? *You* spotted it straight off. We've got three men working on Billy Cunningham, trying to track down friends of his. For some reason they had to kill him, I'd like to know why.'

'Me too, sir. If you want to find out about Cunningham, try his flatmate first.'

'Murdock? Yes, we're talking to him.'

'No, not Murdock, Murdock's girlfriend. I went round there when they reported him missing. There was something about her, something not quite right. Like she was holding back, putting on an act.'

Smylie said, 'I'll take a look.'

'Her and her boyfriend both work with computers. Think that might mean something?'

'I'll take a look,' Smylie repeated. Rebus didn't doubt that he would.

'Ken thinks you should meet Calumn,' Kilpatrick said.

Rebus shrugged. 'Fine by me.'

'Good,' said Kilpatrick. 'Then we'll take a little drive.'

Out in the main office they all looked at him strangely, like they knew precisely what had been said to him in Kilpatrick's den. Well, of course they knew. Their looks told Rebus he was resented more than ever. Even Claverhouse, usually so laid back, was managing a snide little grin.

DI Blackwood rubbed a smooth hand over the hairless crown of his head, then tucked a stray hair back behind his ear. His tonsure was positively monasterial, and it bothered him. In his other hand he held his telephone receiver, listening to someone on the line. He ignored Rebus as Rebus walked past.

At the next desk along, DS Ormiston was squeezing spots on his forehead.

'You two make a picture,' Rebus said. Ormiston didn't appear to get it, but that wasn't Rebus's problem. His problem was that Kilpatrick was taking him into his confidence, and Rebus still didn't know why.

There are lots of warehouses in Sighthill, most of them anonymous. They weren't exactly advertising that one of them had been leased by the Scottish Crime Squad. It was a big old prefabricated building surrounded by a high wire fence and protected by a high barred gate. There was barbed wire strung out across the top of the fence and the gate, and the gatehouse was manned. The guard unlocked the gate and swung it open so they could drive in.

'We got this place for a song,' Kilpatrick explained. 'The market's not exactly thriving just now.' He smiled. 'They even offered to throw in the security, but we didn't think we'd need any help with that.'

Kilpatrick was sitting in the back with Rebus, Smylie acting as chauffeur. The steering wheel was like a frisbee in his paws. But he was a canny driver, slow and considerate. He even signalled as he turned into a parking bay, though there was only one other car in the whole forecourt, parked five bays away. When they got out, the Sierra's suspension groaned upwards. They were standing in front of a normal sized door whose nameplate had been removed. To its right were the much bigger doors of the loading bay. From the rubbish lying around, the impression was of a disused site. Kilpatrick took two keys from his pocket and unlocked the side door.

The warehouse was just that, no offices or partitions off, just one large space with an oily concrete floor and some empty packing cases. A pigeon, disturbed by their entrance, fluttered near the ceiling for a moment before settling again on one of the iron spars supporting the corrugated roof. It had left its mark more than once on the HGV's windshield.

'That's supposed to be lucky,' said Rebus. Not that the articulated lorry looked clean anyway. It was splashed with pale caked-on mud and dust. It was a Ford with a UK licence plate, K registration. The cab door opened and a large man heaved himself out.

He didn't have his brother's moustache and was probably a year or two younger. But he wasn't smiling, and when he spoke his voice was high-pitched, almost cracking from effort.

97

'You must be Rebus.'

They shook hands. Kilpatrick was doing the talking.

'We impounded this lorry two months back, or rather Scotland Yard did. They've kindly loaned it to us.'

Rebus hoisted himself onto the running-plate and peered in the driver's window. Behind the driving seat had been fixed a nude calendar and a dog-eared centrefold. There was space for a bunk, on which a sleeping bag was rolled up ready for use. The cab was bigger than some of the caravans Rebus had stayed in for holidays. He climbed back down.

'Why?'

There was a noise from the back of the lorry. Calumn Smylie was opening its container doors. By the time Rebus and Kilpatrick got there, the two Smylies had swung both doors wide and were standing inside the back, just in front of a series of wooden crates.

'We've taken a few liberties,' said Kilpatrick, hoisting himself into the back beside them, Rebus following. 'The stuff was originally hidden beneath the floor.'

'False fuel tanks,' explained Ken Smylie. 'Good ones too, welded and bolted shut.'

'The Yard cut into them from up here.' Kilpatrick stamped his foot. 'And inside they found what the tip-off had told them they'd find.'

Calumn Smylie lifted the lid off a crate so Rebus could look in. Inside, wrapped in oiled cloths, were eighteen or so AK 47 assault rifles. Rebus lifted one of them out by its folded metal butt. He knew how to handle a gun like this, even if he didn't like doing it. Rifles had gotten lighter since his Army days, but they hadn't gotten any more comfortable. They'd also gotten a deal more lethal. The wooden hand-grip was as cold as a coffin handle.

'We don't know exactly where they came from,' Kilpatrick explained. 'And we don't even know where they were headed. The driver wouldn't say anything, no matter how scary the Anti-Terrorist Branch got with him. He denied all knowledge of the load, and wasn't about to point a finger anywhere else.'

Rebus put the gun back in its crate. Calumn Smylie leaned past him to wipe off any fingerprints with a piece of rag.

'So what's the deal?' Rebus asked. Calumn Smylie gave the answer.

'When the driver was pulled in, there were some phone numbers in his pocket, two in Glasgow, one in Edinburgh. All three of them were bars.'

'Could mean nothing,' Rebus said.

'Or everything,' commented Ken Smylie.

'See,' Calumn added, 'could be those bars are his contacts, maybe his employers, or the people his employers are selling to.'

'So,' said Kilpatrick, leaning against one of the crates, 'we've got men watching all three pubs.'

'In the hope of what?'

It was Calumn's turn again. 'When Special Branch stopped the lorry, they managed to keep it quiet. It's never been reported, and the driver's tucked away somewhere under the Prevention of Terrorism Act and a few minor offences.'

Rebus nodded. 'So his employers or whoever won't know what's happened?' Calumn was nodding too. 'And they might get antsy?' Now Rebus shook his head. 'You should be a sniper.'

Calumn frowned. 'Why?'

'Because that's the longest shot I've ever heard.'

Neither Smylie seemed thrilled to hear this. 'I've already overheard a conversation mentioning The Shield,' Calumn said.

'But you've no idea what The Shield *is*,' Rebus countered. 'Which pub are we talking about anyway?'

'The Dell.'

It was Rebus's turn to frown. 'Just off the Garibaldi Estate?'

'That's the one.'

'We've had some aggro there.'

'Yes, so I hear.'

Rebus turned to Kilpatrick. 'Why do you need the lorry?'

'In case we can operate a sting.'

'How long are you going to give it?'

Calumn shrugged. His eyes were dark and heavy from tension and a lack of sleep. He rubbed a hand through his uncombed hair, then over his unshaven face.

'I can see it's been like a holiday for you,' Rebus said. He knew the plan must have been cooked up by the Smylie brothers. They seemed its real defenders. Kilpatrick's part in it was more uncertain.

'Better than that,' Calumn was saying.

'How so?'

'The holiday I'm having, you don't need to send post-cards.'

Not many people know of Parliament House, home of the High Court of Justiciary, Scotland's highest court for criminal cases. There are few signposts or identifying markers outside, and the building itself is hidden behind St Giles, separated from it by a small anonymous car park containing a smattering of Jaguars and BMWs. Of the many doors facing the prospective visitor, only one normally stands open. This is the public entrance, and leads into Parliament Hall, from off which stretch the Signet Library and Advocates Library.

There were fourteen courts in all, and Rebus guessed he'd been in all of them over the years. He sat on one of the long wooden benches. The lawyers around him were wearing dark pinstripe suits, white shirts with raised collars and white bow ties, grey wigs, and long black cloaks like those his teachers had worn. Mostly the lawyers were talking, either with clients or with each other. If with each other, they might raise their voices, maybe even share a joke. But with clients they were more circumspect. One well-dressed woman was nodding as her advocate talked in an undertone, all the while trying to stop the many files under his arm from wriggling free.

Rebus knew that beneath the large stained glass window there were two corridors lined with old wooden boxes. Indeed, the first corridor was known as the Box Corridor. Each box was marked with a lawyer's name, and each had a slat in the top, though the vast majority of boxes were kept open more or less permanently. Here documents awaited collection and perusal. Rebus had wondered at the openness of the system, the opportunities for theft and espionage. But there had never been any reports of theft, and security men were in any case never far away. He got up now and walked over to the stained glass. He knew the King portrayed was supposed to be James V, but wasn't sure about the rest of it, all the figures or the coats of arms. To his right, through a wooden swing door with glass windows, he could see lawyers poring over books. Etched in gold on the glass were the words PRIVATE ROOM.

He knew another private room close to here. Indeed, just on the other side of St Giles and down some flights of stairs. Billy Cunningham had been murdered not fifty yards from the High Court.

He turned at the sound of heels clicking towards him. Caroline Rattray was dressed for work, from black shoes and stockings to powder-grey wig.

'I wouldn't have recognised you,' he said.

'Should I take that as a compliment?' She gave him a big smile, and held it as she held his gaze. Then she touched his arm. 'I see you've noticed.' She looked up at the stained glass. 'The royal arms of Scotland.' Rebus looked up too. Beneath the large picture there were five smaller square windows, each showing a coat of arms. Caroline Rattray's

101

eyes were on the central panel. Two unicorns held the shield of the red Lion Rampant. Above on a scroll were the words IN DEFENCE, and at the bottom a Latin inscription. Rebus read it.

'*Nemo me impune lacessit.*' He turned to her. 'Never my best subject.'

'You might know it better as "Wha daur meddle wi' me?". It's the motto of Scotland, or rather, the motto of Scotland's kings.'

'A while since we've had any of them.'

'*And* of the Order of the Thistle. Sort of makes you the monarch's private soldier, except they only give it to crusty old sods. Sit down.' She led them back to the bench Rebus had been sitting on. She had files with her, which she placed on the floor rather than the bench, though there was space. Then she gave him her full attention. Rebus didn't say anything, so she smiled again, tipping her head slightly to one side. 'Don't you see?'

'Nemo,' he guessed.

'Yes! Latin for nobody.'

'We already know that, Miss Rattray. Also a character in Jules Verne and in Dickens, plus the letters make the word "omen" backwards.' He paused. 'We've been working, you see. But does it get us any further forward? I mean, was the victim trying to tell us that no one killed him?'

She seemed to puncture, her shoulders sagging. It was like watching an old balloon die after Christmas.

'It could be something,' he offered. 'But it's hard to know what.'

'I see.'

'You could have told me about it on the phone.'

'Yes, I could.' She straightened her back. 'But I wanted you to see for yourself.'

'You think the Order of the Thistle ganged up and murdered Billy Cunningham?' Her eyes were holding his again, no smile on her lips. He broke free, staring past her at the stained glass. 'How's the prosecution game?'

'It's a slow day,' she said. 'I hear the victim's father is a convicted murderer. Is there a connection?'

'Maybe.'

'No concrete motive yet?'

'No motive.' The longer Rebus looked at the royal arms, the more his focus was drawn to its central figure. It was definitely a shield. 'The Shield,' he said to himself.

'Sorry?'

'Nothing, it's just ....' He turned back to her. She was looking eager about something, and hopeful too. 'Miss Rattray,' he said, 'did you bring me here to chat me up?'

She looked horrified, her face reddening; not just her cheeks, but forehead and chin too, even her neck coloured. 'Inspector Rebus,' she said at last.

'Sorry, sorry.' He bowed his head and raised his hands. 'Sorry I said that.'

'Well, I don't know ...' She looked around. 'It's not every day I'm accused of being ... well, whatever. I think I need a drink.' Then, reverting to her normal voice: 'I think you'd better buy me one, don't you?'

They crossed the High Street, dodging the leafleters and mime artists and clowns on stilts, and threaded their way through a dark close and down some worn stone steps into Caro Rattray's preferred bar.

'I hate this time of year,' she said. 'It's such a hassle getting to and from work. And as for parking in town...'

'It's a hard life, all right.'

She went to a table while Rebus stood at the bar. She had taken a couple of minutes to change out of her gown and wig, had brushed her hair out, though the sombre clothes that remained – the accent on black with touches of white – still marked her out as a lawyer in this lawyer's howff.

The place had one of the lowest ceilings of any pub Rebus had ever been in. When he considered, he thought they must be almost directly above some of the shops which led off Mary King's Close. The thought made him change his order.

'Make that whisky a double.' But he added plenty of water.

Caroline Rattray had ordered lemonade with lots of ice and lemon. As Rebus placed her drink on the table, he laughed.

'What's so funny?'

He shook his head. 'Advocate and lemonade, that makes a snowball.' He didn't have to explain to her. She managed a weary smile. 'Heard it before, eh?' he said, sitting beside her.

'And every person who says it thinks they've just invented it. Cheers.'

'Aye, *slainte*.'

'*Slainte*. Do you speak Gaelic?'

'Just a couple of words.'

'I learnt it a few years ago, I've already forgotten most of it.'

'Ach, it's not much use anyway, is it?'

'You wouldn't mind if it died out?'

'I didn't say that.'

'I thought you just did.'

Rebus gulped at his drink. 'Never argue with a lawyer.'

Another smile. She lit a cigarette, Rebus declining.

'Don't tell me,' he said, 'you still see Mary King's Close in your head at night?'

She nodded slowly. 'And during the day. I can't seem to erase it.'

'So don't try. Just file it away, that's all you can do. Admit it to yourself, it happened, you were there, then file it away. You won't forget, but you won't harp on it either.'

'Police psychology?'

'Common sense, hard learnt. That's why you were so excited about the Latin inscription?'

'Yes, I thought I was ... *involved*.'

104

'You'll be involved if we ever catch the buggers. It'll be your job to put them away.'

'I suppose so.'

'Until then, leave it to us.'

'Yes, I will.'

'I'm sorry though, sorry you had to see it. Typical of Curt, dragging you down there. There was no need to. Are you and him ... ?'

Her whoop filled the bar. 'You don't think ... ? We're just acquaintances. He had a spare ticket, I was on hand. Christ almighty, you think I could ... with a *pathologist*?'

'They're human, despite rumours to the contrary.'

'Yes, but he's twenty years older than me.'

'That's not always a consideration.'

'The thought of those hands on me ...' She shivered, sipped her drink. 'What did you say back there about a shield?'

He shook his head. He saw a shield in his mind, and you never got a shield without a sword. *With sword and shield*, that was a line from an Orange song. He slapped the table with his fist, so hard that Caroline Rattray looked frightened.

'Was it something I said?'

'Caroline, you're brilliant. I've got to go.' He got up and walked past the bar, then stopped and came back, taking her hand in his, holding it. 'I'll phone you,' he promised. Then: 'If you like.'

He waited till she'd nodded, then turned again and left. She finished her lemonade, smoked another cigarette, and stubbed it into the ashtray. His hand had been hot, not like a pathologist's at all. The barman came to empty her ashtray into a pail and wipe the table.

'Out hunting again I see,' he said quietly.

'You know too much about me, Dougie.'

'I know too much about everyone, hen,' said Dougie, picking up both glasses and taking them to the bar.

*

Several months back, Rebus had been talking to an acquaintance of his called Matthew Vanderhyde. Their conversation had concerned another case, one involving, as it turned out, Big Ger Cafferty, and apropos of very little Vanderhyde, blind for many years and with a reputation as a white witch, had mentioned a splinter group of the Scottish National Party. The splinter group had been called Sword and Shield, and they'd existed in the late 1950s and early 1960s.

But as a phone call to Vanderhyde revealed, Sword and Shield had ceased to exist around the same time the Rolling Stones were putting out their first album. And at no time, anyway, had they been known as SaS.

'I do believe,' Vanderhyde said, and Rebus could see him in his darkened living room, its curtains shut, slumped in an armchair with his portable phone, 'there exists in the United States an organisation called Sword and Shield, or even Scottish Sword and Shield, but I don't know anything about them. I don't think they're connected to the Scottish Rites Temple, which is a sort of North American Freemasons, but I'm a bit vague.'

Rebus was busy writing it all down. 'No you're not,' he said, 'you're a bloody encyclopaedia.' That was the problem with Vanderhyde: he seldom gave you just the one answer, leaving you more confused than before you'd asked your question.

'Is there anything I can read about Sword and Shield?' Rebus asked.

'You mean histories? I wouldn't know, I shouldn't think they'd bother to issue any as braille editions or talking books.'

'I suppose not, but there must have been something left when the organisation was wound up, papers, documents . . . ?'

'Perhaps a local historian might know. Would you like me to do some sleuthing, Inspector?'

'I'd appreciate it,' said Rebus. 'Would Big Ger Cafferty have had anything to do with the group?'

'I shouldn't think so. Why do you ask?'

'Nothing, forget I said it.' He terminated the call with promises of a visit, then scratched his nose, wondering who to take all this to: Kilpatrick or Lauderdale? He'd been seconded to SCS, but Lauderdale was in charge of the murder inquiry. He asked himself a question: would Lauderdale protect me from Kilpatrick? The answer was no. Then he changed the names around. The answer this time was yes. So he took what he had to Kilpatrick.

And then had to admit that it wasn't much.

Kilpatrick had brought Smylie into the office to join them. Sometimes Rebus wasn't sure who was in charge. Calumn Smylie would be back undercover, maybe drinking in The Dell.

'So,' said Kilpatrick, 'summing up, John, we've got the word Nemo, we've got a Latin phrase –'

'Much quoted by nationalists,' Smylie added, 'at least in its Scots form.'

'And we've got a shield on this coat of arms, all of which reminds you of a group called Sword and Shield who were wound up in the early '60s. You think they've sprung up again?'

Rebus visualised a spring suddenly appearing through the worn covering of an old mattress. He shrugged. 'I don't know, sir.'

'And then this source of yours mentions an organisation in the USA called Sword and Shield.'

'Sir, all I know is, SaS must stand for something. Calumn Smylie's been hearing about an outfit called The Shield who might be in the market for arms. There's also a shield on the Scottish royal arms, as well as a phrase with the word Nemo. I know these are all pretty weak links, but all the same...'

Kilpatrick looked to Smylie, who gave a look indicating he was on Rebus's side.

'Maybe,' Smylie said in proof, 'we could ask our friends in the States to check for us. They'd be doing the work, there's nothing to lose, and with the back-up they've got they could probably give us an answer in a few days. As I say, we haven't lost anything.'

'I suppose not. All right then.' Kilpatrick's hands were ready for prayer. 'John, we'll give it a go.'

'Also, sir,' Rebus added, just pushing his luck a bit, 'we might do some digging into the original Sword and Shield. If the name's been revived, it wasn't just plucked out of the air.'

'Fair point, John. I'll put Blackwood and Ormiston onto it.'

Blackwood and Ormiston: they'd thank him for this, they'd bring him flowers and chocolates.

'Thank you, sir,' said Rebus.

11

Ever since the riot, Father Leary had been trying to contact Rebus, leaving message after message at St Leonard's. So when he got to St Leonard's, Rebus relented and called the priest.

'It hasn't gone too well, father,' he said gamely.

'Then it's God's will.'

For a second, Rebus heard it as God swill. He stuck in his own apostrophe and said, 'I knew you'd say that.' He was watching Siobhan Clarke striding towards him. She had her thumbs up and a big grin spread across her face.

'Got to go, father. Say one for me.'

'Don't I always?'

Rebus put down the receiver. 'What've you got?'

'Cafferty,' she said, throwing the file onto his desk. 'Buried way back.' She produced a sheet of paper and handed it to him. Rebus read through it quickly.

Yes, buried, because it was only a suspicion, one of hundreds that the police had been unable to prove over the course of Cafferty's career.

'Handling dirty money,' he said.

'For the Ulster Volunteer Force.'

Cafferty had formed an unholy alliance with a Glasgow villain called Jinky Johnson, and between them they'd offered a service, turning dirty money into clean at the behest of the UVF. Then Johnson disappeared. Rumour had it he'd either fled with the UVF's cash, or else he'd been skimming a bit and they'd found out and done away with him. Whatever, Cafferty broke his connection.

'What do you think?' Clarke asked.

'It ties Cafferty to the Protestant paramilitaries.'

'And if they thought he knew about Johnson, it'd mean there was no love lost.'

But Rebus had doubts about the time scale. 'They wouldn't wait ten years for revenge. Then again, Cafferty *did* know what SaS stood for. He's heard of it.'

'A new terrorist group?'

'I think so, definitely. And they're here in Edinburgh.' He looked up at Clarke. 'And if we're not careful, Cafferty's men are going to get to them first.' Then he smiled.

'You don't sound overly concerned.'

'I'm so bothered by it all, I think I'll buy you a drink.'

'Deal,' said Siobhan Clarke.

As he drove home, he could smell the cigarettes and booze on his clothes. More ammo for Patience. Christ, there were those videos to take back too. She wouldn't do it, it was up to him. There'd be extra to pay, and he hadn't even watched the bloody things yet.

To defer the inevitable, he stopped at a pub. They didn't come much smaller than the Oxford Bar, but the Ox managed to be cosy too. Most nights there was a party atmosphere, or at the very least some entertaining patter. And there were quarter gills too, of course. He drank just the one, drove the rest of the way to Patience's, and parked in his usual spot near the sports Merc. Someone on Queensferry Road was trying to sing *Tie a Yellow Ribbon*. Overhead, the streetlighting's orange glow picked out the top of the tenements, their chimney pots bristling. The warm air smelt faintly of breweries.

'Rebus?'

It wasn't dark yet, not quite. Rebus had seen the man

110

waiting across the road. Now the man was approaching, hands deep in jacket pockets. Rebus tensed. The man saw the change and brought his hands out to show he was unarmed.

'Just a word,' the man said.

'What about?'

'Mr Cafferty's wondering how things are going.'

Rebus studied the man more closely. He looked like a weasel with misshapen teeth, his mouth constantly open in something that was either a sneer or a medical problem. He breathed in and out through his mouth in a series of small gasps. There was a smell from him that Rebus didn't want to place.

'You want a trip down the station, pal?'

The man grinned, showing his teeth again. Close up, Rebus saw that they were stained so brown from nicotine they might have been made of wood.

'What are the charges?' the weasel said.

Rebus looked him up and down. 'Offence against public decency for a start. They should have kept you in your cage, right at the back of the pet shop.'

'He said you had a way with words.'

'Not just with words.' Rebus started to cross the road to Patience's flat. The man followed, so close he might have been on a leash.

'I'm trying to be pleasant,' the weasel said.

'Tell the charm school to give you a refund.'

'He said you'd be difficult.'

Rebus turned on the man. 'Difficult? You don't know just how difficult I can get if I really try. If I see you here again, you'd better be ready to square off.'

The man narrowed his eyes. 'That'd suit me fine. I'll be sure to mention your co-operation to Mr Cafferty.'

'Do that.' Rebus started down the steps to the garden flat. The weasel leaned down over the rails.

'Nice flat.' Rebus stopped with his key in the lock. He

looked up at the man. 'Shame if anything happened to it.'

By the time Rebus ran back up the steps, the weasel had disappeared.

12

'Have you heard from your brother?'

It was next morning, and Rebus was at Fettes, talking with Ken Smylie.

'He doesn't phone in that often.'

Rebus was trying to turn Smylie into someone he could trust. Looking around him, he didn't see too many potential allies. Blackwood and Ormiston were giving him their double-act filthy look, from which he deduced two things. One, they'd been assigned to look into what, if anything, remained of the original Sword and Shield.

Two, they knew whose idea the job had been.

Rebus, pleased at their glower, decided he wouldn't bother mentioning that Matthew Vanderhyde was looking into Sword and Shield too. Why give them shortcuts when they'd have had him run the marathon?

Smylie didn't seem in the mood for conversation, but Rebus persisted. 'Have you talked to Billy Cunningham's flatmate?'

'She kept going on about his motorbike and what was she supposed to do with it?'

'Is that all?'

Smylie shrugged. 'Unless I want to buy a stripped down Honda.'

'Careful, Smylie, I think maybe you've caught something.'

'What?'

'A sense of humour.'

As Rebus drove to St Leonard's, he rubbed at his jaw

and chin, enjoying the feel of the bristles under his fingertips. He was remembering the very different feel of the AK 47, and thinking of sectarianism. Scotland had enough problems without getting involved in Ireland's. They were like Siamese twins who'd refused the operation to separate them. Only one twin had been forced into a marriage with England, and the other was hooked on self-mutilation. They didn't need politicians to sort things out; they needed a psychiatrist.

The marching season, the season of the Protestant, was over for another year, give or take the occasional small fringe procession. Now it was the season of the International Festival, a festive time, a time to forget the small and insecure country you lived in. He thought again of the poor sods who'd decided to put on a show in the Gar-B.

St Leonard's looked to be joining in the fun. They'd even arranged for a pantomime. Someone had owned up to the Billy Cunningham murder. His name was Unstable from Dunstable.

The police called him that for two reasons. One, he was mentally unstable. Two, he claimed he came from Dunstable. He was a local tramp, but not without resources. With needle and thread he had fashioned for himself a coat constructed from bar towels, and so was a walking sandwich-board for the products which kept him alive and kept him dying.

There were a lot of people out there like him, shiftless until someone (usually the police) shifted them. They'd been 'returned to the community' – a euphemism for dumped – thanks to a tightening of the government's heart and purse-strings. Some of them couldn't tighten their shoe laces without bursting into tears. It was a crying shame.

Unstable was in an interview room now with DS Holmes, being fed hot sweet tea and cigarettes. Eventually they'd turf him out, maybe with a couple of quid in his hand, his technicolor beercoat having no pockets.

Siobhan Clarke was at her desk in the Murder Room. She was being talked at by DI Alister Flower.

So someone had forgotten Rebus's advice regarding the duty roster.

'Well,' Flower said loudly, spotting Rebus, 'if it isn't our man from the SCS. Have you brought the milk?'

Rebus was too slow getting the reference, so Flower obliged.

'The Scottish Co-Operative Society. SCS, same letters as the Scottish Crime Squad.'

'Wasn't Sean Connery a milkman with the Co-Op,' said Siobhan Clarke, 'before he got into acting?' Rebus smiled towards her, appreciating her effort to shift the gist of the conversation.

Flower looked like a man who had comebacks ready, so Rebus decided against a jibe. Instead he said, 'They think very highly of you.'

Flower blinked. 'Who?'

Rebus twitched his head. 'Over at SCS.'

Flower stared at him, then narrowed his eyes. 'Do tell.'

Rebus shrugged. 'What's to tell? I'm serious. The high hiedyins know your record, they've been keeping an eye on you ... that's what I hear.'

Flower shuffled his feet, relaxing his posture. He almost became shy, colour showing in his cheeks.

'They told me to tell you ...' Rebus leaned close, Flower doing likewise, '... that as soon as there's a milk round to spare, they'll give you a call.'

Flower showed two rows of narrow teeth as he growled. Then he stalked off in search of easier prey.

'He's easy to wind up, isn't he?' said Siobhan Clarke.

'That's why I call him the Clockwork Orangeman.'

'Is he an Orangeman?'

'He's been known to march on the 12th.' He considered. 'Maybe Orange Peeler would be a better name for him, eh?'

Clarke groaned. 'What have you got for me from our teuchter friends?'

'You mean the Orkneys. I don't think they'd appreciate being called teuchters.' She tried hard to pronounce the word, but being mostly English, she just failed.

'Remember,' said Rebus, 'teuch is Scots for tough. I don't think they'd mind me calling them tough.' He dragged a chair over to her desk. 'So what did you get?'

She flicked open a paper pad, finding the relevant page. 'Zabriskie House is actually a croft. There's a small cottage, one bedroom and one other room doubling as –'

'I'm not thinking of buying the place.'

'No, sir. The current owners didn't know anything about its past history, but neighbours remembered a chap renting the place for a year or two back in the '70s. He called himself Cuchullain.'

'What?'

'A mythical warrior, Celtic I think.'

'And that was all he called himself?'

'That was all.'

It fitted with the tone of the *Floating Anarchy Factfile*: Celtic hippy. Rebus knew that in the early '70s a lot of young Scots had emulated their American and European cousins by 'dropping out'. But then years later they tended to drop back in again, and did well for themselves in business. He knew because he'd almost dropped out himself. But instead he'd gone to Northern Ireland.

'Anything else?' he asked.

'Bits and pieces. A description that's twenty-odd years old now from a woman who's been blind in one eye since birth.'

'This is your source, is it?'

'Mostly, yes. A police constable went sniffing. He also talked to the man who used to run the sub-post office, and a couple of boatmen. You need a boat to get provisions across to Rousay, and the postman comes by his own boat.

116

He kept himself to himself, grew his own food. There was talk at the time, because people used to come and go at Zabriskie House, young women with no bras on, men with beards and long hair.'

'The locals must've been mortified.'

Clarke smiled. 'The lack of bras was mentioned more than once.'

'Well, a place like that, you have to make your own entertainment.'

'There's one lead the constable is still following up. He'll get back to me today.'

'I won't hold my breath. Have you ever been to the Orkneys?'

'You're not thinking of –' She was interrupted by her telephone. 'DC Clarke speaking. Yes.' She looked up at Rebus and pulled her notepad to her, starting to write. Presumably it was the Old Policeman of Hoy, so Rebus took a stroll around the room. He was reminded again just why he didn't fit, why he was so unsuited to the career life had chosen for him. The Murder Room was like a production line. You had your own little task, and you did it. Maybe someone else would follow up any lead you found, and then someone else after that might do the questioning of a suspect or potential witness. You were a small part of a very large team. It wasn't Rebus's way. He wanted to follow up every lead personally, cross referencing them all, taking them through from first principle to final reckoning. He'd been described, not unkindly, as a terrier, locking on with his jaws and not letting go.

Some dogs, you had to break the jaw to get them off.

Siobhan Clarke came up to him. 'Something?' he asked.

'My constable friend found out Cuchullain used to keep a cow and a pig, plus some chickens. Part of the self-sufficiency thing. He wondered what might have happened to them when Cuchullain moved away.'

'He sounds bright.'

'Turns out Cuchullain sold them on to another crofter, and this crofter keeps records. We got lucky, Cuchullain had to wait for his money, and he gave the crofter a forwarding address in the Borders.' She waved a piece of paper at him.

'Don't get too excited,' warned Rebus. 'We're still talking a twenty year old address for a man whose name we don't know.'

'But we do know. The crofter had a note of that too. It's Francis Lee.'

'Francis Lee?' Rebus sounded sceptical. 'Wasn't he playing for Manchester City in the '70s? Francis Lee ... as in Frank Lee? As in Frank Lee, my dear, I don't give a damn?'

'You think it's another alias?'

'I don't know. Let's get the Borders police to take a look.' He studied the Murder Room. 'Ach, no, on second thoughts, let's go take a look ourselves.'

13

Whenever John Rebus had cause or inclination to drive through any town in the Scottish Borders, one word came to his mind.

Neat.

The towns were simply laid out and almost pathologically tidy. The buildings were constructed from unadorned stone and had a square-built no-nonsense quality to them. The people walking briskly from bank to grocer's shop to chemist's were rosy cheeked and bursting with health, as though they scrubbed their faces with pumice every morning before sitting down to farmhouse fare. The men's limbs moved with the grace of farm machinery. You could present any of the women to your own mother. She'd tell them you weren't good enough for them.

Truth be told, the Borderers scared Rebus. He couldn't understand them. He understood though, that placed many more miles from any large Scottish conurbation than from the English border, there was bound to be some schizophrenia to the towns and their inhabitants.

Selkirk however was definably Scots in character, architecture, and language. Its annual Lammas Fair was not yet just a memory to see the townfolk through the winter. There were still rows of pennants waiting to be taken down, flapping in the slightest breeze. There were some outside the house which abutted the kirkyard wall. Siobhan Clarke checked the address and shrugged.

'It's the manse, isn't it?' Rebus repeated, sure that they had something wrong.

'It's the address I've got here.'

The house was large with several prominent gables. It was fashioned from dull grey stone, but boasted a lush and sweet-smelling garden. Siobhan Clarke pushed open the gate. She searched the front door for a bell but found none, so resorted to the iron knocker which was shaped like an open hand. No one answered. From nearby came the sound of a manual lawnmower, its pull and push as regular as a pendulum. Rebus looked in through the front window of the house, and saw no sign of movement.

'We're wasting our time,' he said. A waste of a long car journey too. 'Let's leave a note and get out of here.'

Clarke peered through the letterbox, then stood up again. 'Maybe we could ask around, now we're here.'

'Fine,' said Rebus, 'let's go talk to the lawnmower man.'

They walked round to the kirkyard gate and took the red gravel path around the perimeter of the church itself. At the back of the soot-blackened building they saw an old man pushing a mower which in Edinburgh might have graced a New Town antique shop.

The gentleman stopped his work when he saw them crossing the trimmed grass towards him. It was like walking on a carpet. The grass could not have been shorter if he'd been using nail scissors. He produced a voluminous handkerchief from his pocket and mopped his suntanned brow. His face and arms were as brown as oak, the face polished with sweat. The elderly skin was still tight across the skull, shiny like a beetle's back. He introduced himself as Willie McStay.

'Is it about the vandalism?' he asked.

'Vandalism? *Here?*'

'They've been desecrating the graves, daubing paint on the headstones. It's the skinheads.'

'Skinheads in Selkirk?' Rebus was not convinced. 'How many skinheads are there, Mr McStay?'

McStay thought about it, grinding his teeth together as though he were chewing tobacco or a particularly tough piece of phlegm. 'Well,' he said, 'there's Alec Tunnock's son for a start. His hair's cropped awful short and he wears those boots wi' the laces.'

'Boots with laces, eh?'

'He hasna had a job since he left school.'

Rebus was shaking his head. 'We're not here about the headstones, Mr McStay. We were wondering about that house.' He pointed towards it.

'The manse?'

'Who lives there, Mr McStay?'

'The minister, Reverend McKay.'

'How long has he lived there?'

'Gracious, I don't know. Fifteen years maybe. Before him it was Reverend Bothwell, and the Bothwells were here for a quarter century or more.'

Rebus looked to Siobhan Clarke. A waste of time.

'We're looking for a man called Francis Lee,' she said.

McStay chomped on the name, jaw chewing from side to side, cheekbones working. He reminded Rebus of a sheep. The old man shook his head. 'Nobody I know of,' he said.

'Well, thanks anyway,' said Rebus.

'A minute,' McStay ordered. Meaning that he wanted to think about it for a minute more. Finally he nodded. 'You've got it the wrong way round.' He leant a hand against the mower's black rubber grip. 'The Bothwells were a lovely couple, Douglas and Ina. Couldn't do enough for this town. When they died, their son sold the house straight off. He wasn't supposed to, Reverend Bothwell told me that often enough. He was supposed to keep it in the family.'

'But it's a manse,' Clarke said. 'Church of Scotland property. How could he sell it?'

'The Bothwells loved the house so much, they bought it

121

off the Church. They were going to live there when Reverend Bothwell retired. The thing is, the son sold it back to the Church. He was a wastrel, that one, took the money and ran. Nobody'd look after their grave if it wasn't for me and a few other old folk here who remember them fondly.' He shook his head. 'Young people, they've no sense of history or commitment.'

'What's this got to do with Francis Lee?' Siobhan Clarke asked. McStay looked at her like she was a child who'd spoken out of turn, and addressed his answer to Rebus.

'Their son was called Lee. I think his middle name was Francis.'

Lee Francis Bothwell: Francis Lee. It was too close to be mere coincidence. Rebus nodded slowly.

'I don't suppose you've any idea,' he said, 'where we might find –' He broke off. 'Frankie Bothwell? Thanks, Mr McStay, thanks for your help.' And he walked towards the gate. It took Siobhan Clarke a moment to catch up with him.

'So are you going to tell me?'

'You don't know Frankie Bothwell?' He watched her try out the name in her mind. She shook her head furiously. 'He owns the Crazy Hose Saloon.'

Now she nodded. 'That Fringe programme in Billy Cunningham's room.'

'Yes, with a show at the Crazy Hose circled. Nice coincidence, eh?' They were at the car now. Rebus opened the passenger door but didn't get in. Instead he rested his elbow on the roof and looked across at her. 'If you believe in coincidence.'

She'd driven them twenty or thirty yards when Rebus ordered her to stop. He'd been looking in his wing mirror, and now got out of the car and started back towards the gates. Siobhan cursed under her breath, drew the car in to the kerb, and followed him. Idling by the gates was a red estate car she'd seen parked further away when they were

122

leaving. Rebus had stopped two men who'd been walking towards Willie McStay.

Neither of the two would have looked out of place in the back of a scrum. Siobhan was in time to catch the end of her superior's argument.

'– and if you don't lay off, so help me, I'll drop you so far in it you'll wish you'd brought a diving bell.' To reinforce this point, Rebus jabbed his finger into the larger man's gut, all the way up to the second joint. The man didn't look like he was enjoying it. His face was a huge ripe plum. But he kept his hands clasped behind his back throughout. He was showing such self control, Siobhan might have taken him for a Buddhist.

Only she'd yet to come across a Buddhist with razor scars carved down both cheeks.

'And what's more,' Rebus was saying, 'you can tell Cafferty we know all about him and the UVF, so he needn't go on acting the innocent about terrorism.'

The bigger of the two men spoke. 'Mr Cafferty's getting very impatient. He wants a result.'

'I don't care if he wants world peace. Now get out of here, and if I hear you've been back asking questions, I'll see you both put away, and I don't care what I've got to do, understood?'

They didn't look overly impressed, but the two men walked away anyway, back to the gates and through them.

'Your fan club?' Siobhan Clarke guessed.

'Ach, they only want me for my body.'

Which, in a sense, was true.

It was late afternoon, and the Crazy Hose was doing no trade at all.

Those in the know just called it the Hose; those not in the know would say, 'Shouldn't it be Horse?' But it was the Hose because its premises were an old decommissioned fire station, left vacant when they built a new edifice just up the street. And it was the Crazy Hose Saloon because it had a wild west theme and country and western music. The main doors were painted gloss black and boasted small square barred windows. Rebus knew the place was doing no trade, because Lee Francis Bothwell was sitting on the steps outside smoking a cigarette.

Although Rebus had never met Frankie Bothwell, he knew the reputation, and there was no mistaking the mess on the steps for anything else. He was dressed like a Las Vegas act, with the face and hair of McGarrett in *Hawaii 5–0*. The hair had to be fake, and Rebus would lay odds some of the face was fake too.

'Mr Bothwell?'

The head nodded without the hair moving one millimetre out of coiffeured place. He was wearing a tan-coloured leather safari jacket, tight white trousers, and an open-necked shirt. The shirt would offend all but the colour blind and the truly blind. It had so many rhinestones on it, Rebus was in no doubt the rhine mines were now exhausted as a result. Around Bothwell's neck hung a simple gold chain, but he would have been better off with a neck-cast. A neck-cast would have disguised the lines, the wrinkles and sags which gave away Bothwell's not insubstantial age.

'I'm Inspector Rebus, this is Detective Constable Clarke.' Rebus had briefed Clarke on the way here, and she didn't look too stunned by the figure in front of her.

'You want a bottle of rye for the police raffle?'

'No, sir. We're trying to complete a collection of magazines.'

'Huh?' Bothwell had been studying the empty street. Just along the road was Tollcross junction, but you couldn't see it from the front steps of the Crazy Hose. Now he looked up at Rebus.

'I'm serious,' Rebus said. 'We're missing a few back issues, maybe you can help.'

'I don't get it.'

'The Floating Anarchy Factfile.'

Frankie Bothwell took off his sunglasses and squinted at Rebus. Then he ground his cigarette-end under the heel of a cowboy boot. 'That was a lifetime ago. How do you know about it?' Rebus shrugged. Frankie Bothwell grinned. He was perking up again. 'Christ, that *was* a long time ago. Up in the Orkneys, peace and love, I had some fun back then. But what's it got to do with anything?'

'Do you know this man?' Rebus handed over a copy of the photo Murdock had given him, the one from the party. It had been cropped to show Billy Cunningham's face only. 'His name's Billy Cunningham.'

Bothwell took a while studying the photo, then shook his head.

'He came here to see a country and western show a couple of weeks back.'

'We're packed most nights, Inspector, especially this time of year. I can ask the bar staff, the bouncers, see if they know him. Is he a regular?'

'We don't know, sir.'

'See, if he's a regular, he'll carry the Cowpoke Card. You get one after three visits in any one month, entitles you to thirty per cent off the admission.' Rebus was shaking his head. 'What's he done anyway?'

'He's been murdered, Mr Bothwell.'

Bothwell screwed up his face. 'Bad one.' Then he looked at Rebus again. 'Not the kid in that underground street?'

Rebus nodded.

Bothwell stood up, brushing dirt from his backside. '*Floating Anarchy* hasn't been in circulation for twenty years. You say this kid had a copy?'

'Issue number three,' Siobhan Clarke confirmed.

Bothwell thought about it. 'Number three, that was a big printing, a thousand or so. There was momentum behind number three. After that ... not so much momentum.' He smiled ruefully. 'Can I keep the photo? Like I say, I'll ask around.'

'Fine, Mr Bothwell. We've got copies.'

'Secondhand shops maybe.'

'Pardon?'

'The magazine, maybe he got it secondhand.'

'That's a thought.'

'A kid that age, Christ.' He shook his head. 'I love kids, Inspector, that's what this place is all about. Giving kids a good time. There's nothing like it.'

'Really, sir?'

Bothwell spread his hands. 'I don't mean anything ... you know ... nothing like that. I've always liked kids. I used to run a football team, local youth club thing. Anything for kids.' He smiled again. 'That's because I'm still a kid myself, Inspector. Me, I'm Peter bloody Pan.'

Still holding the photo, he invited them in for a drink. Rebus was tempted, but declined. The bar would be an empty barn; no place for a drink. He handed Bothwell a card with his office number.

'I'll do my best,' Bothwell said.

Rebus nodded and turned away. He didn't say anything to Siobhan Clarke till they were back in her car.

'Well, what do you think?'

'Creepy,' she said. 'How can he dress like that?'

'Years of practice, I suppose.'

'So what do you reckon to him?'

Rebus thought about this. 'I'm not sure. Let me think about it over a drink.'

'That's very kind, sir, but I'm going out.' She made a show of checking her watch.

'A Fringe show?' She nodded.

'Early Tom Stoppard,' she said.

'Well,' Rebus sniffed, 'I didn't say you were invited anyway.' He paused. 'Who are you going with?'

She looked at him. 'I'm going on my own, not that it's any of your business ... sir.'

Rebus shifted a little. 'You can drop me off at the Ox.'

As they drove past, there was no sign of Frankie Bothwell on the steps of the Crazy Hose Saloon.

The Ox gave Rebus a taste. He phoned Patience, but got the answer-phone. He seemed to remember she was going out tonight, but couldn't recall where. He took the slow route home. In Daintry's Lounge, he stood at the bar listening in on its tough wit. The Festival only touched places like Daintry's insofar as providing posters to advertise the shows. These were as much decoration as the place ever had. He stared at a sign above the row of optics. It said, 'If arseholes could fly, this place would be an airport'.

'Ready for take-off,' he said to the barmaid, proffering his empty glass.

A little later, he found himself approaching Oxford Terrace from Lennox Street, so turned into Lennox Street Lane. What had once been stables in the Lane had now become first floor homes with ground floor garages. The place was always dead. Some of the tenements on Oxford Terrace backed onto the lane. Rebus had a key to Patience's garden gate. He'd let himself in the back door to the flat. As shortcuts went, it wasn't much of one, but he liked the lane.

He was about a dozen paces from the gate when somebody grabbed him. They got him from behind, pulling him by the coat, keeping the grip tight so that he might as well have been wearing a straitjacket. The coat came up over Rebus's head, trapping him, binding his arms. A knee came up into his groin. He lashed out with a foot, which only made it all the easier to unbalance him. He was shouting and swearing as he fell. The attacker had released his grip on the coat. While Rebus struggled to get out of it, a foot

127

caught him on the side of the head. The foot was wearing a plimsoll, which explained why Rebus hadn't heard his attacker following him. It also explained why he was still conscious after the kick.

Another kick dug into his side. And then, just as his head was emerging from his coat, the foot caught him on the chin, and all he could see were the setts beneath him, slick and shining from what light there was. The attacker's hands were on him, rifling pockets. The man was breathing hard.

'Take the money,' Rebus said, trying to focus his eyes. He knew there wasn't much money to take, less than a fiver, all of it in small change. The man didn't seem happy with his haul. It wasn't much for a night's work.

'A'm gonny put you in the hospital.' The accent was Glaswegian. Rebus could make out the man's build – squat – but not yet his face. There was too much shadow. He was rearing up again, coins spilling from his hands to rain down on Rebus.

He'd given Rebus just enough time to shake off the alcohol. Rebus sprang from his crouch and hit the man square in the stomach with his head, propelling his assailant backwards. The man kept his balance, but Rebus was standing too now, and he was bigger than the Glaswegian. There was a glint in the man's hand. A cutthroat razor. Rebus hadn't seen one in years. It flashed in an arc towards him, but he dodged it, then saw that there were two other figures in the lane. They were watching, hands in pockets. He thought he recognised them as Cafferty's men, the ones from the churchyard.

The razor was swinging again, the Glaswegian almost smiling as he went about his business. Rebus slipped his coat all the way off and wrapped it around his left arm. He met the blade with his arm, feeling it cut into the cloth, and lashed out with the sole of his right foot, connecting with the man's knee. The man took a step back, and Rebus struck out again, connecting with a thigh this time. When the man attempted to come back at him, he was limping and easy to sidestep. But instead of aiming with the razor he barrelled into Rebus, pushing him hard against some garage doors. Then he turned and ran.

There was only one exit from the alley, and he took it, running past Cafferty's men. Rebus took a deep breath, then sank to his knees and threw up onto the ground. His coat was ruined, but that was the least of his problems. Cafferty's men were strolling towards him. They lifted him to his feet like he was a bag of shopping.

'You all right?' one asked.

'Winded,' Rebus said. His chin hurt too, but there was no blood. He puked up more alcohol, feeling better for it. The other man had stooped to pick up the money. Rebus didn't get it.

'Your man?' he said. They were shaking their heads. Then the bigger one spoke.

'He just saved us the bother.'

'He was trying to hospitalise me.'

'I think I'd have done the same,' said the big man, holding out Rebus's coins. 'If this is all I'd found.'

Rebus took the money and pocketed it. Then he took a swing at the man. It was slow and tired and didn't connect. But the big man connected all right. His punch took all the remaining fight out of Rebus. He fell to his knees again, palms on the cold ground.

'That's by way of an incentive,' the man said. 'Just in case you were needing one. Mr Cafferty'll be talking to you soon.'

'Not if I can help it,' spat Rebus, sitting with his back to the garage. They were walking away from him, back towards the mouth of the lane.

'He'll be talking to you.'

Then they were gone.

A Glaswegian with a razor, Rebus thought to himself,

happy to sit here till the pain went away. If not Cafferty's man, then whose?

And why?

14

Rebus struggled towards consciousness, even as he picked up the telephone.

'Heathen!' he gasped into it.

'Pardon?'

'To call at this ungodly hour.' He'd recognised DCI Kilpatrick's voice. He ran the palm of his hand down his face, pulling open his eyelids. When he could focus, he tried finding the time on the clock, but in his struggle for the receiver he'd knocked it to the floor. 'What do you want . . . sir?'

'I was hoping you could come in a bit early.'

'What? Cleaners on strike and you're looking for a relief?'

'He sounds like the dead, but he's still cracking jokes.'

'When do you want me?'

'Say, half an hour?'

'You say it, I'll do what I can.' He put down the receiver and found his watch. It was on his wrist. The time was five past six. He hadn't so much slept as drifted into coma. Maybe it was the drink or the vomiting or the beating. Maybe it was just too many late nights catching up with him. Whatever, he didn't feel the worse for it. He checked his side: it was bruised, but not badly. His chin and face didn't feel too bad either, just grazed.

'Who the hell was that?' Patience growled sleepily from beneath her pillow.

'Duty calls,' said Rebus, swinging his unwilling legs out of bed.

They were seated in Kilpatrick's office, Rebus and Ken Smylie. Rebus held his coffee cup the way a disaster victim would, cradling this smallest of comforts. He couldn't have looked worse if there'd been a blanket around his shoulders and a reporter in front of him asking how he felt about the plane crash. His early morning buzz had lasted all the way from the bed to the bathroom. It had been an effort to look in the mirror. Unshaven, you hardly noticed the bruises, but he could feel them on the inside.

Smylie seemed alert enough, not needing the caffeine. And Rebus shouldn't have been drinking it either; it would play merry hell with him later.

It was a minute short of seven o'clock, and they were watching Kilpatrick pretend to reread some fax sheets. At last he was ready. He put down the sheets and interlocked the fingers of both hands. Rebus and Smylie were trying to get a look at what the fax said.

'I've heard from the United States. You were right, Ken, they're quick workers. The gist is, there are two fairly widespread but above board organisations in the US, one's called the Scottish Rites Temple.'

'That's a kind of masonic lodge for Scots,' Rebus said, remembering Vanderhyde's words.

Kilpatrick nodded. 'The other is called Scottish Sword and Shield.' He watched Rebus and Smylie exchange a look. 'Don't get excited. It's much more low-key than Scottish Rites, but it's not into the financing of gun-running. However,' he picked up the fax again, 'there's one final group. It has its main headquarters in Toronto, Canada, but also has branches in the States, particularly in the south and the north-west. It's called The Shield, and you won't find it in any phone book. The FBI have been investigating the US operation for just over a year, as have the American tax people. I had a chat with an FBI agent at their headquarters in Washington.'

'And?'

'And, the Shield is a fund-raiser, only nobody's quite sure what for. Whatever it is, it isn't Catholic. The FBI agent said he'd already passed a lot of this information on to the Royal Ulster Constabulary, in the event of their becoming cognisant of the organisation.'

Ten minutes on the phone to Washington, and already Kilpatrick was aping American speech.

'So,' Rebus said, 'now we talk to the RUC.'

'I already have. That's why I called this meeting.'

'What did they say?'

'They were pretty damned cagey.'

'No surprises there, sir,' said Smylie.

'They did admit to having some information on what they called Sword and Shield.'

'Great.'

'But they won't release it. Usual RUC runaround. They don't like sharing things. Their line is, if we want to see it, we have to go there. Those bastards really are a law unto themselves.'

'No point going higher up with this, sir? *Some*one could order the information out of them.'

'Yes, and it could get lost, or they could lift out anything they didn't feel like letting us see. No, I think we show willing on this.'

'Belfast?'

Kilpatrick nodded. 'I'd like you both to go, it'll only be a day trip.' Kilpatrick checked his watch. 'There's a Loganair flight at seven-forty, so you'd best get going.'

'No time to pack my tour guides,' said Rebus. Inside, two old dreads were warming his gut.

They banked steeply coming down over Belfast harbour, like one of those fairground rides teenagers take to prove themselves. Rebus still had a hum of caffeine in his ears.

'Pretty good, eh?' said Smylie.

'Aye, pretty good.' Rebus hadn't flown in a few years. He'd had a fear of flying ever since his SAS training. Already he was dreading the return trip. It wasn't when he was high up, he didn't mind that. But the take-off and landing, that view of the ground, so near and yet far enough to kill you stone dead if you hit it. Here it came again, the plane dropping fast now, too fast. His fingers were sore against the armrests. There was every chance of them locking there. He could see a surgeon amputating at the wrists . . .

And then they were down. Smylie was quick to stand up. The seat had been too narrow for him, with not enough legroom. He worked his neck and shoulders, then rubbed his knees.

'Welcome to Belfast,' he said.

'We like to give visitors the tour,' Yates said.

He was Inspector Yates of the Royal Ulster Constabulary, and both he and his car were in mufti. He had a face formed of fist-fights or bad childhood infections, scar tissue and things not quite in their right place. His nose veered leftwards, one earlobe hung lower than the other, and his chin had been stitched together not altogether successfully. You'd look at him in a bar and then look away again quickly, not risking the stare he deserved. He had no neck, that was another thing. His head sat on his shoulders like a boulder on the top of a hill.

'That's very kind,' said Smylie, as they sped into town, 'but we'd –'

'Lets you see what we're dealing with.' Yates kept looking in his rearview, conducting a conversation with the mirror. 'The two cities. It's the same in any war zone. I knew this guy, height of the trouble in Beirut, he was recruited as a croupier there. Bombs falling, gunmen on the rampage, and the casinos were still open. Now these,' he nodded out of the windscreen, 'are the recruiting stations.'

They had left the City Airport behind, shaved the city's

commercial centre, and were passing through a wasteland. Until now, you couldn't have said which British city you were in. A new road was being built down by the docks. Old flats, no worse than those in the Gar-B, were being demolished. As Yates had commented, sometimes the divide was hidden.

Not far away, a helicopter hovered high in the sky, watching someone or something. Around them, whole streets had been bulldozed. The kerbstones were painted green and white.

'You'll see red, white and blue ones in other areas.'

On the gable-end of a row of houses was an elaborate painting. Rebus could make out three masked figures, their automatic weapons raised high. There was a tricolour above them, and a phoenix rising from flames above this.

'A nice piece of propaganda,' said Rebus.

Yates turned to Smylie. 'Your man knows what he's talking about. It's a work of art. These are some of the poorest streets in Europe, by the way.'

They didn't look so bad to Rebus. The gable-end had reminded him again of the Gar-B. Only there was more rebuilding going on here. New housing developments were rising from the old.

'See that wall?' said Yates. 'That's called an environmental wall built and maintained by the Housing Executive.' It was a red brick wall, functional, with a pattern in the bricks. 'There used to be houses there. The other side of the wall is Protestant, once you get past the wasteland. They knock down the houses and extend the wall. There's the Peace Line too, that's an ugly old thing, made from iron rather than bricks. Streets like these, they're meat and drink to the paramilitaries. The loyalist areas are the same.'

Eyes were following their slow progress, the eyes of teenagers and children grouped at street corners. The eyes held neither fear nor hate, only mistrust. On a wall, someone had daubed painted messages, old references to the H Block and Bobby Sands, newer additions in praise of the IRA, and promising revenge against the loyalist paramilitaries, the UVF and UFF predominantly. Rebus saw himself patrolling these streets, or streets like them, back when there had been more houses, more people on the move. He'd often been the 'back walker', which meant he stayed at the back of the patrol and faced the rear, his gun pointing towards the people they'd just passed, men staring at the ground, kids making rude gestures, shows of bravado, and mothers pushing prams. The patrol moved as cautiously as in any jungle.

'See, here we are,' Yates was saying, 'we're coming into Protestant territory now.' More gable-ends, now painted with ten-foot-high Williams of Orange riding twenty-foot-high white horses. And then the cheaper displays, the graffiti, exhorting the locals to 'Fuck the Pope and the IRA'. The letters FTP were everywhere. Five minutes before, they had been FKB: Fuck King Billy. They were just routine, a reflex. But of course they were more. You couldn't laugh them off as name-calling, because the people who'd written them wouldn't let you. They kept shooting each other, and blowing each other up.

Smylie read one of the slogans aloud. ' "Irish Out".' He turned to Yates. 'What? All of them?'

Yates smiled. 'The Catholics write "Troops Out", so the loyalists write "Irish Out". They don't see themselves as Irish, they're British.' He looked in the mirror again. 'And they're getting more vicious, loyalist paramilitaries killed more civvies last year than the IRA did. That's a first, so far as I know. The loyalists hate us now, too.'

'Who's us?'

'The RUC. They weren't happy when the UDA was outlawed. Your man, Sir Patrick Mayhew, he lit the fuse.'

'I read about some riots.'

'Only last month, here in the Shankill and elsewhere. They say we're harassing them. We can't really win, can we?'

'I think we get the picture,' said Smylie, anxious to get to work. But Rebus knew the point the RUC man was making: this *was* their work.

'If you think you get the picture,' Yates said, 'then you're not getting the picture. You're to blame, you know.'

'Eh?'

'The Scots. You settled here in the seventeenth century, started pushing around the Catholics.'

'I don't think we need a history lesson,' Rebus said quietly. Smylie was looking like he might explode.

'But it's all about history,' Yates said levelly. 'On the surface at least.'

'And underneath?'

'Paramilitaries are in the business of making money. They can't exist without money. So now they've become gangsters, pure and simple, because that's the easy way to make the money they need. And then it becomes self-perpetuating. The IRA and UDA get together now and then and discuss things. They sit around a table together, just like the politicians want them to, but instead of talking about peace, they talk about carving up the country. You can extort from these taxi firms if we can extort from the building sites. You even get cases where the stuff the one side has stolen is passed on to the other for them to sell in their areas. You get times when the tension's high, then it's back to business as usual. It's like one of those mafia films, the money these bastards are making . . .' Yates shook his head. 'They can't *afford* peace. It'd be bad for business.'

'And bad for your business too.'

Yates laughed. 'Aye, right enough, overtime wouldn't be easy to come by. But then we might live to retirement age, too. That doesn't always happen just now.' Yates had lifted his radio transmitter. 'Two-Six-Zero, I'm about five minutes from base. Two passengers.' The radio spat static.

'Received and understood.'

He put down the receiver. 'Now this,' he said, 'this is

137

Belfast too. South Belfast, you don't hear much about it because hardly anything ever happens here. See what I mean about two cities?'

Rebus had been noticing the change in their surroundings. Suddenly it looked prosperous, safe. There were wide tree-lined avenues, detached houses, some of them very new-looking. They'd passed the university, a red-brick replica of some older college. Yet they were still only ten minutes from 'the Troubles'. Rebus knew this face of the city, too. He'd only spent the one tour of duty here, but he remembered the big houses, the busy city centre, the Victorian pubs whose interiors were regarded as national treasures. He knew the city was surrounded by lush green countryside, winding lanes and farm tracks, at the end of which might sit silent milk-churns packed with explosives.

The RUC station on the Malone Road was a well-disguised affair, tucked away behind a wooden fence, with a discreet lookout tower.

'We have to keep up appearances for the locals,' Yates explained. 'This is a nice part of town, no mesh fences and machine guns.'

The gates had been opened for them, and closed quickly again.

'Thanks for the tour,' Rebus said as they parked. He meant it, something Yates acknowledged with a nod. Smylie opened his door and prised himself out. Yates glanced at the upholstery, then opened the glove compartment and lifted out his holstered pistol, bringing it with him.

'Is your accent Irish?' Rebus asked.

'Mostly. There's a bit of Liverpool in there too. I was born in Bootle, we moved here when I was six.'

'What made you join the RUC?' Smylie asked.

'I've always been a stupid bastard, I suppose.'

He had to sign both visitors into the building, and their identities were checked. Later, Rebus knew, some clerical assistant would add them to a computer file.

Inside, the station looked much like any police station, except that the windows were heavily protected and the beat patrols carried padded vests with them and wore holsters. They'd seen policemen during their drive, but had acknowledged none of them. And they'd passed a single Army patrol, young squaddies sitting at the open rear door of their personnel carrier (known as a 'pig' in Rebus's day, and probably still), automatic rifles held lightly, faces trained not to show emotion. In the station, the windows might be well protected but there seemed little sign of a siege mentality. The jokes were just as blue, just as black, as the ones told in Edinburgh. People discussed TV and football and the weather. Smylie wasn't watching any of it. He wanted the job done and out again as quick as could be.

Rebus wasn't sure about Smylie. The man might be a wonder in the office, as efficient as the day was long, but here he seemed less sure of himself. He was nervous, and showed it. When he took his jacket off, complaining of the heat, there were large sweat marks spreading from beneath his arms. Rebus had thought *he'd* be the nervous one, yet he felt detached, his memories bringing back no new fears. He was all right.

Yates had a small office to himself. They'd bought beakers of tea at a machine, and now sat these on the desk. Yates put his gun into a desk drawer, draped his jacket over his chair, and sat down. Pinned above him on the wall behind the desk was a sheet of computer print-out bearing the oversized words *Nil Illegitimum Non Carborundum*. Smylie decided to take a poke.

'I thought Latin was for the Catholics?'

Yates stared at him. 'There *are* Catholics in the RUC. Don't get us confused with the UDR.' Then he unlocked another drawer and pulled out a file, pushing it across the desk towards Rebus. 'This doesn't leave the room.' Smylie drew his chair towards Rebus's, and they read the contents together, Smylie, the faster reader, fidgeting as he waited for Rebus to catch up.

'This is incredible,' Smylie said at one point. He was right. The RUC had evidence of a loyalist paramilitary force called Sword and Shield (usually just referred to as The Shield), and of a support group working out of the mainland, acting as a conduit through which money and arms could pass, and also raising funds independently.

'By mainland do you mean Scotland?' Rebus asked.

Yates shrugged. 'We're not really taking them seriously, it's just a cover name for the UVF or UFF, got to be. That's the way it works. There are so many of these wee groups, Ulster Resistance, the Red Hands Commando, Knights of the Red Hand, we can hardly keep up with them.'

'But this group is on the mainland,' Rebus said.

'Yes.'

'And we've maybe come up against them.' He tapped the folder. 'Yet nobody thought to tell us any of this.'

Yates shrugged again, his head falling further into his body. 'We leave that to Special Branch.'

'You mean Special Branch were told about this?'

'Special Branch here would inform Special Branch in London.'

'Any idea who the contact would be in London?'

'That's classified information, Inspector, sorry.'

'A man called Abernethy?'

Yates pushed his chair back so he could rock on it, the front two legs coming off the floor. He studied Rebus.

'That's answer enough,' Rebus said. He looked to Smylie, who nodded. They were being screwed around by Special Branch. But why?

'I see something's on your mind,' said Yates. 'Want to tell me about it? I'd like to hear what you know.'

Rebus placed the folder on the desk. 'Then come to Edinburgh some time, maybe we'll tell you.'

Yates placed all four legs of his chair on the floor. When

he looked at Rebus, his face was stone, his eyes fire. 'No need to be like that,' he said quietly.

'Why not? We've wasted a whole day for four sheets of filing paper, all because you wouldn't send it to us!'

'It's nothing personal, Inspector, it's security. Wouldn't matter if you were the Chief fucking Constable. Perspectives tend to change when your arse is in the line of fire.'

If Yates was looking for the sympathy vote, Rebus wasn't about to place a cross in his box. 'The Prods haven't always been as keen as the Provos, have they? What's going on?'

'First off, they're loyalists, not Prods. Prods means Protestants, and we're dealing only with a select few, not with all of them. Second, they're Provies, not Provos. Third ... we're not sure. There's a younger leadership, a keener leadership. Plus like I say, they're not happy just to let the security forces get on with it. See, the loyalist paramilitaries have always had a problem. They're supposed to be on the same side as the security forces, they're supposed to be law-abiding. That's changed. They feel threatened. Just now they're the majority, but it won't always be that way. Plus the British government's more concerned with its international image than with a few hard-line loyalists, so it's paying more attention to the Republic. Put all that together and you get disillusioned loyalists, and plenty of them. The loyalist paramilitaries used to have a bad image. A lot of their operations went wrong, they didn't have the manpower or the connections or the international support of the IRA.

'These days they seem to be better organised though, not so much blatant racketeering. A lot of the thugs have been put off the Road ... that is, put off the Shankill Road, as in banished.'

'But at the same time they're arming themselves,' Rebus said.

'It's true,' added Smylie. 'In the past, whenever we caught them red-handed on the mainland, we used to find gelignite or sodium chlorate, now we're finding rocket launchers and armour-piercing shells.'

'Red-handed.' Yates smiled at that. 'Oh, it's getting heavy duty,' he agreed.

'But you don't know why?'

'I've given you all the reasons I can.'

Rebus wondered about that, but didn't say anything.

'Look, this is a new thing for us,' Yates said. 'We're used to facing off the Provies, not the loyalists. But now they've got Kalashnikovs, RPG-7s, frag grenades, Brownings.'

'And you're taking them seriously?'

'Oh yes, Inspector, we're taking them seriously. That's why I want to know what *you* know.'

'Maybe we'll tell you over a beer,' Rebus said.

Yates took them to the Crown Bar. Across the street, most of the windows in the Europa Hotel were boarded up, the result of another bomb. The bomb had damaged the Crown, too, but the damage hadn't been allowed to linger. It was a Victorian pub, well preserved, with gas lighting and a wall lined with snugs, each with its own table and its own door for privacy. The interior reminded Rebus of several Edinburgh bars, but here he drank stout rather than heavy, and whiskey rather than whisky.

'I know this place,' he said.

'Been here before, eh?'

'Inspector Rebus,' Smylie explained, 'was in the Army in Belfast.'

So then Rebus had to tell Yates all about it, all about 1969. He wasn't getting it out of his system; he could still feel the pressure inside him. He remembered the republican drinking club again, and the way they'd gone in there swinging wildly, some of the toms more enthusiastic than others. What would he say if he met any of the men they'd beaten? Sorry didn't seem enough. He wouldn't talk about it, but he told Yates a few other stories. Talking was okay,

and drinking was okay too. The thought of the return flight
didn't bother him so much after two pints and a nip. By
the time they were in the Indian restaurant eating an early
lunch in a private booth a long way from any other diners,
Smylie had grown loquacious, but it was all mental arm-
wrestling, comparing and contrasting the two police forces,
discussing manpower, back-up, arrest sheets, drug problems.

As Yates pointed out, leaving aside terrorism, Northern
Ireland had one of the lowest crime rates going, certainly
for serious crimes. There were the usual housebreakings
and car-jackings, but few rapes and murders. Even the
rougher housing schemes were kept in check by the paramilitaries, whose punishments went beyond incarceration.

Which brought them back to Mary King's Close. Were
they any nearer, Rebus wondered, to finding out why Billy
Cunningham had been tortured and killed and who had
killed him? The letters SaS on an arm, the word Nemo on
the floor, the style of the assassination and Cunningham's
own sympathies. What did it all add up to?

Yates meantime talked a little more freely, while helping
Smylie polish off the remaining dishes. He admitted they
weren't all angels in the RUC, which did not exactly
surprise Rebus and Smylie, but Yates said they should see
some of the men in the Ulster Defence Regiment, who were
so fair-minded that their patrols had to be accompanied by
RUC men keeping an eye on them.

'You were here in '69, Inspector, you'll remember the B
Specials? The UDR was formed to replace the B Spesh. The
same madmen joined. See, if a loyalist wants to do something for his cause, all he has to do is join the UDR or the
RUC Reserve. That fact has kept the UDA and UVF small.'

'Is there still collusion between the security forces and
the loyalists?'

Yates pondered that one over a belch. 'Probably,' he
said, reaching for his lager. 'The UDR used to be terrible,

so did the Royal Irish Rangers. Now, it's not so widespread.'

'Either that or better hidden,' said Rebus.

'With cynicism like that, you should join the RUC.'

'I don't like guns.'

Yates wiped at his plate with a final sliver of nan bread. 'Ah yes,' he said, 'the essential difference between us. I get to shoot people.'

'It's a big difference,' Rebus suggested.

'All the difference in the world,' Yates agreed.

Smylie had gone quiet. He was wiping his own plate with bread.

'Do the loyalists get aid from overseas?' Rebus asked.

Yates sat back contentedly. 'Not as much as the republicans. The loyalists probably rake in £150,000 a year from the mainland, mostly to help families and convicted members. Two-thirds of that comes from Scotland. There are pockets of sympathisers abroad – Australia, South Africa, the US and Canada. Canada's the big one. The UVF have some Ingrams submachine guns just now that were shipped from Toronto. Why do you want to know?'

Rebus and Smylie shared a look, then Smylie started to talk. Rebus was happy to let him: this way, Yates only got to know what Smylie knew, rather than what Rebus suspected. Toronto: headquarters of The Shield. When Smylie had finished, Rebus asked Yates a question.

'This group, Sword and Shield, I didn't see any names on the file.'

'You mean individuals?' Rebus nodded. 'Well, it's all pretty low-key. We've got suspicions, but the names wouldn't mean anything to you.'

'Try me.'

Yates considered, then nodded slowly. 'Okay.'

'For instance, who's the leader?'

'We haven't breached their command structure ... not yet.'

'But you have your suspicions?'

Yates smiled. 'Oh yes. There's one bastard in particular.' His voice, already low, dropped lower still. 'Alan Fowler. He was UVF, but left after a disagreement. A right bad bastard, I think the UVF were glad to be shot of him.'

'Can I have a photo? A description?'

Yates shrugged. 'Why not? He's not my problem just now anyway.'

Rebus put down his glass. 'Why's that?'

'Because he took the ferry to Stranraer last week. A car picked him up and drove him to Glasgow.' Yates paused. 'And that's where we lost him.'

15

Ormiston was waiting at the airport with a car.

Rebus didn't like Ormiston. He had a huge round face marked with freckles, and a semi-permanent grin too close to a sneer for comfort. His hair was thickly brown, always in need of a comb or a cut. He reminded Rebus of an overgrown schoolboy. Seeing him at his desk next to the bald and schoolmasterly Blackwood was like seeing the classroom dunce placed next to the teacher so an eye could be kept on his work.

But there was something particularly wrong with Ormiston this afternoon. Not that Rebus really cared. All he cared about was the headache which had woken him on the approach to Edinburgh. A midday drinking headache, a glare behind the eyes and a stupor further back in the brain. He'd noticed at the airport, the way Ormiston was looking at Smylie, Smylie not realising it.

'Got any paracetamol on you?' Rebus asked.

'Sorry.' And he caught Rebus's eye again, as if trying to communicate something. Normally he was a nosy bugger, yet he hadn't asked about their trip. Even Smylie noticed this.

'What is it, Ormiston? A vow of *omerta* or something?'

Ormiston still wasn't talking. He concentrated on his driving, giving Rebus plenty of time for thought. He had things to tell Kilpatrick ... and things he wanted to keep to himself for the time being.

When Ormiston stopped the car at Fettes, he turned to Rebus.

'Not you. We've got to meet the Chief somewhere.'

'What?'

Smylie, half out of his door, stopped. 'What's up?'

Ormiston just shook his head. Rebus looked to Smylie. 'See you later then.'

'Aye, sure.' And Smylie got out, relieving the car's suspension. As soon as he'd closed the door, Ormiston moved off.

'What is it, Ormiston?'

'Best if the Chief tells you himself.'

'Give me a clue then.'

'A murder,' Ormiston said, changing up a gear. 'There's been a murder.'

The scene had been cordoned off.

It was a narrow street of tall tenements. St Stephen Street had always enjoyed a rakish reputation, something to do with its mix of student flats, cafes and junk shops. There were several bars, one of them catering mainly to bikers. Rebus had heard a story that Nico, ex-Velvet Underground, had lived here for a time. It could be true. St Stephen Street, connecting the New Town to Raeburn Place, was a quiet thoroughfare which still managed to exude charm and seediness in equal measures.

The tenements either side of the street boasted basements, and a lot of these were flats with their own separate stairwells and entrances. Patience lived in just such a flat not seven minutes' walk away. Rebus walked carefully down the stone steps. They were often worn and slippy. At the bottom, in a sort of damp courtyard, the owner or tenant of the flat had attempted to create a garden of terracotta pots and hanging baskets. But most of the plants had died, probably from lack of light, or perhaps from rough treatment at the hands of the builders. Scaffolding stretched

147

up the front of the tenement, much of it covered with thick polythene, crackling in the breeze.

'Cleaning the façade,' someone said. Rebus nodded. The front door of the flat faced a whitewashed wall, and in the wall were set two doors. Rebus knew what these were, they were storage areas, burrowed out beneath the surface of the pavement. Patience had almost identical doors, but never used the space for anything; the cellars were too damp. One of the doors stood open. The floor was mostly moss, some of which was being scraped into an evidence-bag by a SOCO.

Kilpatrick, watching this, was listening to Blackwood, who ran his left hand across his pate, tucking an imaginary hair behind his ear. Kilpatrick saw Rebus.

'Hello, John.'

'Sir.'

'Where's Smylie?'

Ormiston was coming down the steps. Rebus nodded towards him. 'The Quiet Man there dropped him at HQ. So what's the big mystery?'

Blackwood answered. 'Flat's been on the market a few months, but not selling. Owner decided to tart it up a bit, see if that would do the trick. Builders turned up yesterday. Today one of them decided to take a look at the cellars. He found a body.'

'Been there long?'

Blackwood shook his head. 'They're doing the post-mortem this evening.'

'Any tattoos?'

'No tattoos,' said Kilpatrick. 'Thing is, John, it was Calumn.' The Chief Inspector looked genuinely troubled, almost ready for tears. His face had lost its colour, and had lengthened as though the muscles had lost all motivation. He massaged his forehead with a hand.

'Calumn?' Rebus shook away his hangover. 'Calumn Smylie?' He remembered the big man, in the back of the

148

HGV with his brother. Tried to imagine him dead, but couldn't. Especially not here, in a cellar...

Kilpatrick blew his nose loudly, then wiped it. 'I suppose I'd better get back and tell Ken.'

'No need, sir.'

Ken Smylie was standing at street level, gripping the gloss-black railings. He looked like he might uproot the lot. Instead he arched back his head and gave a high-pitched howl, the sound swirling up into the sky as a smattering of rain began to fall.

Smylie had to be ordered to go home, they couldn't shift him otherwise. Everyone else in the office moved like automatons. DCI Kilpatrick had some decisions to make, chief among them whether or not to tie together the two murder inquiries.

'He was stabbed,' he told Rebus. 'No signs of a struggle, certainly no torture, nothing like that.' There was relief in his voice, a relief Rebus could understand. 'Stabbed and dumped. Whoever did it probably saw the For Sale sign outside the flat, didn't reckon on the body being found for a while.' He had produced a bottle of Laphroaig from the bottom drawer of his desk, and poured himself a glass.

'Medicinal,' he explained. But Rebus declined the offer of a glass. He'd taken three paracetamol washed down with Irn-Bru. He noticed that the level in the Laphroaig bottle was low. Kilpatrick must have a prescription.

'You think he was rumbled?'

'What else?' said Kilpatrick, dribbling more malt into his glass.

'I'd have expected another punishment killing, something with a bit of ritual about it.'

'Ritual?' Kilpatrick considered this. 'He wasn't killed there, you know. The pathologist said there wasn't enough blood. Maybe they held their "ritual" wherever they killed him. Christ, and I let him go out on a limb.' He took out a handkerchief and blew his nose, then took a deep breath. 'Well, I've got a murder inquiry to start up, the high hiedyins are going to be asking questions.'

'Yes, sir.' Rebus stood up, but stopped at the door. 'Two murders, two cellars, two lots of builders.'

Kilpatrick nodded, but said nothing. Rebus opened the door.

'Sir, who knew about Calumn?'

'How do you mean?'

'Who knew he was undercover? Just this office, or anyone else?'

Kilpatrick furrowed his brow. 'Such as?'

'Special Branch, say.'

'Just this office,' Kilpatrick said quietly. Rebus turned to leave. 'John, what did you find out in Belfast?'

'That Sword and Shield exists. That the RUC know it's operating here on the mainland. That they told Special Branch in London.' He paused. 'That DI Abernethy probably knows all about it.'

Having said which, Rebus left the room. Kilpatrick stared at the door for a full minute.

'Christ almighty,' he said. His telephone was ringing. He was slow to answer it.

'Is it true?' Brian Holmes asked. Siobhan Clarke was waiting for an answer too.

'It's true,' said Rebus. They were in the Murder Room at St Leonard's. 'He was working on something that might well be connected to Billy Cunningham.'

'So what now, sir?'

'We need to talk to Millie and Murdock again.'

'We've talked to them.'

'That's why I said "again". Don't you listen? And after that, let's fix up a little chat with some of the Jaffas.'

'Jaffas?'

Rebus tutted at Siobhan Clarke. 'How long have you lived here? Jaffas are Orangemen.'

'The Orange Lodge?' said Holmes. 'What can they tell us?'

'The date of the Battle of the Boyne for a start.'

'1690, Inspector.'

'Yes, sir.'

'The date, of course, means more than a mere *annus mirabilis*. One-six-nine-o. One and six make seven, nine plus nought equals nine, seven and nine being crucial numbers.' He paused. 'Do you know anything of numerology, Inspector?'

'No, sir.'

'What about the lassie?'

Siobhan Clarke bristled visibly. 'It's sort of a crank science, isn't it?' she offered. Rebus gave her a cooling look. Humour him, the look ordered.

'Not crank, no. It's ancient, with the ring of truth. Can I get you something to drink?'

'No, thanks, Mr Gowrie.'

They were seated in Arch Gowrie's 'front room', a parlour kept for visitors and special occasions. The real living room, with comfortable sofa, TV and video, drinks cabinet, was elsewhere on this sprawling ground floor. The house was at least three storeys high, and probably boasted an attic conversion too. It was sited in The Grange, a leafy backwater of the city's southern side. The Grange got few visitors, few strangers, and never much traffic, since it was not a well-known route between any two other areas of the city. A lot of the huge detached houses, one-time merchants' houses with walled grounds and high wooden or metal gates, had been bought by the Church of Scotland or other religious denominations. There was a retirement home to one side of Gowrie's own residence, and what Rebus thought was a convent on the other side.

151

Archibald Gowrie liked to be called 'Arch'. Everyone knew him as Arch. He was the public face of the Orange Lodge, an eloquent enough apologist (not that he thought there was anything to apologise for), but by no means that organisation's most senior figure. However, he was high enough, and he was easy to find – unlike Millie and Murdock, who weren't home.

Gowrie had agreed readily to a meeting, saying he'd be free between seven and quarter to eight.

'Plenty of time, sir,' Rebus had said.

He studied Arch Gowrie now. The man was big and fiftyish and probably attractive to women in that way older men could be. (Though Rebus noticed Siobhan Clarke didn't seem too enthralled.) Though his hair – thinning nicely – was silver, his thick moustache was black. He wore his shirt with the sleeves rolled up, showing darkly haired arms. He was always ready for business. In fact, 'open for business' had been his public motto, and he worked tirelessly whenever he got his teeth into a new development.

From what Rebus knew, Gowrie had made his money initially as director of a company which had nippily shifted its expertise from ships and pipelines to building exploration platforms and oil rigs for the North Sea. That was back in the early '70s. The company had been sold at vast profit, and Gowrie had disappeared for several years before reappearing in the guise of property developer and invest-ment guru. He was still a property developer, his name on several projects around the city as well as further afield. But he had diversified into wildly different areas: film production, hi-fi design, edible algae, forestry, two country house hotels, a woollen mill, and the Eyrie restaurant in the New Town. Probably Arch was best known for his part-ownership of the Eyrie, the city's best restaurant, certainly its most exclusive, by far its most expensive. You wouldn't find nutritious Hebridean Blue Algae on its menu, not even written in French.

Rebus knew of only one large loss Gowrie had taken, as money man behind a film set predominantly in Scotland. Even boasting Rab Kinnoul as its star, the film had been an Easter turkey. Still, Gowrie wasn't shy: there was a framed poster for the film hanging in the entrance hall.

'*Annus mirabilis*,' Rebus mused. 'That's Latin, isn't it?'

Gowrie was horrified. 'Of course it's Latin! Don't tell me you never studied Latin at school? I though we Scots were an educated bunch. Miraculous year, that's what it means. Sure about that drink?'

'Maybe a small whisky, sir.' Kill or cure.

'Nothing for me, sir,' said Siobhan Clarke, her voice coming from the high moral ground.

'I won't be a minute,' said Gowrie. When he'd left the room, Rebus turned to her.

'Don't piss him off!' he hissed. 'Just keep your gob shut and your ears open.'

'Sorry, sir. Have you noticed?'

'What?'

'There's nothing green in this room, nothing at all.'

He nodded again. 'The inventor of red, white and blue grass will make a fortune.'

Gowrie came back into the room. He took a look at the two of them on the sofa, then smiled to himself and handed Rebus a crystal tumbler.

'I won't offend you by offering water or lemonade with that.'

Rebus sniffed the amber liquid. It was a West Highland malt, darker, more aromatic than the Speysides. Gowrie held his own glass up.

'*Slainte*.' He took a sip, then sat in a dark blue armchair. 'Well now,' he said, 'how exactly can I help you?'

'Well, sir –'

'It's nothing to do with us, you know. We've told the Chief Constable that. They're an offshoot of the Grand Lodge, less than that even, now that we've disbarred them.'

153

Rebus suddenly knew what Gowrie was talking about. There was to be a march along Princes Street on Saturday, organised by the Orange Loyal Brigade. He'd heard about it weeks ago, when the very idea had provoked attacks from republican sympathisers and anti-right wing associations. There were expected to be confrontations during the march.

'When did you disbar the group exactly, sir?'

'April 14th. That was the day we had the disciplinary hearing. They belonged to one of our district lodges, and at a dinner-dance they'd sent collecting tins round for the LPWA.' He turned to Siobhan Clarke. 'That's the Loyalist Prisoners' Welfare Association.' Then back to Rebus. 'We can't have that sort of thing, Inspector. We've denounced it in the past. We'll have no truck with the paramilitaries.'

'And the disbarred members set up the Orange Loyal Brigade?'

'Correct.'

Rebus was feeling his way. 'How many do you think will be on the march?'

'Ach, a couple of hundred at most, and that's including the bands. I think they've got bands coming from Glasgow and Liverpool.'

'You think there'll be trouble?'

'Don't you? Isn't that why you're here?'

'Who's the Brigade's leader?'

'Gavin MacMurray. But don't you know all this already? Your Chief Constable asked if I could intervene. But I told him, they're nothing to do with the Orange Lodge, nothing at all.'

'Do they have connections with the other right-wing groups?'

'You mean with fascists?' Gowrie shrugged. 'They deny it, of course, but I wouldn't be surprised to see a few skinheads on the march, even ones with Sassenach accents.'

Rebus left a pause before asking, 'Do you know if there's any link-up between the Orange Brigade and The Shield?'

Gowrie frowned. 'What shield?'

'Sword and Shield. It's another splinter group, isn't it?'

Gowrie shook his head. 'I've never heard of it.'

'No?'

'Never.'

Rebus placed his whisky glass on a table next to the sofa. 'I just assumed you'd know something about it.' He got to his feet, followed by Clarke. 'Sorry to have bothered you, sir.' Rebus held out his hand.

'Is that it?'

'That's all, sir, thanks for your help.'

'Well ...' Gowrie was clearly troubled. 'Shield ... no, means nothing to me.'

'Then don't worry about it, sir. Have a good evening now.'

At the front door, Clarke turned and smiled at Gowrie. 'We'll let you get back to your wee numbers. Goodbye, sir.'

They heard the door close behind them with a solid click as they walked back down the short gravel path to the driveway.

'I've only got one question, sir: what was all that about?'

'We're dealing with lunatics, Clarke, and Gowrie isn't a lunatic. A zealot maybe, but not a madman. Tell me, what do you call a haircut in an asylum?'

By now Clarke knew the way her boss's mind worked. 'A lunatic fringe?' she guessed.

'*That's* who I want to talk to.'

'You mean the Orange Loyal Brigade?'

Rebus nodded. 'And every one of them will be taking a stroll along Princes Street on Saturday.' He smiled without humour. 'I've always enjoyed a parade.'

16

Saturday was hot and clear, with a slight cooling breeze, just enough to make the day bearable. Shoppers were out on Princes Street in numbers, and the lawns of Princes Street Gardens were as packed as a seaside beach, every bench in full use, a carousel attracting the children. The atmosphere was festive if frayed, with the kids squealing and tiring as their ice-cream cones melted and dropped to the ground, turning instantly into food for the squirrels, pigeons, and panting dogs.

The parade was due to set off from Regent Road at three o'clock, and by two-fifteen the pubs behind Princes Street were emptying their cargo of brolly-toting white-gloved elders, bowler hats fixed onto their sweating heads, faces splotched from alcohol. There was a show of regalia, and a few large banners were being unfurled. Rebus couldn't remember what you called the guy at the front of the march, the one who threw up and caught the heavy ornamental staff. He'd probably known in his youth. The flute players were practising, and the snare drummers adjusted their straps and drank from cans of beer.

People outside the Post Office on Waterloo Place could hear the flutes and drums, and peered along towards Regent Road. That the march was to set off from outside the old Royal High School, mothballed site for a devolved Scottish parliament, added a certain something to the affair.

Rebus had been in a couple of the bars, taking a look at the Brigade members and supporters. They were a varied crew, taking in a few Doc Marten-wearing skinheads (just as Gowrie had predicted) as well as the bowler hats. There were also the dark suit/white shirt/dark tie types, their shoes as polished as their faces. Most of them were drinking like fury, though they didn't seem completely mortal yet. Empty cans were being kicked along Regent Road, or trodden on and left by the edges of the pavement. Rebus wasn't sure why these occasions always carried with them the air of threat, of barely suppressed violence, even before they started. Extra police had been drafted in, and were readying to stop traffic from coming down onto Princes Street. Metal-grilled barriers waited by the side of the road, as did the small groups of protesters, and the smaller group of protesters who were protesting against the protesters. Rebus wondered, not for the first time, which maniac on the Council had pushed through the okay for the parade.

The marching season of course had finished, the main parades being on and around the 12th of July, date of the Battle of the Boyne. Even then the biggest marches were in Glasgow. What was the point of this present parade? To stir things up, of course, to make a noise. To be noticed. The big drum, the *lambeg*, was being hammered now. There was competition from a few bagpipe buskers near Waverley Station, but they'd be silenced by the time the parade reached them.

Rebus wandered freely among the marchers as they drank and joked with each other and adjusted their uniforms. A Union Jack was unfurled, then ordered to be rolled up again, bearing as it did the initials of the British National Party. There didn't seem to be any collecting tins or buckets, the police having pressed for a quick march with as little interaction with the public as possible. Rebus knew this because he'd asked Farmer Watson, and the Farmer had confirmed that it would be so.

'Here's tae King Billy!' A can was raised. 'God bless the Queen and King William of Orange!'

157

'Well said, son.'

The bowler hats said little, standing with the tips of their umbrellas touching the ground, hands resting lightly on the curved wooden handles. It was easy to dismiss these unsmiling men too lightly. But God help you if you started an argument with one of them.

'Why dae yis hate Catholics?' a pedestrian yelled.

'We don't!' somebody yelled back, but she was already bustling away with her shopping bags. There were smiles, but she'd made her point. Rebus watched her go.

'Hey, Gavin, how long now?'

'Five minutes, just relax.'

Rebus looked towards the man who had just spoken, the man who was probably called Gavin MacMurray and therefore in charge. He seemed to have appeared from nowhere. Rebus had read the file on Gavin MacMurray: two arrests for breach of the peace and actual bodily harm, but a lot more information to his name than that. Rebus knew his age (38), that he was married and lived in Currie, and that he ran his own garage. He knew Inland Revenue had no complaints against him, that he drove a red Mercedes Benz (though he made his money from more prosaic Fords, Renaults and the like), and that his teenage son had been in trouble for fighting, with two arrests after pitched battles outside Rangers matches and one arrest after an incident on the train home from Glasgow.

So Rebus assumed the teenager standing close beside Gavin MacMurray must be the son, Jamesie. Jamesie had pretensions of all obvious kinds. He wore sunglasses and a tough look, seeing himself as his father's lieutenant. His legs were apart, shoulders back. Rebus had never seen anyone itching so badly for action of some kind. He had his father's low square jaw, the same black hair cut short at the front. But while Gavin MacMurray was dressed in chainstore anonymity, Jamesie wanted people to look at him. Biker boots, tight black jeans, white t-shirt and black leather jacket. He wore a red bandana around his right wrist, a studded leather strap around the left. His hair, long and curling at the back, had been shaved above both ears.

Turning from son to father was like turning from overt to covert strength. Rebus knew which he'd rather tackle. Gavin MacMurray was chewing gum with his front teeth, his head and eyes constantly in movement, checking things, keeping things in check. He kept his hands in his windcheater pockets, and wore silver-framed spectacles which magnified his eyes. There seemed little charisma about him, little of the rouser or orator. He looked chillingly ordinary.

Because he *was* ordinary, they all were, all these semi-inebriated working men and retired men, quiet family types who might belong to the British Legion or their local Ex-Servicemen's Club, who might inhabit the bowling green on summer evenings and go with their families on holiday to Spain or Florida or Largs. It was only when you saw them in groups like this that you caught a whiff of something else. Alone, they had nothing but a nagging complaint; together, they had a voice: the sound of the *lambeg*, dense as a heartbeat; the insistent flutes; the march. They always fascinated Rebus. He couldn't help it. It was in his blood. He'd marched in his youth. He'd done a lot of things back then.

There was a final gathering of lines, MacMurray readying his troops. A word with the policeman in charge, a conversation by two-way radio, then a nod from MacMurray. The opening fat-fry of snare drums, the *lambeg* pumping away, and then the flutes. They marched on the spot for a few moments, then moved off towards Princes Street, where traffic had been stopped for them, where the Castle glared down on them, where a lot of people but by no means everyone paused to watch.

A few months back, a pro-republican march had been banned from this route. That was why the protesters were particularly loud in their jeers, thumbs held down. Some of them were chanting Na-Zis, Na-Zis, and then being told to shut up by uniformed police. There would be a few arrests, there always were. You hadn't had a good day out at a march unless there'd been at least the threat of arrest.

Rebus followed the march from the pavement, sticking to the Gardens side, which was quieter. A few more marchers had joined in, but it was still small beer, hardly worth the bother. He was beginning to wonder what he'd thought would happen. His eyes moved back through the procession from the tosser at the front, busy with his muckle stick, through the flutes and drums, past bowler hats and suits, to the younger marchers and stragglers. A few pre-teenage kids had joined in on the edges, loving every minute. Jamesie, right near the back, told them in no uncertain terms that they should leave, but they didn't listen to him.

'Tough' always was a relative term.

But now one of the stragglers clutched Jamesie's arm and they shared a few words, both of them grinning. The straggler was wearing sunglasses with mirrored lenses, and a denim jacket with no shirt beneath.

'Hello,' said Rebus quietly. He watched Jamesie and Davey Soutar have their conversation, saw Jamesie pat Davey on the shoulder before Davey moved away again, falling back until he left the procession altogether, squeezing between two of the temporary barriers and vanishing into the crowd.

Jamesie seemed to relax a bit after this. His walk became looser, less of an act, and he swung his arms in time to the music. He seemed to be realising that it was a bright summer's day, and at last peeled off his leather jacket, slinging it over one shoulder, showing off his arm muscles and several tattoos. Rebus walked a bit faster, keeping close to the edge of the pavement. One of the tattoos was professional, and showed the ornately overlaid letters RFC: Rangers Football Club. But there was also the maroon emblem of Heart of Midlothian FC, so obviously Jamesie liked to play safe. Then there was a kilted, busby-wearing piper, and further down his arm towards the leather wrist-band a much more amateur job, the usual shaky greeny-blue ink.

The letters SaS.

Rebus blinked. It was almost too far away for him to be sure. Almost. But he *was* sure. And suddenly he didn't want to talk to Gavin MacMurray any more. He wanted a word with his son.

He stopped on the pavement, letting the march pull away from him. He knew where they were heading. A left turn into Lothian Road, passing the windows of the Caledonian Hotel. Something for the rich tourists to get a picture of. Then another left into King's Stables Road, stopping short of the Grassmarket. Afterwards, they'd probably head down into the Grassmarket itself for the post-march analysis and a few more beers. The Grassmarket being trendy these days, there'd be a lot of Fringe drinkers there too. A fine cocktail of cultures for a Saturday afternoon.

He followed the trail to one of the rougher pubs on the Cowgate, just the other side of Candlemaker Row from the Grassmarket. At one time, they'd hung miscreants from the gallows in the Grassmarket. It was a cheerier prospect these days, though you wouldn't necessarily know it from a visit to the Merchant's Bar where, at ten p.m. each night, the pint glasses were switched for flimsy plastic imposters, relieving the bar of ready weapons. It was that kind of place.

Inside, the bar was airless, a drinkers' fug of smoke and television heat. You didn't come here for a good time, you came out of necessity. The regulars were like dragons, each mouthful cooling the fire inside them. As he entered the bar, he saw no one he recognised, not even the barman. The barman was a new face, just out of his teens. He poured pints with an affected disdain, and took the money like it was a bribe. From the sounds of atonal song, Rebus knew the marchers were upstairs, probably emptying the place.

Rebus took his pint – still in a glass glass – and headed up to the dance hall. Sure enough, the marchers were about all there was. They'd shed jackets, ties, and inhibitions, and were milling around, singing to off-key flutes and downing pints and shorts. Getting the drink in had become a logistical nightmare, and more marchers were coming in all the time.

Rebus took a deep breath, carved a smile into his face, and waded in.

'Magic, lads.'

'Aye, ta, pal.'

'Nae bother, eh?'

'Aye, nae bother right enough.'

'All right there, lads?'

'Fine, aye. Magic.'

Gavin MacMurray hadn't arrived yet. Maybe he was off elsewhere with his generals. But his son was on the stage pretending he held a microphone stand and a crowd's attention. Another lad clambered onto the stage and played an invisible guitar, still managing to hold his pint glass. Lager splashed over his jeans, but he didn't notice. That was professionalism for you.

Rebus watched with the smile still on his face. Eventually they gave up, as he'd known they would, there being no audience, and leapt down from the stage. Jamesie landed just in front of Rebus. Rebus held his arms wide.

'Whoah there! That was brilliant.'

Jamesie grinned. 'Aye, ta.' Rebus slapped him on the shoulder.

'Get you another?'

'I think I'm all right, ta.'

'Fair enough.' Rebus looked around, then leant close to Jamesie's ear. 'I see you're one of us.' He winked.

'Eh?'

The tattoo had been covered by the leather jacket, but Rebus nodded towards it. 'The Shield,' he said slyly. Then he nodded again, catching Jamesie's eye, and moved away. He went back downstairs and ordered two pints. The bar was busy and noisy, both TV and jukebox blaring, a couple of arguments rising above even these. Half a minute later, Jamesie was standing beside him. The boy wasn't very bright, and Rebus weighed up how much he could get away with.

'How do you know?' Jamesie asked.

'There's not much I don't know, son.'

'But I don't know you.'

Rebus smiled into his drink. 'Best keep it that way.'

'Then how come you know me?'

Rebus turned towards him. 'I just do.' Jamesie looked around him, licking his lips. Rebus handed him one of the pints. 'Here, get this down you.'

'Ta.' He lowered his voice. 'You're in The Shield?'

'What makes you think that?' Now Jamesie smiled. 'How's Davey, by the way?'

'Davey?'

'Davey Soutar,' said Rebus. 'You two know each other, don't you?'

'I know Davey.' He blinked. 'Christ, you *are* in The Shield. Hang on, did I see you at the parade?'

'I bloody hope so.'

Now Jamesie nodded slowly. 'I thought I saw you.'

'You're a sharp lad, Jamesie. There's a bit of your dad in you.'

Jamesie started at this. 'He'll be here in five minutes. You don't want him to see us . . .'

'You're right. He doesn't know about The Shield then?'

'Of course not.' Jamesie looked slighted.

'Only sometimes the lads tell their dads.'

'Not me.'

Rebus nodded. 'You're a good one, Jamesie. We've got our eyes on you.'

'Really?'

'Absolutely.' Rebus supped from his pint. 'Shame about Billy.'

Jamesie became a statue, the glass inches from his lips. He recovered with effort. 'Pardon?'

'Good lad, say nothing.' Rebus took another sup. 'Good parade, wasn't it?'

'Oh aye, the best.'

'Ever been to Belfast?'

Jamesie looked like he was having trouble keeping up with the conversation. Rebus hoped he was. 'Naw,' he said at last.

'I was there a few days ago, Jamesie. It's a proud city, a lot of good people there, *our* people.' Rebus was wondering, how long can I keep this up? A couple of teenagers, probably a year or two beneath the legal drinking age, had already come to the stairs looking for Jamesie to join them.

'True,' Jamesie said.

'We can't let them down.'

'Absolutely not.'

'Remember Billy Cunningham.'

Jamesie put down his glass. 'Is this ...' his voice had become a little less confident, 'is this a ... some sort of warning?'

Rebus patted the young man's arm. 'No, no, you're all right, Jamesie. It's just that the polis are sniffing around.' It was amazing where a bit of confident bull's keech could get you.

'I'm no squealer,' said Jamesie.

The way he said it, Rebus knew. 'Not like Billy?'

'Definitely not.'

Rebus was nodding to himself when the doors burst open and Gavin MacMurray swaggered in, a couple of his generals squeezing through the doorway in his wake. Rebus

became just another punter at the bar, as MacMurray slung
a heavy arm around his son's neck.

'Awright, Jamesie boy?'

'Fine, Dad. My shout.'

'Three export then. Bring them up back, aye?'

'No bother, Dad.'

Jamesie watched the three men walk to the stairs. He
turned towards his confidant, but John Rebus had already
left the bar.

17

Every chain, no matter how strong, has one link weaker than the rest. Rebus had hopes of Jamesie MacMurray, as he walked out of the Merchant's. He was halfway to his car when he saw Caro Rattray walking towards him.

'You were going to call me,' she said.

'Work's been a bit hectic.'

She looked back at the pub. 'Call that work, do you?'

He smiled. 'Do you live here?'

'On the Canongate. I've just been walking my dog.'

'Your dog?' There was no sign of a leash, never mind the animal. She shrugged.

'I don't actually like dogs, I just like the idea of walking them. So I have an imaginary dog.'

'What's he called?'

'Sandy.'

Rebus looked down at her feet. 'Good boy, Sandy.'

'Actually, Sandy's a girl.'

'Hard to tell at this distance.'

'And I don't talk to her.' She smiled. 'I'm not mad, you know.'

'Right, you just go walking with a pretend dog. So what are you and Sandy doing now?'

'Going home and having a drink. Fancy joining us?'

Rebus thought about it. 'Sure,' he said. 'Drive or walk?'

'Let's walk,' said Caroline Rattray. 'I don't want Sandy shedding on your seats.'

*

She lived in a nicely furnished flat, tidy but not obsessive. There was a grandfather clock in the hall, a family heirloom. Her surname was engraved on the brass face.

A dividing wall had been taken away so that the living room had windows to front and back. A book lay open on the sofa, next to a half-finished box of shortbread. Solitary pleasures, thought Rebus.

'You're not married?' he said.

'God, no.'

'Boyfriend?'

She smiled again. 'Funny word that, isn't it? Especially when you get to my age. I mean, a boyfriend should be in his teens or twenties.'

'Gentleman friend then,' he persisted.

'Doesn't have the same connotations though, does it?' Rebus sighed. 'I know, I know,' she said, 'never argue with an advocate.'

Rebus looked out of the back window onto a drying-green. Overhead, the few clouds were basking in the space they had. 'Sandy's digging up your flower bed.'

'What do you want to drink?'

'Tea, please.'

'Sure? I've only got decaf.'

'That's perfect.' He meant it. While she made noises in the kitchen, he walked through the living room. Dining-table and chairs and wall units at the back, sofa, chairs, bookcases towards the front. It was a nice room. From the small front window, he looked down onto slow-walking tourists and a shop selling tartan teddy-bears.

'This is a nice part of town,' he said, not really meaning it.

'Are you kidding? Ever tried parking round here in the summer?'

'I never try parking anywhere in the summer.'

He moved away from the window. A flute and some sheet music sat on a spindly music-stand in one corner. On

167

a unit were small framed photos of the usual gap-toothed kids and kind-looking old people.

'Family,' she said, coming back into the room. She lit a cigarette, took two deep puffs on it, then stubbed it into an ashtray, exhaling and wafting the smoke away with her hand. 'I hate smoking indoors,' she explained.

'Then why do it?'

'I smoke when I'm nervous.' She smiled slyly and returned to the kitchen, Rebus following. The aroma of the cigarette mingled with the richer aroma of the perfume she wore. Had she just applied some? It hadn't been this strong before.

The kitchen was small, functional. The whole flat had the look of recent but not radical redecoration.

'Milk?'

'Please. No sugar.' Their conversation, he realised, was assuming a studied banality.

The kettle clicked off. 'Can you take the mugs?'

She had already poured a splash of milk into either plain yellow mug. There wasn't much room at all in the kitchen, something Rebus realised as he went to pick up the mugs. He was right beside her as she stirred the teabags in the pot. Her head was bent down, affording a view of the long black hairs curling from her nape, and the nape of her neck itself. She half turned her face towards him, smiling, her eyes finally finding his. Then she moved her body around too. Rebus kissed her forehead first, then her cheek. She had closed her eyes. He burrowed his face in her neck, inhaling deeply: shampoo and perfume and skin. He kissed her again, then came up for air. Caroline opened her eyes slowly.

'Well now,' she said.

He felt suddenly as though he'd been flung down a tunnel, watching the circle of light at the entrance shrink to a full stop. He tried desperately to think of something to say. There was perfume in his lungs.

'Well now,' she repeated. What did that mean? Was she pleased, shocked, bemused? She turned back to the teapot and put its lid on.

'I better go,' Rebus said. She became very still. He couldn't see her face, not enough of it. 'Hadn't I?'

'I've no commitments, John.' Her hands were resting lightly on the work surface, either side of the pot. 'What about you?'

He knew what she meant; she meant Patience. 'There's someone,' he said.

'I know, Dr Curt told me.'

'I'm sorry, Caroline, I shouldn't have done that.'

'What?' She turned to him.

'Kissed you.'

'I didn't mind.' She gave him her smile again. 'I'll never drink a whole pot of tea on my own.'

He nodded, realising he was still holding the mugs. 'I'll take them through.'

He walked out of the kitchen on unsteady legs, his heart shimmying. He'd kissed her. Why had he kissed her? He hadn't meant to. But it had happened. It was real now. The photographs smiled at him as he put the mugs down on a small table which already had coffee-rings on it. What was she doing in the kitchen? He stared at the doorway, willing her to come, willing her not to come.

She came. The teapot was on a tray now, a tea-cosy in the shape of a King Charles spaniel keeping in the heat.

'Is Sandy a King Charles?'

'Some days. How strong do you like it?'

'As it comes.'

She smiled again and poured, handed him a mug, then took one herself and sat in her chair. She didn't look very comfortable. Rebus sat opposite her on the sofa, not resting against the back of it but leaning forward.

'There's some shortbread,' she said.

'No, thanks.'

169

'So,' she said, 'any progress on Nemo?'

'I think so.' This was good; they were talking. 'SaS is a loyalist support group. They're buying and shipping arms.'

'And the victim in Mary King's Close, he was killed by paramilitaries, nothing to do with his father?'

Rebus shrugged again. 'There's been another murder. It could be linked.'

'That man they found in the cellar?' Rebus nodded. 'Nobody told me they were connected.'

'It's being kept a bit quiet. He was working undercover.'

'How was he found?'

'The flat was having some building work done. One of the labourers opened the cellar door.'

'That's a coincidence.'

'What?'

'There was building work going on in Mary King's Close too.'

'Not the same firm.'

'You've checked?'

Rebus frowned. 'Not me personally, but yes, we've checked.'

'Oh well.' She took another cigarette from her packet and made to light it, but stopped herself. She took the cigarette from her mouth and examined it. 'John,' she said, 'if you'd like to, we can make love any time you want.'

There were none of Cafferty's men waiting for him outside Patience's flat, nothing to delay him. He'd been hoping for the Weasel. Right now, he felt ready for some hands-on with the Weasel.

But it wasn't Cafferty's man he was angry with.

Inside, the long hallway was cool and dark, the only light coming from three small panes of glass above the front door. 'Patience?' he called, hoping she'd be out. Her car was outside, but that didn't mean anything. He wanted to run a bath, steep in it. He turned on both taps, then

went to the bedroom, picked up the phone, and rang Brian
Holmes at home. Holmes's partner Nell picked up the call.

'It's John Rebus,' he told her. She said nothing, just put
the receiver to one side and went off to fetch Brian.
There was no love lost these days between Rebus and Nell
Stapleton, something Holmes himself realised but couldn't
bring himself to query ...

'Yes, sir?'

'Brian, those two building companies.'

'Mary King's Close and St Stephen Street?'

'How thoroughly have we checked them?'

'Pretty well.'

'And we've cross-referenced? There's no connection
between them.'

'No, why?'

'Can you check them again yourself?'

'I can.'

'Humour me then. Do it Monday.'

'Anything in particular I should be looking for?'

'No.' He paused. 'Yes, start with casual labour.'

''I thought you wanted Siobhan and me to go see
Murdock?'

'I did. I'll take your place. Have a nice evening.' Rebus
put down the phone and went back to the bathroom. There
was good pressure in the pipes, and the bath was practically
full already. He turned off the cold and reduced the hot to
a trickle. The kitchen was through the living room, and he
fancied some milk from the fridge.

Patience was in the kitchen, chopping vegetables.

'I didn't know you were here,' Rebus said.

'I live here, remember? This is my flat.'

'Yes, I know.' She was angry with him. He opened the
fridge door, took out the milk, and managed to pass her
without touching her. He put the milk on the breakfast
table and got a glass from the draining board. 'What are
you cooking?'

'Why the interest? You never eat here.'

'Patience...'

She came to the sink, scraping peelings into a plastic container. It would all go onto her compost heap. She turned to him. 'Running a bath?'

'Yes.'

'It's Giorgio, isn't it?'

'Sorry?'

'That perfume.' She leaned close, sniffed his shirt. 'Giorgio of Beverly Hills.'

'Patience...'

'You'll have to tell me about her one of these days.'

'You think I'm seeing someone?'

She threw the small sharp kitchen knife at the sink and ran from the room. Rebus stood there, listening until he heard the front door slam. He poured the milk down the sink.

He took back the videos – still unwatched – then went for a drive. The Dell Bar sat on an unlovely stretch of main road outside the Gar-B. It didn't get much passing trade, but there was a line of cars parked outside. Rebus slowed as he drove past. He could go in, but what good would it do? Then he saw something, and pulled his car up kerbside. Next to him a van was parked, with fly-posters pasted on its sides. The posters advertised the play which was soon to go on in the Gar-B gang hut. The theatre group was called Active Resistance. Some of them must be drinking inside. A few vehicles further on was the car he wanted. He bent down at the driver's side window. Ken Smylie tried to ignore him, then wound the window down angrily.

'What are you doing here?' he asked.

'I was about to ask the same,' said Rebus.

Smylie nodded towards the Dell. He had his hands on the steering-wheel. They weren't just resting on it, they were squeezing it. 'Maybe there's someone drinking in there killed Calumn.'

'Maybe there is,' Rebus said quietly: he didn't fancy being Smylie's punchbag. 'What are you going to do about it?'

Smylie stared at him. 'I'm going to sit here.'

'And then what? Break the neck of every man who comes out? You know the score, Ken.'

'Leave me alone.'

'Look, Ken –' Rebus broke off as the Dell's door swung open and two punters sauntered out, cigarettes in mouths, sharing some joke between them. 'Look,' he said, 'I know how you feel. I've got a brother too. But this isn't doing any good.'

'Just go away.'

Rebus sighed, straightened up. 'Fair enough then. But if there's any hassle, radio for assistance. Just do that for me, okay?'

Smylie almost smiled. 'There won't be any trouble, believe me.'

Rebus did, the way he believed TV advertising and weather reports. He walked back towards his car. The two drinkers were getting into their Vauxhall. As the passenger yanked open his door, it nearly caught Rebus.

The man didn't bother to apologise. He gave Rebus a look like it was Rebus's fault, then got into his seat.

Rebus had seen the man before. He was about five-ten, broad in the chest, wearing jeans and black t-shirt and a denim jacket. He had a face shiny with drink, sweat on his forehead and in his wavy brown hair. But it wasn't until Rebus was back in his own car and halfway home that he put a name to the face.

The man Yates had told him about, shown him a photo of, the ex-UVF man they'd lost in Glasgow. Alan Fowler. Drinking in the Gar-B like he owned the place.

Maybe he did at that.

Rebus retraced his route, cruising some of the narrow streets, checking parked cars. But he'd lost the Vauxhall. And Ken Smylie's car was no longer outside the Dell.

18

Monday morning at St Leonard's, Chief Inspector Lauderdale was having to explain a joke he'd just made.

'See, the squid's so meek, Hans can't bring himself to thump it either.' He caught sight of Rebus walking into the Murder Room. 'The prodigal returns! Tell us, what's it like working with the glamour boys?'

'It's all right,' said Rebus. 'I've already had one return flight out of them.'

Lauderdale clearly had not been expecting this...

'So it's true then,' he said, recovering well, 'they're all high flyers over at SCS.' He captured a few laughs for his trouble. Rebus didn't mind being the butt. He knew the way it was. In a murder inquiry, you worked as a team. Lauderdale, as team manager, had the job of boosting morale, keeping things lively. Rebus wasn't part of the team, not exactly, so he was open to the occasional low tackle with studs showing.

He went to his desk, which more than ever resembled a rubbish tip, and tried to see if any messages had been left for him. He had spent the rest of his weekend, when not avoiding Patience, trying to track down Abernethy or anyone else in Special Branch who'd talk to him. Rebus had left message after message, so far without success.

DI Flower, teeth showing, advanced on Rebus's desk.

'We've got a confession,' he said, 'to the stabbing in St Stephen Street. Want to talk to the man?'

Rebus was wary. 'Who is it?'

'Unstable from Dunstable. He's off his trolley this time, keeps asking for a curry and talking about cars. I told him he'd have to settle for a bridie and his bus fare.'

'You're all heart, Flower.' Rebus saw that Siobhan Clarke had finished getting ready. 'Excuse me.'

'Ready, sir?' Clarke asked.

'Plenty ready. Let's go before Lauderdale or Flower can think of another gag at my expense. Not that *their* jokes ever cost me more than small change.'

They took Clarke's cherry-red Renault 5, following bus after bus west through the slow streets until they could take a faster route by way of The Grange, passing the turn-off to Arch Gowrie's residence.

'And you said The Grange didn't lead anywhere,' Clarke said, powering through the gears. True enough, it was the quickest route between St Leonard's and Morningside. It was just that as a policeman, Rebus had never had much cause to heed Morningside, that genteel backwater where old ladies in white face powder, like something out of a Restoration play, sat in tea shops and pondered aloud their next choice from the cake-stand.

Morningside wasn't exclusive the way Grange was. There were students in Morningside, living at the top of roadside tenements, and people on the dole, in rented flats housing too many bodies, keeping the rent down. But when you thought of Morningside you thought of old ladies and that peculiar pronunciation they had, like they'd all under-studied Maggie Smith in *The Prime of Miss Jean Brodie*. The Glaswegians joked about it. They said Morningside people thought sex was what the coal came in. Rebus doubted there were coal fires in Morningside any longer, though there would certainly be some wood-burning stoves, brought in by the young professionals who probably out-numbered the old ladies these days, though they weren't nearly so conspicuous.

It was to serve these young professionals, as well as to

175

cater for local businesses, that a thriving little computer shop had opened near the corner of Comiston Road and Morningside Drive.

'Can I help you?' the male assistant asked, not looking up from his keyboard.

'Is Millie around?' Rebus asked.

'Through the arch.'

'Thanks.'

There was a single step up to the arch, through which was another part of the shop, specialising in contract work and business packages. Rebus almost didn't recognise Millie, though there was no one else there. She was seated at a terminal, thinking about something, tapping her finger against her lips. It took her a second to place Rebus. She hit a key, the screen went blank, and she rose from her seat.

She was dressed in an immaculate combination of brilliant white skirt and bright yellow blouse, with a single string of crystals around her neck.

'I just can't shake you lot off, can I?'

She did not sound unhappy. Indeed, she seemed almost *too* pleased to see them, her smile immense. 'Can I fix you some coffee?'

'Not for me, thanks.'

Millie looked to Siobhan Clarke, who shook her head. 'Mind if I make some for myself?' She went to the arch. 'Steve? Cuppa?'

'Wouldn't say no.'

She came back. 'No, but he might say please, just once.' There was a cubby-hole at the back of the shop, leading to a toilet cubicle. In the cubbyhole sat a percolator, a packet of ground coffee, and several grim-looking mugs. Millie got to work. While she was occupied, Rebus asked his first question.

'Billy's mum tells us you were good enough to pack up all his stuff.'

'It's still sitting in his room, three bin liners. Not a lot to show for a life, is it?'

'What about his motorbike?'

She smiled. 'That thing. You could hardly call it a bike. A friend of his asked if he could have it. Billy's mum said she didn't mind.'

'You liked Billy?'

'I liked him a lot. He was genuine. You never got bullshit with Billy. If he didn't like you, he'd tell you to your face. I hear his dad's some kind of villain.'

'They didn't know one another.'

She slapped the coffee-maker. 'This thing takes ages. Is that what you want to ask me about, Billy's dad?'

'Just a few general questions. Before he died, did Billy seem worried about anything?'

'I've been asked already, more than once.' She looked at Clarke. 'You first, and then that big bastard with the voice like something caught in a mousetrap.' Rebus smiled: it was a fair description of Ken Smylie. 'Billy was just the same as ever, that's all I can say.'

'Did he get along okay with Mr Murdock?'

'What sort of question is that? Christ, you're scraping the barrel if you think Murdock would've done anything to Billy.'

'You know what it's like in mixed flats though, where there's a couple plus one, jealousy can be a problem.'

An electric buzzer announced the arrival of a customer. They could hear Steve talking to someone.

'We've got to ask, Millie,' Clarke said soothingly.

'No you don't. It's just that you *like* asking!'

So much for the good mood. Even Steve and the customer seemed to be listening. The coffee machine started dolloping boiled water into the filter.

'Look,' said Rebus, 'let's calm down, eh? If you like, we can come back. We could come to the flat –'

'It never ends, does it? What is this? Trying to get a

confession out of me?' She clasped her hands together. 'Yes, I killed him. It was me.'

She held her hands out, wrists prominent.

'I've forgotten my cuffs,' Rebus said, smiling. Millie looked to Siobhan Clarke, who shrugged.

'Great, I can't even get myself arrested.' She sloshed coffee into a mug. 'And I thought it was the easiest thing in the world.'

'Are we really so bad, Millie?'

She smiled, looked down at her mug. 'I suppose not, sorry about that.'

'You're under a lot of strain,' said Siobhan Clarke, 'we appreciate that. Maybe if we sit down, eh?'

So they sat at Millie's desk, like customers and assistant. Clarke, who liked computers, had actually picked up a couple of brochures.

'That's got a twenty-five megahertz microprocessor,' Millie said, pointing to one of the brochures.

'What size memory?'

'Four meg RAM, I think, but you can select a hard disk up to one-sixty.'

'Does this one have a 486 chip?'

Good girl, thought Rebus. Clarke was calming Millie down, taking her mind off both Billy Cunningham and her recent outburst. Steve brought the customer through to show him a certain screen. He gave the three of them a look full of curiosity.

'Sorry, Steve,' said Millie, 'forgot your coffee.' Her smile would not have passed a polygraph.

Rebus waited till Steve and the customer had retreated. 'Did Billy ever bring friends back to the flat?'

'I've given you a list.'

Rebus nodded. 'Nobody else you've thought of since?'

'No.'

'Can I try you with a couple of names? Davey Soutar and Jamesie MacMurray.'

178

'Last names don't mean much in our flat. Davey and Jamesie ... I don't think so.'

Rebus willed her to look at him. She did so, then looked away again quickly. You're lying, he thought.

They left the shop ten minutes later. Clarke looked up and down the pavement. 'Want to go see Murdock now?'

'I don't think so. What do you suppose it was she didn't want us to see?'

'Sorry?'

'You look up, see the police coming towards you, why do you blank your computer screen pronto and then come flying off your seat all bounce and flounce?'

'You think there was something on the computer she didn't want us to see?'

'I thought I just said that,' said Rebus. He got into the Renault's passenger seat and waited for Clarke. 'Jamesie MacMurray knows about The Shield. They killed Billy.'

'So why aren't we pulling him in?'

'We've nothing on him, nothing that would stick. That's not the way to work it.'

She looked at him. 'Too mundane?'

He shook his head. 'Like a golf course, too full of holes. We need to get him scared.'

She thought about this. 'Why did they kill Billy?'

'I think he was about to talk, maybe he'd threatened to come to us.'

'Could he be that stupid?'

'Maybe he had insurance, something he thought would save his skin.'

Siobhan Clarke looked at him. 'It didn't work,' she said.

Back at St Leonard's, there was a message for him to call Kilpatrick.

'Some magazine,' Kilpatrick said, 'is about to run with a story about Calumn Smylie's murder, specifically that he was working undercover at the time.'

'How did they get hold of that?'

'Maybe someone talked, maybe they just burrowed deep enough. Whatever, a certain local reporter has made no friends for herself.'

'Not Mairie Henderson?'

'That's the name. You know her, don't you?'

'Not particularly,' Rebus lied. He knew Kilpatrick was fishing. If someone in the notoriously tight-lipped SCS was blabbing, who better to point the finger at than the new boy?

He phoned the news desk while Siobhan fetched them coffee. 'Mairie Henderson, please. What? Since when? Right, thanks.' He put the phone down. 'She's resigned,' he said, not quite believing it. 'Since last week. She's gone freelance apparently.'

'Good for her,' said Siobhan, handing over a cup. But Rebus wasn't so sure. He called Mairie's home number, but got her answering machine. Its message was succinct:

'I'm busy with an assignment, so I can't promise a quick reply unless you're offering work. If you *are* offering work, leave your number. You can see how dedicated I am. Here comes the beep.'

Rebus waited for it. 'Mairie, it's John Rebus. Here are three numbers you can get me on.' He gave her St Leonard's, Fettes, and Patience's flat, not feeling entirely confident about this last, wondering if any message from a woman would reach him with Patience on the intercept.

Then he made an internal call to the station's liaison officer.

'Have you seen Mairie Henderson around?'

'Not for a wee while. The paper seems to have switched her for someone else, a right dozy wee nyaff.'

'Thanks.'

Rebus thought about the last time he'd seen her, in the corridor after Lauderdale's conference. She hadn't mentioned any story, or any plan of going freelance. He made one more call, external this time. It was to DCI Kilpatrick.

'What is it, John?'

'That magazine, sir, the one doing the story about Calumn Smylie, what's it called?'

'It's some London rag ...' There were sounds of papers being shuffled. 'Yes, here it is. *Snoop*.'

'*Snoop?*' Rebus looked to Siobhan Clarke, who nodded, signalling she'd heard of it. 'Right, thank you, sir.' He put the receiver down before Kilpatrick could ask any questions.

'Want me to phone them and ask?'

Rebus nodded. He saw Brian Holmes come into the room. 'Just the man,' he said. Holmes saw them and wiped imaginary sweat from his brow.

'So,' said Rebus, 'what did you get from the builders?'

'Everything but an estimate for repointing my house.' He took out his notebook. 'Where do you want me to start?'

19

Davey Soutar had agreed to meet Rebus in the community hall.

On his way to the Gar-B, Rebus tried not to think about Soutar. He thought instead about building firms. All Brian Holmes had been able to tell him was that the two firms were no cowboys, and weren't admitting to use of casual, untaxed labour. Siobhan Clarke's call to the office of *Snoop* magazine had been more productive. Mairie Henderson's piece, which they intended publishing in their next issue, had not been commissioned specially. It was part of a larger story she was working on for an American magazine. Why, Rebus wondered, would an American magazine be interested in the death of an Edinburgh copper? He thought he had a pretty good idea.

He drove into the Gar-B car park, bumped his car up onto the grass, and headed slowly past the garages towards the community hall. The theatre group hadn't bothered with the car park either. Maybe someone had had a go at their van. It was now parked close by the hall's front doors. Rebus parked next to it.

'It's the filth,' someone said. There were half a dozen teenagers on the roof of the building, staring down at him. And more of them sitting and standing around the doors. Davey Soutar had not come alone.

They let Rebus past. It was like walking through hate. Inside the hall, there was an argument going on.

'I never touched it!'

'It was there a minute ago.'

'You calling me a liar, pal?'

Three men, who'd been constructing a set on the stage, had stopped to watch. Davey Soutar was talking with another man. They were standing close, faces inches apart. Clenched fists and puffed-out chests.

'Is there a problem?' Rebus said.

Peter Cave, who'd been sitting with head in hands, now stood up.

'No problem,' he said lightly.

The third man thought there was. 'The wee bastard,' he said, meaning Davey Soutar, 'just lifted a packet of fags.'

Soutar looked ready to hit something. It was interesting that he didn't hit his accuser. Rebus didn't know what he'd been expecting from the theatre company. He certainly hadn't been expecting this. The accuser was tall and wiry with long greasy hair and several days' growth of beard. He didn't look in the least scared of Soutar, whose reputation must surely have preceded him. Nor did the workers on the stage look unwilling to enter any fray. He reached into his pocket and brought out a fresh pack of twenty, which he handed to Davey Soutar.

'Here,' he said, 'take these, and give the gentleman back his ciggies.'

Soutar turned on him like a zoo leopard, not happy with its cage. 'I don't need your ...' The roar faded. He looked at the faces around him. Then he laughed, a hysterical giggling laugh. He slapped his bare chest and shook his head, then took the cigarettes from Rebus and tossed another pack onto the stage.

Rebus turned to the accuser. 'What's your name?'

'Jim Hay.' The accent was west coast.

'Well, Jim, why don't you take those cigarettes outside, have a ten-minute break?'

Jim Hay looked ready to protest, but then thought better of it. He gestured to his crew and they followed him outside.

Rebus could hear them getting into the van. He turned his attention to Davey Soutar and Peter Cave.

'I'm surprised you came,' said Soutar, lighting up.

'I'm full of surprises, me.'

'Only, last time I saw you here, you were heading for the hills. You owe Peter an apology, by the way.' Soutar had changed completely. He looked like he was enjoying himself, like he hadn't lost his temper in weeks.

'I don't think that's strictly necessary,' Peter Cave said into the silence.

'Apology accepted,' said Rebus. He dragged over a chair and sat down. Soutar decided this was a good idea. He found a chair for himself and sat with a hard man's slump, legs wide apart, hands stuffed into the tight pockets of his denims, cigarette hanging from his lips. Rebus wanted a cigarette, but he wasn't going to ask for one.

'So what's the problem, Inspector?'

Soutar had agreed to a meeting here, but hadn't mentioned Peter Cave would be present. Maybe it was coincidence. Whatever, Rebus didn't mind an audience. Cave looked tired, pale. There was no question who was in charge, who had power over whom.

'I just have a few things to ask, there's no question of charges or anything criminal, all right?' Soutar obliged with a grunt, examining the laces of his basketball boots. He was shirtless again, still wearing the worn denim jacket. It was filthy, and had been decorated with pen drawings and dark-inked words, names mostly. Grease and dirt were erasing most of the messages and symbols, a few of which had already been covered with fresh hieroglyphs in thicker, darker ink. Soutar slid a hand from his pocket and ran it down his chest, rubbing the few fair curling hairs over his breast bone. He was giving Rebus a friendly look, his lips slightly parted. Rebus wanted to smash him in the face.

'I can walk any time I want?' he said to Rebus.

'Any time.'

The chair grated against the floor as Soutar pushed it back and stood up. Then he laughed and sat down again, wriggling to get comfortable, making sure his crotch was visible. 'Ask me a question then,' he said.

'You know the Orange Loyal Brigade?'

'Sure. That was easy, try another.'

But Rebus had turned to Cave. 'Have you heard of it, too?'

'I can't say I –'

'Hey! It's me the questions are for!'

'In a second, Mr Soutar.' Davey Soutar liked that: *Mr* Soutar. Only the dole office and the census taker had ever called him Mr. 'The Orange Loyal Brigade, Mr Cave, is an extreme hardline Protestant group, a small force but an organised one, based in east central Scotland.'

Soutar confirmed this with a nod.

'The Brigade were kicked out of the Orange Lodge for being too extreme. This may give you some measure of them. Do you know what they're committed to, Mr Cave? Maybe Mr Soutar can answer.'

Mr again! Soutar chuckled. 'Hating the Papes,' he said.

'Mr Soutar's right.' Rebus's eyes hadn't moved from Cave's since he'd first turned to him. 'They hate Catholics.'

'Papes,' said Soutar. 'Left-footers, Tigs, bogmen, Paddies.'

'And a few more names beside,' added Rebus. He left a measured pause. 'You're a Roman Catholic, aren't you?' As if he'd forgotten. Cave merely nodded, while Soutar slid his eyes sideways to look at him. Suddenly Rebus turned to Soutar. 'Who's head of the Brigade, Davey?'

'Er ... Ian Paisley!' He laughed, and got a smile from Rebus.

'No, but really.'

'I haven't a clue.'

'No? You don't know Gavin MacMurray?'

'MacMurray? Is he the one with the garage in Currie?'

'That's him. He's the Supreme Commander of the Orange Loyal Brigade.'

'I'll take your word for it.'

'And his son's the Provost-Marshall. Lad called Jamesie, be a year or two younger than you.'

'Oh aye?'

Rebus shook his head. 'Short term memory loss, that's what a bad diet does.'

'Eh?'

'All the chips and crisps, the booze you put away, not exactly brain food, is it? I know what it's like on estates like the Gar-B, you eat rubbish and you inject yourselves with anything you can get your paws on. Your body'll wither and die, probably before your brain does.'

The conversation had clearly taken an unexpected turn. 'What are you talking about?' Soutar yelled. 'I don't do drugs! I'm as fit as fuck, pal!'

Rebus looked at Soutar's exposed chest. 'Whatever you say, Davey.'

Soutar sprang to his feet, the chair tumbling behind him. He threw off his jacket and stood there, chest inflated, pulling both arms up and in to show the swell of muscle.

'You could punch me in the guts and I wouldn't flinch.'

Rebus could believe it, too. The stomach was flat except for ripples of musculature, looking so solid they might have been sculpted from marble. Soutar relaxed his arms, held them in front of him.

'Look, no tracks. Drugs are for mugs.'

Rebus held up a pacifying hand. 'You've proved your point, Davey.'

Soutar stared at him for a moment longer, then laughed and picked his jacket up off the floor.

'Interesting tattoos, by the way.'

They were the usual homemade jobs in blue ink, with one larger professional one on the right upper arm. It showed the Red Hand of Ulster, with the words No Surrender beneath. Below it the self-inflicted tattoos were just letters and messages: UVF, UDA, FTP, and SaS.

Rebus waited till Soutar had put on his jacket. 'You know Jamesie MacMurray,' he stated.

'Do I?'

'You bumped into him last Saturday when the Brigade was marching on Princes Street. You were there for the march, but you had to leave. However, you said hello to your old friend first. You knew Mr Cave was a Catholic right from the start, didn't you? I mean, he didn't hide the fact?'

Soutar was looking confused. The questions were all over the place, it was hard to keep up.

'Pete was straight with us,' he admitted. He was staying on his feet.

'And that didn't bother you? I mean, you came to his club, bringing your gang with you. And the Catholic gang came along too. What did Jamesie say about that?'

'It's nothing to do with him.'

'You could see it was a good thing though, eh? Meeting the Catholic gang, divvying up the ground between you. It's the way it works in Ulster, that's what you've heard. Who told you? Jamesie? His dad?'

'His *dad*?'

'Or was it The Shield?'

'I never even –' Davey Soutar stopped. He was breathing hard as he pointed at Rebus. 'You're in shite up past the point of breathing.'

'Then I must be standing on your shoulders. Come on, Davey.'

'It's *Mr* Soutar.'

'Mr Soutar then.' Rebus had his hands open, palms up. He was sitting back in his chair, rocking it on its back legs. 'Come on, sit down. It's no big deal. Everybody knows about The Shield, knows you're part of it. Everybody except Mr Cave here.' He turned to Peter Cave. 'Let's just say that

The Shield is even more extreme than the Orange Loyal Brigade. The Shield collects money, mostly by violence and extortion, and it sends arms to Northern Ireland.' Soutar was shaking his head.

'You're nothing, you've *got* nothing.'

'But you've got something, Davey. You've got your hate and your anger.' He turned to Cave again. 'See, Mr Cave? You've got to be asking, how come Davey puts up with a committed worker for the Church of Rome, or the Whore of Rome as Davey himself might put it? A question that has to be answered.'

When he looked round, Soutar was on the stage. He pushed over the sets, kicking them, stomping them, then jumped down again and made for the doors. His face was orange with anger.

'Was Billy a friend too, Davey?' That stopped him dead. 'Billy Cunningham, I mean.'

Soutar was on the move.

'Davey! You've forgotten your fags!' But Davey Soutar was out the door and screaming things which were unintelligible. Rebus lit a cigarette for himself.

'That laddie's got too much testosterone for his own good,' he said to Cave.

'Look who's talking.'

Rebus shrugged. 'Just an act, Mr Cave. Method acting, you might say.' He blew out a plume of smoke. Cave was staring at his hands, which were clasped in his lap. 'You need to know what you've gotten into.'

Cave looked up. 'You think I condone sectarian hate?'

'No, my theory's much simpler. I think you get off on violence and young men.'

'You're sick.'

'Then maybe all you are, Mr Cave, is misguided. Get out while you can. A policeman's largesse never lasts.' He walked over to Cave and bent down, speaking quietly. 'They've swallowed you, you're in the pit of the Gar-B's stomach. You can still crawl out, but maybe there's not as much time as you think.' Rebus patted Cave's cheek. It was cold and soft, like chicken from the fridge.

'Look at yourself some time, Rebus. You might find you'd make a bloody good terrorist yourself.'

'Thing is, I'd never be tempted. What about you?'

Cave stood up and walked past him towards the doors. Then he walked through them and kept going. Rebus blew smoke from his nose, then sat on the edge of the stage, finishing the cigarette. Maybe he'd tripped Soutar's fuse too early. If it had come out right, he'd have learned something more about The Shield. At the moment, it was all cables and coiled springs, junctions from which spread different coloured wires. Hard to defuse when you didn't know which wire to attack first.

The doors were opening again, and he looked up. Davey Soutar was standing there. Behind him there were others, more than a dozen of them. Soutar was breathing hard. Rebus glanced at his watch and hoped it was right. There was an Emergency Exit at the other end of the hall, but where did Rebus go from there? Instead, he climbed onto the stage and watched them advance. Soutar wasn't saying anything. The whole procession took place in silence, except for breathing and the shuffle of feet on the floor. They were at the front of the stage now. Rebus picked up a length of wood, part of the broken set. Soutar, his eyes on the wood, began to climb onto the stage.

He stopped when he heard the sirens. He froze for a moment, staring up at Rebus. The policeman was smiling.

'Think I'd come here without my cavalry, Davey?' The sirens were drawing closer. 'Your call, Davey,' Rebus said, managing to sound relaxed. 'If you want another riot, here's your chance.'

But all Davey Soutar did was ease himself back off the stage. He stood there, eyes wide and unblinking, as if sheer will of thought might cause Rebus to implode. A final snarl, and he turned and walked away. They followed him, all of them. Some looked back at Rebus. He tried not to look too relieved, lit another cigarette instead. Soutar was crazy, a force gone mad, but he was strong too. Rebus was just beginning to realise how very strong he was.

He went home exhausted that evening, 'home' by now being a very loose term for Patience's flat.

He was still shaking a bit. When Soutar had left the hall that first time, he'd taken it all out on Rebus's car. There were fresh dents, a smashed headlamp, a chipped wind-screen. The actors in the van looked like they'd witnessed a frenzy. Then Rebus had told them about their sets.

He'd thought about the theatre group on his way, under police escort, out of the Gar-B. They'd been parked outside the Dell the night he'd seen the Ulsterman there. He still had their flyer, the one that had doubled as a paper plane.

At St Leonard's, he found them in the Fringe programme, Active Resistance Theatre; active as opposed to passive, Rebus supposed. He placed a couple of calls to Glasgow. Someone would get back to him. The rest of the day was a blur.

As he was locking what was left of his car, he sensed a shape behind him.

'Damn you, weasel-face!'

But he turned to see Caroline Rattray.

'Weasel-face?'

'I thought you were someone else.'

She put her arms round him. 'Well I'm not, I'm me. Remember me? I'm the one who's being trying to phone you for God knows how long. I know you got my messages, because someone in your office told me.'

That would be Ormiston. Or Flower. Or anyone else with a grudge.

'Christ, Caro.' He pulled away from her. 'You must be crazy.'

'For coming here?' She looked around. 'This is where she lives?'

She sounded completely unconcerned. Rebus didn't need this. His head felt like it was splitting open above the eyes. He needed to bathe and to stop thinking, and it would take a great effort to stop him thinking about this case.

'You're tired,' she said. Rebus wasn't listening. He was too busy looking at Patience's parked car, at her gateway, then along the street, willing her not to appear. 'Well, I'm tired too, John.' Her voice was rising. 'But there's always room in the day for a little consideration!'

'Keep your voice down,' he hissed.

'Don't you dare tell me what to do!'

'Christ, Caro ...' He squeezed shut his eyes and she relented for a moment. It was long enough to appraise his physical and psychic state.

'You're exhausted,' she concluded. She smiled and touched his face. 'I'm sorry, John. I just thought you'd been avoiding me.'

'Who'd want to do that, Caro?' Though he was starting to wonder.

'What about a drink?' she said.

'Not tonight.'

'All right,' she said, pouting. A moment ago, she had been all tempest and cannon fire, and now she was a surface as calm as any doldrums could produce. 'Tomorrow?'

'Fine.'

'Eight o'clock then, in the Caly bar.' The Caly being the Caledonian Hotel. Rebus nodded assent.

'Great,' he said.

'See you then.' She leaned into him again, kissing his lips. He drew away as quickly as he could, remembering her perfume. One more waft of that, and Patience would go nuclear.

'See you, Caro.' He watched her get into her car, then walked quickly down the steps to the flat.

The first thing he did was run a bath. He looked at himself in the mirror and got a shock. He was looking at his father. In later years, his father had grown a short grey beard. There was grey in Rebus's stubble too.

'I look like an old man.'

There was a knock at the bathroom door. 'Have you eaten?' Patience called.

'Not yet. Have you?'

'No, shall I stick something in the microwave?'

'Sure, great.' He added foam-bath to the water.

'Pizza?'

'Whatever.' She didn't sound too bad. That was the thing about being a doctor, you saw so much pain every day, it was easy to shrug off the more minor ailments like arguments at home and suspected infidelities. Rebus stripped off his clothes and dumped them in the laundry basket. Patience knocked again.

'By the way, what are you doing tomorrow?'

'You mean tomorrow night?' he called back.

'Yes.'

'Nothing I know of. I might be working...'

'You better not be. I've invited the Bremners to dinner.'

'Oh, good,' said Rebus, putting his foot in the water without checking the temperature. The water was scalding. He lifted the foot out again and screamed silently at the mirror.

20

They had breakfast together, talking around things, their conversation that of acquaintances rather then lovers. Neither spoke his or her thoughts. We Scots, Rebus thought, we're not very good at going public. We store up our true feelings like fuel for long winter nights of whisky and recrimination. So little of us ever reaches the surface, it's a wonder we exist at all.

'Another cup?'

'Please, Patience.'

'You'll be here tonight,' she said. 'You won't be working.' It was neither question nor order, not explicitly.

So he tried phoning Caro from Fettes, but now she was the one having messages left for her: one on her answering machine at home, one with a colleague at her office. He couldn't just say, 'I'm not coming', not even to a piece of recording tape. So he'd just asked her to get in touch. Caro Rattray, elegant, apparently available, and mad about him. There *was* something of the mad in her, something vertiginous. You spent time with her and you were standing on a cliff edge. And where was Caro? She was standing right behind you.

When his phone rang, he leapt for it.

'Inspector Rebus?' The voice was male, familiar.

'Speaking.'

'It's Lachlan Murdock.' Lachlan: no wonder he used his last name.

'What can I do for you, Mr Murdock?'

'You saw Millie recently, didn't you?'

'Yes, why?'

'She's gone.'

'Gone where?'

'I don't know. What the hell did you say to her?'

'Are you at your flat?'

'Yes.'

'I'm coming over.'

He went alone, knowing he should take some back-up, but loath to approach anyone. Out of the four – Ormiston, Blackwood, 'Bloody' Claverhouse, Smylie – Smylie would still be his choice, but Smylie was as predictable as the Edinburgh weather, even now turning overcast. The pavements were still Festival busy, but not for much longer, and as recompense September would be quiet. It was the city's secret month, a retreat from public into private.

As if to reassure him, the cloud swept away again and the sun appeared. He wound down his window, until the bus fumes made him roll it back up again. The back of the bus advertised the local newspaper, which led him to thoughts of Mairie Henderson. He needed to find her, and it wasn't often a policeman thought that about a reporter.

He parked the car as close to Murdock's tenement as he could find a space, pressed the intercom button beside the main door, and got the answering buzz which unlocked the door.

Your feet made the same sound on every tenement stairwell, like sandpaper on a church floor. Murdock had opened the door to his flat. Rebus walked in.

Lachlan Murdock did not look in good fettle. His hair was sprouting in clumps from his head, and he pulled on his beard like it was a fake he'd glued on too well. They were in the living room. Rebus sat down in front of the TV. It was where Millie had been sitting the first time he'd visited. The ashtray was still there, but the sleeping bag had gone. And so had Millie.

'I haven't seen her since yesterday.' Murdock was standing, and showed no sign of sitting down. He walked to the window, looked out, came back to the fireplace. His eyes were everywhere that wasn't Rebus.

'Morning or evening?'

'Morning. I got back last night and she'd packed and left.'

'Packed?'

'Not everything, just a holdall. I thought maybe she'd gone to see a pal, she does that sometimes.'

'Not this time?'

Murdock shook his head. 'I phoned Steve at her work this morning, and he said the police had been to see her yesterday, a young woman and an older man. I thought of you. Steve said she was in a terrible state afterwards, she'd to come home early. What did you say to her?'

'Just a few questions about Billy.'

'Billy.' The dismissive shake of the head told Rebus something.

'She got on better with Billy than you did, Mr Murdock?'

'I didn't dislike the guy.'

'Was there anything between the two of them?'

But Murdock wasn't about to answer that. He paced the room again, flapping his arms as though attempting flight. 'She hasn't been the same since he died.'

'It was upsetting for her.'

'Yes, it was. But to run off...'

'Can I see her room?'

'What?'

Rebus smiled. 'It's what we usually do when someone goes missing.'

Murdock shook his head again. 'She wouldn't want that. What if she comes back, and sees someone's been through her stuff? No, I can't let you do that.' Murdock looked ready for physical resistance if necessary.

'I can't force you,' Rebus said calmly. 'Tell me a bit more about Billy.'

This quietened Murdock. 'Like what?'

'Did he like computers?'

'Billy? He liked video games, so long as they were violent. I don't know, I suppose he was interested in computers.'

'He could work one?'

'Just about. What are you getting at?'

'Just interested. Three people sharing a flat, two of them work with computers, the third doesn't.'

Murdock nodded. 'You're wondering what we had in common. Look around the city, Inspector, you'll see flats full of people who're only there because they need a room or the rent money. In an ideal world, I wouldn't have needed someone in the spare room at all.'

Rebus nodded. 'So what should we do about Miss Docherty?'

'What?'

'You called me, I came, where do we go from here?' Murdock shrugged. 'Normally we'd wait another day or so before listing her missing.' He paused. 'Unless there's reason to suspect foul play.'

Murdock seemed lost in thought, then recovered. 'Let's wait another day then.' He started nodding. 'Maybe I'm overreacting. I just ... when Steve told me...'

'I'm sure it wasn't anything I said to her,' Rebus lied, getting to his feet. 'Can I have another look at Billy's room while I'm here?'

'It's been gutted.'

'Just to refresh my memory.' Murdock said nothing. 'Thanks,' said Rebus.

The small room had indeed been gutted, the bed stripped of duvet and sheet and pillowcase, though the pillow still lay there. It was stained brown, leaking feathers. The bare mattress was pale blue with similar brown patches. There seemed a little more space in the room, but not much. Still,

Rebus doubted Murdock would have any trouble finding a new tenant, not with the student season approaching.

He opened the wardrobe to a clanging of empty wire hangers. There was a fresh sheet of newspaper on the floor. He closed the wardrobe door. Between the corner of the bed and the wardrobe there was a clear patch of carpet. It lay hard up against the skirting-board beneath the still unwashed window. Rebus crouched down and tugged at the carpet's edge. It wasn't tacked, and lifted an inch or so. He ran his fingers underneath it, finding nothing. Still crouched, he lifted the mattress, but saw only bedsprings and the carpet beneath, thick balls of dust and hair marking the furthest reach of the hoover.

He stood up, glancing at the bare walls. There were small rips in the wallpaper where Blu-Tak had been removed. He looked more closely at one small pattern of these. The wallpaper had come away in two longer strips. Wasn't this where the pennant had hung? Yes, you could see the hole made by the drawing-pin. The pennant had hung from a maroon cord which had been pinned to the wall. Meaning the pennant had been hiding these marks. They didn't look so old. The lining paper beneath was clean and fresh, as though the Sellotape had been peeled off recently.

Rebus put his fingers to the two stripes. They were about three inches apart and three inches long. Whatever had been taped there, it had been square and thin. Rebus knew exactly what would fit that description.

Out in the hall, Murdock was waiting to leave.

'Sorry to keep you waiting, sir,' Rebus said.

The Carlton sounded like another old ladies' tea-room, but in fact was a transport cafe with famed large helpings. When Mairie Henderson finally got back to Rebus, he suggested taking her to lunch there. It was on the shore at Newhaven, facing the Firth of Forth just about where that broad inlet became inseparable from the North Sea.

Lorries bypassing Edinburgh or heading to Leith from the north would usually pause for a break outside the Carlton. You saw them in a line by the sea wall, between Starbank Road and Pier Place. The drivers thought the Carlton well worth a detour, even if other road users and the police didn't always appreciate their sentiments.

Inside, the Carlton was a clean well-lit place and as hot as a truck engine. For air conditioning, they kept the front door wedged open. You never ate alone, which was why Rebus phoned in advance and booked a table for two.

'The one between the counter and the toilets,' he specified.

'Did I hear you right? *Book* a table?'

'You heard me.'

'Nobody's *booked* a table all the years we've been open.' The chef held the phone away from his face. 'Hiy, Maggie, there's somebody here wants tae *book* a table.'

'Cut the shite, Sammy, it's John Rebus speaking.'

'Special occasion is it, Mr Rebus? Anniversary? I'll bake yis a cake.'

'Twelve o'clock,' said Rebus, 'and make sure it's the table I asked for, okay?'

'Yes, sir.'

So when Rebus walked into the Carlton, and Sammy saw him, Sammy whipped a dishtowel off the stove and came sauntering between the tables, the towel over his arm.

'Your table is ready, sir, if you'll follow me.'

The drivers were grinning, a few of them offering encouragement. Maggie stood there holding a pillar of empty white plates, and attempted a curtsy as Rebus went past. The small Formica-topped table was laid for two, with a bit of card folded in half and the word RESERVED written in blue biro. There was a clean sauce bottle, into the neck of which someone had pushed a plastic carnation.

He saw Mairie look through the cafe window, then come in through the door. The drivers looked up.

'Room here, sweetheart.'

'Hiy, hen, sit on my lap, no' his.'

They grinned through the smoke, cigarettes never leaving their mouths. One of them ate camel-style, lower jaw moving in sideways rotation while his upper jaw chewed down. He reminded Rebus so strongly of Ormiston, he had to look away. Instead he looked at Mairie. Why not, everyone else was. They were staring without shame at her bum as she moved between the tables. True to form, Mairie had worn her shortest skirt. At least, Rebus hoped it was her shortest. And it was tight, one of those black Lycra numbers. She wore it with a baggy white t-shirt and thick black tights whose vertical seams showed pinpricks of white leg flesh. She'd pushed her sunglasses onto the top of her head, and swung her shoulder-bag onto the floor as she took her seat.

'I see we're in the members' enclosure.'

'It took money but I thought it was worth it.'

Rebus studied her while she studied the wall-board which constituted the Carlton's menu.

'You look good,' he lied. Actually, she looked exhausted.

'Thanks. I wish I could say the same.'

Rebus winced. 'I looked as good as you at your age.'

'Even in a mini-skirt?' She leaned down to lift a pack of cigarettes from her bag, giving Rebus a view of her lace-edged bra down the front of her t-shirt. When she came up again he was frowning.

'Okay, I won't smoke.'

'It stunts your growth. And speaking of health warnings, what about that story of yours?'

But Maggie came over, so they went through the intricacies of ordering. 'We're out of Moët Shandy,' Maggie said.

'What was that about?' Mairie asked after Maggie had gone.

'Nothing,' he said. 'You were about to tell me...?'

'Was I?' She smiled. 'How much do you know?'

'I know you've been working on a story, a chunk of which you've sold to *Snoop* but the bulk of which is destined for some US magazine.'

'Well, you know quite a lot then.'

'You took the story to your own paper first?'

She sighed. 'Of course I did, but they wouldn't print it. The company lawyers thought it was close to libel.'

'Who were you libelling?'

'Organisations rather than individuals. I had a blow-up with my editor about it, and handed in my resignation. His line was that the lawyers were paid to be over-cautious.'

'I bet their fees aren't over-cautious.' Which reminded him: Caro Rattray. He still had to contact her.

'I was planning on going freelance anyway, just not quite so soon. But at least I'm starting with a strong story. A few months back I got a letter from a New York journalist. His name's Jump Cantona.'

'Sounds like a car.'

'Yes, a four-by-four, that's just what I thought. Anyway, Jump's a well known writer over there, investigations with a capital I. But then of course it's easier in the US.'

'How's that?'

'You can go further before someone starts issuing writs. Plus you've got more freedom of information. Jump needed someone this end, following up a few leads. His name comes first in the main article, but any spin-offs I write, I get sole billing.'

'So what have you found?'

'A can of worms.' Maggie was coming with their food. She heard Mairie's closing words and gave her a cold look as she placed the fry-up in front of her. For Rebus, there was a half-portion of lasagne and a green salad.

'How did Cantona find you?' Rebus asked.

'Someone I met when I was on a journalism course in New York. This guy knew Cantona was looking for someone who could do some digging in Scotland. I was the obvious choice.' She attacked four chips with her fork. Chewing, she reached for the salt, vinegar, and tomato sauce. After momentary consideration, she poured some brown sauce on as well.

'I knew you'd do that,' Rebus said. 'And it still disgusts me.'

'You should see me with mustard and mayonnaise. I hear you got moved to SCS.'

'It's true.'

'Why?'

'If I didn't know better, I'd say they were keeping an eye on me.'

'Only, they were there at Mary King's Close, a murder that looks like an execution. Then next thing you're off to SCS, and I know SCS are investigating gun-running with an Irish slant.' Maggie arrived with two cans of Irn-Bru. Mairie checked hers was cold enough before opening it. 'Are we working on the same story?'

'The police don't have stories, Mairie, we have cases. And it's hard to answer your question without seeing your story.'

She slipped a hand into her shoulder-bag and pulled out several sheets of neatly typed paper. The document had been stapled and folded in half. Rebus could see it was a photocopy.

'Not very long,' he said.

'You can read it while I eat.'

He did. But all it did was put a lot of speculative meat on the bones he already had. Mostly it concentrated on the North American angle, mentioning the IRA fundraising in passing, though the Orange Loyal Brigade was mentioned, as was Sword and Shield.

'No names,' Rebus commented.

'I can give you a few, off the record.'

'Gavin and Jamesie MacMurray?'

'You're stealing my best lines. Do you have anything on them?'

'What do you think we'll find, a garden shed full of grenade launchers?'

'That could be pretty close.'

'Tell me.'

She took a deep breath. 'We can't put anything in print yet, but we think there's an Army connection.'

'You mean stuff from the Falklands and the Gulf? Souvenirs?'

'There's too much of it for it to be souvenirs.'

'What then? The stuff from Russia?'

'Much closer to home. You know stuff walks out of Army bases in Northern Ireland?'

'I've heard of it happening.'

'Same thing happened in the '70s in Scotland, the Tartan Army got stuff from Army bases. We think it's happening again. At least, Jump thinks it is. He's spoken to someone who used to be in American Shield, sending money over here. It's easier to send money here than arms shipments. This guy told Jump the money was buying *British* armaments. See, the IRA has good links with the East and Libya, but the loyalist paramilitaries don't.'

'You're telling me they're buying guns from the Army?' Rebus laughed and shook his head. Mairie managed a small smile.

'There's another thing. I know there's nothing to back this up. Jump knows it too. It's just one man's word, and that man isn't even willing to go public. He's afraid American Shield would get to him. Anyway, who'd believe him: he's being paid to tell Jump this stuff. He could be making it all up. Journalists like a juicy conspiracy, we lap them up like cream.'

'What are you talking about, Mairie?'

'A policeman, a detective, someone high up in The Shield.'

'In America?'

She shook her head. 'At the UK end, no name or anything. Like I say, just a story.'

'Aye, just a story. How did you find out we had a man undercover?'

'That was strange. It was a phone call.'

'Anonymous of course?'

'Of course. But who could have known?'

'Another policeman, obviously.'

Mairie pushed her plate away. 'I can't eat all these chips.'

'They should put up a plaque above the table.'

Rebus needed a drink, and there was a good pub only a short walk away. Mairie went with him, though she complained she didn't have room for a drink. Still, when they got there she found space for a white wine and soda. Rebus had a half-pint and a nip. They sat by the window, with a view out over the Forth. The water was battleship grey, reflecting the sky overhead. Rebus had never seen the Forth look other than forbidding.

'What did you say?' He'd missed it completely.

'I said, I forgot to say.'

'Yes, but the bit after that?'

'A man called Moncur, Clyde Moncur.'

'What about him?'

'Jump has him pegged as one of The Shield's hierarchy in the US. He's also a big-time villain, only it's never been proven in a court of law.'

'And?'

'And he flies into Heathrow tomorrow.'

'To do what?'

'We don't know.'

'So why aren't you down in London waiting for him?'

'Because he's booked on a connecting flight to Edinburgh.'

Rebus narrowed his eyes. 'You weren't going to tell me.'

'No, I wasn't.'

'What changed your mind?'

She gnawed her bottom lip. 'It may be I'll need a friend sometime soon.'

'You're going to confront him?'

'Yes ... I suppose so.'

'Jesus, Mairie.'

'It's what journalists do.'

'Do you know anything about him? I mean *anything*?'

'I know he's supposed to run drugs into Canada, brings illegal immigrants in from the Far East, a real Renaissance man. But on the surface, all he does is own a fish-processing plant in Seattle.' Rebus was shaking his head. 'What's wrong?'

'I don't know,' he said. 'I suppose I just feel ... gutted.'

It took her a moment to get the joke.

21

'Caro, thank God.'

Rebus was back in Fettes, at his desk, on the phone, having finally tracked Caroline Rattray to ground.

'You're calling off our drink,' she said coldly.

'I'm sorry, something's cropped up. Work, you know how it is. The hours aren't always social.' The phone went dead in his hand. He replaced the receiver like it was spun sugar. Then, having requested five minutes of his boss's time, he went to Kilpatrick's office. As ever there was no need to knock; Kilpatrick waved him in through the glass door.

'Take a seat, John.'

'I'll stand, sir, thanks all the same.'

'What's on your mind?'

'When you spoke to the FBI, did they mention a man called Clyde Moncur?'

'I don't think any names were mentioned.' Kilpatrick wrote the name on his pad. 'Who is he?'

'He's a Seattle businessman, runs his own fish-processing plant. Possibly also a gangster. He's coming to Edinburgh on holiday.'

'Well, we need the tourist dollars.'

'And he may be high up in The Shield.'

'Oh?' Kilpatrick casually underlined the name. 'What's your source?'

'I'd rather not say.'

'I see.' Kilpatrick underlined the name one last time. 'I don't like secrets, John.'

'Yes, sir.'

'Well, what do you want to do?'

'Put a tail on him.'

'Ormiston and Blackwood are good.'

'I'd prefer someone else.'

Kilpatrick threw down his pen. 'Why?'

'I just would.'

'You can trust me, John.'

'I know that, sir.'

'Then tell me why you don't want Ormiston and Black-wood on the tail.'

'We don't get on. I get the feeling they might muck things up just to make me look bad.' Lying was easy with practice, and Rebus had years of practice at lying to superiors.

'That sounds like paranoia to me.'

'Maybe it is.'

'I've got a *team* here, John. I need to know that they can work as a team.'

'You brought me in, sir. I didn't ask for secondment. Teams always resent the new man, it just hasn't worn off yet.' Then Rebus played his ace. 'You could always move me back to St Leonard's.' Not that he wanted this. He liked the freedom he had, flitting between the two stations, neither Chief Inspector knowing where he was.

'Is that what you want?' Kilpatrick asked.

'It's not down to me, it's what *you* want that matters.'

'Quite right, and I want you in SCS, at least for the time being.'

'So you'll put someone else on the tail?'

'I take it you've got people in mind?'

'Two more from St Leonard's. DS Holmes and DC Clarke. They work well together, they've done this sort of thing before.'

'No, John, let's keep this to SCS.' Which was Kilpatrick's way of reasserting his authority. 'I know two good men

206

over in Glasgow, no possible grudge against you. I'll get them over here.'

'Right, sir.'

'Sound all right to you, Inspector?'

'Whatever you think, sir.'

When Rebus left the office, the two typists were discussing famine and Third World debt.

'Ever thought of going into politics, ladies?'

'Myra's a local councillor,' one of them said, nodding to her partner.

'Any chance of getting my drains cleared?' Rebus asked Myra.

'Join the queue,' Myra said with a laugh.

Back at his desk Rebus phoned Brian Holmes to ask him a favour, then he went to the toilets down the hall. The toilet was one of those design miracles, like Dr Who's time machine. Somehow two urinals, a toilet cubicle, and washhand basin had been squeezed into a space smaller than their total cubic volume.

So Rebus wasn't thrilled when Ken Smylie joined him. Smylie was supposed to be taking time off work, only he insisted on coming in.

'How are you doing, Ken?'

'I'm all right.'

'Good.' Rebus turned from his urinal and headed for the sink.

'You seem to be working hard,' Smylie said.

'Do I?'

'You're never here, I assume you're working.'

'Oh, I'm working.' Rebus shook water from his hands.

'Only I never see any notes.'

'Notes?'

'You never write down your case notes.'

'Is that right?' Rebus dried his hands on the cotton roller-towel. This was his lucky day: a fresh roll had just been

207

fitted. He still had his back to Smylie. 'Well, I like to keep my notes in my head.'

'That's not procedure.'

'Tough.'

He'd just got the word out, and was preparing for another intake of breath, when Smylie's arms gripped him with the force of a construction crane around his chest. He couldn't breathe, and felt himself being lifted off the ground. Smylie pushed his face against the wall next to the roller-towel. His whole weight was sandwiching Rebus against the wall.

'You're on to something, aren't you?' Smylie said in his high whistling voice. 'Tell me who it is.' He released his bear hug just enough so Rebus could speak.

'Get the fuck off me!'

The grip tightened again, Rebus's face pressing harder into the wall. I'll go through it in a minute, he thought. My head'll be sticking out into the corridor like a hunting trophy.

'He was my brother,' Smylie was saying. '*My* brother.'

Rebus's face was full of blood which wanted to be somewhere else. He could feel his eyes bulging out of their sockets, his eardrums straining. My last view, he thought, will be of this damned roller-towel. Then the door swung inwards, and Ormiston was standing there, cigarette gawping. The cigarette dropped to the floor as Ormiston flung his own arms around Smylie's. He couldn't reach all the way round, but enough to dig his thumbs into the soft flesh of the inner elbows.

'Let go, Smylie!'

'Get off me!'

Rebus felt the pressure on him ease, and used his own shoulders to throw Smylie off. There was barely room for all three men, and they danced awkwardly, Ormiston still holding Smylie's arms. Smylie threw him off with ease. He was on Rebus again, but now Rebus was ready. He kneed the big man in the groin. Smylie groaned and slumped to his knees. Ormiston was picking himself up.

'What the hell sparked this?'

Smylie pulled himself to his feet. He looked angry, frustrated. He nearly took the handle off the door as he pulled it open.

Rebus looked in the mirror. His face was that sunburnt cherry colour some fair-skinned people go, but at least his eyes had retreated back into their sockets.

'Wonder what my blood pressure got up to,' he said to himself. Then he thanked Ormiston.

'I was thinking of me, not you,' Ormiston retorted. 'With you two wrestling,' he stooped to pick up his cigarette, 'there wasn't room for me to have a quiet puff.'

The cigarette itself survived the mêlée, but after inspecting it Ormiston decided to flush it anyway and light up a fresh one.

Rebus joined him. 'That may be the first time smoking's saved someone's life.'

'My grandad smoked for sixty years, died in his sleep at eighty. Mind you, he was bedridden for thirty of them. So what was all that about?'

'Filing. Smylie doesn't like my system.'

'Smylie likes to know everything that's going on.'

'He shouldn't even be here. He should be at home, bereaving.'

'But that's what he *is* doing,' argued Ormiston. 'Just because he looks like a big cuddly bear, a gentle giant, don't be fooled.' He took a drag on his cigarette. 'Let me tell you about Smylie.'

And he did.

Rebus was home at six o'clock, much to Patience Aitken's surprise. He had a shower rather than a bath and came into the living room dressed in his best suit and wearing a shirt Patience had given him for Christmas. It wasn't till

209

he'd tried it on that they both discovered it required cuff links, so then he'd had to buy some.

'I can never do these up by myself,' he said now, flapping his cuffs and brandishing the links. Patience smiled and came to help him. Close up, she smelt of perfume.

'Smells wonderful,' he said.

'Do you mean me or the kitchen?'

'Both,' said Rebus. 'Equally.'

'Something to drink?'

'What are you having?'

'Fizzy water till the cooking's done.'

'Same for me.' Though really he was dying for a whisky. He'd lost the shakes, but his ribs still hurt when he inflated his lungs. Ormiston said he'd once seen Smylie bear-hug a recalcitrant prisoner into unconsciousness. He also told Rebus that before Kilpatrick had come on the scene, the Smylie brothers had more or less run the Edinburgh Crime Squad.

He drank the water with ice and lime and it tasted fine. When the preparations were complete and the table laid and the dishwasher set to work on only the first of the evening's loads, they sat down together on the sofa and drank gin with tonic.

'Cheers.'

'Cheers.'

And then Patience led him by the hand out into the small back garden. The sun was low over the tops of the tenements, the birds easing off into evensong. She examined every plant as she passed it, like a general assessing her troops. She'd trained Lucky the cat well; it now went over the wall into the neighbouring garden when it needed the toilet. She named some of the flowers for him, like she always did. He could never remember them from one day to the next.

The ice clinked in Patience's glass as she moved. She had changed into a long patterned dress, all flowing folds and squares of colour. With her hair up at the back, the dress worked well, showing off her neck and shoulders and the contours of her body. It had short sleeves to show arms tanned from gardening.

Though the bell was a long way off, he heard it. 'Front door,' he said.

'They're early.' She looked at her watch. 'Well, not much actually. I'd better get the potatoes on.'

'I'll let them in.'

She squeezed his arm as they separated, and Rebus made his way down the hallway towards the front door. He straightened himself, readying the smile he'd be wearing all evening. Then he opened the door.

'Bastard!'

Something hissed, a spray-can, and his eyes stung. He'd closed them a moment too late, but could still feel the spray dotting his face. He thought it must be Mace or something similar, and swiped blindly, trying to knock the can out of his assailant's hand. But the feet were already on the stone steps, shuffling upwards and away. He didn't want to open his eyes, so staggered blindly towards the bathroom, his hands feeling the hallway walls, past the bedroom door then hitting the lightswitch. He slammed the door and locked it as Patience was coming into the hall.

'John? John, what is it?'

'Nothing,' he said through his teeth. 'It's all right.'

'Are you sure? Who was at the door?'

'They were looking for the upstairs neighbours.' He was running water into the sink. He got his jacket off and plunged his head into the warm water, letting the sink fill, wiping at his face with his hands.

Patience was still waiting on the other side of the bathroom door. 'Something's wrong, John, what is it?'

He didn't say anything. After a few moments, he pried open one eye, then shut it again. Shit, that stung! He swabbed again with the water, opening his eyes underwater this time. The water seemed murky to him. And when he looked at his hands, they were red and sticky.

Oh Christ, he thought. He forced himself to look in the mirror above the sink. He was bright red. It wasn't like earlier in the day when Smylie had attacked him. It was ... paint. That's what it was, red paint. From an aerosol can. Jesus Christ. He staggered out of his clothes and got into the shower, turning his face up to the spray, shampooing his hair as hard as he could, then doing it again. He scrubbed at his face and neck. Patience was at the door again, asking him what the hell he was up to. And then he heard her voice change, rising on the final syllable of a name.

The Bremners had arrived.

He got out of the shower and rubbed himself down with a towel. When he looked at himself again, he'd managed to get a lot of the colour off, but by no means all of it. Then he looked at his clothes. His jacket was dark, and didn't show the paint too conspicuously; conspicuously enough though. As for his good shirt, it was ruined, no question about that. He unlocked the bathroom door and listened. Patience had taken the Bremners into the living room. He padded down the hall into the bedroom, noticing on the way that his hands had left red smears on the wallpaper. In the bedroom he changed quickly into chinos, yellow t-shirt and a linen jacket Patience had bought him for summer walks by the river which they never took.

He looked like a has-been trying to look trendy. It would do. The palms of his hands were still red, but he could say he'd been painting. He popped his head round the living room door.

'Chris, Jenny,' he said. The couple were seated on the sofa. Patience must be in the kitchen. 'Sorry, I'm running a bit late. I'll just dry my hair and I'll be with you.'

'No rush,' said Jenny as he retreated into the hall. He took the telephone into the bedroom and called Dr Curt at home.

'Hello?'

'It's John Rebus here, tell me about Caroline Rattray.'

'Pardon?'

'Tell me what you know about her.'

'You sound smitten,' Curt said, amusement in his voice.

'I'm smitten all right. She's just sprayed me with a can of paint.'

'I'm not sure I caught that.'

'Never mind, just tell me about her. Like for instance, is she the jealous type?'

'John, you've met her. Would you say she's attractive?'

'Yes.'

'And she has a very good career, plenty of money, a lifestyle many would envy?'

'Yes.'

'But does she have any beaux?'

'You mean boyfriends, and the answer is I don't know.'

'Then take it from me, she does not. That's why she can be at a loose end when I have ballet tickets to spare. Ask yourself, why should this be? Answer, because she scares men off. I don't know *what's* wrong with her, but I know that she's not very good at relationships with the opposite sex. I mean, she *has* relationships, but they never last very long.'

'You might have told me.'

'I didn't realise you two were an item.'

'We're not.'

'Oh?'

'Only she thinks we are.'

'Then you're in trouble.'

'It looks like it.'

'Sorry I can't be more help. She's always been all right with me, perhaps I could have a word with her ... ?'

'No thanks, that's my department.'

'Goodbye then, and good luck.'

Rebus waited till Curt had put his receiver down. He

listened to the line, then heard another click. Patience had been listening on the kitchen extension. He sat on the bed, staring at his feet, till the door opened.

'I heard,' she said. She had an oven glove in one hand. She knelt down in front of him, her hands on his knees. 'You should have told me.'

He smiled. 'I just did.'

'Yes, but to my face.' She paused. 'There was nothing between the two of you, nothing happened?'

'Nothing happened,' he said without blinking. There was another moment's silence.

'What are we going to do?'

He took her hands. 'We,' he said, 'are going to join our guests.' Then he kissed her on the forehead and pulled her with him to her feet.

22

At nine-thirty next morning, Rebus was sitting in his car outside Lachlan Murdock's flat.

When he'd washed his eyes last night, it had been like washing behind them as well. Always it came to this, he tried to do things by the books and ended up cooking them instead. It was easier, that was all. Where would the crime detection rates be without a few shortcuts?

He had tried Murdock's number from a callbox at the end of the road. There was no one there, just an answering machine. Murdock was at work. Rebus got out of the car and tried Murdock's intercom. Again, no answer. So he picked the lock, the way he'd been taught by an old lag when he'd gone to the man for lessons. Once inside, he climbed the stairwell briskly, a regular visitor rather than an intruder. But no one was about.

Murdock's flat was on the Yale rather than a deadlock, so it was easy to open too. Rebus slipped inside and closed the door after him. He went straight to Murdock's bedroom. He didn't suppose Millie would have left the computer disk behind, but you never knew. People with no access to safe deposit boxes sometimes mistook their homes for one.

The postman had been, and Murdock had left the mail strewn on the unmade bed. Rebus glanced at it. There was a letter from Millie. The envelope was postmarked the previous day, the letter itself written on a single sheet of lined writing paper.

'Sorry I didn't say anything. Don't know how long I'll

be away. If the police ask, say nothing. Can't say more just now. Love you. Millie.'

Rebus left the letter lying where it was and pulled on a pair of surgical gloves stolen from Patience. He walked over to Murdock's workdesk and switched on the computer, then started going through the computer disks. There were dozens of them, kept in plastic boxes, most of them neatly labelled. The majority had labels with spidery black handwriting, which Rebus guessed was Murdock's. The few that remained he took to be Millie's.

He went through these first, but found nothing to interest him. The unlabelled disks proved to be either blank or corrupted. He started searching through drawers for other disks. Parked on the floor one side of the bed were the plastic binliners containing Billy's things. He looked through these, too. Murdock's side of the bed was a chaos of books, ashtray, empty cigarette packets, but Millie's side was a lot neater. She had a bedside cupboard on which sat a lamp, alarm clock, and a packet of throat lozenges. Rebus crouched down and opened the cupboard door. Now he knew why Millie's side of the bed was so neat: the cupboard was like a wastepaper bin. He sifted through the rubbish. There were some crumpled yellow Post-It notes in amongst it. He picked them out and unpeeled them. They were messages from Murdock. The first one contained a seven-digit phone number and beneath it the words 'Why don't you call this bitch?' As Rebus unpeeled the others, he began to understand. There were half a dozen telephone messages, all from the same person. Rebus had thought he recognised the phone number, but on the rest of the messages the caller's name was printed alongside.

Mairie Henderson.

Back at St Leonard's he was pleased to find that both Holmes and Clarke were elsewhere. He went to the toilets and splashed water on his face. His eyes were still irritated, red at their rims and bloodshot. Patience had taken a close look at them last night and pronounced he'd live. After the Bremners had gone home happy, she'd also helped him scrub the rest of the red out of his hair and off his hands. Actually, there was still some on his right palm.

'Cuchullain of the Red Hand,' Patience had said. She'd been great really, considering. Trust a doctor to be calm in a crisis. She'd even managed to calm him down when, late in the evening, he'd considered going round to Caroline Rattray's flat and torching it.

'Here,' she'd said, handing him a whisky, 'set fire to yourself instead.'

He smiled at himself in the toilet mirror. There was no Smylie here, about to grope him to death, no jeering Ormiston or preening Blackwood. This was where he belonged. He wondered again just what he was doing at Fettes. Why had Kilpatrick scooped him up?

He thought now that he had a bloody good idea.

Edinburgh's Central Lending Library is situated on George IV Bridge, across the street from the National Library of Scotland. This was student territory, and just off the Royal Mile, and hence at the moment also Festival Fringe territory. Pamphleteers were out in force, still enthusing, sensing audiences to be had now that the least successful shows had packed up and headed home. For the sake of politeness, Rebus took a lurid green flyer from a teenage girl with long blonde hair, and read it as far as the first litter bin, where it joined many more identical flyers.

The Edinburgh Room was not so much a room as a gallery surrounding an open space. Far below, readers in another section of the library were at their desks or browsing among the bookshelves. Not that Mairie Henderson was reading books. She was poring over local newspapers, seated at one of the few readers' tables. Rebus stood beside Mairie, reading over her shoulder. She had a neat portable

217

computer with her, flipped open and plugged into a socket in the library floor. Its screen was milky grey and filled with notes. It took her a minute to sense that there was someone standing over her. She looked round slowly, expecting a librarian.

'Let's talk,' said Rebus.

She saved what she'd been writing and followed him out onto the library's large main staircase. A sign told them not to sit on the window ledges, which were in a dangerous condition. Mairie sat on the top step, and Rebus sat a couple of steps down from her, leaving plenty of room for people to get past.

'I'm in a dangerous condition, too,' he said angrily.

'Why? What's happened?' She looked as innocent as stained glass.

'Millie Docherty.'

'Yes?'

'You didn't tell me about her.'

'What exactly should I have told you?'

'That you'd been trying to talk to her. Did you succeed?'

'No, why?'

'She's run off.'

'Really?' She considered this. 'Interesting.'

'What did you want to talk to her about?'

'The murder of one of her flatmates.'

'That's all?'

'Shouldn't it be?' She was looking interested.

'Funny she does a runner when you're after her. How's the research?' She'd told him over their drink in Newhaven that she was looking into what she called 'past loyalist activity' in Scotland.

'Slow,' she admitted. 'How's yours?'

'Dead stop,' he lied.

'Apart from Ms Docherty's disappearance. How did you know I wanted to talk to her?'

'None of your business.'

She raised her eyebrows. 'Her flatmate didn't tell you?'

'No comment at this time.'

She smiled.

'Come on,' said Rebus, 'maybe you'll talk over a coffee.'

'Interrogation by scone,' Mairie offered.

They walked the short walk to the High Street and took a right towards St Giles Cathedral. There was a coffee shop in the crypt of St Giles, reached by way of an entrance which faced Parliament House. Rebus glanced across the car park, but there was no sign of Caroline Rattray. The coffee shop though was packed, having not many tables to start with and this still being the height of the tourist season.

'Try somewhere else?' Mairie suggested.

'Actually,' said Rebus, 'I've gone off the idea. I've got a bit of business across the road.' Mairie tried not to look relieved. 'I'd caution you,' he warned her, 'not to piss me about.'

'Caution received and understood.'

She waved as she walked off back towards the library. Rebus watched her good legs recede from view. They stayed good-looking all the way out of his vision. Then he threaded his way between the lawyers' cars and entered the court building. He had an idea he was going to leave a note for Caroline Rattray in her box, always supposing she had one. But as he walked into Parliament Hall he saw her talking with another lawyer. There was no chance to retreat; she spotted him immediately. She kept up the conversation for a few more moments, then put her hand on her colleague's shoulder, said a brief farewell, and headed towards Rebus.

It was hard to reconcile her, in her professional garb, with the woman who had spray-painted him the previous night. She left her colleague with a faint smile on her lips, and met Rebus with that same smile. Under her arm were the regulation files and documents.

'Inspector, what brings you here?'

'Can't you guess?'

'Ah yes, of course, I'll send a cheque.'

He had kept telling himself all the way across the car park that he wasn't going to let her get under his skin. Now he found she was already there, like a half inch of syringe.

'Cheque?'

'For the dry cleaning or whatever.' A passing lawyer nodded to her. 'Hullo, Mansie. Oh, Mansie?' She spoke with the lawyer for a few moments, her hand on his elbow.

She was offering a cheque for the dry cleaning. Rebus was glad of a few moments in which to cool off. But now someone was tapping his shoulder. He turned to find Mairie Henderson standing there.

'I forgot,' she said, 'the American's in town.'

'Yes, I know. Have you done anything about him?'

She shook her head. 'Biding my time.'

'Good, no use scaring him off.' Caroline Rattray was looking interested in this new arrival, so much so that she was losing the thread of her own conversation. She dismissed Mansie halfway through a sentence and turned to Rebus and Mairie. Mairie smiled at her, the two women waiting for an introduction.

'See you then,' Rebus said to Mairie.

'Oh, right.' Mairie walked backwards a step or two, just in case he'd change his mind, then turned. As she turned, Caroline Rattray took a step forward, her hand out as though she were about to make her own introduction, but Rebus really didn't want her to, so he grabbed the hand and held her back. She shrugged his grip off and glared at him, then looked back through the doorway. Mairie had already left the building.

'You seem to have quite a little stable, Inspector.' She tried rubbing at her wrist. It wasn't easy with the files still precariously pressed between her elbow and stomach

'Better stable than unstable,' he said, regretting the dig

immediately. He should just have denied the charge.

'Unstable?' she echoed. 'I don't know what you mean.'

'Look, let's forget it, eh? I mean, forget *everything*. I've told Patience all about it.'

'I find that difficult to believe.'

'That's your problem, not mine.'

'You think so?' She sounded amused.

'Yes.'

'Remember something, Inspector.' Her voice was level and quiet. '*You* started it. And then *you* told the lie. My conscience is clear, what about yours?'

She gave him a little smile before walking away. Rebus turned and found himself confronting a statue of Sir Walter Scott, seated with his feet crossed and a walking-cane held between his open knees. Scott looked as though he'd heard every word but wasn't about to pass judgment.

'Keep it that way,' Rebus warned, not caring who might hear.

He phoned Patience and invited her to an early evening drink at the Playfair Hotel on George Street.

'What's the occasion?' she asked.

'No occasion,' he said.

He was restless the rest of the day. Glasgow came back to him, but only to say that they'd nothing on either Jim Hay or Active Resistance Theatre. He turned up early at the Playfair, making across its entrance hall (all faded glory, but *studied* faded glory, almost too perfect) to the bar beyond. It called itself a 'wet bar', which was okay with Rebus. He ordered a Talisker, hoisted himself onto a well-padded barstool and dipped a hand into the bowl of peanuts which had appeared at his approach.

The bar was empty, but would be filled soon enough with prosperous businessmen on their way home, other businessmen who wanted to look prosperous and didn't mind spending money on it, and the hotel clientele, enjoying a snifter before a pre-dinner stroll. A waitress stood idly against the end of the bar, not far from the baby grand. The piano was kept covered with a dustsheet until evening, so for now there was wallpaper music, except that whoever was playing trumpet wasn't half bad. He wondered if it was Chet Baker.

Rebus paid for his drink and tried not to think about the amount of money he'd just been asked for. After a bit, he changed his mind and asked if he could have some ice. He wanted the drink to last. Eventually a middle-aged couple came into the bar and sat a couple of seats away from him. The woman put on elaborate glasses to study the cocktail list, while her husband ordered Drambuie, pronouncing it Dramboo-i. The husband was short but bulky, given to scowling. He was wearing a white golfing cap, and kept glancing at his watch. Rebus managed to catch his eye, and toasted him.

'Slainte.'

The man nodded, saying nothing, but the wife smiled. 'Tell me,' she said, 'are there many Gaelic speakers left in Scotland?'

Her husband hissed at her, but Rebus was happy to answer. 'Not many,' he conceded.

'Are you from Edinburgh?' Head-in-burrow, it sounded like.

'Pretty much.'

She noticed that Rebus's glass was now all melting ice. 'Will you join us?' The husband hissed again, something about her not bothering people who only wanted a quiet drink.

Rebus looked at his watch. He was calculating whether he could afford to buy a round back. 'Thank you, yes, I'll have a Talisker.'

'And what is that?'

'Malt whisky, it comes from Skye. There are some Gaelic speakers over there.'

The wife started humming the first few notes of the *Skye Boat Song*, all about a French Prince who dressed in drag. Her husband smiled to cover his embarrassment. It couldn't be easy, travelling with a madwoman.

'Maybe you can tell me something,' said Rebus. 'Why is a wet bar called a wet bar?'

'Could be because the beer's draught,' the husband offered grudgingly, 'not just bottled.'

The wife had perched her shiny handbag on the bar and now opened it, taking out a compact so she could check her face. 'You're not the mystery man, are you?' she asked.

Rebus put down his glass. 'Sorry?'

'Ellie!' her husband warned.

'Only,' she said, putting away her compact, 'Clyde had a message to meet someone in the bar, and you're the only person here. They didn't leave a name or anything.'

'A misunderstanding, that's all,' said Clyde. 'They got the wrong room.' But he looked at Rebus anyway. Rebus obliged with a nod.

'Mysterious, certainly.'

The fresh glass was put before Rebus, and the barman decided he merited another bowl of nuts too.

'*Slainte*,' said Rebus.

'*Slainte*,' said husband and wife.

'Am I late?' said Patience Aitken, running her hands up Rebus's spine. She slipped onto the stool which separated Rebus from the tourists. For some reason, the man now removed his cap, showing a good amount of hair slicked back from the forehead.

'Patience,' Rebus said, 'I'd like to introduce you to...'

'Clyde Moncur,' said the man, visibly relaxing. Rebus obviously posed no threat. 'This is my wife Eleanor.'

Rebus smiled. 'Dr Patience Aitken, and I'm John.'

Patience looked at him. He seldom used 'Dr' when introducing her, and why had he left out his own surname?

'Listen,' Rebus was saying, staring right past her,

223

'wouldn't we be more comfortable at a table?'

They took a table for four, the waitress appearing with a little tray of nibbles, not just nuts but green and black olives and chipsticks too. Rebus tucked in. The drinks might be expensive, but you had to say the food was cheap.

'You're on holiday?' Rebus said, opening the conversation.

'That's right,' said Eleanor Moncur. 'We just love Scotland.' She then went on to list everything they loved about it, from the skirl of the bagpipes to the windswept west coast. Clyde let her run on, taking sips from his drink, occasionally swirling the ice around. He sometimes looked up from the drink to John Rebus.

'Have you ever been to the United States?' Eleanor asked.

'No, never,' said Rebus.

'I've been a couple of times,' Patience said, surprising him. 'Once to California, and once to New England.'

'In the fall?' Patience nodded. 'Isn't that just heaven?'

'Do you live in New England?' Rebus asked.

Eleanor smiled. 'Oh no, we're way over the other side. Washington.'

'Washington?'

'She means the state,' her husband explained, 'not Washington DC.'

'Seattle,' said Eleanor. 'You'd like Washington, it's wild.'

'As in wilderness,' Clyde Moncur added. 'I'll put that on our room, miss.'

Patience had ordered lager and lime, which the waitress had just brought. Rebus watched as Moncur took a room key from his pocket. The waitress checked the room number.

'Clyde's ancestors came from Scotland,' Eleanor was saying. 'Somewhere near Glasgow.'

'Kilmarnock.'

'That's right, Kilmarnock. There were four brothers, one went to Australia, two went to Northern Ireland, and Clyde's great-grandfather sailed from Glasgow to Canada with his wife and children. He worked his way across Canada and settled in Vancouver. It was Clyde's grandfather who came down into the United States. There are still offshoots of the family in Australia and Northern Ireland.'

'Where in Northern Ireland?' Rebus asked casually.

'Portadown, Londonderry,' she went on, though Rebus had directed the question at her husband.

'Ever visit them?'

'No,' said Clyde Moncur. He was interested in Rebus again. Rebus met the stare squarely.

'The north west's full of Scots,' Mrs Moncur rattled on. 'We have ceilidhs and clan gatherings and Highland Games in the summer.'

Rebus lifted his glass to his lips and seemed to notice it was empty. 'I think we need another round,' he said. The drinks arrived with their own scalloped paper coasters, and the waitress took away with her nearly all the money John Rebus had on him. He'd used the anonymous message to get Moncur down here, and Patience to put him off his guard. In the event, Moncur was sharper than Rebus had given him credit for. The man didn't need to say a word, his wife spoke enough for two, and nothing she said could prove remotely useful.

'So you're a doctor?' she asked Patience now.

'General practice, yes.'

'I admire doctors,' said Eleanor. 'They keep Clyde and me alive and ticking.' And she gave a big grin. Her husband had been watching Patience while she'd been speaking, but as soon as she finished he turned his gaze back to Rebus. Rebus lifted his glass to his lips.

'For some time,' Eleanor Moncur was saying now, 'Clyde's grandaddy was captain of a clipper. His wife gave birth on board while the boat was headed to pick up ... what was it, Clyde?'

'Timber,' Clyde said. 'From the Philippines. She was eighteen and he was in his forties. The baby died.'

'And know what?' said Eleanor. 'They preserved the body in brandy.'

'Embalmed it?' Patience offered.

Eleanor Moncur nodded. 'And if that boat had been a temperance vessel, they'd've used tar instead of brandy.'

Clyde Moncur spoke to Rebus. 'Now *that* was hard living. Those are the people who built America. You had to be tough. You might be conscientious, but there wasn't always room for a conscience.'

'A bit like in Ulster,' Rebus offered. 'They transplanted some pretty hard Scots there.'

'Really?' Moncur finished his drink in silence.

They decided against a third round, Clyde reminding his wife that they had yet to take their pre-prandial walk down to Princes Street Gardens and back. They exchanged handshakes outside, Rebus taking Patience's arm and leading her downhill, as though they were heading into the New Town.

'Where's your car?' he asked.

'Back on George Street. Where's yours?'

'Same place.'

'Then where are we going?'

He checked over his shoulder, but the Moncurs were out of sight. 'Nowhere,' he said, stopping.

'John,' said Patience, 'next time you need me as a cover, have the courtesy to ask first.'

'Can you lend me a few quid, save me finding a cash-point?'

She sighed and dug into her bag. 'Twenty enough?'

'Hope so.'

'Unless you're thinking of returning to the Playfair bar.'

'I've been up braes that weren't as steep as that place.'

He told her he'd be back late, perhaps very late, and pecked her on the cheek. But she pulled him to her and took her fair share of mouth to mouth.

'By the way,' she said, 'did you talk to the action painter?'

'I told her to get lost. That doesn't mean she will.'

'She better,' said Patience, pecking him a last time on the cheek before walking away.

He was unlocking his car when a heavy hand landed on his own. Clyde Moncur was standing next to him.

'Who the fuck are you?' the American spat, looking around him.

'Nobody,' Rebus said, shaking off the hand.

'I don't know what all that shit was about at the hotel, but you better stay far away from me, friend.'

'That might not be easy,' said Rebus. 'This is a small place. *My* town, not yours.'

Moncur took a step back. He'd be in his late-60s, but the hand he'd placed on Rebus's had stung. There was strength there, and determination. He was the sort of man who normally got his own way, whatever the cost.

'Who *are* you?'

Rebus pulled open the car door. He drove away without saying anything at all. Moncur watched him go. The American stood legs apart, and raised a hand to pat his jacket at chest height, nodding slowly.

A gun, Rebus thought. He's telling me he's got a gun. And he's telling me he'd use it, too.

23

Mairie Henderson had a flat in Portobello, on the coast east of the city. In Victorian times a genteel bathing resort, 'Porty' was still used by day trippers in summer. Mairie's tenement was on one of the streets between High Street and the Promenade. With his window rolled down, Rebus caught occasional wafts of salt air.

When his daughter Sammy was a kid they'd come to Porty beach for walks. The beach had been cleaned up by then, or at least covered with tons of sand from elsewhere. Rebus used to enjoy those walks, trouser legs rolled up past the ankles, feet treading the numbing water at the edge of the louring North Sea.

'If we kept walking, Daddy,' Sammy would say, pointing to the skyline, 'where would we go?'

'We'd go to the bottom of the sea.'

He could still see the dreadful look on her face. She'd be twenty this year. Twenty. He reached under his seat and let his hand wander till it touched his emergency pack of cigarettes. One wouldn't do any harm. Inside the pack, nestling amongst the cigarettes, was a slim disposable lighter.

The light was still on in Mairie's first-floor window. Her car was parked right outside the tenement's front door. He knew the back door led to a small enclosed drying-green. She'd have to come out the front. He hoped she'd bring Millie Docherty with her.

He didn't quite know why he thought Mairie was hiding

Millie; it was enough that he thought it. He'd had wrong hunches before, enough for a convention of the Quasimodo fan club, but you always had to follow them up. If you stopped being true to instinct, you were lost. His stomach rumbled, reminding him that olives and chipsticks did not a meal make. He thought of the Portobello chip shops, but sucked on his cigarette instead. He was across the road from the tenement and about six cars down. It was eleven o'clock and dark; no chance of Mairie spotting him.

He thought he knew why Clyde Moncur was in town. Same reason the ex-UVF man was here. He just didn't want to go public with his thoughts, not when he didn't know who his friends were.

At quarter past eleven, the tenement door opened and Mairie came out. She was alone, wearing a Burberry-style raincoat and carrying a bulging shopping bag. She looked up and down the street before unlocking her car and getting in.

'What are you nervous about, kid?' Rebus asked, watching her headlights come on. He lit another cigarette, just to wash down the first, and started his engine.

She took the Portobello Road back into the city. He hoped she wasn't going far. Tailing a car, even in the dark, wasn't as easy as the movies made it look, especially when the person you were tailing knew your car. The roads were quiet, making things trickier still, but at least she stuck to the main routes. If she'd used side streets and rat runs, she'd have spotted him for sure.

On Princes Street, the bikers were out in summer-night force, hitting the late-opening burger bars and revving up and down the straight. He wondered if Clyde Moncur was out for a post-prandial stroll. With the burgers and bikes, he'd probably feel right at home. Moncur was tough the way old people could get; seeming to shrink as they got older but that was only because they were losing juice, becoming rock-hard as a result. There was nothing soft left of Clyde Moncur. He had a handshake like a saloon-bar challenge. Even Patience had complained of it.

The night was delicious, perfect for a walk, and that's what most people were enjoying. Too bad for the Fringe shows: who wanted to sit in an airless, dark theatre for two hours while the real show was outside, continuous and absolutely free?

Mairie turned left at the west end, heading up Lothian Road. The street was already reeling with drunks. They'd probably be heading for a curry house or pizza emporium. Later, they'd regret this move. You saw the evidence each morning on the pavements. Just past the Tollcross lights, Mairie signalled to cross the oncoming traffic. Rebus wondered where the hell she was headed. His question was soon answered. She parked by the side of the road and turned off her lights. Rebus hurried past while she was locking her door, then stopped at the junction ahead. There was no traffic coming, but he sat there anyway, watching in his rearview.

'Well, well,' he said as Mairie crossed the road and went into the Crazy Hose Saloon. He put the car into reverse, brought it back, and squeezed in a few cars ahead of Mairie. He looked across at the Crazy Hose. The sign above was yellow and red flashing neon, which must be fun for the people in the tenement outside which Rebus was parked. A short flight of steps led to the main doors, and on these steps stood two bouncers. The Hose's wild west theme had passed the bouncers by, and they were dressed in regulation black evening suits, white shirts and black bow ties. Both had cropped hair to match their IQs, and held their hands behind their backs, swelling already prodigious chests. Rebus watched them open the doors for a couple of stetson-tipping cowpokes and their mini-dressed partners.

'In for a dime, I suppose.' He locked his car and walked purposefully across the road, trying to look like a man looking for a good time. The bouncers eyed him suspiciously, and did not open the door. Rebus decided he'd played enough games today, so he opened his ID and stuck it in the tallest bouncer's face. He wondered if the man could read.

'Police,' he said helpfully. 'Don't I get the door opened for me?'

'Only on your way out,' the smaller bouncer said. So Rebus pulled open the door and went in. The admission desk had been done up like an old bank, with vertical wooden bars in front of the smiling female face.

'Platinum Cowpoke Card,' Rebus said, again showing his ID. Past the desk was a fair-sized hallway where people were playing one-armed bandits. There was a large crowd around an interactive video game, where some bearded actor on film invited you to shoot him dead if you were quick enough on the draw. Most of the kids in front of the machine were dressed in civvies, though a few sported cowboy boots and bootlace ties. Big belt-buckles seemed mandatory, and both males and females wore Levi and Wrangler denims with good-sized turn-ups. The toilets were out here too, always supposing you could work out which you were, a Honcho or Honchette.

A second set of doors led to the dance hall and four bars, one in each corner of the vast arena. Plenty of money had been spent on the decor, with the choicest pieces being spotlit behind Perspex high up out of reach on the walls. There was a life-size cigar-store Indian, a lot of native head-dresses and jackets and the like, and what Rebus hoped was a replica of a Gatling-gun. Old western films played silently on a bank of TV screens set into one wall, and there was a bucking bronco machine against another wall. This was disused now, ever since a teenager had fallen from it and been put in a coma. They'd nearly shut the place down for that. Rebus didn't like to think about why they hadn't. He kept coming up with friends in the right places and money changing hands. There was something that looked like a font near one of the bars, but Rebus knew it was a spittoon. He noticed that the bar closest to it wasn't doing great business.

Rebus wasn't hard to pick out in a crowd. Although there were people there his own age, they were all wearing western dress to some degree, and they were nearly all dancing. There was a stage which was spotlit and full of instruments but empty of bodies. Instead the music came through the PA. A DJ in an enclosed box next to the stage babbled between songs; you could have heard him halfway to Texas.

'Can I help you?'

Not hard to pick out in the crowd, and of course the bouncers had sent word to the floor manager. He was in his late-twenties with slick black hair and a rhinestone waistcoat. The accent was strictly Lothian.

'Is Frankie in tonight?' If Bothwell were in the dancehall, he'd have spotted him. Bothwell's clothes would have drowned out the PA.

'I'm in charge.' The smile told Rebus he was as welcome as haemorrhoids at a rodeo.

'Well, there's no trouble, son, so I can put your mind at rest straight off. I'm just looking for a friend, only I didn't fancy paying the admission.'

The manager looked relieved. You could see he hadn't been in the job long. He'd probably been promoted from behind the bar. 'My name's Lorne Strang,' he said.

'And mine's Lorne Sausage.'

Strang smiled. 'My real name's Kevin.'

'Don't apologise.'

'Drink on the house?'

'I'd rather drink on a bar-stool, if that's all right with you.'

Rebus had given the dance floor a good look, and Mairie wasn't there, which meant she was either trapped in the Honchettes' or was somewhere behind the scenes. He wondered what she could be doing behind the scenes at Frankie Bothwell's club.

'So,' said Kevin Strang, 'who are you looking for?'

'Like I say, a friend. She said she'd be here. Maybe I'm a bit late.'

'The place is only just picking up now. We're open another two hours. What'll you have?' They were at the bar. The bar staff wore white aprons covering chest and legs and gold-coloured bands around their sleeves to keep their cuffs out of the way.

'Is that so they can't palm any notes?' asked Rebus.

'Nobody cheats the bar here.' One of the staff broke off serving someone to attend to Kevin Strang.

'Just a beer, please,' Rebus said.

'Draught? We only serve half pints.'

'Why's that?'

'There's more profit in it.'

'An honest answer. I'll have a bottle of Beck's.' He looked back to the dance floor. 'The last time I saw this many cowboys was at a builders' convention.'

The record was fading out. Strang patted Rebus's back. 'That's my cue,' he said. 'Enjoy yourself.'

Rebus watched him move through the dancers. He climbed onto the stage and tapped the microphone, sending a whump through the on-stage PA. Rebus didn't know what he was expecting. Maybe Strang would call out the steps of the next barn dance. But instead all he did was speak in a quiet voice, so people had to be quiet to hear him. Rebus didn't think Kevin Strang had much future as floor manager at the Crazy Hose.

'Dudes and womenfolk, it's a pleasure to see you all here at the Crazy Hose Saloon. And now, please welcome onto the Deadwood Stage our band for this evening's hoedown ... Chaparral!'

There was generous applause as the band emerged through a door at the back of the stage. A few of the arcade junkies had come in from the foyer. The band was a six-piece, barely squeezing onto the stage. Guitar/vocals, bass, drums, another guitar and two backing singers. They started into their first number a little shakily, but had warmed up by the end, by which time Rebus was finishing his drink and thinking about heading back to the car.

Then he saw Mairie.

No wonder she'd had a raincoat around her. Underneath she must have been wearing a tasselled black skirt, brown leather waistcoat, white blouse cut just above the chest and up around the shoulders, leaving a lot of bare flesh. She wasn't wearing a stetson, but there was a red kerchief around her throat and she was singing her heart out.

She was one of the backing singers.

Rebus ordered another drink and gawped at the stage. After a few songs, he could differentiate between Mairie's voice and that of the other backing singer. He noticed that most of the men were watching this singer. She was much taller than Mairie and had long straight black hair, plus she was wearing a much shorter skirt. But Mairie was the better singer. She sang with her eyes closed, swaying from the hips, knees slightly bent. Her partner used her hands a lot, but didn't gain much from it.

At the end of their fourth song, the male singer/guitarist gave a short spiel while the others in the band caught their breath, retuned, swigged drinks or wiped their faces. Rebus didn't know about C&W, but Chaparral seemed pretty good. They didn't just play mush about pet dogs, dying spouses or standing by your lover. Their songs had a harder, much urban feel, with lyrics to match.

'And if you don't know Hal Ketchum,' the singer was saying, 'you better get to know him. This is one of his, it's called Small Town Saturday Night.'

Mairie took lead vocal, her partner patting a tambourine and looking on. At the end of the song, the cheers were loud. The singer came back to his mike and raised his arm towards Mairie.

'Katy Hendricks, ladies and gentlemen.' The cheers resumed while Mairie took her bow.

After this they started into their own material, two songs whose intention was always ahead of ability. The singer mentioned that both were available on the band's first cassette, available to buy in the foyer.

'We're going to take a break now. So you can all go away for the next fifteen minutes, but be sure to come back.'

Rebus went into the foyer and dug six pounds out of his pocket. When he came back in, the band were at one of the bars, hoping to be bought drinks if half-time refreshments weren't on the house. Rebus shook the cassette in Mairie's ear.

'Miss Hendricks, would you autograph this, please?'

The band looked at him and so did Mairie. She took him by the lapels and propelled him away from the bar.

'What are you doing here?'

'Didn't you know? I'm a big country and western fan.'

'You don't like anything but sixties rock, you told me so yourself. Are you following me?'

'You sang pretty well.'

'*Pretty* well? I was great.'

'That's my Mairie, never one to hide her light under a tumbleweed. Why the false name?'

'You think I wanted those arseholes at the paper to find out?' Rebus tried to imagine the Hose full of drunken journos cheering their singer-scribe.

'No, I don't suppose so.'

'Anyway, everyone in the band uses an alias, it makes it harder for the DSS to find out they've been working.' She pointed at the tape. 'You bought that?'

'Well, they didn't hand it over as material evidence.'

She grinned. 'You liked us then?'

235

'I really did. I know I shouldn't be, but I'm amazed.'

She was almost persuaded onto this tack, but not quite. 'You still haven't said why you're following me.'

He put the tape in his pocket. 'Millie Docherty.'

'What about her?'

'I think you know where she is.'

'What?'

'She's scared, she needs help. She might just run to the reporter who's being wanting to see her. Reporters have been known to hide their sources away, protect them.'

'You think I'm hiding her?'

He paused. 'Has she told you about the pennant?'

'What pennant?'

Mairie had lost her cowgirl singer look. She was back in business.

'The one on Billy Cunningham's wall. Has she told you what he had hidden behind it?'

'What?'

Rebus shook his head. 'I'll make a deal,' he said. 'We'll talk to her together, that way neither of us is hiding anything. What do you say?'

The bassist handed Mairie an orange juice.

'Thanks, Duane.' She gulped it down until only ice was left. 'Are you staying for the second set?'

'Will it be worth my while?'

'Oh yes, we do a cracking version of "Country Honk".'

'That'll be the acid test.'

She smiled. 'I'll see you after the set.'

'Mairie, do you know who owns this place?'

'A guy called Boswell.'

'It's Bothwell. You don't know him?'

'Never met him. Why?'

The second set was paced like a foxtrot: two slow dances, two fast, then a slow, sad rendering of 'Country Honk' to end with. The floor was packed for the last dance, and

Rebus was flattered when a woman a good few years younger than him asked him up. But then her man came back from the Honchos', so that was the end of that.

As the band played a short upbeat encore, one fan climbed onstage and presented the backing singers with sheriff's badges, producing the loudest cheer of the night as both women pinned them on their chests. It was a good natured crowd, and Rebus had spent worse evenings. He couldn't see Patience enjoying it though.

When the band finished, they went back through the door they'd first appeared through. A few minutes later, Mairie reappeared, still dressed in all her gear and with the raincoat folded up in her shopping bag along with her flat-soled driving shoes.

'So?' Rebus said.

'So let's go.'

He started for the exit, but she was making towards the stage, gesturing for him to follow.

'I don't really want her to see me like this,' she said. 'I'm not sure the outfit conveys journalistic clout and professionalism. But I can't be bothered changing.'

They climbed onto the stage, then through the door. It led into a low-ceilinged passage of broom closets, crates of empty bottles, and a small room where in the evening the band got ready and during the day the cleaner could stop for a cup of tea. Beyond this was a dark stairwell. Mairie found the light switch and started to climb.

'Where exactly are we going?'

'The Sheraton.'

Rebus didn't ask again. The stairs were steep and twisting. They reached a landing where a padlocked door faced them, but Mairie kept climbing. At the second landing she stopped. There was another door, this time with no lock. Inside was a vast dark space, which Rebus judged to be the building's attic. Light infiltrated from the street through a skylight and some gaps in the roof, showing the solid forms of rafters.

'Watch you don't bump your head.'

The roofspace, though huge, was stifling. It seemed to be filled with tea chests, ladders, stacks of cloth which might have been old firemen's uniforms.

'She's probably asleep,' Mairie whispered. 'I found this place the first night we played here. Kevin said she could stay here.'

'You mean Lorne? He knows?'

'He's an old pal, he got us this residency. I told him she was a friend who'd come up for the Fringe but had nowhere to stay. I said I had eight people in my flat as it was. That's a lie by the way, I like my privacy. Where else was she going to stay? The city's bursting at the seams.'

'But what does she do all day?'

'She can go downstairs and boil a kettle, there's a loo there too. The club itself's off limits, but she's so scared I don't think she'd risk it anyway.'

She had led them past enough obstacles for a game of crazy golf, and now they were close to the front of the building. There were some small window panes here, forming a long thin arch. They were filthy, but provided a little more light.

'Millie? It's only me.' Mairie peered into the gloom. Rebus's eyes had become accustomed to the dark, but even so there were places enough she could be hiding. 'She's not here,' Mairie said. There was a sleeping bag on the floor: Rebus recognised it from the first time he'd met Millie. Beside it lay a torch. Rebus picked it up and switched it on. A paperback book lay face down on the floor.

'Where's her bag?'

'Her bag?'

'Didn't she have a bag of stuff?'

'Yes.' Mairie looked around. 'I don't see it.'

'She's gone,' said Rebus. But why would she leave the

sleeping-bag, book and torch? He moved the beam around the walls. 'This place is a junk shop.' An old red rubberised fire-hose snaked cross the floor. Rebus followed it with the beam all the way to a pair of feet.

He moved the beam up past splayed legs to the rest of the body. She was propped against the corner in a sitting position. 'Stay here,' he ordered, approaching the body, trying to keep the torch steady. The fire-hose was coiled around Millie Docherty's neck. Someone had tried strangling her with it, but they hadn't succeeded. The perished rubber had snapped. So instead they'd taken the brass nozzle and stuffed it down her throat. It was still there, looking like the mouth of a funnel. And that's what they'd used it as. Rebus put his nose close to the funnel and sniffed.

He couldn't be sure, but he thought they'd used acid. They'd tipped it down into her while she'd been choking on the nozzle. If he looked closer, he'd see her throat burnt away. He didn't look. He shone the torch on the floor instead. Her bag was lying there, its contents emptied onto the floorboards. There was something small and crumpled beside a wooden chest. He picked it up and flattened it out. It was the sleeve for a computer disk. Written on it were the letters SaS.

'Looks like they got what they wanted,' he said.

Nobody was dancing in the Crazy Hose Saloon.

Everyone had been sent home. Because the Hose was in Tollcross, it was C Division's business. They'd sent officers out from Torphichen Place.

'John Rebus,' one of the CID men said. 'You get around more than a Jehovah's Witness.'

'But I never try to sell you religion, Shug.'

Rebus watched DI Shug Davidson climb onto the stage and disappear through the door. They were all upstairs; the action was upstairs. They were setting up halogen lamps on tripods to assist the photographers. No key could be found for the first floor padlock, so they'd taken a sledgehammer to it. Rebus didn't like to ask who or what they thought they'd find hidden behind a door padlocked from the outside. He doubted it would be germane to the case. Only one thing was germane, and it was standing at the bar near the spittoon, drinking a long cold drink. Rebus walked over.

'Have you talked to your boss yet, Kevin?'

'I keep getting his answering machine.'

'Bad one.'

Kevin Strang nearly bit through the glass. 'How do you mean?'

'Bad for business.'

'Aye, right enough.'

'Mairie tells me you and her are friends?'

'Went to school together. She was a couple of years above me, but we were both in the school orchestra.'

'That's good, you'll have something to fall back on.'

'Eh?'

'If Bothwell sacks you, you can always busk for a living. Did you ever see her? Talk to her?'

Kevin knew who he meant. He was shaking his head before Rebus had finished asking.

'No?' Rebus persisted. 'You weren't even a wee bit curious? Didn't want to see what she looked like?'

'Never thought about it.'

Rebus looked across to the distant table where Mairie was being questioned by one of the Torphichen squad, with a WPC in close attendance. 'Bad one,' he said again. He leaned closer to Kevin Strang. 'Just between us, Kevin, who did you tell?'

'I didn't tell anyone.'

'Then you're going down, son.'

'How do you mean?'

'They didn't find her by accident, Kevin. They *knew* she

240

was there. Only two people could have provided that information: Mairie or you. C Division are hard bastards. They'll want to know all about you, Kevin. You're about the only suspect they've got.'

'I'm not a suspect.'

'She died about six hours ago, Kevin. Where were you six hours ago?' Rebus was making this up: they wouldn't know for sure until the pathologist took body temperature readings. But he reckoned it was a fair guess all the same.

'I'm telling you nothing.'

Rebus smiled. 'You're just snot, Kevin. Worse, you're hired snot.' He made to pat Kevin Strang's face, but Strang flinched, staggered back, and hit the spittoon. They watched it tip with a crash to the floor, rock to and fro, and then lie there. Nothing happened for a second, then with a wet sucking sound a thick roll of something barely liquid oozed out. Everyone looked away. The only thing Strang found to look at was Rebus. He swallowed.

'Look, I had to tell Mr Bothwell, just to cover myself. If I hadn't told him, and he'd found out ...'

'What did he say?'

'He just shrugged, said she was *my* responsibility.' He shuddered at the memory.

'Where were you when you told him?'

'In the office, off the foyer.'

'This morning?' Strang nodded. 'Tell me, Kevin, did Mr Bothwell go check out the lodger?'

Strang looked down at his empty glass. It was answer enough for Rebus.

There were strict rules covering the investigation of a serious crime such as murder. For one, Rebus should talk to the officer in charge and tell him everything he knew about Millie Docherty. For two, he should also mention his conversation with Kevin Strang. For three, he should then leave well alone and let C Division get on with it.

But at two in the morning, he was parked outside Frankie Bothwell's house in Ravelston Dykes, giving serious thought to going and ringing the doorbell. If nothing else, he might learn whether Bothwell's night attire was as gaudy as his daywear. But he dismissed the idea. For one thing, C Division would be speaking with Bothwell before the night was out, always supposing they managed to get hold of him. They would not want to be told by Bothwell that Rebus had beaten them to it.

For another, he was too late. He heard the garage doors lift automatically, and saw the dipped headlights as Bothwell's car, a gloss-black Merc with custom bodywork, bounced down off the kerb onto the road and sped away. So he'd finally got the message, and was on his way to the Hose. Either that or he was fleeing.

Rebus made a mental note to do yet more digging on Lee Francis Bothwell.

But for now, he was relieved the situation had been taken out of his hands. He drove back to Oxford Terrace at a sedate pace, trying hard not to fall asleep at the wheel. No one was waiting in ambush outside, so he let himself in quietly and went to the living room, his body too tired to stay awake but his mind too busy for sleep. Well, he had a cure for that: a mug of milky tea with a dollop of whisky in it. But there was a note on the sofa in Patience's handwriting. Her writing was better than most doctors', but not by much. Eventually Rebus deciphered it, picked up the phone, and called Brian Holmes.

'Sorry, Brian, but the note said to call whatever the time.'

'Hold on a sec.' He could hear Holmes getting out of bed, taking the cordless phone with him. Rebus imagined Nell Stapleton awake in the bed, rolling back over to sleep and cursing his name. The bedroom door closed. 'Okay,' said Holmes, 'I can talk now.'

'What's so urgent? Is it about our friend?'

'No, all's quiet on that front. I'll tell you about it in the morning. But I was wondering if you'd heard the news?'

'I was the one who found her.'

Rebus heard a fridge opening, a bottle being taken out, something poured into a glass.

'Found who?' Brian asked.

'Millie Docherty. Isn't that what we're talking about?' But of course it wasn't; Brian couldn't possibly know so soon. 'She's dead, murdered.'

'They're piling up, aren't they? What happened to her?'

'It's not a bedtime story. So what's your news?'

'A breakout from Barlinnie. Well, from a van actually, stopped between Barlinnie and a hospital. The whole thing was planned.'

Rebus sat down on the sofa. 'Cafferty?'

'He does a good impersonation of a perforated ulcer. It happened this evening. The prison van was sandwiched between two lorries. Masks, sawn-offs and a miracle recovery.'

'Oh Christ.'

'Don't worry, there are patrols all up and down the M8.'

'If he's coming back to Edinburgh, that's the last road he'll use.'

'You think he'll come back?'

'Get a grip, Brian, of course he's coming back. He's going to have to kill whoever butchered his son.'

24

He didn't get much sleep that night, in spite of the tea and whisky. He sat by the recessed bedroom window wondering when Cafferty would come. He kept his eyes on the stairwell outside until dawn came. His mind made up, he started packing. Patience sat up in bed.

'I hope you've left a note,' she said.

'We're both leaving, only not together. What's the score in an emergency?'

'My dream was making more sense than this.'

'Say you had to go away at very short notice?'

She was rubbing her hair, yawning. 'Someone would cover for me. What did you have in mind, elopement?'

'I'll put the kettle on.'

When he came back from the kitchen carrying two mugs of coffee, she was in the shower.

'What's happening?' she asked afterwards, rubbing herself dry.

'You're going to your sister's,' he told her. 'So drink your coffee, phone her, get dressed, and start packing.'

She took the mug from him. 'In that order?'

'Any order you like.'

'And where are you going?'

'Somewhere else.'

'Who'll feed the pets?'

'I'll get someone to do it, don't worry.'

'I'm not worried.' She took a sip of coffee. 'Yes I am. What *is* going on?'

'A bad man's coming to town.' Something struck him. 'There you are, that's another old film I like: *High Noon.*'

Rebus booked into a small hotel in Bruntsfield. He knew the night manager and phoned first, checking they had a room.

'You're lucky, we've one single.'

'How come you're not full?'

'The old gent who was in it, he's been coming here for years, he died of a stroke yesterday afternoon.'

'Oh.'

'You're not superstitious or anything?'

'Not if it's your only room.'

He climbed the steps to street level and looked around. When he was happy, he gestured for Patience to join him. She carried a couple of bags. Rebus was already holding her small suitcase. They put the stuff in the back of her car and embraced hurriedly.

'I'll call you,' he said. 'Don't try phoning me.'

'John . . .'

'Trust me on this if on nothing else, Patience, please.'

He watched her drive off, then hung around to make sure no one was following her. Not that he could be absolutely sure. They could pick her up on Queensferry Road. Cafferty wouldn't hesitate to use her, or anyone, to get to him. Rebus got his own bag from the flat, locked the flat tight, and headed for his car. On the way he stopped at the next door neighbour's door, dropping an envelope through the letterbox. Inside were keys to the flat and feeding instructions for Lucky the cat, the budgie with no name, and Patience's goldfish.

It was still early morning, the quiet streets unsuitable for a tail. Even so, he took every back route he could think of. The hotel was just a big family house really, converted into a small family hotel. Out front, where a garden once separated it from the pavement, tarmac had been laid, making a car park for half a dozen cars. But Rebus drove round the back and parked where the staff parked. Monty, the night manager, brought him in the back way, then led him straight up to his room. It was at the top of the house, all the way up one of the creakiest staircases Rebus had ever climbed. No one would be able to tiptoe up there without him and the woodworm knowing about it.

He lay on the solid bed wondering if lying on a dead man's bed was like stepping into his shoes. Then he started to think about Cafferty. He knew he was taking half-measures only. How hard would it be for Cafferty to track him down? A few men staked outside Fettes and St Leonard's and in a few well-chosen pubs, and Rebus would be in the gangster's hands by the end of the day. Fine, he just didn't want Patience involved, or Patience's home, or those of his friends.

Didn't most suicides do the same thing, come to hotels so as not to involve family and friends?

He could have gone home of course, back to his flat in Marchmont, but it was still full of students working in Edinburgh over the summer. He liked his tenants, and didn't want them meeting Cafferty. Come to that, he didn't want Monty the night manager meeting Cafferty either.

'He's not after *me*,' he kept reminding himself, hands behind his head as he stared at the ceiling. There was a clock radio by the bed, and he switched it on, catching the news. Police were still searching for Morris Gerald Cafferty. 'He's not after me,' he repeated. But in a sense, Cafferty *was*. He'd know Rebus was his best bet to finding the killers. There was a short item about the body at the Crazy Hose, though no gruesome details. Not yet, anyway.

When the news finished, he washed and went downstairs. He got a black cab to take him to St Leonard's. Once told the destination, the driver switched off his meter.

'On the house,' he said.

Rebus nodded and sat back. He'd commandeer someone's

car during the course of the day, either that or find a spare car from the pool. No one would complain. They all knew who'd put Cafferty in Barlinnie. At St Leonard's, he walked smartly into the station and went straight to the computer, tapping into Brains. Brains had a direct link to PNC2, the UK mainland police database at Hendon. As he'd expected, there wasn't much on Lee Francis Bothwell, but there was a note referring him to files kept by Strathclyde Police in Partick.

The officer he talked to in Partick was not thrilled.

'All that old stuff's in the attic,' he told Rebus. 'I'll tell you, one of these days the ceiling'll come down.'

'Just go take a look, eh? Fax it to me, save yourself a phone call.'

An hour later, Rebus was handed several fax sheets relating to activities of the Tartan Army and the Workers' Party in the early 1970s. Both groups had enjoyed short anarchic lives, robbing banks to finance their arms purchases. The Tartan Army had wanted independence for Scotland, at any price. What the Workers' Party had wanted Rebus couldn't recall, and there was no mention of their objectives in the fax. The Tartan Army had been the bigger terror of the two, breaking into explosives stores and Army bases, building up an arms cache for an insurrection which never came.

Frankie Bothwell was mentioned as a Tartan Army supporter, but with no evidence against him of illegal acts. Rebus reckoned this would be just before his move to the Orkneys and rebirth as Cuchullain. Cuchullain of the Red Hand.

Arch Gowrie was probably at breakfast when Rebus caught him. He could hear the clink of cutlery on plate.

'Sorry to disturb you so early, sir.'

'More questions, Inspector? Maybe I should start charging a consultancy fee.'

'I was hoping you could help me with a name.' Gowrie

made a noncommittal noise, or maybe he was just chewing.

'Lee Francis Bothwell.'

'Frankie Bothwell?'

'You know him?'

'I used to.'

'He was a member of the Orange Lodge?'

'Yes, he was.'

'But he got kicked out?'

'Not quite. He left voluntarily.'

'Might I ask why, sir?'

'You might.' There was a pause. 'He was ... unpredictable, had a temper on him. Most of the time he was fine. He coached the youth football teams for a couple of district lodges, he seemed to enjoy that.'

'Was he interested in history?'

'Yes, Scottish and Irish history.'

'Cuchullain?'

'Amongst other things. I think he wrote a couple of articles for *Ulster*, that's the magazine of the UDA. He did them under a pseudonym, so we couldn't discipline him, but the style was his. Loyalists, Inspector, are very interested in Irish pre-history. Bothwell was writing about the Cruithin. He was very bright like that, but he –'

'Did he have any links with the Orange Loyal Brigade?'

'Not that I know of, but it wouldn't surprise me. Gavin MacMurray's interested in pre-history too.' Gowrie sighed. 'Frankie left the Orange Lodge because he didn't feel we went far enough. That's as much as I'll say, but maybe it tells you something about him.'

'It does, Mr Gowrie, yes. Thanks for your help.'

Rebus put the phone down and thought it over. Then he shook his head sadly.

'You picked some place to hide her, Mairie. Some fucking place.'

His desk now looked like a skip, and he decided to do something about it. He filled his waste bin with empty cups, plates, crumpled papers and packets. Until, only slightly buried, he came to an A4-size manila envelope. His name was written on it in black marker pen. The envelope was fat. It hadn't been opened.

'Who left this here?'

But nobody seemed to know. They were too busy discussing another call made to the newspaper by the lunatic with the Irish accent. Nobody knew about The Shield, of course, not the way Rebus knew. The media had stuck to the theory that the body in Mary King's Close was that of the caller, a rogue from an IRA unit who'd been disciplined by his masters. It didn't make any sense now, but that didn't matter. There'd been another call now, another morning headline. '"Shut the Whole Thing Down," says Threat Man.' Rebus had considered what benefit SaS could derive from disrupting the Festival. Answer: none.

He looked at the envelope a final time, then ran his finger under the flap and eased out a dozen sheets of paper, photocopies of reports, news stories. American, the lot of them, though whoever had done the copying had been careful, leaving off letter headings, addresses, phone numbers. As Rebus read, he couldn't be sure where half the stories originated. But one thing *was* clear, they were all about one man.

Clyde Moncur.

There were no messages, nothing handwritten, nothing to identify the sender. Rebus checked the envelope. It hadn't been posted. It had been delivered by hand. He asked around again, but nobody owned up to having ever seen the thing before. Mairie was the only source he could think of, but she wouldn't have sent the stuff like this.

He read through the file anyway. It reinforced his impression of Clyde Moncur. The man was a snake. He ran drugs up into Vancouver and across to Ontario. His boats brought in immigrants from the Far East, or often didn't, though they were known to have picked up travellers along the way. What happened to them, these people who paid to be transported to a better life? The bottom of the deep blue sea, seemed to be the inference.

There were other murky areas to Moncur's life, like his undeclared interest in a fish processing plant outside Toronto ... Toronto, home of The Shield. The US Internal Revenue had been trying for years to get to the bottom of it all, and failing.

Buried in all the clippings was the briefest mention of a Scottish salmon farm.

Moncur had imported Scottish smoked salmon into the USA, though the Canadian stuff was just a mite closer to hand. The salmon farm he used was just north of Kyle of Lochalsh. Its name struck home. Rebus had come across the name very recently. He went back to the files on Cafferty, and there it was. Cafferty had been legitimate part-owner of the farm in the 1970s and early 80s ... around the time him and Jinky Johnson were washing and drying dirty money for the UVF.

'This is beautiful,' Rebus said to himself. He hadn't just squared the circle, he'd created an unholy triangle out of it.

He got a patrol car to take him to the Gar-B.

From the back seat, he had a more relaxed view of the whole of Pilmuir. Clyde Moncur had talked about the early Scottish settlers. The new settlers, of course, took on just as tough a life, moving into the private estates which were being built around and even *in* Pilmuir. This was a frontier life, complete with marauding natives who wanted the intruders gone, border skirmishes, and wilderness experiences aplenty. These estates provided starter homes for those making the move from the rented sector. They also provided starter courses in basic survival.

Rebus wished the settlers well.

When they got to the Gar-B, Rebus gave the uniforms their instructions and sat in the back seat enjoying the stares of passers-by. They were away a while, but when they came back one of them was pulling a boy by his forearm and pushing the boy's bike. The other one had two kids, no bikes. Rebus looked at them. He recognised the one with the bike.

'You can let the others go,' he said. 'But him, I want in here with me.'

The boy got into the car reluctantly. His pals ran as soon as the officers released them. When they were far enough away, they turned to watch. They wanted to know what would happen.

'What's your name, son?' Rebus asked.

'Jock.'

Maybe it was true and maybe it wasn't. Rebus wasn't bothered. 'Shouldn't you be at school, Jock?'

'We've no' started back yet.'

This too could be true; Rebus didn't know. 'Do you remember me, son?'

'It wasnae me did your tyres.'

Rebus shook his head. 'That's all right. I'm not here about that. But you remember when I came here?' The boy nodded. 'Remember you were with a pal, and he thought I was someone else. Remember? He asked me where my flash car was.' The boy shook his head. 'And you told him that I wasn't who he thought I was. Who did he think I was, son?'

'I don't know.'

'Yes you do.'

'I don't.'

'But someone a bit like me, eh? Similar build, age, height? Fancier clothes though, I'll bet.'

'Maybe.'

'What about his car, the swanky car?'

'A custom Merc.'

Rebus smiled. There were some things boys just had eyes and a memory for. 'What colour Merc?'

'Black, all of it. The windows too.'

'Seen him here a lot?'

'Don't know.'

'Nice car though, eh?'

The boy shrugged.

'Right, son, on you go.'

The boy knew from the pleased look on the policeman's face that he'd made a mistake, that he'd somehow helped. His cheeks burned with shame. He snatched his bike from the constable and ran with it, looking back from time to time. His pals were waiting to question him.

'Get what you were looking for, sir?' asked one of the uniforms, getting back into the car.

'Exactly what I was looking for,' said Rebus.

25

He went to see Mairie, but a friend was looking after her and Mairie herself was sleeping. The doctor had given her a few sleeping pills. Left alone in the flat with an unconscious Mairie, he could have gone through her notes and computer files, but the friend didn't even let him over the threshold. She had a pinched face with prominent cheeks and a few too many teeth in her quiet but determined mouth.

'Tell her I called,' Rebus said, giving up. He had retrieved his car from the back of the hotel. Cafferty would find him, with or without the rust-bucket to point the way. He drove to Fettes where DCI Kilpatrick had an update on the Clyde Moncur surveillance.

'He's acting the tourist, John, no more or less. He and his wife are admiring the sights, taking bus tours, buying souvenirs.' Kilpatrick sat back in his chair. 'The men I put on it are restless. Like they say, it's hardly likely he's here on business when his wife's with him.'

'Or else it's the perfect cover.'

'A couple more days, John, that's all we can give it.'

'I appreciate it, sir.'

'What about this body at the Crazy Hose?'

'Millie Docherty, sir.'

'Yes, any ideas?'

Rebus just shrugged. Kilpatrick didn't seem to expect an answer. Part of his mind was still on Calumn Smylie. They were about to open an internal inquiry. There would be questions to answer about the whole investigation.

'I hear you had a run in with Smylie,' Kilpatrick said.

So Ormiston had been talking. 'Just one of those things, sir.'

'Watch out for Smylie, John.'

'That's all I seem to do these days, sir, watch out for people.' But he knew now that Smylie was the least of his problems.

At St Leonard's, DCI Lauderdale was fighting his corner, arguing that his team should take on the Millie Docherty investigation from C Division. So he was too busy to come bothering Rebus, and that was fine by Rebus.

Officers were out at Lachlan Murdock's flat, talking to him. He was being treated as a serious suspect now; you didn't lose two flatmates to hideous deaths and not come under the microscope. Murdock would be on the petri dish from now till the case reached some kind of conclusion. Rebus returned to his desk. Since he'd last been there, earlier in the day, people had started using it as a rubbish bin again.

He phoned London, and waited to be passed along the line. It was not a call he could have made from Fettes.

'Abernethy speaking.'

'About bloody time. It's DI Rebus here.'

'Well well. I wondered if I'd hear from you.'

Rebus could imagine Abernethy leaning back in his chair. Maybe his feet were up on the desk in front of him. 'I must have left a dozen messages, Abernethy.'

'I've been busy, what about you?' Rebus stayed silent. 'So, Inspector Rebus, how can I help?'

'I've got a few questions. How much stuff is the Army losing?'

'You've lost me.'

'I don't think so.' Someone walking past offered Rebus a cigarette. Without thinking he accepted it. But then the donor walked away, leaving Rebus without a light. He sucked on the filter anyway. 'I think you know what I'm talking about.' He opened the desk drawers, looking for matches or a lighter.

'Well, I don't.'

'I think material has been going missing.'

'Really?'

'Yes, really.' Rebus waited. He didn't want to speculate too wildly, and he certainly didn't want Abernethy to know any more than was necessary. But there was silence on the other end of the line. 'Or you suspect it's going missing.'

'That would be a matter for Army Intelligence or the security service.'

'Yes, but you're Special Branch, aren't you? You're the public arm of the security service. I think you came up here in a hurry because you damned well know what's going on. The question is, why did you disappear again in such a hurry too?'

'You've lost me again. Maybe I'd better pack my bag for a trip, what do you say?'

Rebus didn't say anything, he just put down the phone. 'Anyone got a light?' Someone tossed a box of matches onto the desk. 'Cheers.' He lit the cigarette and inhaled, the smoke rattling his nerves like they were dice in a cup.

He knew Abernethy would come.

He kept moving, the most difficult kind of target. He was trusting to his instincts; after all, he had to trust something. Dr Curt was in his office at the university. To get to the office you had to walk past a row of wooden boxes marked with the words 'Place Frozen Sections Here'. Rebus had never looked in the boxes. In the Pathology building, you kept your eyes front and your nostrils tight. They were doing some work in the quadrangle. Scaffolding had been erected, and a couple of workmen were belying their name by sitting on it smoking cigarettes and sharing a newspaper.

'Busy, busy, busy,' Curt said, when Rebus reached his office. 'You know, most of the university staff are on holiday.

I've had postcards from the Gambia, Queensland, Florida.' He sighed. 'I am cursed with a vocation while others get a vacation.'

'I bet you were awake all night thinking up that one.'

'I was awake half the night thanks to your discovery at the Crazy Hose Saloon.'

'Post-mortem?'

'Not yet complete. It was a corrosive of some kind, the lab will tell us exactly which. I am constantly surprised by the methods murderers will resort to. The fire hose was new to me.'

'Well, it stops the job becoming routine, I suppose.'

'How's Caroline?'

'I'd forgotten all about her.'

'You must pray that she'll let you.'

'I stopped praying a long time ago.'

He walked back down the stairs and out into the quadrangle, wondering if it was too soon in the day for a drink at Sandy Bell's. The pub was just round the corner, and he hadn't been there in months. He noticed someone standing in front of the Frozen Sections boxes. They had the flap open, like they'd just made a deposit. Then they turned around towards Rebus and smiled.

It was Cafferty.

'Dear God.'

Cafferty closed the flap. He was dressed in a baggy black suit and open-necked white shirt, like an undertaker on his break. 'Hello, Strawman.' The old nickname. It was like an ice-pack on Rebus's spine. 'Let's talk.' There were two men behind Rebus, the two from the churchyard, the two who'd watched him taking a beating. They escorted him back to a newish Rover parked in the quadrangle. He caught the licence number, but felt Cafferty's hand land on his shoulder.

'We'll change plates this afternoon, Strawman.' Someone was getting out of the car. It was weasel-face. Rebus and Cafferty got into the back of the car, weasel-face and one

256

of the heavies into the front. The other heavy stood outside, blocking Rebus's door. He looked towards where the scaffolding stood. The workmen had vanished. There was a sign on the scaffolding, just the name of a firm and their telephone number. A light came on in practically the last dark room in Rebus's head.

Big Ger Cafferty had made no effort at disguise. His clothes didn't look quite right – a bit large and not his style – but his face and hair were unchanged. A couple of students, one Asian and one Oriental, walked across the quadrangle towards the Pathology building. They didn't so much as glance at the car.

'I see your stomach cleared up.'

Cafferty smiled. 'Fresh air and exercise, Strawman. You look like you could do with both.'

'You're crazy coming back here.'

'We both know I had to.'

'We'll have you inside again in a matter of days.'

'Maybe I only need a few days. How close are you?'

Rebus stared through the windscreen. He felt Cafferty's hand cover his knee.

'Speaking as one father to another . . .'

'You leave my daughter out of this!'

'She's in London, isn't she? I've a lot of friends in London.'

'And I'll tear them to shreds if she so much as stubs a toe.'

Cafferty smiled. 'See? See how easy it is to get worked up when it's family?'

'It's not family with you, Cafferty, you said so yourself. It's business.'

'We could do a trade.' Cafferty looked out of his window, as though thinking. 'Say someone's been bothering you, could be an old flame. Let's say she's been disrupting your life, making things awkward.' He paused. 'Making you see red.'

Rebus nodded to himself. So weasel-face had witnessed the little scene with the spray-can.

'My problem, not yours.'

Cafferty sighed. 'Sometimes I wonder how hard you really are.' He looked at Rebus. 'I'd like to find out.'

'Try me.'

'I will, Strawman, one day. Trust me on that.'

'Why not now? Just you and me?'

Cafferty laughed. 'A square go? I haven't the time.'

'You used to shuffle cash around for the UVF, didn't you?' The question caught Cafferty unaware. 'Did I?'

'Till Jinky Johnson disappeared. You were in pretty tight with the terrorists. Maybe that's where you heard of the SaS. Billy was a member.'

Cafferty's eyes were glassy. 'I don't know what you're saying.'

'No, but you know what I'm talking about. Ever heard the name Clyde Moncur?'

'No.'

'That sounds like another lie to me. What about Alan Fowler?'

Now Cafferty nodded. 'He was UVF.'

'Not now he isn't. Now he's SaS, and he's here. They're *both* here.'

'Why are you telling me?' Rebus didn't answer. Cafferty moved his face closer. 'It's not because you're scared. There's something else ... What's on your mind, Rebus?' Rebus stayed silent. He saw Dr Curt coming out of the Pathology building. Curt's car, a blue Saab, was parked three cars away from the Rover.

'You've been busy,' Cafferty said.

Now Curt was looking over towards the Rover, at the big man standing there and the men seated inside.

'Any more names?' Cafferty was beginning to sound impatient, losing all his cool veneer. 'I want *all of them*!' His right hand lashed around Rebus's throat, his left hand pushing him deep into the corner of the seat. 'Tell me all of it, all of it!'

258

Curt had turned as though forgetting something, and was walking back towards the building. Rebus blinked away the water in his eyes. The stooge outside thumped on the bodywork. Cafferty released his grip and watched Curt going back into Pathology. He used both hands to grasp Rebus's face, turning it towards his, holding Rebus with the pressure of his palms on Rebus's cheekbones.

'We'll meet again, Rebus, only it won't be like in the song.' Rebus felt like his head was going to crack, but then the pressure stopped.

The heavy outside opened the door and he got out fast. As the heavy got in, the driver gunned the engine. The back window went down, Cafferty looking at him, saying nothing.

The car sped off, tyres screeching as it turned into the one-way traffic on Teviot Place. Dr Curt appeared in the Pathology doorway, then came briskly across the quadrangle.

'Are you all right? I've just phoned the police.'

'Do me a favour, when they get here tell them you were mistaken.'

'What?'

'Tell them anything, but don't tell them it was me.'

Rebus started to move off. Maybe he'd have that drink at Sandy Bell's. Maybe he'd have three.

'I'm not a very good liar,' Dr Curt called after him.

'Then the practice will be good for you,' Rebus called back.

Frankie Bothwell shook his head again.

'I've already spoken with the gentlemen from Torphichen Place. You want to ask anyone, ask them.'

He was being difficult. He'd had a difficult night, what with being dragged from his bed and then staying up till all hours dealing with the police, answering their questions, explaining the stash of cased spirits they'd found on the first floor. He didn't need this.

'But you knew Miss Murdoch was upstairs,' Rebus persisted.

'Is that right?' Bothwell wriggled on his barstool and tipped ash onto the floor.

'You were told she was upstairs.'

'Was I?'

'Your manager told you.'

'You've only got his word for that.'

'You deny he said it? Maybe if we could get the two of you together?'

'You can do what you like, he's out on his ear anyway. I sacked him first thing. Can't have people dossing upstairs like that, bad for the club's image. Let them sleep on the streets like everyone else.'

Rebus tried to imagine what resemblance the kid at the Gar-B had seen between himself and Frankie Bothwell. He was here because he was feeling reckless. Plus he'd put a few whiskies away in Sandy Bell's. He was here because he quite fancied beating Lee Francis Bothwell to a bloody mush on the dance floor.

Stripped of music and flashing lights and drink and dancers, the Crazy Hose had as much life as a warehouse full of last year's fashions. Bothwell, appearing to dismiss Rebus from his mind, lifted one foot and began to rub some dust from a cowboy boot. Rebus feared the white trousers would either split or else eviscerate their wearer. The boot was black and soft with small puckers covering it like miniature moon craters. Bothwell caught Rebus looking at it.

'Ostrich skin,' he explained.

Meaning the craters were where each feather had been plucked. 'Look like a lot of little arseholes,' Rebus said admiringly. Bothwell straightened up. 'Look, Mr Bothwell, all I want are a couple of answers. Is that so much to ask?'

'And then you'll leave?'

'Straight out the door.'

Bothwell sighed and flicked more ash onto the floor. 'Okay then.'

Rebus smiled his appreciation. He rested his hand on the bar and leaned towards Bothwell.

'Two questions,' he said. 'Why did you kill her and who's got the disk?'

Bothwell stared at him, then laughed. 'Get out of here.'

Rebus lifted his hand from the bar. 'I'm going,' he said. But he stopped at the doors to the foyer, holding them open. 'You know Cafferty's in town?'

'Never heard of him.'

'That's not the point. The point is, has *he* heard of *you*? Your father was a minister. Did you ever learn Latin?'

'What?'

'*Nemo me impune lacessit.*' Bothwell didn't even blink. 'Never mind, it won't worry Cafferty one way or the other. See, you didn't just meddle with him, you meddled with his family.'

He let the doors swing shut behind him. This was the way he should have worked it throughout, using Cafferty – the mere threat of Cafferty – to do his work for him. But would Cafferty be enough to scare the American and the Ulsterman?

Somehow, John Rebus doubted it.

Back at St Leonard's, Rebus first phoned the scaffolding company, then placed a call to Peter Cave.

'Something I've been meaning to ask you, sir,' he said.

'Yes?' Cave sounded tired, deep down inside.

'Since the Church stopped supporting the youth club, how do you survive?'

'We manage. Everyone who comes along has to pay.'

'Is it enough?'

'No.'

'You're not subsidising the place out of your own pocket?' Cave laughed at this. 'What then? Sponsorship?'

261

'In a way, yes.'

'What sort of way?'

'Just someone who saw the good the club was doing.'

'Someone you know?'

'Never met him, as a matter of fact.'

Rebus took a stab. 'Francis Bothwell?'

'How did you know that?'

'Someone told me,' Rebus lied.

'Davey?'

So Davey Soutar *did* know Bothwell. Yes, it figured. Maybe from a district lodge football team, maybe some other way. Time to change track.

'What does Davey do by the way?'

'Works in an abattoir.'

'He's not a builder then?'

'No.'

'One last thing, Mr Cave. I got a name from a scaffolding company: Malky Haston. He's eighteen, lives in the Gar-B.'

'I know Malky, Inspector. And he knows you.'

'How's that?'

'Heavy metal fan, always wears a band t-shirt. You've spoken with him.'

Black t-shirt, thought Rebus, Davey Soutar's pal. With white flecks in his hair that Rebus had mistaken for dandruff.

'Thank you, Mr Cave,' Rebus said, 'I think that's everything.'

Everything he needed.

A uniform approached as he put down the phone, and handed Rebus the information he'd requested on recent and not-so-recent break-ins. Rebus knew what he was looking for, and it didn't take long. Acid wasn't that easy to come by, not unless you had a plausible reason for wanting it. Easier to steal the stuff if you could. And where could you find acid?

Break-ins at Craigie Comprehensive School were fairly

standard. It was like pre-employment training for the unrulier pupils. They learned to slip a window-catch and jemmy open a door, some graduated to lock-picking, and others became fences for the stolen goods. It was always a buyers' market, but then economics was not a strong point with these junior careerists. Three months back, Craigie had been entered at the dead of night and the tuck shop emptied.

They'd also broken into the science rooms, physics and chemistry. The chemistry stock room had a different lock, but they took that out too, and made off with a large jar of methylated spirits, a few other choice cocktail ingredients, and three thick glass jars of various acids.

The caretaker, who lived in a small pre-fabricated house on the school grounds, saw and heard nothing. He'd been watching a special comedy night on the television. Probably he wouldn't have ventured out of doors anyway. Craigie Comprehensive wasn't exactly full of pupils with a sense of humour or love for their elders.

What could you expect from a school whose catchment area included the infamous Garibaldi Estate?

He was putting the pieces together when Chief Inspector Lauderdale came over.

'As if we're not stretched thin enough,' Lauderdale complained.

'What's that?'

'Another anonymous threat, that's twice today. He says our time's up.'

'Shame, I was just beginning to enjoy myself. Any specifics?'

Lauderdale nodded distractedly. 'A bomb. He didn't say where. He says it's so big there'll be no hiding place.'

'Festival's nearly over,' Rebus said.

'I know, that's what worries me.' Yes, it worried Rebus too.

Lauderdale turned to walk away, just as Rebus's phone rang.

'Inspector, my name's Blair-Fish, you won't remember me...'

'Of course I remember you, Mr Blair-Fish. Have you called to apologise about your grand-nephew again?'

'Oh no, nothing like that. But I'm a bit of a local historian, you see.'

'Yes.'

'And I was contacted by Matthew Vanderhyde. He said you wanted some information about Sword and Shield.'

Good old Vanderhyde: Rebus had given up on him. 'Go on, please.'

'It's taken me a while. There was thirty years of detritus to wade through...'

'What have you got, Mr Blair-Fish?'

'Well, I've got notes of some meetings, a treasurer's report, minutes and things like that. Plus the membership lists. I'm afraid they're not complete.'

Rebus sat forward in his chair. 'Mr Blair-Fish, I'd like to send someone over to collect everything from you. Would that be all right?' Rebus was reaching for pen and paper.

'Well, I suppose ... I don't see why not.'

'Let's look on it as final atonement for your grand-nephew. Now if you'll just give me your address...'

Locals called it the Meat Market, because it was sited close to the slaughterhouse. Workers from the slaughterhouses wandered in at lunchtime for pints, pies and cigarettes. Sometimes they wore flecks of blood; the owner didn't mind. He'd been one of them once, working the jet-air gun at a chicken factory. The pistol, hooked up to a compressor, had taken the heads off several hundred stunned chickens per hour. He ran the Meat Market with the same unruffled facility.

It wasn't lunchtime, so the Market was quiet – two old

men drinking slow half pints at opposite ends of the bar, ignoring one another so studiously that there had to be a grudge between them, and two unemployed youths shooting pool and trying to make each game last, their pauses between shots the stuff of chess games. Finally, there was a man with sparks in his eyes. The proprietor was keeping a watch on him. He knew trouble when he saw it. The man was drinking whisky and water. He looked the sort of drinker, when he was mortal you wouldn't want to get in his way. He wasn't getting mortal just now; he was making the one drink last. But he didn't look like he was enjoying anything about it. Finally he finished the quarter gill.

'Take care,' the proprietor said.

'Thanks,' said John Rebus, heading for the door.

Slaughterhouse workers are a different breed.

They worked amid brain and offal, thick blood and shit, in a sanitised environment of whitewash and piped radio music. A huge electrical unit reached down from the ceiling to suck the smell away and pump in fresh air. The young man hosing blood into a drain did so expertly, spraying none of the liquid anywhere other than where he wanted it. And afterwards he turned down the pressure at the nozzle and hosed off his black rubber boots. He wore a white rubberised apron round his neck and stretching down to his knees, as did most of those around him. Aprons to Rebus meant barmen, masons and butchers. He was reminded only of this last as he walked across the floor.

They were working with cattle. The cows looked young and fearful, eyes bulging. They'd probably already been injected with muscle relaxants, so moved drunkenly along the line. A jolt of electricity behind either ear numbed them, and quickly the wielder of the bolt-gun took aim with the cold muzzle hard against each skull. Their back legs seemed to crumple first. Already the light was vanishing from behind their eyes.

He'd been told Davey Soutar was working near the back of the operation, so he had to pick his way around the routine. Men and women speckled with blood smiled and nodded as he passed. They all wore hats to keep their hair off the meat.

Or perhaps to keep the meat off their hair.

Soutar was by the back wall, resting easily against it, hands tucked into the front of his apron. He was talking to a girl, chatting her up perhaps.

So romance isn't dead, thought Rebus.

Then Soutar saw him, just as Rebus slipped on a wet patch of floor. Soutar placed him immediately, and seemed to raise his head and roll his eyes in defeat. Then he ran forward and picked something up from a shiny metal table. He was fumbling with it as Rebus advanced. It was only when Soutar took aim and the girl screamed that Rebus realised it was a bolt-gun. There was the sound of a two-pound hammer hitting a girder. The bolt flew, but Rebus dodged it. Soutar threw the gun at him and dived for the rear wall, hitting the bar of the emergency exit. The door swung open then closed again behind him. The girl was still screaming as Rebus ran towards her, pushed the horizontal bar to unlock the door, and stumbled into the abattoir's back yard.

There were a couple of large transporters in the middle of disgorging their doomed cargo. The animals were sending out distress calls as they were fed into holding pens. The entire rear area was walled in, so nobody from the outside world could glimpse the spectacle. But if you went around the transporters, a lane led back to the front of the building. Rebus was about to head that way when the blow felled him. It had come from behind. On his hands and knees, he half-turned his head to see his attacker. Soutar had been hiding behind the door. He was holding a long metal stick, a cattle prod. It was this which he had swung at Rebus's head, catching him on the left ear. Blood dropped onto the ground. Soutar lunged with the pole, but Rebus caught it and managed to pull himself up. Soutar kept moving forwards, but though wiry and young he did not possess the older man's bulk and strength. Rebus twisted the pole from his hands, then dodged the kick which Soutar aimed at him. Kick-fighting wasn't so easy with rubber boots on.

Rebus wanted to get close enough to land a good punch or kick of his own, or even to wrestle Soutar to the ground. But Soutar reached into his apron and came out with a gold-coloured butterfly knife, flicking its two moulded wings to make a handle for the vicious looking blade.

'There's more than one way to skin a pig,' he said, grinning, breathing hard.

'I like it when there's an audience,' Rebus said. Soutar turned for a second to take in the sight of the cattle herders, all of whom had stopped work to watch the fight. By the time he looked back, Rebus had caught the knife hand with the toe of his shoe, sending the knife clattering to the ground. Soutar came straight for him then, butting him on the bridge of the nose. It was a good hit. Rebus's eyes filled with tears, he felt energy earth out of him into the ground, and blood ran down his lips and chin.

'You're dead!' Soutar screamed. 'You just don't know it yet!' He picked up his knife, but Rebus had the metal pole, and swung it in a wide arc. Soutar hesitated, then ran for it. He took a short cut, climbing the rail which funnelled the cattle into the pens, then leaping one of the cows and clearing the rail at the other side.

'Stop him!' Rebus called, spraying blood. 'I'm a police officer!' But by then Davey Soutar was out of sight. All you could hear were his rubber boots flapping as he ran.

The doctor at the Infirmary had seen Rebus several times before, and tutted as usual before getting to work. She confirmed what he knew: the nose was not broken. He'd been lucky. The cut to his ear required two stitches, which she did there and then. The thread she used was thick and black and ugly.

'Whatever happened to invisible mending?'

'It wasn't a deterrent.'

'Fair point.'

'If it stings, you can always get your girlfriend to lick your wounds.'

Rebus smiled. Was that a chat-up line? Well, he had enough problems without adding another to the inventory. So he didn't say anything. He acted the good patient, then went to Fettes and filed the assault.

'You look like Ken Buchanan on a good night,' said Ormiston. 'Here's the stuff you wanted. Claverhouse has gone off in a huff; he didn't like being turned into a messenger boy.'

Ormiston patted the heavy package on Rebus's desk. It was a large brown cardboard box, smelling of dust and old paper. Rebus opened it and took out the ledger book which served as a membership record for the original Sword and Shield. The blue fountain-ink had faded, but each surname was in capitals so it didn't take him long. He sat staring at the two names, managing a short-lived smile. Not that he'd anything to smile about, not really. There was nothing to be proud of. His desk drawer didn't lock, but Ormiston's did. He took the ledger with him.

'Has the Chief seen this?' Ormiston shook his head.

'He's been out of the office since before it arrived.'

'I want it kept safe. Can you lock it in your drawer?' He watched Ormiston open the deep drawer, drop the package in, then shut it again and lock it.

'Tighter than a virgin's,' Ormiston confirmed.

'Thanks. Listen, I'm going out hunting.'

Ormiston drew the key out of the lock and pocketed it. 'Count me in,' he said.

26

Not that Rebus expected to find Davey Soutar at home; he doubted Soutar was quite that daft. But he did want to take a look, and now he had the excuse. He also had Ormiston, who looked threatening enough to dissuade anyone who might look like complaining. Ormiston, cheered by the story of how Rebus came by his cuts and bruises (his eyes were purpling and swelling nicely, a consequence of the head butt), was further cheered by the news that they were headed for the Gar-B.

'They should open the place as a safari park,' he opined. 'Remember those places? They used to tell you to keep your car doors locked and your windows rolled up. Same advice I'd give to anyone driving through the Gar-B. You never know when the baboons will stick their arses in your face.'

'Did you ever find anything about Sword and Shield?'

'You never expected us to,' Ormiston said. When Rebus looked at him, he laughed coldly. 'I might look daft, but I'm not. You're not daft either, are you? Way you're acting, I'd say you think you've cracked it.'

'Paramilitaries in the Gar-B,' Rebus said quietly, keeping his eyes on the road. 'And Soutar's in it up to his neck and beyond.'

'He killed Calumn?'

'Could be. A knife's his style.'

'Not Billy Cunningham though?'

'No, he didn't kill Billy.'

'Why are you telling me all this?'

Rebus turned to him for a moment. 'Maybe I just want someone else to know.'

Ormiston weighed this remark. 'You think you're in trouble?'

'I can think of half a dozen people who'd throw confetti at my funeral.'

'You should take this to the Chief.'

'Maybe. Would you?'

Ormiston thought about this. 'I haven't known him long, but I heard good things from Glasgow, and he seems pretty straight. He expects us to show initiative, work off our own backs. That's what I like about SCS, the leeway. I hear you like a bit of leeway yourself.'

'That reminds me, Lee Francis Bothwell: know him?'

'He owns that club, the one with the body in it?'

'That's him.'

'I know he should change the music.'

'What to?'

'Acid house.'

It was worth a laugh, but Rebus didn't oblige. 'He's an acquaintance of my assailant.'

'What is he, slumming it?'

'I'd like to ask him, but I can't see him answering. He's been putting money into the youth club.' Rebus was measuring each utterance, wondering how much to feed Ormiston.

'Very civic minded of him.'

'Especially for someone who got kicked out of the Orange Lodge on grounds of zeal.'

Ormiston frowned. 'How are you doing for evidence?'

'The youth club leader's admitted the connection. Some kids I spoke to a while back thought I was Bothwell, only my car wasn't flash enough. He drives a customised Merc.'

'How do you read it?'

'I think Peter Cave blundered with good intention into

something that was already happening. I think something very bad is happening in the Gar-B.'

They had to take a chance on parking the car and leaving it. If Rebus had thought about it, he'd have brought one other man, someone to guard the wheels. There were kids loitering by the parking bays, but not the same kids who'd done his tyres before, so he handed over a couple of quid and promised a couple more when he came back.

'It's dearer than the parking in town,' Ormiston complained as they headed for the high-rises. The Soutars' high-rise had been renovated, with a sturdy main door added to stop undesirables congregating in the entrance hall or on the stairwells. The entrance hall had been decorated with a green and red mural. Not that you would know any of this to look at the place. The lock had been smashed, and the door hung loosely on its hinges. The mural had been all but blocked out by penned graffiti and thick black coils of spray paint.

'Which floor are they on?' Ormiston asked.

'The third.'

'Then we'll take the stairs. I don't trust the lifts in these places.'

The stairs were at the end of the hall. Their walls had become a winding scribble-pad, but they didn't smell too bad. At each turn in the stairs lay empty cider cans and cigarette stubs. 'What do they need a youth club for when they've got the stairwell?' Ormiston asked.

'What've you got against the lift?'

'Sometimes the kids'll wait till you're between floors then shut off the power.' He looked at Rebus. 'My sister lives in one of those H-blocks in Oxgangs.'

They entered the third floor at the end of a long hallway which seemed to be doubling as a wind tunnel. There were fewer scribbles on the walls, but there were also smeared patches, evidence that the inhabitants had been cleaning the stuff off. Some of the doors offered polished brass name

271

plaques and bristle doormats. But most were also protected by a barred iron gate, kept locked shut when the flats were empty. Each flat had a mortice deadlock as well as a Yale, and a spyhole.

'I've been in jails with laxer security.'

But conspicuously, the door with the name Soutar on it had no extra security, no gate or spyhole. This fact alone told Rebus a lot about Davey Soutar, or at least about his reputation amongst his peers. Nobody was going to break into Davey's flat.

There was neither bell nor knocker, so Rebus banged his fist against the meat of the door. After a wait, a woman answered. She peered out through a chink, then opened the door wide.

'Fuckin' polis,' she said. It was a statement of fact rather than a judgment. 'Davey, I suppose?'

'It's Davey,' said Rebus.

'He did that to you?' She meant Rebus's face, so he nodded. 'And what were you doing to him?'

'Just the usual, Mrs Soutar,' Ormiston interrupted. 'A length of lead pipe on the soles of the feet, a wet towel over the face, you know how it is.'

Rebus nearly said something, but Ormiston had judged her right. Mrs Soutar smiled tiredly and stepped back into her hall. 'You'd better come in. A bit of steak would stop those eyes swelling, but all I've got is half a pound of mince, and it's the economy stuff. You'd get more meat from a butcher's pencil. This is my man, Dod.'

She had led them along the short narrow hall and into a small living room where a venerable three-piece suite took up too much space. Along the sofa, his shoeless feet resting on one arm of it, lay an unshaven man in his forties, or perhaps even badly nurtured thirties. He was reading a war comic, his lips moving with the words on the page.

'Hiy, Dod,' Mrs Soutar said loudly, 'these are the polis. Davey's just put the heid on one of them.'

'Good for him,' Dod said without looking up. 'No offence, like.'

'None taken.' Rebus had wandered over to the window, wondering what the view was like. The window, however, was a botched piece of double glazing. Condensation had crept between the panes, frosting the glass.

'It wasn't much of a view to start with,' Mrs Soutar said. He turned and smiled at her. He didn't doubt she would see through any scheme, any lie. She was a short, strong-looking woman, big boned with a chiselled jaw but a pleasant face. If she didn't smile often, it was because she had to protect herself. She couldn't afford to look weak. In the Gar-B, the weak didn't last long. Rebus wondered how much influence she'd had over her son while he was growing up here. A lot, he'd say. But then the father would be an influence too.

She kept her arms folded while she talked, unfolding them only long enough to slap Dod's feet off the end of the sofa so she could sit herself down on the arm.

'So what's he done this time?'

Dod put down his comic and reached into his packet of cigarettes, lighting one for himself and handing the pack to Mrs Soutar.

'He's assaulted a police officer for a start,' Rebus said. 'That's a pretty serious offence, Mrs Soutar. It could land him a spell in the carpentry shop.'

'You mean the jail?' Dod pronounced it, 'jyle'.

'That's what I mean.'

Dod stood up, then half doubled over, seized by a cough which crackled with phlegm. He went into the kitchenette, separated from the living room by a breakfast bar, and spat into the sink.

'Run the tap!' Mrs Soutar ordered. Rebus was looking at her. She was looking sad but resilient. It took her only a moment to shrug off the idea of the prison sentence. 'He'd be better off in jail.'

'How's that?'

'This is the Gar-B, or hadn't you noticed? It does things to you, to the young ones especially. Davey'd be better off out of the place.'

'What has it done to him, Mrs Soutar?'

She stared at him, considering how long an answer to give. 'Nothing,' she said finally. Ormiston was standing by the wall unit, studying a pile of cassettes next to the cheap hi-fi system. 'Put some music on if you like,' she told him. 'Might cheer us up.'

'Okay,' said Ormiston, opening a cassette case.

'I was joking.'

But Ormiston just smiled, slammed the tape home, and pressed play. Rebus wondered what he was up to. Then the music started, an accordion at first, joined by flutes and drums, and then a quavering voice, using vibrato in place of skill.

The song was 'The Sash'. Ormiston handed the cassette case to Rebus. The cover was a cheap Xeroxed drawing of the Red Hand of Ulster, the band's name scratched on it in black ink. They were called the Proud Red Hand Marching Band, though it was hard to conceive of anyone marching to an accordion.

Dod, who had returned from the sink, started whistling along and clapping his hands. 'It's a grand old tune, eh?'

'What do you want to put that on for?' Mrs Soutar asked Ormiston. He shrugged, saying nothing.

'Aye, a grand old tune.' Dod collapsed onto the sofa. The woman glared at him.

'It's bigotry's what it is. I've nothing against the Catholics.'

'Well neither have I,' Dod countered. He winked at Ormiston. 'But there's no shame in being proud of your roots.'

'What about Davey, Mr Soutar? Does he have anything against Catholics?'

'No.'

'No? He seems to run around with Protestant gangs.'

'It's the Gar-B,' Mr Soutar said. 'You have to belong.'

Rebus knew what he was saying. Dod Soutar sat forward on the sofa.

'Ye see, it's history, isn't it? The Protestants have run Ulster for hundreds of years. Nobody's going to give that up, are they? Not if the other lot are sniping away and planting bombs and that.' He realised that Ormiston had turned off the tape. 'Well, isn't that right? It's a religious war, you can't deny it.'

'Ever been there?' Ormiston asked. Dod shook his head. 'Then what the fuck do you know about it?'

Dod gave a challenging look, and stood up. 'I know, pal, don't think I don't.'

'Aye, right,' Ormiston said.

'I thought you were here to talk about my Davey?'

'We are talking about Davey, Mrs Soutar,' Rebus said quietly. 'In a roundabout way.' He turned to Dod Soutar. 'There's a lot of you in your son, Mr Soutar.'

Dod Soutar turned his combative gaze from Ormiston. 'Oh aye?'

Rebus nodded. 'I'm sorry, but there it is.'

Dod Soutar's face creased into an angry scowl. 'Wait a fuckn minute, pal. Think you can walk in here and fuckn –'

'People like you terrify me,' Rebus said coolly. He meant it, too. Dod Soutar, hacking cough and all, was a more horrifying prospect than a dozen Caffertys. You couldn't change him, couldn't argue with him, couldn't touch his mind in any way. He was a closed shop, and the management had all gone home.

'My son's a good boy, brought up the right way,' Soutar was saying. 'Gave him everything I could.'

'Some folk are just born lucky,' said Ormiston.

That did it. Soutar launched himself across the narrow width of the room. He went for Ormiston with his head low and both fists out in front of him, but collided with the shelf unit when Ormiston stepped smartly aside. He turned back towards the two policemen, swinging wildly, swearing barely coherent phrases. When he went for Rebus, and Rebus arched back so that the swipe missed, Rebus decided he'd had enough. He kneed Soutar in the crotch.

'Queensferry Rules,' he said, as the man went down.

'Dod!' Mrs Soutar ran to her husband. Rebus gestured to Ormiston.

'Get out of my house!' Mrs Soutar screamed after them. She came to the front door and kept on yelling and crying. Then she went indoors and slammed her door.

'The cassette was a nice touch,' Rebus said on his way downstairs.

'Thought you'd appreciate it. Where to now?'

'While we're here,' said Rebus, 'maybe the youth club.'

They walked outside and didn't hear anything until the vase hit the ground beside them, smashing into a thousand pieces of shrapnel. Mrs Soutar was at her window.

'Missed!' Rebus yelled at her.

'Jesus Christ,' Ormiston said, as they walked away.

The usual lacklustre teenagers sat around outside the community hall, propping their backs against its door and walls. Rebus didn't bother to ask about Davey Soutar. He knew what the response would be; it had been drilled into them like catechism. His ear was tingling, not hurting exactly, but there was a dull throbbing pain in his nose. When they recognised Rebus, the gang got to their feet.

'Afternoon,' Ormiston said. 'You're right to stand up, by the way. Sitting on concrete gives you piles.'

In the hall, Jim Hay and his theatre group were sitting on the stage. Hay too recognised Rebus.

'Guess what?' he said. 'We have to mount a guard, otherwise they rip the stuff off.'

Rebus didn't know whether to believe him or not. He was more interested in the youth sitting next to Hay.

'Remember me, Malky?'

Malky Haston shook his head.

'I've got a few questions for you, Malky. Want to do it here or down the station?'

Haston laughed. 'You couldn't take me out of here, not if I didn't want to go.'

He had a point. 'We'll do it here then,' said Rebus. He turned to Hay, who raised his hands.

'I know, you want us to take a fag break.' He got up and led his troupe away. Ormiston went to the door to stop anyone else coming in.

Rebus sat on the stage next to Haston, getting close, making the teenager uncomfortable.

'I've done nothing, and I'm saying nothing.'

'Have you known Davey a while?'

Haston said nothing.

'I'd imagine since you were kids,' Rebus answered. 'Remember the first time we met? You had bits in your hair. I thought it was dandruff, but it was plaster. I spoke to ScotScaf. They hire out scaffolding to building contractors, and when it comes back it's your job to clean it. Isn't that right?'

Haston just looked at him.

'You're under orders not to talk, eh? Well, I don't mind.' Rebus stood up, facing Haston. 'There was ScotScaf scaffolding at the two murder sites, Billy's and Calumm Smylie's. You told Davey, didn't you? You knew where building work was going on, empty sites, all that.' He leaned close to Haston's face. 'You *knew*. That makes you an accessory at the very least. And that means we're going to throw you in jail. We'll pick out a nice Catholic wing for you, Malky, don't worry. Plenty of the green and white.'

277

Rebus turned his back and lit a cigarette. When he turned back to Haston, he offered him one. Ormiston was having a bit of bother at the door. The gang wanted in. Haston took a cigarette. Rebus lit it for him.

'Doesn't matter what you do, Malky. You can run, you can lie, you can say nothing at all. You're going away, and we're the only friends you'll ever have.'

He turned away and walked towards Ormiston. 'Let them in,' he ordered. The gang came crashing through the doors, fanning out across the hall. They could see Malky Haston was all right, though he was sitting very still on the edge of the stage. Rebus called to him.

'Thanks for the chat, Malky. We'll talk again, any time you want.' Then he turned to the gang. 'Malky's got his head screwed on,' he told them. '*He* knows when to talk.'

'Lying bastard!' Haston roared, as Rebus and Ormiston walked into the daylight.

Rebus met Lachlan Murdock at the Crazy Hose, despite Bothwell's protests.

Murdock's uncombed hair was wilder than ever, his clothes sloppy. He was waiting in the foyer when Rebus arrived.

'They all think I had something to do with it,' Murdock protested as Rebus led him into the dancehall.

'Well, you did, in a way,' Rebus said.

'What?'

'Come on, I want to show you something.'

He led Murdock up to the attic. In the daytime, the attic was a lot lighter. Even so, Rebus had brought a torch. He didn't want Murdock to miss anything.

'This,' he said, 'is where I found her. She'd suffered, believe me.' Already, Murdock was close to fresh tears, but sympathy could wait, the truth couldn't. 'I found this on the floor.' He handed over the disk cover. 'This is what they killed her for. A computer disk, same size as would fit your machine at home.' He walked up close to Murdock's slouched figure. 'They killed her for *this*!' he hissed. He waited a moment, then moved away towards the windows.

'I thought maybe she'd have made a copy. She wasn't daft, was she? But I went to the shop, and there's nothing there. Maybe in your flat?' Murdock just sniffed. 'I can't believe she –'

'There was a copy,' Murdock groaned. 'I wiped it.'

Rebus walked back towards him. 'Why?'

Murdock shook his head. 'I didn't think it ...' He took a deep breath. 'It reminded me ...'

Rebus nodded. 'Ah yes, Billy Cunningham. It reminded you of the pair of them. When did you begin to suspect?'

Murdock shook his head again.

'See,' said Rebus, 'I know most of it. I know enough. But I don't know it all. Did you look at the files on the disk?'

'I looked.' He wiped his red-rimmed eyes. 'It was Billy's disk, not hers. But a lot of the stuff on it was hers.'

'I don't understand.'

Murdock managed a weak smile. 'You're right, I did know about the two of them. I didn't want to know, but I knew all the same. When I wiped the disk, I was angry, I was *so* angry.' He turned to look at Rebus. 'I don't think he could have done it without Millie. You need quite a set-up to hack into the kinds of systems they were dealing with.'

'Hacking?'

'They probably used the stuff in her shop. They hacked into Army and police computers, bypassed security, invaded datafiles, then marched out again without leaving any trace.'

'So what did they do?'

Murdock was talking now, enjoying the release. He wiped tears from below his glasses. 'They monitored a couple of police investigations and altered a few inventories. Believe me, once they were in, they could have done a lot more.'

The way Murdock went on to explain it, it was almost ludicrously simple. You could steal from the Army (with inside assistance, there had to be inside assistance), and then erase the theft by altering the computer records to show stocks as they stood, not as they had been. Then, if SCS or Scotland Yard or anyone else took an interest, you could monitor their progress or lack of it. Millie: Millie had been the key throughout. Whether or not she knew what she was doing, she got Billy Cunningham in. He placed her in the lock and turned. The disk had contained instructions on their hacking procedures, tips for bypassing security checks, the works.

Rebus didn't doubt that the further Billy Cunningham got in, the more he wanted out. He'd been killed because he wanted out. He'd probably mentioned his little insurance policy in the hope they would let him leave quietly. Instead, they'd tried to torture its whereabouts out of him, before delivering the final silencing bullet. Of course, The Shield knew Billy wasn't hacking alone. It wouldn't have taken them long to get to Millie Docherty. Billy had stayed silent to protect her. She must have known. That's why she'd run.

'There was stuff about this group, too, The Shield,' Murdock was saying. 'I thought they were just a bunch of hackers.'

Rebus tried him with a few names. Davey Soutar and Jamesie MacMurray hit home. Rebus reckoned that in an interview room he could crack Jamesie like a walnut under a hammer. But Davey Soutar . . . well, he might need a real hammer for that. The final file on the computer was all about Davey Soutar and the Gar-B.

'This Soutar,' Murdock said, 'Billy seemed to think he'd been skimming. That was the word he used. There's some stuff stashed in a lock-up out at Currie.'

Currie: the lock-up would belong to the MacMurrays.

Murdock looked at Rebus. 'He didn't say what was being skimmed. Is it money?'

'I underestimated you, Davey,' Rebus said aloud. 'All down the line. It might be too late now, but I swear I won't underestimate you again.' He thought of how Davey and his kind hated the Festival. Hated it with a vengeance. He thought of the anonymous threats.

'Not money, Mr Murdock. Weapons and explosives. Come on, let's get out of here.'

Jamesie talked like a man coming out of silent retreat, especially when his father, hearing the story from Rebus, ordered him to. Gavin MacMurray was incensed, not that his son should be in trouble, but that the Orange Loyal Brigade hadn't been enough for him. It was a betrayal.

Jamesie led Rebus and the other officers to a row of wooden garages on a piece of land behind MacMurray's Garage. Two Army men were on hand. They checked for booby traps and trip wires and it took them nearly half an hour to get round to going in. Even then, they did not enter by the door. Instead, they climbed a ladder to the roof and cut through the asphalt covering, then dropped through and into the lock-up. A minute later, they gave the all clear, and a police constable broke open the door with a crowbar. Gavin MacMurray was with them.

'I haven't been in here for years,' he said. He'd said it before, as if they didn't believe him. 'I never use these garages.'

They had a good look round. Jamesie didn't know the precise location of the cache, only that Davey had said he needed a place to keep it. The garage had operated as a motorcycle workshop – that was how Billy Cunningham had got to know Jamesie, and through him Davey Soutar, in the first place. There were long rickety wooden shelves groaning with obscure metal parts, a lot of them rusted brown with age, tools covered with dust and cobwebs, and tins of paint and solvent. Each tin had to be opened, each tool examined. If you could hide Semtex in a transistor radio, you could certainly hide it in a tool shed. The Army had offered a specialised sniffer dog, but it would have to come from Aldershot. So instead they used their own eyes and noses and instinct.

Hanging from nails on the walls were old tyres and wheels and chains. Forks and handlebars lay on the floor along with engine parts and mouldy boxes of nuts, bolts and screws. They scraped at the floor, but found no buried boxes. There was a lot of oil on the ground.

'This place is clean,' said a smudged Army man. Rebus nodded agreement.

'He's been and cleared the place out. How much was there, Jamesie?'

But Jamesie MacMurray had been asked this before, and he didn't know. 'I swear I don't. I just said he could use the space. He got his own padlock fitted and everything.'

Rebus stared at him. These young hard men, Rebus had been dealing with them all his life and they were pathetic, like husks in suits of armour. Jamesie was about as hard as the *Sun* crossword. 'And he never showed you?'

Jamesie shook his head. 'Never.'

His father was staring at him furiously. 'You stupid wee bastard,' Gavin MacMurray said. 'You stupid, stupid wee fool.'

'We'll have to take Jamesie down the station, Mr Mac-Murray.'

'I know that.' Then Gavin MacMurray slapped his son's face. With a hand callused by years of mechanical work, he loosened teeth and sent blood curdling from Jamesie's mouth. Jamesie spat on the dirt floor but said nothing. Rebus knew Jamesie was going to tell them everything he knew.

Outside, one of the Army men smiled in relief. 'I'm glad we didn't find anything.'

'Why?'

'Keeping the stuff in an environment like that, it's bound to be unstable.'

'Just like the guy who's got it.' Unstable ... Rebus thought of Unstable from Dunstable, confessing to the St Stephen Street killing, raving to DI Flower about curry and cars ... He walked back into the garage and pointed to the stain on the floor.

'That's not oil,' he said, 'not all of it.'

'What?'

'Everybody out, I want this place secured.'

They all got out. Flower should have listened to Unstable from Dunstable. The tramp had been talking about Currie, not curry. And he'd said cars because of the garages. He must have been sleeping rough nearby and seen or heard something that night.

'What is it, sir?' one of the officers asked Rebus.

'If I'm right, this is where they killed Calumn Smylie.'

That evening, Rebus moved out of the hotel and back into Patience's flat. He felt exhausted, like a tool that had lost its edge. The stain on the garage floor had been a mixture of oil and blood. They were trying to separate the two so they could DNA-test the blood against Calumn Smylie's. Rebus knew already what they'd find. It all made sense when you thought about it.

He poured a drink, then thought better of it. Instead he phoned Patience and told her she could come home in the next day or two. But she was determined to return in the morning, so he told her why she shouldn't. She was very quiet for a moment.

'Be careful, John.'

'I'm still here, aren't I?'

'Let's keep it that way.'

He rang off when he heard the doorbell. The manhunt for Davey Soutar was in full swing, under the control of CI

Lauderdale at St Leonard's. Arms would be issued as and when necessary. Though they didn't know the extent of Soutar's cache, no chances would be taken. Rebus had been asked if he'd like a bodyguard.

'I'll trust to my guardian angel,' he'd said.

The doorbell rang again. He felt naked as he walked down the long straight hall towards the door. The door itself was inch-and-a-half thick wood, but most guns could cope with that and still leave enough velocity in the bullet to puncture human flesh. He listened for a second, then put his eye to the spy-hole. He let his breath out and unlocked the door.

'You've got things to tell me,' he said, opening the door wide.

Abernethy produced a bottle of whisky from behind his back. 'And I've brought some antiseptic for those cuts.'

'Internal use only,' Rebus suggested.

'The money it cost me, you better believe it. Still, a nice drop of Scotch is worth all the tea in China.'

'We call it whisky up here.' Rebus closed the door and led Abernethy back down the hall into the living room. Abernethy was impressed.

'Been taking a few back-handers?'

'I live with a doctor. It's her flat.'

'My mum always wanted me to be a doctor. A respectable job, she called it. Got some glasses?'

Rebus fetched two large glasses from the kitchen.

27

Frankie Bothwell couldn't afford to close the Crazy Hose.

The Festival and Fringe had only a couple more days to go. All too soon the tourists would be leaving. But over the past fortnight he'd really been packing them in. Advertising and word of mouth helped, as had a three-night residency by an American country singer. The club was making more money than ever before, but it wouldn't last. The Crazy Hose was unique, every bit as unique as Frankie himself. It deserved to do well. It *had* to do well. Frankie Bothwell had commitments, financial commitments. They couldn't be broken or excused because of low takings. Every week needed to be a good week.

So he was not best pleased to see Rebus and another cop walk into the bar. You could see it in his eyes and the smile as frozen as a Crazy Hose daiquiri.

'Inspector, how can I help you?'

'Mr Bothwell, this is DI Abernethy. We'd like a word.'

'It's a bit hectic just now. I haven't had a chance to replace Kevin Strang.'

'We insist,' said Abernethy.

With two conspicuous police officers on the premises, trade at the bars wasn't exactly brisk, and nobody was dancing. They were all waiting for something to happen. Bothwell took this in.

'Let's go to my office.'

Abernethy waved bye-bye to the crowd as he followed Rebus and Bothwell into the foyer. They went behind the admission desk and Bothwell unlocked a door. He sat behind his desk and watched them squeeze their way into the space that was left.

'A big office is a waste of space,' he said by way of apology. The place was like a cleaning cupboard. There were spare till rolls and boxes of glasses on a shelf above Bothwell's head, framed cowboy posters stacked against a wall, bric-a-brac and debris like everything had just spilled out of a collision at a car boot sale.

'We might be more comfortable talking in the toilets,' Rebus said.

'Or down the station,' offered Abernethy.

'I don't think we've met,' Bothwell said to him, affably enough.

'I usually only meet shit when I wipe my arse.'

That took the smile off Bothwell's face.

'Inspector Abernethy,' Rebus said, 'is Special Branch. He's here investigating The Shield.'

'The Shield?'

'No need to be coy, Mr Bothwell. You're not being charged, not yet. We just want you to know we're on to you in a big way.'

'And we're not about to let go,' Abernethy said on cue.

'Though it might help your case if you told us about Davey Soutar.' Rebus placed his hands in his lap and waited. Abernethy lit a cigarette and blew the smoke across the strewn desk. Frankie Bothwell looked from one man to the other and back again.

'Is this a joke? I mean, it's a bit early for Halloween, that's when you're supposed to scare people without any reason.'

Rebus shook his head. 'Wrong answer. What you should have said was, "Who's Davey Soutar?"'

Bothwell sat back in his chair. 'All right then, who's Davey Soutar?'

'I'm glad you asked me that,' said Rebus. 'He's your

lieutenant. Maybe he's also your recruiting officer. And now he's on the run. Did you know he's been keeping back some of the explosives and guns for himself? We've got a confession.' It was a blatant lie, and caused Bothwell to smile. That smile sealed Bothwell's guilt in Rebus's mind.

'Why have you been funding the Gar-B youth centre?' he asked. 'Is it a useful recruiting station? You took the name Cuchullain when you were an anarchist. He's the great Ulster hero, the original Red Hand. That was no accident. You were dismissed from the Orange Lodge for being a bit over-zealous. In the early '70s your name was linked to the Tartan Army. They used to break into Army bases and steal weapons. Maybe that's what gave you the idea.'

Bothwell was still smiling as he asked, 'What idea?'

'You know.'

'Inspector, I haven't understood a word you've said.'

'No? Then understand this, we're a bollock-hair's breadth away from you. But more importantly, we want to find Davey Soutar, because if he's gone rogue with rifles and plastic explosives...'

'I still don't know what you're –'

Rebus jumped from his seat and grabbed Bothwell's lapels, pulling him tight against the desk. Bothwell's smile evaporated.

'I've been to Belfast, Bothwell, I've spent time in the North. The last thing that place needs is cowboys like you. So put away your forked tongue and tell us where he is!'

Bothwell wrenched himself out of Rebus's grip, his lapel tearing down the middle in the process. His face was purple, eyes blazing. He stood with his knuckles on the edge of the desk, leaning over it, his face close to Rebus's.

'Nobody meddles wi' me!' he spat. 'That's my motto.'

'Aye,' said Rebus, 'and you know the Latin for it too. Did you get a kick that night in Mary King's Close?'

'You're crazy.'

'We're the police,' Abernethy said lazily. 'We're paid to be crazy, what's your excuse?'

Bothwell considered the two of them and sat down slowly. 'I don't know anyone called Davey Soutar. I don't know anything about bombs or Sword and Shield or Mary King's Close.'

'I didn't say Sword and Shield,' said Rebus. 'I just said The Shield.'

Bothwell sat in silence.

'But now you mention it, I see your father the minister was in the original Sword and Shield. His name's on file. It was an offshoot of the Scottish National Party; I don't suppose you know anything about it?'

'Nothing.'

'No? Funny, you were in the youth league.'

'Was I?'

'Did your dad get you interested in Ulster?'

Bothwell shook his head slowly. 'You never stop, do you?'

'Never,' said Rebus.

The door opened. The two bouncers from the main door stood there, hands clasped in front of them, legs apart. They'd obviously been to the bouncers' school of etiquette. And, just as obviously, Bothwell had summoned them with some button beneath the lip of his desk.

'Escort these bastards off the premises,' he ordered.

'Nobody escorts me anywhere,' said Abernethy, 'not unless she's wearing a tight skirt and I've paid for her.' He got up and faced the bouncers. One of them made to take his arm. Abernethy grabbed the bouncer at the wrist and twisted hard. The man fell to his knees. There wasn't much room for the other bouncer, and he looked undecided. He was still looking blank as Rebus pulled him into the room and threw him over the desk. Bothwell was smothered beneath him. Abernethy let the other bouncer go and followed Rebus outside with a real spring in his step, breathing deeply of Edinburgh's warm summer air. 'I enjoyed that.'

'Aye, me too, but do you think it worked?'

'Let's hope so. We're making liabilities of them. I get the feeling they're going to implode.'

Well, that was the plan. Every good plan, however, had a fall-back. Theirs was Big Ger Cafferty.

'Is it too late to grab a curry?' Abernethy added.

'You're not in the sticks now. The night's young.'

But as Rebus led Abernethy towards a good curry house, he was thinking about liabilities and risks ... and dreading tomorrow's showdown.

28

The day dawned bright, with blue skies and a breeze which would soon warm. It was expected to stay good all day, with a clear night for the fireworks. Princes Street would be bursting at the seams, but it was quiet as DCI Kilpatrick drove along it. He was an early riser, but even he had been caught by Rebus's wake-up call.

The industrial estate was quiet too. After being cleared by the guard on the gate, he drove up to the warehouse and parked next to Rebus's car. The car was empty, but the warehouse door stood open. Kilpatrick went inside.

'Morning, sir.' Rebus was standing in front of the HGV.

'Morning, John. What's with all the cloak and dagger?'

'Sorry about that, sir. I hope I can explain.'

'I hope so too, going without breakfast never puts me in the best of moods.'

'It's just that there's something I had to tell you, and this seems as quiet a place as any.'

'Well, what is it?'

Rebus had started walking around the lorry, Kilpatrick following him. When they were at the back of the vehicle, Rebus pulled on the lever and swung the door wide open. On top of the boxes inside sat Abernethy.

'You didn't warn me it was a party,' Kilpatrick said.

'Here, let me help you up.'

Kilpatrick looked at Rebus. 'I'm not a pensioner.' And he pulled himself into the back, Rebus clambering after him.

'Hello again, sir,' Abernethy said, putting his hand out

for Kilpatrick to shake. Kilpatrick folded his arms instead.

'What's this all about, Abernethy?'

But Abernethy shrugged and nodded towards Rebus.

'Notice anything, sir?' said Rebus. 'I mean, about the load.'

Kilpatrick put on a thoughtful face and looked around. 'No,' he said finally, adding: 'I never was one for party games.'

'No games, sir. Tell me, what happens to all this stuff if we're not going to use it in a sting operation?'

'It goes to be destroyed.'

'That's what I thought. And the papers go with it, don't they?'

'Of course.'

'But since the stuff has been under our stewardship, those papers will be from the City of Edinburgh Police?'

'I suppose so. I can't see –'

'You will, sir. When the stuff came here, there was a record with it, detailing what it was and how much of it there was. But we replace that record with one of our own, don't we? And if the first record goes astray, well, there's always *our* record.' Rebus tapped one of the boxes. 'There's less here than there was.'

'What?'

Rebus lifted the lid from a crate. 'When you showed me around before with Smylie, there were more AK 47s than this.'

Kilpatrick looked horrified. 'Are you sure?' He looked inside the crate.

'Yet the current inventory shows twelve AK 47s, and that's how many are here.'

'Twelve,' Abernethy confirmed, as Rebus got out the sheet of paper and handed it to Kilpatrick.

'Then you must have made a mistake,' said Kilpatrick.

'No, sir,' said Rebus, 'with all due respect. I've checked with Special Branch. They hold a record of the original delivery. Two dozen AK 47s. The other dozen are missing. There's other stuff too: a rocket launcher, some of the ammo . . .'

'You see, sir,' said Abernethy, 'normally nobody would bother to backtrack, would they? The stuff is going for disposal, and there's a chitty says everything checks. No one ever looks back down the line.'

'But it's impossible.' Kilpatrick still held the sheet of paper, but he wasn't looking at it.

'No, sir,' said Rebus, 'it's dead easy. *If* you can alter the record. You're in charge of this load, it's your name on the sheet.'

'What are you saying?'

Rebus shrugged and slipped his hands into his pockets. 'The surveillance on the American, that was your operation too, sir.'

'As requested by you, Inspector.'

Rebus nodded. 'And I appreciated it. It's just, I can't understand a few things. Such as how your trusted team from Glasgow didn't spot me and a friend of mine having a drink with Clyde Moncur and his wife.'

'What?'

'The details you gave me, sir, there was nothing about that. I didn't think there would be. That's partly why I did it. Nor was there any mention of a meeting between Clyde Moncur and Frankie Bothwell. All your men say is that Moncur and his wife go for walks, see the sights, act the perfect tourists. But there *is* no surveillance, is there? I know because I put a couple of colleagues onto Moncur myself. You see, I knew something was up the minute I met Inspector Abernethy here.'

'You put an unofficial surveillance on Moncur?'

'And I've the pictures to prove it.' On cue, Abernethy rustled a white paper bag, one side of which was clear cellophane. The black and white photos could be seen inside.

'There's even one here,' Abernethy said, 'of you meeting Moncur in Gullane. Maybe you were talking about golf?'

'You must have promised The Shield some of these arms before I came along,' Rebus went on. 'You brought me into the investigation to keep an eye on me.'

'But why would I bring you here in the first place?'

'Because Ken Smylie asked you to. And you didn't want to raise *his* suspicions. There's not much gets past Ken.'

Rebus had expected Kilpatrick to deflate, but he didn't, if anything he grew bigger. He plunged his hands into his jacket pockets and slid his shoulders back. His face showed no emotion, and he wasn't about to talk.

'We've been looking at you for a while,' Abernethy continued. 'Those Prod terrorists you let slip through your fingers in Glasgow ...' He shook his head slowly. 'That's one reason we moved you from Glasgow, to see if you could still operate. When news of the six-pack reached me, I knew you were still lending a hand to your friends in The Shield. They've always relied on inside help, and by Christ they've been getting it.'

'You thought it was a drugs hit,' Kilpatrick argued.

Abernethy shrugged. 'I'm a good actor. When you seconded Inspector Rebus, I knew it was because you saw him as a threat. You needed to keep an eye on him. Luckily he came to the same conclusion.' Abernethy peered into the bag of photographs. 'And here's the result.'

'Funny, sir,' said Rebus, 'when we were talking about Sword and Shield, the old Sword and Shield I mean, you never mentioned that you were a member.'

'What?'

'You didn't think there were any records, but I managed to track some down. Back in the early '60s you were in their youth league. Same time Frankie Bothwell was. Like I say, funny you never mentioned it.'

'I didn't think it was relevant.'

'Then I was attacked by someone trying to put me out

of the game. The man was a pro, I'd swear to that, a street-slugger with a cutthroat razor. He had a Glasgow accent. You must have met a few hard men during your stint over there.'

'You think I hired him?'

'With all respect,' Rebus locked eyes with Kilpatrick, 'you must be off your rocker.'

'Madness comes from the head, not the blood, not the heart.' Kilpatrick rested against a box. 'You think you can trust Abernethy, John? Well, good luck to you. I'm waiting.'

'For what?'

'Your next gimmick.' He smiled. 'If you wanted to make a case against me, we wouldn't be meeting like this. You know as well as I do that a filing mistake and an innocent photograph don't make a case. They don't make anything.'

'You could be kicked off the force.'

'With my record? No, I might retire early, say on health grounds, but no one's going to sack me. It doesn't happen that way, I thought two experienced officers would know that. Now answer me this, Inspector Rebus, you set up an illicit surveillance: how much trouble can that get *you* in? With your record of insubordination and bucking the rules, we could kick you off the force for not wiping your arse properly.' He rose from the box and walked to the edge of the lorry, then dropped to the ground and turned towards them. 'You haven't proved anything to me. If you want to try your act with someone else, be my guests.'

'You cold bastard,' Abernethy said. He made it sound like a compliment. He walked to the edge of the lorry and faced Kilpatrick, then slowly began to pull his shirt out from his trousers. He lifted it up, showing bare flesh and sticking plasters and wires. He was miked up. Kilpatrick stared back at him.

'Anything to add, sir?' Abernethy said. Kilpatrick turned and walked away. Abernethy turned to Rebus. 'Quiet all of a sudden, isn't it?'

Rebus leapt from the lorry and walked briskly to the door. Kilpatrick was getting into his car, but stopped when he saw him.

'Three murders so far,' Rebus said. 'Including a police officer, one of your own. That's a madness of the blood.'

'That wasn't me,' Kilpatrick said quietly.

'Yes, it was,' Rebus said. 'There'd be none of it without you.'

'I don't know how they got to Calumn Smylie.'

'They hack into computers. Your secretary uses one.'

Kilpatrick nodded. 'And there's a file on the operation in the computer.' He shook his head slowly. 'Look, Rebus...' But Kilpatrick stopped himself. He shook his head again and got into the car, shutting the door.

Rebus bent down to the driver's-side window, and waited for Kilpatrick to wind it down.

'Abernethy's told me what it's about, why the loyalists are suddenly arming themselves. It's Harland and Wolff.' This being a shipyard, one of the biggest employers in the province, its workforce predominantly Protestant. 'They think it's going to be wound up, don't they? The loyalists are taking it as a symbol. If the British government lets Harland and Wolff go to the wall, then it's washing its hands of the Ulster Protestants. Basically, it's pulling out.' Hard to know whether Kilpatrick was listening. He was staring through the windscreen, hands on the steering wheel. 'At which point,' Rebus went on anyway, 'the loyalists are set to explode. You're arming them for civil war. But worse than that, you've armed Davey Soutar. He's a walking anti-personnel mine.'

Kilpatrick's voice was hard, unfeeling. 'Soutar's not my problem.'

'Frankie Bothwell can't help. Maybe he could control Soutar once upon a time, but not now.'

'There's only one person Soutar respects,' Kilpatrick said quietly, 'Alan Fowler.'

'The UVF man?'

Kilpatrick had started the engine.

'Wait a minute,' said Rebus. As Kilpatrick moved off, Rebus kept a grip of the window-frame. Kilpatrick turned to him.

'Nine tonight,' he said. 'At the Gar-B.'

Then he sped out of the compound.

Abernethy was just behind Rebus.

'What was he telling you?' he asked.

'Nine o'clock at the Gar-B.'

'Sounds like a nice little trap to me.'

'Not if we take the cavalry.'

'John,' Abernethy said with a grin, 'I've got all the cavalry we'll need.'

Rebus turned to face him. 'You've been playing me like a pinball machine, haven't you? That first time we met, all that stuff you told me about computers being the future of crime. You knew back then.'

Abernethy shrugged. He pulled up his shirt again and started to pull off the wires. 'All I did was point you in the general direction. Look at the way I got on your tits that first time. *That's* how I knew I could trust you. I nettled you and you let it show. You'd nothing to hide.' He nodded to himself. 'Yes, I knew, I've known for a long time. Proving it was the bugger.' Abernethy looked at the compound gates. 'But Kilpatrick's got enemies, remember that, not just you and me any more.'

'What do you mean?'

But Abernethy just winked and tapped his nose. 'Enemies,' he said.

Rebus had pulled Siobhan Clarke off the Moncur surveillance and put her on to Frankie Bothwell. But Frankie Bothwell had disappeared. She apologised, but Rebus only shrugged. Holmes had kept with Clyde Moncur, but Moncur and his wife were off on some bus tour, a two-day trip to the Highlands. Moncur could always get off the bus and double back, but Rebus discontinued the tail anyway.

'You seem a bit glum, sir,' Siobhan Clarke told him. Maybe she was right. The world seemed upside down. He'd seen bad cops before, of course he had. But he had never before seen anything like Kilpatrick's lack of an explanation or a decent defence. It was as if he didn't feel he needed one, as if he'd just been doing the right thing; in the wrong way perhaps, but the right thing all the same.

Abernethy had told him how deep the suspicions went, how long they'd been accumulating. But it was hard to investigate a policeman who, on the surface, seemed to be doing nearly everything right. Investigation required co-operation, and the co-operation wasn't there. Until Rebus had come along.

At the Gar-B lock-ups, outside the blocks of flats, police and Army experts were opening doors, just in case the stolen cache was inside one of the garages. Door to door inquiries were going on, trying to pin down Davey's friends, trying to get someone to talk or to admit they were hiding him. Meantime, Jamesie MacMurray was already being charged. But they were minnows, their flesh not enough to merit the hook. Kilpatrick, too, had disappeared. Rebus had phoned Ormiston and found that the CI hadn't returned to his office, and no one answered at his home.

Holmes and Clarke returned from the warrant search of Soutar's home, Holmes toting a plain cardboard box, obviously not empty. Holmes put the box on Rebus's desk.

'Let's start,' Holmes said, 'with a jar of acid, carefully concealed under Soutar's bed.'

'His mother says he never lets her in to clean his room,' Clarke explained. 'He's got a padlock on the door to prove it. We had to break the lock. His mum wasn't best pleased.'

'She's a lovely woman, isn't she?' said Rebus. 'Did you meet the dad?'

'He was at the bookie's.'

'Lucky for you. What else have you got?'

'Typhoid probably,' Holmes complained. 'The place was like a Calcutta rubbish tip.'

Clarke dipped in and pulled out a few small polythene bags; everything in the box had been wrapped first and labelled. 'We've got knives, most of them illegal, one still with what looks like dried blood on it.' Some of it Calumn Smylie's blood, Rebus didn't doubt. She dipped in again. 'Mogadon tablets, about a hundred of them, and some unopened cans of cola and beer.'

'The Can Gang?'

Clarke nodded. 'Looks like it. There are wallets, credit cards ... it'll take us two minutes to check. Oh, and we found this little booklet.' She held it up for him. It was poorly Xeroxed, with its A4-sized sheets folded in half and stapled. Rebus read the title.

'*The Total Anarchy Primer*. Wonder who gave him this?'

'Looks like it's been translated from another language, maybe German. Some of the words they couldn't find the English for, so they've left them in the original.'

'Some primer.'

'It tells you how to make bombs,' said Clarke, 'in case you were wondering. Mostly fertiliser bombs, but there's a section on timers and detonators, just in case you found yourself with any plastique.'

'The perfect Christmas gift. Are they checking the bedroom for traces?'

Holmes nodded. 'They were at it when we left.'

Rebus nodded. A special forensic unit had been sent in to test for traces of explosive materials. The same unit had been working at the MacMurray lock-up. They knew now that the garage had held a quantity of plastic explosive, probably Semtex. But they couldn't say how much. Usually, as one of the team had explained, Semtex was quite difficult to prove, being colourless and fairly scentless. But it looked like Soutar had been playing with his toys, unwrapping at least one of the packages the better to have a look at it. Traces had been left on the surface of the workbench.

'Were there detonators in the cache?' Rebus asked. 'That's the question.'

Holmes and Clarke looked at one another.

'A rhetorical one,' Rebus added.

29

The city was definitely coming out to play.

It was the start of September, and therefore the beginning of that slow slide into chill autumn and long dark winter. The Festival was winding down for another year, and everyone was celebrating. It was on days like this that the city, so often submerged like Atlantis or some subaqua Brigadoon, bubbled to the surface. The buildings seemed less dour and the people smiled, as though cloud and rain were unknowns.

Rebus might have been driving through a thunderstorm for all the notice he took. He was a hunter, and hunters didn't smile. Abernethy had just admitted being Marie's anonymous caller, the one who'd put her on to Calumn Smylie.

'You knew you were putting his life in danger?' Rebus asked.

'Maybe I thought I was saving it.'

'How did you know about Mairie anyway? I mean, how did you know to contact *her*?'

Abernethy just smiled.

'You sent me that stuff about Clyde Moncur, didn't you?'

'Yes.'

'You could have warned me what I was getting into.'

'You were more effective the way you were.'

'I've been a walking punch-bag.'

'But you're still here.'

'I bet you'd lose a lot of sleep if I wasn't.'

The sun had finally given up. The street lights were on. There were a lot of people on the streets tonight. Hogmanay apart, it was the city's biggest night of the year. The traffic was all headed into town, where most of the parking spaces had been grabbed hours ago.

'Families,' Rebus explained, 'on their way to the fireworks.'

'I thought *we* were on our way to the fireworks,' Abernethy said, smiling again.

'We are,' said Rebus quietly.

There were never signposts to places like the Gar-B, the inference being that if you wanted to go there, you must already know the place. People didn't just visit on a whim. Rebus took the slip-road past the gable end – ENJOY YOUR VISIT TO THE GAR-B – and turned into the access road.

'Nine o'clock, he said.'

Abernethy checked his watch. 'Nine it is.'

But Rebus wasn't listening. He was watching a van roaring towards them. The road was barely wide enough for two vehicles, and the van driver didn't seem to be paying much attention. He was crouched down, eyes on his wing mirror. Rebus slammed on the brakes and the horn and whipped the steering wheel around. The rust bucket slew sideways like it was on ice. That was the problem with bald tyres.

'Out!' Rebus called. Abernethy didn't need telling twice. The driver had finally seen them. The van was skidding to an uncertain stop. It hit the driver's side door, shuddered, and was still. Rebus pulled open the van door and hauled out Jim Hay. He'd heard of people looking white as a sheet, white as a ghost, but Jim Hay looked whiter than that. Rebus held him upright.

'He's gone off his fucking head!' Hay yelled.

'Who has?'

'Soutar.' Hay was looking behind him, back down the

road which curled snake-like into the Gar-B. 'I'm only the delivery man, not this ... not this.'

Dusting himself off, Abernethy joined them. He'd lost the knees out of his denims.

'You deliver the stuff,' Rebus was saying to Hay, 'the explosives, the arms?'

Hay nodded.

Yes, the perfect delivery man, in his little theatre van, all boxes and props, costumes and sets, guns and grenades. Delivered east coast to west, where another connection would be made, another switch.

'Hold him,' Rebus ordered. Abernethy looked like he didn't understand. 'Hold him!'

Then Rebus let Jim Hay go, got into the van, and reversed it out of his car's bodywork and back into the Gar-B. When he reached the car park, he turned the van and bumped it at speed onto the grass, heading for the youth centre.

There was nobody about, not a soul. The door-to-door had been wound up for the day, having yielded nothing. The Gar-B simply didn't speak to the 'polis'. It was a rule of life, like remembering to breathe. Rebus was breathing hard. The garages he passed had been searched and declared safe, though one of them had contained a suspicious number of TV sets, videos, and camcorders, and another showed evidence of sniffed glue and smoked crack.

No neighbours were out discussing the day's events. There was even silence at the community centre. He doubted the Gar-B tribe were the kind to be attracted to a firework display ... not normally.

The doors were open, so Rebus walked in. A bright trail of blood led in an arc across the floor from the stage to the far wall. Kilpatrick was slumped against the wall, almost but not quite sitting up. He'd removed his necktie halfway across the room, maybe to help him breathe. He was still alive, but he'd lost maybe a pint of blood already. When Rebus crouched down beside him, Kilpatrick clutched at him with wet red fingers, leaving a bloody handprint on Rebus's shirt. His other hand was protecting his own stomach, source of the wound.

'I tried to stop him,' he whispered.

Rebus looked around him. 'Was the stuff hidden here?'

'Under the stage.'

Rebus looked at the small stage, a stage he'd sat on and stood on.

'Hay's gone to fetch an ambulance,' Kilpatrick said.

'He was running like a rabbit,' Rebus said.

Kilpatrick forced a smile. 'I thought he might.' He licked his lips. They were cracked, edged with white like missed toothpaste. 'They've gone with him.'

'Who? His gang?'

'They'll follow Davey Soutar to hell. He made those phone calls. He told me so. Just before he did this.' Kilpatrick tried to look down at his stomach. The effort was almost too much for him.

Rebus stood up. Blood flushed around his system, making him dizzy. 'The Fireworks? He's going to blow up the Fireworks?' He ran out of the hall and into the nearest tower block. The first front door he came to, he kicked it in. It took him three good hits. Then he marched into the living room, where two terrified pensioners were watching TV.

'Where's your phone?'

'We dinnae have one,' the man eventually said.

Rebus walked back out and kicked in the next door. Same procedure. This time the single mother with the two shrieking kids did have a phone. She hurled abuse at Rebus as he pressed the buttons.

'I'm the police,' he told her. It made her angrier still. She quietened, though, when she heard Rebus order an ambulance. She was shushing the kids as he made his second call.

'It's DI Rebus here,' he said. 'Davey Soutar and his gang

303

are on their way to Princes Street with a load of high explosives. We need that area *sealed*.'

He half-smiled an apology as he left the flat and half-ran back to the van. Still nobody had come to investigate, to see what all the noise and the fuss were. Like Edinburghers of old, they could become invisible to trouble. In olden times, they'd hidden in the catacombs below the Castle and the High Street. Now they just shut their windows and turned up the TV. They were Rebus's employers, whose taxes paid his salary. They were the people he was paid to protect. He felt like telling them all to go to hell.

When he got back to his car, Abernethy was standing there with Jim Hay, not a clue what to do with him. Rebus yanked the steering wheel and pulled the van onto the grass.

'An ambulance is on its way,' he said, trying to pull open his car door. It groaned like something in a scrapyard crusher, but eventually gave, and he squeezed through the gap into his seat, brushing aside the glass chippings.

'Where are you going?' Abernethy asked.

'Stay here with him,' Rebus said, starting the car and reversing back up the access road.

The Glenlivet Fireworks: every year there was a firework display from the Castle ramparts, accompanied by a chamber orchestra in Princes Street Gardens' bandstand and watched by crowds in the Gardens and packed into Princes Street itself. The concert usually started around ten-fifteen, ten-thirty. It was now ten o'clock on a balmy dry evening. The area would be full to bursting.

Wild Davey Soutar. He and his kind detested the Festival. It took away from them *their* Edinburgh and propped something else in its place, a façade of culture which they didn't need and couldn't understand. There was no underclass in Edinburgh, they'd all been pushed out into schemes on the city boundaries. Isolated, exiled, they had every right to resent the city centre with its tourist traps and temporary playtime.

Not that that's why Soutar was doing it. Rebus thought Soutar had some simpler reasons. He was showing off, he was showing even his elders in The Shield that they couldn't control him, that *he* was the boss. He was, in fact, quite mad.

'Make a run for it, Davey,' Rebus said to himself. 'Get a grip. Use your sense. Just ...' But he couldn't think of the words.

He didn't often drive fast; dangerously ... almost never. It was car smashes that did it, being on the scene at car smashes. You saw heads so messed up you didn't know which side was the face until it opened its mouth to scream.

Nevertheless, Rebus drove back into town like he was attempting the land-speed record.

His car seemed to sense the absolute urgency, the necessity, and for once didn't black out or choke up. It whined its own argument, but kept moving.

Princes Street and the three main streets leading down to it from George Street had been cordoned off as a matter of course, stopping traffic from coming anywhere near the thousands of spectators. On a night like this, there'd be quarter of a million souls watching the display, the majority of them in and around Princes Street. Rebus took his car as far as he could, then simply stopped in the middle of the road, got out, and ran. Police were setting up new barriers. Lauderdale and Flower were there. He made straight for them.

'Any news?' he spat.

Lauderdale nodded. 'There was a convoy of cars on West Coates, running red lights, travelling at speed.'

'That's them.'

'We've put up a diversion to bring them here.'

Rebus looked around, wiping sweat from his eyes. The

305

street was lined with shops at street level, offices above. Uniformed officers were moving civilians out of the area. An Army vehicle sat roadside.

'Bomb disposal,' Lauderdale explained. 'Remember, we've been ready for this.'

More barriers were being erected, and Rebus saw van doors open and half a dozen police marksmen appear, their chests covered by black body armour.

'Is Kilpatrick okay?' Lauderdale asked.

'Should be, depends on the ambulance.'

'How much stuff does Soutar have?'

Rebus tried to remember. 'It's not just explosives, he's probably toting AK 47s, pistols and ammo, maybe grenades . . .'

'Christ almighty.' Lauderdale spoke into his radio. 'Where are they?'

The radio crackled to life. 'Can't you see them yet?'

'No.'

'They're right in front of you.'

Rebus looked up. Yes, here they came. Maybe they were expecting a trap, maybe not. Whichever, it was still a suicide mission. They might get in, but they weren't going to get out.

'Ready!' Lauderdale called. The marksmen checked their guns and pointed them ahead. There were police cars behind the barriers. The uniforms had stopped moving people away. They wanted to watch. More onlookers were arriving all the time, keen for this preliminary event.

In the lead car, Davey Soutar was alone. He seemed to think about ramming the barricade, then braked hard instead, bringing his car to a stop. Behind him, four other cars slowed and halted. Davey sat frozen in his seat. Lauderdale lifted a megaphone.

'Bring your hands where we can see them.'

The car doors behind Davey were opening. Metal clattered to the ground as guns were thrown down. Some of the

Gar-B started to run for it, others, seeing the armed police, got out slowly with hands held high. Others were awaiting instructions. One of them, a young kid, no older than fourteen, lost his nerve and ran straight for the police lines.

Overhead, the first fireworks burst into brief life with a noise like old-fashioned gunfire and mortar. The sky sizzled, the glow lighting the scene.

At the first noise, most people flinched instinctively. The armed police dropped to a crouch, others spread themselves on the ground. The kid who'd been running towards the barriers started screaming in fright, then fell to his hands and knees.

Behind him, Davey Soutar's car was empty.

He'd shuffled into the passenger seat, opened the door, and made a dash to the pavement. Running low, it took him only seconds to disappear into the mass of pedestrians.

'Did anyone see? Did he have a gun?'

The Army personnel moved in warily on the lead car, while police started rounding up the Gar-B. More weapons were jettisoned. Lauderdale moved in to supervise his men.

And John Rebus was after Soutar.

The one place there wasn't much of a crowd was George Street: you couldn't see the fireworks from there. So Rebus had little trouble following Soutar. The sky turned from red to green to blue, with small pops and the occasional huge explosion. Each explosion had Rebus squirming, thinking of the bomb disposal unit busy back at Soutar's car. When the wind changed, it carried with it wafts of musical accompaniment from the orchestra in the Gardens. Chase music it wasn't.

Soutar ran with loose energy, almost bouncing. He covered a lot of ground, but it wasn't a straight line. He did a lot of weaving from side to side, covering most of the width of the pavement. Rebus concentrated on closing the gap, moving forwards like he was on rails. His eyes were on Soutar's hands. As long as he could see those hands, see they weren't carrying anything, he was content.

For all Soutar's crazy progress, Rebus was losing ground on the younger man, except when Soutar turned to look back at his pursuer. That's what he was doing when he ran out into the road and bounced off a taxi cab. The cab was on St Andrew's Square. The driver stuck his head out the window, then pulled it in again fast when Soutar drew his gun.

It looked like a service revolver to Rebus. Soutar fired a shot through the cab window, then started running again. He was slower now, with a slouch announcing a damaged right leg.

Rebus glanced in at the cab driver. He'd thrown up all over his knees, but was unhurt.

Give it up, Rebus thought, his lungs on fire. Give it up.

But Soutar kept moving. He ran through the bus station, dodging the single-deckers as they moved in and out of their ranks. The few waiting passengers could see he was armed, and stared in horror as he flew past them, jacket flapping, for all the world like a scarecrow come to life.

Rebus followed him up James Craig Walk, across the top of Leith Street, and into Waterloo Place. Soutar stopped for a moment, as though trying to come to a decision. His right hand still gripped the revolver. He saw Rebus moving steadily in his direction, and dropped to one knee, taking two-handed aim with the revolver. Rebus stepped into a doorway and waited for a shot that didn't come. When he peered out again, Soutar had vanished.

Rebus walked slowly towards where Soutar had been. He was nowhere on the street, but a couple of yards further on was a gateway, and beyond it some steps. The steps led to the top of Calton Hill. Rebus took a final deep breath and accepted the challenge.

The rough steps up to the summit were busy with people climbing and descending. Most of them were young and had been drinking. Rebus couldn't even summon the breath to yell something, 'Stop him' or 'Get out of his way'. He knew if he tried to spit, the stuff would be like paste. All he could do was follow.

At the top, Calton Hill was crowded with people sitting on the grass, all eyes turned towards the Castle. The view would have been breathtaking, had Rebus had any breath to spare. The music was being piped up here too. Smoke drifted south across the city, followed by more tinsel colour and rockets. It was like being the onlooker at a medieval siege. A lot of people were drunk. Some were stoned. It wasn't gunpowder you could smell up here.

Rebus had a good look around. He'd lost Davey Soutar.

There was no street lighting here, and crowds of people, mostly young and dressed in denim. Easy to lose someone.

Too damned easy.

Soutar could be heading down the other side of the hill, or snaking back down the roadway to Waterloo Place. Or he could be hiding amongst people who looked just like him. Except that the night air was chill. Rebus could feel it turning his sweat cold. And Soutar was only wearing a denim jacket.

As a huge firework burst over the Castle, and everyone stared up at the sky and gasped and cheered, Rebus looked for the one person who wasn't watching. The one person with his head down. The one person shivering like he'd never get warm again. He was sitting on the grass verge, next to a couple of girls who were drinking from cans and waving what looked like luminous rubber tubes. The girls had moved away from him a little, so that he looked the way he was: all alone in the world. Behind him on the grass was a gang of bikers, all muscle and gut. They were shouting and swearing, proclaiming hate of the English and all things foreign.

Rebus walked up to Davey Soutar, and Davey Soutar looked up.

And it wasn't him.

This kid was a couple of years younger, strung out on something, his eyes unable to focus.

'Hey,' one of the bikers yelled, 'you trying to pick up my pal?'

Rebus held up his hands. 'My mistake,' he said.

He turned around fast. Davey Soutar was behind him. He'd slipped off his jacket and had wound it around his right arm, all the way down to the wrist and the hand. Rebus knew what was in the hand, disguised now by the grubby denim.

'Okay, pigmeat, let's walk.'

Rebus knew he had to get Soutar away from the crowd. There were probably five bullets still in the revolver. Rebus didn't want any more bodies, not if he could help it.

They walked to the car park. There was a hot-food van doing good business, and a few cars, their drivers and passengers biting into burgers. It was darker here, and quieter. There wasn't much action here.

'Davey,' Rebus said, coming to a stop.

'This as far as you want to go?' Soutar said. He'd turned to face Rebus.

'No point me answering that, Davey, you're in charge now.'

'I've been in charge all along!'

Rebus nodded. 'That's right, skimming without your bosses knowing about it. Planning all this.' He nodded towards the fireworks. 'Could have been quite something.'

Soutar soured his face. 'You couldn't let it go, could you? Kilpatrick knew you were trouble.'

'You didn't have to stab him.' A car was making its way slowly up to the car park from Regent Road. Soutar had his back to it, but Rebus could see it. It was a marked police car, its headlights off.

'He tried to stop me,' Soutar sneered. 'No guts.'

If the music was anything to go by, the fireworks were coming to their climax. Rebus fixed his eyes on Soutar, watching the face turn from gold to green to blue.

'Put the gun away, Davey. It's finished.'

'Not till I say so.'

'Look, enough! Just put it down.'

The police car was at the top of the rise now. Davey Soutar unwound the jacket from his arm and threw it to the ground. A girl at the hot-food van started to scream. Behind Soutar, the police driver switched his headlamps on full-beam, lighting Soutar and Rebus like they were on stage. The passenger door was open, someone leaning out of it. Rebus recognised Abernethy. Soutar pivoted, aiming the gun. It was all the incentive Abernethy needed. The report from his gun was as loud as anything from the Castle. Meantime, the crowd was applauding again, unaware of the drama behind them.

Soutar was knocked backwards, taking Rebus with him. They fell in a heap, Rebus feeling the young man's damp hair brushing his face, his lips. He swore impressively as he pulled himself out from under the suddenly prone, suddenly still figure. Abernethy was pulling the revolver from Soutar's hand, his foot heavy on the youth's wrist.

'No need for that,' Rebus hissed. 'He's dead.'

'Looks like,' said Abernethy, putting away his own gun. 'So here's my story: I saw a flash, heard a bang, and assumed he'd fired. Sound reasonable?'

'Are you authorised to carry that cannon?'

'What do you think?'

'I think you're...'

'As bad as him?' Abernethy raised an eyebrow. 'I don't think so. And hey, don't mention it.'

'What?'

'Saving your fucking life! After that stunt you pulled, leaving me in the Gar-B.' He paused. 'You've got blood on you.'

Rebus looked. There was plenty of blood. 'There goes another shirt.'

'Trust a Jock to make a comment like that.'

The police driver had got out of the car to look, and a useful crowd was growing, now that the fireworks had finished. Abernethy began to check Soutar's pockets. Best get it over with while the body was warm. It was more pleasant that way. When he got to his feet again, Rebus was gone, and so was the car. He looked in disbelief at his driver.

'Not again.'

Yes, again.

30

Rebus had the police radio on as he drove. The bomb disposal team were halfway through lifting five small packages from the boot of Soutar's car. The packages had been fitted with detonators, and the Semtex was of advanced age, possibly unstable. There were pistols, automatic and bolt-action rifles too. God knew what he'd been planning to use them for.

The fireworks over, the buildings no longer glowed. They'd returned to their normal sooty hue. Crowds were moving through the streets, making their way home or towards last drinks, late suppers. People were smiling, wrapping arms around themselves to keep warm. They'd all enjoyed a good night out. Rebus didn't like to think about how close the whole night had come to disaster.

He switched on his siren and emergency lights to clear people from the roadway, then pulled past the line of cars in front of him. It was a few minutes before he realised he was shivering. He pulled the damp shirt away from his back and turned up the heating in the car. Not that heat would stop him shivering. He wasn't shivering from cold. He was headed for Tollcross, the Crazy Hose. He was headed for final business.

But when he arrived, siren and lights off, he saw smoke seeping out through the front doors. He pulled his car hard onto the pavement and ran to the doors, kicking them open. It wasn't rule one in the firefighter's manual, but he didn't have much choice. The fire was in the dancehall.

Only the smoke had so far reached the foyer and beyond. There was no one about. A sign on the front door gave abrupt notice that the club was closed 'due to unforeseen circumstances'.

That's me, thought Rebus, I'm unforeseen circumstances.

He headed for Frankie Bothwell's office. Where else was he going to go?

Bothwell was sitting in his chair, prevented from movement by a sudden case of death. His neck flopped over to one side in a way necks shouldn't. Rebus had seen broken necks before. There was bruising on the throat. Strangulation. He hadn't been dead long, his forehead was still warm. But then it was getting warm in the office. It was getting warm everywhere.

The new fire station was at the top of the road. Rebus wondered where the fire crew was.

As he came back into the foyer, he saw that more smoke was belching from the dance hall. The door had been opened. Clyde Moncur was dragging himself into the foyer. He was still alive and wanted to stay that way. Rebus checked Moncur wasn't carrying a gun, then got hold of him by the neck of his jacket and hauled him across the floor. Moncur was trying hard to breathe. He was having a little trouble. He felt light as Rebus dragged him. He kicked open the doors and deposited Moncur at the top of the steps.

Then he went in again.

Yes, the blaze had started here, here in the dance hall. Flames had taken control of the walls and ceiling. All Bothwell's gewgaws and furnishings were melting or turning to ash. The carpet in the seating area had caught. The bottles of alcohol hadn't exploded yet, but they would. Rebus looked around, but couldn't see much. The smoke was too thick, there was too much of it. He wrapped his handkerchief around his face, but even so he couldn't stop coughing. He could hear a rhythmic thumping sound coming from somewhere. Somewhere up ahead.

It was the little self-contained box where the DJ sat, over beyond the stage. There was someone in there now. He tried the door. It was locked, so sign of a key. He took a few steps back so he could run at it.

Then the door flew open. Rebus recognised the Ulsterman, Alan Fowler. He's used his head to butt the door open, his arms being tied firmly to the back of a chair. They were still tied to the chair as, head low, he came barrelling from the box. He caught Rebus a blow to the stomach and Rebus went down. Rebus rolled and came to his knees, but Fowler was up too, and he was blind mad. For all he knew, it was Rebus who was trying to roast him. He butted Rebus again, this time in the face. It was a sore one, but Rebus had ridden a Glasgow Kiss before. The blow caught him on his cheek.

The power of it snapped Rebus's head back, sending him staggering. Fowler was like a bull, the chair legs sticking up like swords from his back. Now that he was more or less upright, he went for Rebus with his feet. One caught Rebus on his damaged ear, tearing it, sending a white jab of pain bouncing through his brain. That gave Fowler time for another kick, and this one was going to shatter Rebus's knee ... Until a blow in the face with an empty bottle knocked him sideways. Rebus looked up to see his saviour, his knight in shining armour. Big Ger Cafferty was still wearing his funeral suit and open shirt. He was busy making sure Fowler was down and out. Then he took one look at Rebus, and produced the hint of a smile, looking every bit as amused as a butcher who finds the carcass he's working on is still alive.

He spent a precious few seconds, life and death seconds, weighing up his options. Then he slung Rebus's arm over his shoulder and walked with him out of the dance hall, through the foyer, and into the night air, the clean, breathable air. Rebus took in huge gulps of it, falling onto the pavement, sitting there, head bowed, his feet on the road. Cafferty sat down beside him. He seemed to be studying his own hands. Rebus knew why, too.

And now the fire engines were arriving, men leaping out of cabs, doing things with hoses. One of them complained about the police car. The keys were in the ignition, so the fireman backed it up.

At last Rebus could speak. 'You did that?' he asked. It was a stupid question. Hadn't he given Cafferty nearly all the information he'd needed?

'I saw you going in,' Cafferty said, his voice raw. 'You were gone a long time.'

'You could have let me die.'

Cafferty looked at him. 'I didn't come in for *you*. I came in to stop you bringing out that bastard Fowler. As it is, Moncur's done a runner.'

'He can't run far.'

'He better try. He knows I won't give up.'

'You knew him, didn't you? Moncur, I mean. He's an old pal of Alan Fowler's. When Fowler was UVF, the UVF laundered money using your salmon farm. Moncur bought the salmon with his good US dollars.'

'You never stop.'

'It's my business.'

'Well,' said Cafferty, glancing back at the club, 'this was business, too. Only, sometimes you have to cut a few corners. I know *you* have.'

Rebus was wiping his face. 'Problem is, Cafferty, when you cut a corner, it bleeds.'

Cafferty studied him. There was blood on Rebus's ear, sweat cloying his hair. Davey Soutar's blood still spattered his shirt, mixed now with smoke. And Kilpatrick's handprint was still there. Cafferty stood up.

'Not thinking of going anywhere?' Rebus said.

'You going to stop me?'

'You know I'll try.'

A car drew up. In it were Cafferty's men, the two from the kirkyard plus weasel-face. Cafferty walked to the car. Rebus was still sitting on the pavement. He got up slowly now, and walked towards the police car. He heard Cafferty's car door shutting, and looked at it, noting the licence plate. As the car passed him, Cafferty was looking at the road ahead. Rebus opened his own car and got on the radio, giving out the licence number. He thought about starting his engine and giving chase, but just sat there instead, watching the firemen go about their business.

I played it by the rules, he thought. I cautioned him and then I called in. It didn't say in the rules that you had to have a go when there were four of them and only one of you.

Yes, he'd played it by the rules. The good feeling started to wear off after only minutes, and damned few minutes at that.

They finally picked Clyde Moncur up at a ferry port. Special Branch in London were dealing with him. Abernethy was dealing with him. Before he'd left, Rebus had asked a simple question.

'Will it happen?'

'Will what happen?'

'Civil war.'

'What do you think?'

So much for that. The story was simple. Moncur was visiting town to see how the money from US Shield was being spent. Fowler was around to make sure Moncur was happy. The Festival had seemed the perfect cover for Moncur's trip. Maybe Billy had been executed to show the American just how ruthless SaS could be . . .

In hospital, recovering from his stab wounds, DCI Kilpatrick was smothered to death with his pillow. Two of his ribs had been cracked from the weight of his attacker pressing down on him.

'Must've been the size of a grizzly,' Dr Curt announced.

'Not many grizzlies about these days,' said Rebus.

He phoned the Procurator Fiscal's office, just to check on Caro Rattray. After all, Cafferty had spoken of her. He just wanted to know she was okay. Maybe Cafferty was out there tying up a lot of loose ends. But Caro had gone.

'What do you mean?'

'Some private practice in Glasgow offered her a partnership. It's a big step up, she grabbed it, anyone would.'

'Which office is it?'

Funny, it was the office of Cafferty's own lawyers. It might mean something or nothing. After all, Rebus *had* given Cafferty some names. Mairie Henderson had gone down to London to try to follow up the Moncur story. Abernethy phoned Rebus one night to say he thought she was terrific.

'Yes,' said Rebus, 'you'd make a lovely couple.'

'Except she hates my guts.' Abernethy paused. 'But she might listen to you.'

'Spit it out.'

'Just don't tell her too much, all right? Remember, Jump Cantona will take most of the credit anyway, and wee Mairie's been paid upfront. She doesn't *have* to bust a gut. Most of what she'd say wouldn't get past the libel lawyers and the Official Secrets Act anyway.'

Rebus had stopped listening. 'How do you know about Jump Cantona?' He could almost hear Abernethy easing his feet up onto the desk, leaning back in his chair.

'The FBI have used Cantona before to put out a story.'

'And you're in with the FBI?'

'I'll send them a report.'

'Don't cover yourself with too much glory, Abernethy.'

'You'll get a mention, Inspector.'

'But not star billing. That's how you knew about Mairie, isn't it? Cantona told the FBI? It's how you had all the stuff on Clyde Moncur to hand?'

'Does it matter?'

Probably not. Rebus broke the connection anyway.

He shopped for a coming home meal, pushing the trolley around a supermarket close to Fettes HQ. He wouldn't be going back to Fettes. He'd phoned his farewell to Ormiston and told him to tell Blackwood to cut off his remaining strands of hair and be done with it.

'He'd have a seizure if I told him that,' said Ormiston. 'Here, what about the Chief? You don't think ...?'

But Rebus had rung off. He didn't want to talk about Ken Smylie, didn't want to think about it. He knew as much as he needed to. Kilpatrick had been on the fringe; he was more useful to The Shield that way. Bothwell was the executioner. He'd killed Billy Cunningham and he'd ordered the deaths of Millie Docherty and Calumn Smylie. Soutar had done his master's bidding in both cases, except Millie had proved messy, and Soutar had left her where he'd killed her. Bothwell must have been furious about that, but of course Davey Soutar had other things on his mind, other plans. Bigger things.

Rebus bought the makings for the meal and added bottles of rosé champagne, malt whisky and gin to the trolley. A mile and a half to the north, the shops on the Gar-B estate would be closing for the evening, pulling down heavy metal shutters, fixing padlocks, double-checking alarm systems. He paid with plastic at the check-out and drove back up the hill to Oxford Terrace. Curiously, the rust bucket was sounding healthier these days. Maybe that knock from Hay's van had put something back into alignment. Rebus had replaced the glass, but was still debating the door-frame.

At the flat, Patience was waiting for him, back from Perth earlier than expected.

'What's this?' she said.

'It was meant to be a surprise.' He put down the bags

and kissed her. She drew away from him slowly afterwards.

'You look an absolute mess,' she said.

He shrugged. It was true, he'd seen boxers in better shape after fifteen rounds. He'd seen punchbags in better shape.

'So it's over?' she said.

'Finishes today.'

'I don't mean the Festival.'

'I know you don't.' He pulled her to him again. 'It's over.'

'Did I hear a clink from one of those bags?'

Rebus smiled. 'Gin or champagne?'

'Gin and orange.'

They took the bags into the kitchen. Patience got ice and orange juice from the fridge, while Rebus rinsed two glasses. 'I missed you,' she said.

'I missed you, too.'

'Who else do I know who tells awful jokes?'

'Seems a while since I told a joke. It's a while since I heard one.'

'Well, my sister told me one. You'll love it.' She arched back her head, thinking. 'God, how does it go?'

Rebus unscrewed the top from the gin bottle and poured liberally.

'Whoah!' Patience said. 'You don't want us getting mortal.'

He splashed in some orange. 'Maybe I do.'

She kissed him again, then pulled away and clapped her hands. 'Yes, I've got it now. There's this octopus in a restaurant, and it's –'

'I've heard it,' said Rebus, dropping ice into her glass.

All Orion/Phoenix titles are available at your local bookshop or from the following address:

Littlehampton Book Services
Cash Sales Department L
14 Eldon Way, Lineside Industrial Estate
Littlehampton
West Sussex BN17 7HE
telephone 01903 721596, *facsimile* 01903 730914

Payment can either be made by credit card (Visa and Mastercard accepted) or by sending a cheque or postal order made payable to *Littlehampton Book Services*.

DO NOT SEND CASH OR CURRENCY.

Please add the following to cover postage and packing

UK and BFPO:
£1.50 for the first book, and 50P for each additional book to a maximum of £3.50

Overseas and Eire:
£2.50 for the first book plus £1.00 for the second book and 50p for each additional book ordered

----

BLOCK CAPITALS PLEASE

name of cardholder ....   *delivery address*
        ....   *(if different from cardholder)*
address of cardholder ....
        ....
        ....
        ....
        postcode ....   *postcode* ....

☐ I enclose my remittance for £....................

☐ please debit my Mastercard/Visa (delete as appropriate)

card number ☐☐☐☐☐☐☐☐☐☐☐☐☐☐☐☐☐☐

expiry date ☐☐☐☐

signature ....

prices and availability are subject to change without notice